Ma

MW01135068

Made in Savannah
Cozy Mysteries Series (Books 1-3)

Hope Callaghan

hopecallaghan.com

*****

Visit my website for new releases and special offers:
hopecallaghan.com

Thank you to these wonderful ladies who help make my books shine - Peggy H., Cindi G., Jean P., Wanda D. and Barbara W. and for the extra sets of eyes and for catching all of my mistakes.

A special THANKS to my reader review teams, here in the U.S., and those across the pond, over the border and an ocean away!

Alice, Amary, Barbara, Becky, Becky B, Brinda, Cassie, Charlene, Christina, Debbie, Dee, Denota, Devan, Grace, Jan, Jo-Ann, Joeline, Joyce, Jean K., Jean M., Katherine, Lynne, Megan, Melda, Kat, Linda, Lynne, Pat, Patsy, Paula, Rebecca, Renate, Rita, Shelba, Tamara, Valerie and Vicki.

Allie, Anca, Angela, Ann, Anne, Bev, Bobbi, Bonny, Carol, Carmen, David, Debbie, Diana, Elaine, Elizabeth, Gareth, Ingrid, Jane, Jayne, Jean, Joan, Karen, Kate, Kathy, Lesley, Margaret, Marlene, Patricia, Pauline, Sharon, Sheila and Susan.

CONTENTS

Cast of Characters

Carlita Garlucci. The widow of a mafia "made" man, Carlita promised her husband on his deathbed to get their sons out of the "family" business, so she moves from New York to the historic city of Savannah, Georgia. But escaping the family isn't as easy as she hoped it would be and trouble follows Carlita to her new home.

Mercedes Garlucci. Carlita's daughter and the first to move to Savannah with her mother. An aspiring writer, Mercedes has a knack for finding mysteries and adventure.

Vincent Garlucci, Jr. Carlita's oldest son and a younger version of his father, Vinnie is deeply entrenched in the "family business" and is not interested in leaving New York.

Tony Garlucci. Carlita's middle son and the first to follow his mother to Savannah. Tony is protective of both his mother and his sister, which is a good thing since the Garlucci women are always in some sort of a predicament.

Paulie Garlucci. Carlita's youngest son. Mayor of the small town of Clifton Falls, NY, Paulie never joined the "family business," and is content to live his life with his wife and young children far away from a life of crime. Gina, Paulie's wife, rules the family household with an iron fist.

1-Key to Savannah

Made in Savannah

Cozy Mysteries Series Book 1

Hope Callaghan

hopecallaghan.com
Copyright © 2016
All rights reserved.

*****

Visit my website for new releases and special offers: hopecallaghan.com

Thank you, Peggy H., Cindi G., Jean P. and Rosmarie H. for taking the time to preview *Key to Savannah*, for the extra sets of eyes and for catching all my mistakes.

A special thanks to my reader review team: Alice, Amary, Barbara, Becky, Becky B, Brinda, Cassie, Christina, Cyndi, Debbie, Denota, Devan, Francine, Grace, Jo-Ann, Joeline, Joyce, Jean K., Jean M., Kathy, Lynne, Megan, Melda, Kat, Lynne, Pat, Patsy, Renate, Rita, Rita P, Shelba, Tamara, Vicki and Wanda

Prologue

Carlita Garlucci straightened her 4' 10" frame and stared at her husband as she steeled herself for the inevitable. Vincent "Vinnie" Garlucci was dying.

The rasp of the ventilator and beep of the machines that were keeping him alive filled the room and her head. Carlita closed her eyes for a second and the room began to spin. She swayed slightly and reached out to steady herself, grasping the edge of the bed, her hand brushing against Vinnie's hand.

He wiggled his fingers at her touch and Carlita's eyes flew open. The doctors had told her that her beloved Vinnie was near death, unable to respond.

Carlita caressed the top of her husband's cold hand before gently holding it. She leaned in so that her face was mere inches from his. "Vinnie. It's me. Carlita." Her voice began to crack and tears burned the back of her eyes.

She said it again, this time a little louder. "Vinnie."

Vinnie squeezed her hand, and Carlita could've sworn she saw his lips move so she leaned in even closer, so close that their cheeks almost touched.

"Promise..." Vinnie Garlucci moaned through parched lips. "Promise..."

"Anything Vinnie. I love you with all my heart," Carlita whispered, her voice raw with emotion. "I'll promise you anything. Don't go. Please Vinnie," she begged.

Vinnie tried to lift his head and his mouth began moving again. "Get my sons...out. Get them out."

A lone tear rolled down Carlita's cheek. "I swear, Vinnie. I'll get them out." As soon as she uttered the words, Vinnie loosened his grip, his head fell back on the pillow and the machines that had kept Carlita's husband alive grew silent.

The screen flat lined. Vincent Garlucci was gone.

Chapter 1

Carlita Garlucci flung her closet door open, determined to start the day by sorting through Vinnie's clothes, something she had been putting off since her husband's sudden death several months earlier.

She quickly formed three piles. A pile to donate to charity, a pile to keep for her sons to sort through and the smallest pile, the precious mementos she couldn't bear to part with.

Carlita quickly finished the task, the ache in her heart still fresh. She sorted through his ties, his shoes and his accessories. She was almost finished when she spotted the white plastic bag shoved in the far corner. It contained the clothes Vinnie had been wearing the day he was admitted to the hospital.

She slowly unfolded the top of the bag and reached inside to pull out Vinnie's dress slacks. Carlita set the slacks in the donate pile. His shirt was next and she carefully placed it in the same pile. The last item she pulled out was the jacket he'd been wearing. It was his favorite one.

Carlita eased one arm, and then the other into the jacket, pulling it tight across her chest. She lifted the lapel, closed her eyes and breathed deeply. She could smell the lingering scent of Vinnie's cologne, and it was almost as if he was with her again. She would keep the jacket.

Carlita shrugged out of the jacket and reached for a hanger when she noticed something poking out of the front pocket. She stuck her hand inside and pulled out a white envelope.

"What's this?" she muttered under her breath as she unfolded it. On the front of the envelope was her name, scrawled in Vinnie's familiar handwriting. She slid the tip of her finger under the seal and flipped the flap.

Inside the envelope was a keyring with an odd shaped key. There was also a round tag with a set of numbers etched on one side.

She dropped the keyring back inside the envelope, folded it in half and shoved it in her back pocket before carefully sliding the jacket on the hanger and placing it on the closet rod.

After bagging the designated clothes headed to a local charity, Carlita carried them to the breezeway.

She had already planned to call a taxi to pick her up so she could run some errands and mentally added dropping off the clothes to her to-do list.

Vinnie's sudden death had been a blow to her children and Carlita's three sons called almost every day to check on their mother. After several months, she had finally managed to settle into a daily routine and the calls were coming less frequently.

Carlita had not forgotten her promise to her husband, Vinnie, on his deathbed to get her sons "out." He hadn't come right out and said it, but she was certain Vinnie meant getting them out of the "family." Every time she brought it up, her sons cut her off, refusing to discuss leaving the "family" business.

Carlita dropped the folded envelope on the kitchen table and headed back down the hall. She started to pass by her daughter, Mercedes', bedroom door when she heard a muffled sound on the other side.

"I'm going to eat breakfast. Want to join me?" Carlita asked through the closed door.

The door swung open and Carlita gazed at her youngest child, her only daughter, Mercedes Marie Garlucci.

3

Mercedes nodded, a long strand of jet-black hair falling across one eye. "Sure."

Mercedes had been a daddy's girl. Whatever Mercedes wanted, Mercedes got, but one thing she didn't get, was to be included in the family business.

Bored with her dead-end, part-time job as a cashier, Mercedes had started what she hoped would be an exciting new career...an author. She had always wanted to be a writer, although she kept it a secret from her family, not that she didn't think they would support her dream. It was the story she was working on that they wouldn't approve of. She was writing about living the life as a mobster's daughter.

"Whatcha doing?" Carlita asked.

"Killing people."

"Huh?" Carlita lifted a brow.

"Never mind," Mercedes mumbled as she slipped into the hall, closing the bedroom door behind her. She followed her mother to the kitchen. "I didn't get much sleep last night."

"Me either." Carlita set the box of corn flakes and milk on the table before sliding into one of the chairs.

4

"What's this?" Mercedes picked up the envelope Carlita had just placed on the table and turned it over.

"Some sort of key. I found it in the jacket your father wore to the hospital."

Mercedes opened the envelope and pulled out the keyring. She turned the key over and rubbed her thumb across the metal ring. "Five forty-nine." She flipped the tag over. "FNB. This looks like a safe deposit box key."

She set the key next to her and reached for a bowl. "I'm gonna do a little research. Did Pop ever mention a safe deposit box?"

"No." Carlita shook her head. There were many things Carlita didn't know about her husband and probably didn't want to know.

"It must be something valuable," Mercedes theorized. "Otherwise, why wouldn't he have just used the wall safe?"

Years ago, Vinnie had installed a hidden safe in the living room, behind a large oil painting of the Tuscan countryside.

Mercedes quickly ate her bowl of cereal and then dumped the milk down the kitchen drain before placing the dirty dish in the dishwasher. "I'll see what I can find out."

Carlita had just finished straightening the kitchen when Mercedes bounded into the kitchen. "This is a First National Bank safe deposit box key."

Vinnie and Carlita had banked at First National Bank for decades. "You're sure?"

"Yeah," Mercedes said. "We need to go check it out."

Chapter 2

Mercedes dangled the keyring in her hand as she breezed into the kitchen. "I called a taxi to take us to the bank."

Carlita had never learned how to drive. Vinnie had always driven her wherever she wanted or needed to go. Vinnie's baby, his shiny black 1970's four-door Lincoln town car, was parked in the garage. The car was her husband's prized possession and he never let anyone, including his sons, drive it.

Every Sunday afternoon, weather permitting, Vinnie would park the car in the drive where he would wash it, wax it, wipe down the leather seats and polish the chrome rims. He refused to take it to a drive-thru car wash, explaining to his wife that the brushes they used would scratch the paint.

Carlita's sons, Vinnie Jr., Anthony and Paulie all knew how to drive, and on their 17th birthdays, each of them had been given a nearly new car as a birthday present.

Mercedes had gotten her driver's license a few years back, but showed no interest in driving or owning a vehicle. Like her mother, she depended on the men in the family or on occasion, a taxi to take her wherever she needed to go, including her former part-time job.

Beep. Beep. The taxi honked out front and Carlita slipped her sweater on and grabbed her purse before heading out the front door.

Mercedes had gone ahead and stood waiting for her mother on the curb. She opened the car door for her mom and waited for her to climb in before sliding into the seat next to her. "First National Bank, East and Seventy Third," Mercedes told the driver as she pulled the door shut.

The women were silent as they rode out of their neighborhood. Carlita rarely left the area where she had lived for the past thirty plus years, preferring to shop at Guido's Meat Market on the corner or Stefano's drug store two blocks over.

The only time Carlita left the neighborhood was every once in a blue moon when Paulie, her youngest son, and Gina, her daughter-in-law, invited them to their home in Clifton Falls, usually to celebrate a birthday or milestone event in her grandchildren's lives.

Carlita suspected that Gina didn't approve of the family's business and who could blame her? It was an unsettling life to an outsider.

The taxi driver eased into a spot in front of the bank and shifted the vehicle into park. "That'll be forty seven dollars and eighty-two cents plus tip." He climbed out of the taxi and opened the back door.

Carlita eyes widened as she stared at her daughter. She hadn't brought enough cash. Mercedes shot her mother a glance. "Don't worry Ma. I got it." She reached inside her front pocket, pulling out two twenties and a ten. "Highway robbery," she muttered under her breath as she handed the cash to the driver. "This is all I've got."

Mercedes hopped out of the taxi and waited for her mother to join her. "I should start driving Pop's car." She slipped her arm through her mother's as they strode down the sidewalk and made their way inside the bank.

"We'll start there." Mercedes pointed to a tall counter. They snaked their way through the twined ropes and then waited for the next available teller, who motioned them forward.

"We have a lock box key and would like to inspect the contents," Carlita said when they reached the counter. The teller, a blonde man with wire-rimmed glasses and a serious expression, pointed to the right. "Wait over there and I'll get someone to take you to the back."

Mother and daughter stepped to the side and out of earshot. "What if they ask for ID or ask if it's our box?" Carlita whispered under her breath.

Mercedes didn't have time to answer. A tall man dressed in a navy blue business suit made his way over. "I'm Derek Wilder. You're here to inspect the contents of a safe deposit box?"

"Yes," Mercedes nodded.

"Do you have the key?"

"We do." Carlita pulled the keyring from her purse and handed it to the bank employee.

He flipped the small metal ring over and studied the tag. "Follow me."

Carlita and Mercedes trailed behind Derek Wilder as he strode across the gleaming polished floors to a small office in the corner.

He stepped to the side and motioned them into the room. "I'll need to see picture ID."

Carlita and Mercedes exchanged a quick glance. "My husband died a few months ago. I...I'm not sure if my name is on the box."

"I'll check." Derek Wilder settled in behind a small desk and began tapping on the computer keys. He slowly shook his head. "Vincent Garlucci is the only name on the box."

"But..." Carlita wasn't ready to give up.

"Wait! There's a note attached to the file." Derek Wilder scrunched his brow as he studied the screen. "It looks as if Mr. Garlucci added a Carlita Garlucci to the box back in December."

Carlita's hand flew to her chest. "I'm Carlita Garlucci." She fumbled inside her purse for her picture ID and handed it to Derek Wilder, who glanced at the identification card and then back at the screen. "Thank you, Mrs. Garlucci. I'll need you to sign a form and then follow me.

Carlita quickly signed the document he slid across the desk, and she and Mercedes followed Derek to the other side of the bank, to a door with thick metal bars. He pulled a key from his pocket, inserted the key in the lock and swung the door open. "This way."

They passed by several large doors until reaching the end of the corridor. Derek unlocked a second door and swung it open. Inside the room was row after row of small metal drawers.

"It's over here." Derek shifted to the right and pointed at a drawer with two locks. He inserted his key to unlock one of the locks. "You'll need to open the other lock with your key."

Carlita inserted her key and unlocked the box before Mr. Wilder slid it out. "You can view the contents over here." He led them to the other side of the room and a small table in the corner. "I'll wait for you near the exit." He made his way toward the door while Carlita and Mercedes crowded around the box.

Carlita reached inside and pulled out an 8x10 manila envelope. Her hand trembled as she handed it to her daughter. "I'm too nervous. You look at it."

Mercedes reached inside the envelope, pulled out a thick set of papers, her eyes scanning the top sheet. "This is a deed to property..." She thrust the pile of papers toward her mother. "The property is in Savannah, Georgia."

Chapter 3

"Property?" Carlita blinked rapidly and stared at the papers in disbelief. "I own property in Savannah, Georgia?"

"I think so." Mercedes frowned and then glanced at Derek Wilder. "Maybe he knows." She took the papers from her mother and approached the bank employee. "Can you look at this?"

Mercedes handed the papers to Mr. Wilder, who quickly skimmed the front page. "This appears to be a quitclaim deed from a Vincent Robert Garlucci to a Carlita Lenore Garlucci."

Derek handed the papers back to Mercedes. "It would appear Mrs. Garlucci is the rightful owner of property in Savannah Georgia, but you'll have to contact a probate attorney in the State of Georgia to verify the validity of the document. I'm no attorney."

"Thank you," Carlita said. "By the way, where exactly is Savannah, Georgia?"

"In the south," Mercedes and Derek Wilder said in unison.

"Near the east coast," Derek Wilder added.

Mercedes carefully slid the papers inside the envelope. "Thank you Mr. Wilder."

Derek nodded. "You're welcome. I'll go shut the drawer. " He stepped over to the safe deposit box, lifted it from the table and it made a tinkling noise. He turned back. "Are you sure it's empty?"

Mother and daughter glanced at each other. "I thought it was empty," Carlita said.

Mr. Wilder set the box down and resumed his position by the door. "You may want to take another look."

Carlita lifted the top on the box. Tucked in the back, behind the hinge was a small black velvet pouch. It was the same color as the inside of the box.

"Huh." Carlita pulled it out, tugged on the drawstrings and opened the bag. She dumped the contents into the palm of her hand. "These look like gems," she whispered to her daughter.

"Put them in your purse," Mercedes whispered back and then raised her voice. "We're all set."

On the way out Carlita signed a second form, stating that the safe deposit box contents had been removed.

When they reached the bank lobby, Carlita glanced behind her. "I thought your father made me to promise to get our sons out of the family business. What if he meant out of the city?"

The key to the deposit box had been in the jacket pocket Vinnie had worn to the hospital. Had he planned to tell her about the property, but never got around to it? "Why in the world would he want us to move to Savannah?"

***

Mercedes and Carlita paused when they reached the sidewalk.

"Vinnie and Tony are not going to like this," Mercedes warned. She thought of her own dilemma, her mob novel, still in the early stages of writing. "This is the only life we've ever known."

A taxi crept by. Mercedes darted to the edge of the sidewalk and waved her hand. She waited for the taxi to pull to the curb before reaching for the door handle. "Not only that, we've never been to Savannah."

Carlita slid into the back seat and reached for her seatbelt. "True." She had only briefly glanced at the papers. "I wonder what we own."

The conversation ended as Carlita recited their address,"22-15 172nd Street, Queens," she told the driver.

Home. The three bedroom, two bath ranch Vinnie and she had lived in for decades, and raised their four children.

Carlita mulled over her promise to her husband. It would be difficult, if not impossible, for her to convince her sons to honor their father's dying wish to leave the family business, even though it was a well-known fact that a "made man" was also a "marked man."

The more she thought about it, the more determined she became to fulfill her beloved Vinnie's dying wish. The "how" was going to be the tricky part.

The taxi driver pulled to the curb a short time later and shifted into park.

Carlita leaned forward to talk to him when something caught her eye.

Mercedes noticed, too. "Did you see that? Someone just ran out the side porch door." Her daughter quickly scrambled out of the back of the taxi, and raced down the drive and into the backyard. "Hey!"

It was too late. The person, wearing a black jacket and denim jeans, jumped the back fence and disappeared over the other side.

"Not again!" Carlita shifted in the seat and turned her attention to the taxi driver a second time. "I have to go inside to get some cash so I can pay you." She didn't wait for an answer as she hopped out of the taxi and headed in through the door the intruder had just exited.

When she returned, she approached the driver's side window, handed the taxi driver a fifty, thanked him for waiting and headed to the backyard where her daughter stood, studying the back fence. "This is crazy."

This wasn't the first time someone had broken into their house. The day Vinnie died someone had broken in and had torn the place apart.

"We aren't safe in our own home anymore," Mercedes groaned. "Whoever it was is long gone."

Carlita headed back inside. "At least they didn't tear the place apart this time," she said as she set her purse on the kitchen counter. A few of the kitchen cabinets were open but other than that, nothing was out of place. "It's time for a family meeting."

Mercedes tapped the manila envelope on the edge of the kitchen table. "I'm gonna do a little research on the property while you talk to the others." She disappeared down the hall and into her room, closing the door behind her.

Carlita checked to make sure there wasn't a second intruder before heading to the kitchen phone. Vinnie had bought Carlita a cell phone a couple years back, telling her she needed to learn to how to use it and to keep it with her in case of an emergency.

She had humored her husband, but Carlita still preferred to use the house phone. She called her eldest son, Vinnie, first. The call went to voice mail.

Her middle son, Tony, didn't answer, either.

Paulie, her youngest son, answered on the first ring. "Hi Ma. I was gonna call to find out how you're doin' today."

"I'm fine Paulie. Mercedes and I caught someone sneaking out of the house when we returned home from running an errand. They ran out through the side door and jumped the back fence."

"You oughta get better locks on the doors now that Pop is gone," Paulie advised. "You have any idea what they were lookin' for?"

Carlita reached inside her purse and pulled out the bag of gems. "Maybe. Listen, we need to have a family meeting. I have something important to discuss."

The other end of the line grew quiet. Paulie hated driving to Queens. Carlita knew Paulie's wife, Gina, hated it even more.

"Please. It's important to me," Carlita pleaded.

"Okay," Paulie caved. "I'm not sure if Gina will come. The kids are keepin' us hopping this school year what with all their after school activities."

"It's okay. I understand." Carlita let out the breath she'd been holding. One down, two to go. "How 'bout around dinnertime? I'll make a big dish of your favorite spaghetti and meatballs," she promised, in an attempt to sweeten the invitation.

After hanging up the phone, Carlita opened the velvet pouch, tipped it upside down and dumped the contents onto the counter. The gems, all different sizes, made small *pinging* noises as they bounced lightly on the Formica countertop.

She reached inside her purse, pulled out her reading glasses and slipped them on. "One, two, three..." There were a dozen gems in all. She picked up the largest one, a diamond, and rolled it between her fingers. "This has to be at least three carats," she murmured.

The house phone began ringing and Carlita carefully set the gem next to the others. It was her oldest son, Vinnie, who told her he'd already planned to stop by.

When she mentioned that Mercedes and she had scared off another intruder, her son let loose a string of cuss words. "I'll bring some heavy duty deadbolts with me and change the locks. I bet it was that weasel, Carmine Tonesci, nosing around, thinkin' Pop left something behind."

Carlita frowned. Her son had no idea. "That's part of the reason I'm calling the family meeting."

"You're still not thinkin' crazy thoughts about selling the place," Vinnie guessed. Thankfully, another call was coming in and Carlita cut him off.

"I got another call, Vinnie. We'll talk about it after dinner tonight. Spaghetti and meatballs," she rattled off before disconnecting the line. "Hello?"

It was Tony, who didn't seem at all pleased that his mother was calling a family meeting, but Carlita played on her middle son's sympathies and it worked like a charm. "Mercedes and I ran an errand earlier. Someone broke into the house again. They were running out the door as our taxi pulled up."

"No kidding," Tony said. "It's probably that snake, Frank Delmario. I heard him 'n Pops got into it a couple weeks before he died, down at Gino's Pizzeria and Frank told Pop he was gonna burn him."

Carlita's pulse quickened. "Burn" was another term for kill.

Tony went on. "Frank is nothing but a crumb so I didn't think too much about it."

A "crumb" was lingo for a member of "legit" society. In other words, it was a working man and someone who was not in the business.

Carlita thought about the deed to the Savannah property. "Do you think Frank owed your father money?" Had her husband obtained the property through underhanded, illegal means? If so, perhaps the person who was breaking into her house was after the deed.

"It's possible," Tony said. "I wouldn't rule anyone out."

Vinnie, Carlita's husband, had been a shylock. He had never come right out and told her that he was a shylock, but she had heard whispered rumors and finally, looked it up for herself.

A shylock was a financial racketeer who loaned money to others at a high rate of interest, so high that the person who took out the loan was never able to pay it back.

It was a type of indenture used by the mob to pay off other loans. Many of the people who took out the loans were in a tight spot and desperate to pay someone off lest they become a mark.

She often wondered where Vinnie came up with the money to loan others in the first place. One day, not long after they married, she point blank asked him.

Vinnie tried to skirt the question, but eventually told her he had placed several lucky bets on horses and had managed to accumulate some cold, hard cash.

Carlita never pressed the issue after that and, at least in her mind, loaning money was a little more on the up and up than some of the other "careers" the made men took up...drug trafficking, fencing, counterfeiting and blackmailing, to name a few.

Tony offered to bring a new set of locks but Carlita told him that Vinnie was already on it. "You can help your brother," she said. "He mentioned a Carmine Tonesci. The name sounds vaguely familiar."

"Carmine Tonesci is a snake, too. I wouldn't put it past him to break into a widow's house and rob her," Tony said. "Maybe I should pay a visit to Carmine's dry cleaning business."

"Please don't go looking for trouble." Even as she said the words, Carlita knew they sounded absurd. Her sons were made men, part of the mafia. Trouble was a daily occurrence.

After Carlita told her son good-bye, she scooped the gems off the counter and carefully dropped them back inside the velvet bag before placing the bag in the safest place she could think of...her bra.

Mercedes emerged from her bedroom as Carlita set the phone in the cradle. "I was able to dig up information on the Savannah property. There is more than one deed and I think there are several properties. I did a Google drive by and..." Mercedes's voice trailed off.

Carlita could tell from the look on her daughter's face there was more. "And what?" she prompted.

"Let's just say the properties need a little work. They're fixer uppers for sure. The good news is the properties appear to be in historic downtown Savannah."

Mercedes laced her fingers together and lifted both arms over her head. "I left the street view on my computer if you want to take a look."

On the one hand, Carlita wanted to see what they had inherited, but on the other, she was almost afraid to. She was pinning her hopes, her promise to her husband to get their children out of the city, on this property. "I guess I need to see it."

Carlita reluctantly followed Mercedes down the hall and into her bedroom.

"Have a seat," Mercedes waved to the small office chair in front of the computer desk.

Mercedes had been teaching her mother basic computer skills, but her skills were limited to playing solitaire, reading local news stories and researching Italian recipes.

Carlita slid into the chair and stared at the dark screen.

"Wiggle the mouse," Mercedes pointed at the mouse.

Her mother wiggled the small device and the dark screen disappeared, replaced by a picture of a large, dilapidated brick building. Almost all of the windows were boarded up and graffiti spray-painted on the sheets of plywood covering what had been windows. "It's hard to tell what this is. Is there a way to get a closer look?"

"Sure." Mercedes clicked the mouse a couple times and zoomed in. One of the buildings was a two story. Off to one side was a fire escape. "This place has a lot of potential," she said excitedly. "Think about it. We could sell the gems and use the money to fix the place up and start a business. Maybe we could convert the upper floors to apartments."

Carlita frowned. "I don't know. What if it's in a rough neighborhood?"

"That's the beauty of it, Ma. I did a virtual drive by. This place is in the historic district. Not right in the center, but on the edge. We need to go down there to check it out. Kind of a reconnaissance mission."

There was no way Carlita's sons would be onboard to make a trip to Savannah to check out a dump their father had left them. "Your brothers won't go."

Mercedes straightened her back, her eyes still fixed on the screen. "So? If they won't go, we'll go by ourselves."

Carlita shifted in the chair and studied the look of determination in her daughter's eyes. As much as she believed the property was a gift from God, and a move to Savannah was destined, there was no way her sons would drive them there. "I don't drive Mercedes. You have your license, but when is the last time you drove a car?"

"Well," Mercedes tugged on a strand of hair thoughtfully. "Probably about a year or so, but I was thinking, I can start practicing, you know drive around the block and stuff. I figure if I practice enough, I'll be ready for a road trip in a couple days, which will give us enough time to find a place to stay in Savannah."

She could see her mother was beginning to warm to the idea and quickly continued. "I say we don't tell Vinnie, Tony or Paulie. You know they will be dead set against going with us and just as dead set against us going by ourselves."

Carlita eased out of the chair. "Let me think about it." She shifted her gaze and stared at the screen. "In the meantime, I need to start working on my meatballs for dinner."

She made her way out of her daughter's room and down the hall to the kitchen where she pulled mixing bowls from the cupboard and then realized she was out of milk and breadcrumbs.

Carlita grabbed her purse and headed for the door before hollering to the back of the house. "I'm walking down to Sal's to pick up some groceries."

"Okay," Mercedes hollered back.

Carlita stepped out onto the front porch, locking the door behind her. The bright afternoon sun was blinding. She reached inside her purse for her sunglasses.

It was a couple blocks to Sal's Market and Deli, and the walk gave Carlita time to think. She needed to contact an attorney to review the papers.

Even if they made the trip to Savannah, and even if the property was salvageable, Carlita would be fighting an uphill battle with her sons.

Vinnie had left her with an almost unsurmountable task. Cosa Nostra, the mob, was a part of their lives...all of their lives, including hers. Moving away, starting fresh was almost unheard of. She picked up the pace, Sal's place in view now.

Sal's Market and Deli was larger than most local groceries, taking up the entire corner of Packett and Stock Avenue. The bell jingled as Carlita pushed the door open and stepped inside, the smell of freshly baked bread filled the air.

Sal was in the back.

"My timing is perfect."

Sal lifted his head at the sound of her voice. When he saw who it was, he set the butcher knife he was holding on the wooden cutting block and leaned his arms on the counter. "Carlita. Good to see you out and about. How you doin'?"

Carlita adjusted the strap of her purse. "Fine except that someone broke into my house again today. This is the second time since Vinnie's death." She crossed her arms and rubbed the sides. "I don't feel safe in my own home."

Sal lifted a hand and smoothed his thick, black moustache thoughtfully. "I heard about the first break-in. I'm sorry to hear someone is still botherin' ya."

He went on. "Carmine was in here earlier, said Vito gave Vinnie some swag to deliver right before he died but it never got there."

Carlita knew a lot of the lingo, but swag was a new one, at least to her. "Swag?"

"You know. Stolen goods he was supposed to deliver," Sal said. "According to Carmine, it was a big drop."

Chapter 4

The front door bell chimed and Sal looked over
Carlita's shoulder toward the door. "So what can I
getcha?"

"I need a pound and a half of ground beef. I have a
couple other things to pick up, too." Carlita waited for Sal
to package the meat.

He slid it across the counter and she placed the
package in the bottom of her basket. "Thanks Sal." She
grabbed a bag of breadcrumbs and a half-gallon of milk
before making her way to the small counter near the
front.

Victoria, Sal's wife, was working the cash register. She
took the grocery basket from Carlita and set it on the
counter. "I heard you tell Sal someone broke into your
house again." Victoria tsk-tsked and lowered her voice.
"I'll keep an ear out and let you know if I hear anything."

"Thanks Victoria. I would appreciate that." Carlita
paid for her purchases and then headed out of the store,
her head spinning.

Sal had mentioned Vito and Carmine. Could it be one
of them was searching for the gems?

The velvet bag she'd hidden inside her bra shifted. She needed to find a safer place to hide the goods.

Carlita's skin began to crawl when she noticed a dark sedan with tinted windows and a spotlight on the driver's side creep past her on the street. She got the eerie feeling the car was following her so she picked up the pace, almost jogging the rest of the way home.

When she got to the front door, the car that had followed her sped off. Carlita darted inside, quickly locked the door and leaned against it.

Mercedes bounded into the living room and flopped down on the living room sofa. "I'm ready to take that drive. Do you want to go with me?"

Carlita gazed into the kitchen at the stack of dishes she'd assembled to start working on her made-from-scratch meatballs. "If you can wait until I make the meatballs, I'll go with you," she bargained.

"Sounds good," Mercedes sat upright. "Do you need help?"

The women headed to the kitchen and began mixing the ground beef and other ingredients. Carlita made a double batch since all of her children would be there for dinner. It had been a long time since the whole family had eaten together.

Carlita's eyes shifted to the kitchen table and Vinnie's seat at the head of the table. Not everyone would be there. She blinked back the unexpected tears and Mercedes, noting the look on her mom's face, hugged her. "Pop would be proud of you," she said.

"You're right, which is why I'm determined to honor my vow and get the family out of the city and out of the business."

After Carlita placed the bowl of meatballs in the fridge and tidied the kitchen, she headed to the living room and the wall safe.

She could put the valuable gems in the safe, but Carlita's sons knew of the safe's existence and even knew the combination. Vinnie had always kept a couple thousand in cash inside for emergencies, along with a small arsenal of weapons.

She opened the safe, reached inside and pulled out a gun. Carlita's knowledge of guns was limited. Vinnie had taken her to the shooting range to teach her how to use a gun, but that had been years ago.

Mercedes, who had gone back to her room to grab her purse, walked into the living room. "What are you doing?"

"We need to practice shooting. I thought maybe you and I could find a gun shooting range nearby and take a few practice shots."

"Sounds like fun." Mercedes snaked around the side of her mother, reached inside the safe and pulled out a gun. It was a small silver gun with a pearl handle. "This one will do."

She turned the gun over in her hand, lifted it as she'd seen in the movies and gazed down the barrel, squeezing one eye shut. "What about bullets?"

Mercedes didn't wait for an answer as she lowered the gun, handed it to her mother and stuck her hand inside the safe a second time, pulling out a box of bullets. "I wonder if these will work." She set them on the coffee table nearby and reached back inside, pulling out two more boxes of bullets.

Carlita picked up one of the boxes. "Maybe we should take them all. Surely someone at the shooting range can help us figure it out."

"We'll need a bigger handbag to carry the goods." Mercedes darted to her room, returning moments later with a large Gucci bag. The women carefully placed the boxes of bullets in the bottom of the bag and then set the guns on top.

"Be careful carrying that. The guns might be loaded." Carlita said, which created a new set of concerns. Was it legal to carry a loaded handgun in a vehicle? Deciding ignorance was bliss, the women reached for their purses, the extra bag containing the weaponry and headed to the garage.

Carlita stopped abruptly in front of the garage door. "We need the keys and the garage door opener."

"Check." Mercedes held up a key fob. She pressed the button and the door silently opened. Vinnie's black Lincoln town car filled the entire single stall garage. There was no room for Carlita to squeeze through the narrow opening to reach the passenger side.

"Your father always backed the car out of the garage before I got in," Carlita told her daughter.

"Good idea." Mercedes hurried into the garage, opened the driver's side door and slid into the driver's seat.

Carlita stepped off to the side and waited while her daughter started the vehicle and then revved up the engine. "I don't..." She was going to tell her daughter not to rev it up, but the car windows were shut and there was no way she could hear.

The car, tires squealing, lurched forward. *Clunk!*

"Oh my gosh." Carlita started toward the rear of the car when suddenly, the tires squealed again and the black beast tore out of the garage.

Carlita ran for cover, squeezing her eyes shut and waiting for another crash, which never came.

Mercedes slammed on the brakes and the car screeched to a halt in the driveway.

"Dear God, please protect us." Carlita reached for the door handle, opened the door and slid into the passenger seat. "What did you hit?" she asked her daughter as she reached for her seatbelt.

"An old metal barrel. It's fine. I only put a small dent in it." Mercedes patted the dashboard. "This baby is built like a tank. Probably not even a scratch on it."

Carlita raised a brow but kept silent. Vinnie would have blown a gasket.

Mercedes closed the garage door and slowly backed out of the driveway. "I know there's a shooting range a couple blocks away," she said. "Shoot Great or something like that." She shifted the car into drive and pressed her foot on the gas pedal.

Carlita watched as the houses whizzed by and leaned over to check the car's speed. Her daughter was cruising at almost forty-five miles an hour. "Mercedes! The speed limit is only twenty-five."

"Sorry." Mercedes eased her foot off the gas and the car slowed. "We're not far now." She studied the buildings to her left.

Carlita's eyes widened in horror as they blew through a stop sign. "Mercedes!"

"What?"

"You just ran a stop sign," her mother gasped, clutching her chest. She might not live long enough to have to worry about properly shooting a gun.

"I can't drive and look for the gun place at the same time," Mercedes argued.

"You drive, I'll look." Carlita shifted her head back and forth, as she studied the buildings. "I see it up ahead on the right."

Mercedes tapped the brakes to slow for the upcoming turn but not enough. She jerked the wheel and the car careened to the right, jumping the curb. She pulled into a parking spot and stomped the brakes.

Carlita's head jerked forward and her neck made a small popping noise.

Mercedes shifted into park and turned the engine off. "See? Safe and sound. A couple more practice runs and I'll be ready for the open road." She hopped out of the car and reached back inside to grab the Gucci...err, gun bag and the women headed for the front entrance.

Carlita eased out of the car and slammed the passenger door shut. "I think I'll walk home," she said, only half-joking and then turned her attention to the building.

Carlita never would've guessed the nondescript, plain vinyl-sided building was a shooting range had there not been a sign out front.

Mercedes strode to the door and held it open while her mother stepped inside.

From somewhere in the back, Carlita could hear the *pop, pop* of gunfire. Not far from the front door was a small counter and standing behind the counter was a bald man she guessed to be close to her age. "Can I help you?"

"Yes." Mercedes approached the counter and set the bag of guns on top. "My mother and I need to practice shooting. Well, she needs more practice. I've never shot a gun before."

The man studied Carlita then Mercedes. "You're in the right place." He extended his hand. "I'm Bud Little. This is my shooting range and it's your lucky day. Someone cancelled on me and I have enough time to fit you gals in for a quick lesson."

"Perfect," Carlita said.

"That'll be sixty-five dollars each for an hour lesson," he said.

"What if we do half an hour each?" Mercedes bargained as she reached for her purse.

"Okay," Bud shrugged. "Sixty-five bucks for half an hour for two of you."

Mercedes had grabbed a stack of cash along with the guns and ammo. She pulled four twenties from the banded stack inside her purse and handed them to Bud. He counted the bills, opened the cash register and counted out the change, placing the bills in Mercedes's open palm.

"Follow me." He led the women through a door to the right of the front desk and down a short corridor. At the end of the corridor was another door and on the other side of that, a large room with open stalls. Plexiglass walls divided the stalls.

They shuffled over to the first open stall on the left and Bud pointed to Mercedes's bags. "You can put your stuff in the corner. Did you bring guns? If not, I have some, but I'll have to charge you extra."

Mercedes patted the Gucci bag. "They're in here." She gave her mother a quick glance. "We weren't sure what to bring since my pop owned a small arsenal." She opened the bag and Bud peered inside. He stuck his hand in the bag and pulled out a box of bullets. "How much shootin' you plan to do?"

"Just a few rounds," Carlita said. "We weren't sure which bullets belonged to which guns so we brought a variety."

"No kidding." Bud set the box of bullets on the small shelf next to him and then reached inside and pulled out the gun with the pearl handle. He turned it over in his hand and inspected the side. "You got a gem here. This is a collector's piece."

"What kind of gun is it?" Carlita took a step closer. Maybe it was worth some money and they could sell it.

"Special order pearl-handled gold and silver plated Colt." Bud tugged on the magazine. "This baby is loaded." He shifted his gaze to Mercedes. "You're carrying around a loaded gun?"

Mercedes shrank back. "I-I had no idea it was loaded."

"Neither did I," Carlita confessed.

"You two really do need lessons," Bud shook his head. "Gather round." He motioned them closer and began showing them the different parts of the gun. He also showed them how to check the magazine, and how to latch and unlatch the safety. He even showed them how to carry the gun.

Afterwards, he let them fire off a few rounds from both the Colt and the other gun, which, according to Bud, was another Colt. When they finished shooting several rounds, he supervised as the women safely disarmed the weapons and carefully placed them inside the bag.

They followed him out of the shooting area and to the front. "Thank you for fitting us in," Carlita said gratefully. "We might come back soon for another lesson."

At least now, Carlita was confident she could fire a weapon and possibly hit her target, if necessary.

They told Bud good-bye and then headed back to the car. Mercedes placed the gun bag on the backseat and then climbed behind the wheel. "That was fun."

Mercedes circled a few more blocks and managed to run one more stop sign before they headed back to the house.

Carlita spotted her son, Vinnie, as soon as they rounded the corner and pulled onto their street. He was leaning against the trunk of his car and watched as his sister steered their father's car into the drive.

Mercedes stopped in the driveway to let her mother out. "Be sure to go slow when you pull into the garage," Carlita told her daughter before slamming the passenger side door shut.

"Got it." Mercedes peered over the steering wheel and eased into the garage. "Piece of cake," she muttered to herself as she shifted into park, turned the engine off and hopped out of the car.

Vinnie marched up the drive. "What do you think you're doing driving Pop's car?"

Chapter 5

"Cool your jets big bro." Mercedes shifted the bags. "I have Ma's permission."

Vinnie began to pace as he listed a slew of reasons why they should not be driving his father's car. His reasons included not knowing how to pump gas. (Carlita agreed he had a point and made a mental note to have one of her sons take her to a local gas station to show Mercedes and her how to pump gas.)

He also pointed out that they didn't even know if the vehicle was insured and if they ended up in a car accident, they could be sued. Another valid point Carlita vowed to look into before they cruised around town again.

He ended with the lame reasoning that his father would not approve.

Carlita was saved from having to answer by the toot of a car horn. She watched as her youngest son pulled his SUV into the drive. "I better get inside and start on dinner." She left her three children, along with her youngest son, Paulie's wife, Gina, standing in the drive and hurried indoors.

If Vinnie was freaking out about Mercedes and Carlita taking the town car around the neighborhood, there was no way he would approve of them driving halfway across the country.

Carlita filled a large pot with water, added a couple shakes of salt, turned her front stove burner on high and set the pot on top. While the water warmed, she began mixing her homemade spaghetti sauce and when she finished, she set it aside to start cooking the meatballs. The aroma of garlic, Italian spices and sizzling meat filled the kitchen.

"Smells delicious Ma." Tony, Carlita's middle son, wandered into the kitchen, stopping to kiss his mother's cheek. He stared down at the frying pan. "I stopped by Carmine Tonesci's on my way here."

Carlita shifted. "Yeah?"

"He may have had something to do with Pop's death," Tony said softly.

"Don't go getting yourself murdered. Nothing you do will bring your father back." She set the fork she was holding on top of a folded paper towel. "Mercedes and I have some errands to run tomorrow if you're gonna be around."

Mercedes stepped into the kitchen and Vinnie trailed behind, catching the tail end of the conversation. "Or maybe Mercedes and Ma will drive themselves," Vinnie said.

Tony shot his older brother a dark look. "Pop would be proud of Mercedes and Ma for trying to take care of themselves," he argued. "We can't be here all the time, Vinnie. What if something were to happen to us?"

Paulie, who had followed his older brother inside, added his two cents. "Tony is right. Pop would be pleased."

"I don't see the harm," Gina added.

Vinnie glared at his brothers and stalked into the living room. Carlita heard the television blaring local news, and Tony and Paulie joined their brother moments later. She could hear them arguing but it wasn't loud enough to make out what was being said.

The pasta had finished cooking and a small sample assured Carlita it was a perfect al dente. She sawed off thick slices of the Italian bread she had picked up at Sal's earlier and arranged them in a breadbasket.

"Dinner is ready," she hollered into the living room as she set the bread on the table, next to the large bowl of piping hot spaghetti and meatballs.

The arguing abruptly stopped and Vinnie led the way to the kitchen. He glanced at his father's chair and then slid into an empty seat next to it.

Paulie eased into a seat next to Carlita and clasped his hands. "I'll say grace," he offered. The family bowed their heads in prayer and after praying, Carlita swiped at the tear that had trickled down her cheek.

Paulie reached out and squeezed her hand. "I'm sorry Ma. Pop chose his way of life and it ended up being his downfall."

The statement got the other two brothers, Vinnie and Tony, riled up and an argument ensued. The only ones who didn't join in the fray were mother, daughter and Paulie's wife, Gina. They remained silent.

Finally, they all calmed, agreeing to disagree. "Nothing you can say – or do - will bring your father back," Carlita said as she studied her children's faces.

Vinnie was the spitting image of his old man, right down to his jet black, slicked back hair, piercing gray eyes and pointed trademark Garlucci nose. Not only was Vinnie the spitting image of his father, he was a "mini" Vinnie with the same mannerisms, same walk, same shrewd business savvy, not to mention wise crack sense of humor.

Carlita's second oldest, Anthony "Tony" Garlucci, was the complete opposite of his father and older brother. He was a mama's boy. Tony loved the finer things in life, fine wine, beautiful women. He also had a penchant for expensive sports cars and an obsession with thoroughbred racehorses, just like his father.

What Tony didn't love was the "family business" and the messy way the family made a living. In fact, Tony tried to stay on the fringes of the family, unless of course, he was called to "clip" someone, but he was fastidious. Get in. Get the job done. Get out.

Vinnie and Carlita's youngest son, Paul or "Paulie" hadn't worked in the "family" business for decades. He had gone clean and, in fact, had become the mayor of nearby Clifton Falls, New York.

Paulie loved his suburban life and suburban wife, Gina, and their three young children, Gracie, Noel and Paulie, Jr. They lived in a nondescript, two-story brick home in the town of Clifton Falls. Gina, a homemaker, handled the day-to-day upkeep and running of their home.

The couple rarely left Clifton Falls, attending Mass at St. Patrick's Catholic Church in their hometown. Paulie and Gina only drove to New York when absolutely necessary.

Paulie reached for the basket of bread. "What you want to talk about Ma? Pop's will? His possessions?"

"I have some of his things I want you to go through, but I also want to discuss his dying wish." Carlita sucked in a deep breath. "Your father's wish that I get his sons, our children, out of Queens, out of New York and start a new life somewhere else."

The words were no more out of her mouth and Vinnie began to argue. "Where we gonna go? We don't know nothin' except for New York."

Carlita gave Mercedes a quick glance. "We're going to Savannah, Georgia."

Chapter 6

Everyone began talking at once, her boys arguing with her that there was no way they were moving to the south with excuses ranging from the oppressive heat, larger than life bugs and lack of public transportation, although Carlita wasn't sure where that came from since all of her sons owned vehicles. Mercedes and she were the only ones who used public transportation.

Tony wiped his mouth with his napkin, dropped it on top of his empty dinner plate and pushed his chair back. "That's crazy. Why Savannah?"

Mercedes placed her fork on the table. "Because Pop left us...property in Savannah. From what we can tell, they appear to be abandoned businesses. One of the buildings is a multi-level and we're thinking we can turn the top floor into apartments."

"How..." Paulie started to ask.

Carlita explained how she had found an envelope inside Vinnie's jacket with her name on it, that there'd been a safe deposit box key inside the envelope. "Inside the safe deposit box was a quitclaim deed to property in Savannah." She left out the part about the gems.

"So sell the property and use the money to live on," Tony shrugged.

Carlita's sons started arguing again while Carlita, Mercedes and Gina cleared the table. It quickly became apparent her sons had no intention of ever setting foot in Savannah, let alone moving there.

Vinnie, Tony and Paulie headed outside to change the door locks, which didn't take long and it made Carlita feel a smidgen safer.

She was glad her children had come for dinner, but by the time they all left, Carlita was exhausted. Mercedes was in the living room watching television when Carlita slumped into the recliner. "That went well," she joked.

Mercedes muted the television and turned to face her mother. "We're going to go ahead as planned. With a few more driving practices under my belt, I'll be ready to drive to Savannah."

"I agree. We'll have to sneak off and maybe let the boys know we've gone after we get there." Carlita smoothed her dark hair and leaned back in the recliner. "In the meantime, we better keep the guns close at hand. Hard telling if someone is going to break in and try to get their hands on the..."

Mercedes waved her hand wildly, making a zipping motion across her lips. She ran into the kitchen and returned moments later with a pad of paper and pen. She scribbled on the pad and turned it so that her mother could read the words. "What if someone bugged the house?"

Carlita slowly nodded. She wouldn't put it past anyone, including her sons, to bug her home. She watched her daughter make her way back into the kitchen and then plucked the bag of gems from her bra.

She twirled the end of the strings thoughtfully. Her son, Vinnie, had mentioned Carmine Tonesci. Carlita had met Carmine a few times and he had always given her an odd feeling, as if he was sizing her up.

Carmine had always been polite when they had bumped into one another at various functions. Carmine's wife, Luciana, was friendly. She owned a small nail salon not far from the house.

Carlita had never gone inside the salon, but had ridden past on occasion, and she had always wondered if Carmine used his wife's nail salon as a front for his nefarious business transactions.

Next on the list was Frank Delmario. Tony had told her that Frank and her Vinnie had gotten into it inside Gino's

Pizzeria days before his death and Frank had threatened to kill Vinnie. Tony had used another term but Carlita couldn't remember what it was.

Everyone knew Frank wasn't in the business, but he was a local businessman. Had he borrowed money from Vinnie, Vinnie had called the payment due and when Frank couldn't pay, he panicked and took a hit on her husband?

Last, but not least, was Vito Castellini. If Vito had given Vinnie a drop and the drop was the bag of gems, someone, including Vito, would want those gems back.

Carlita wished she had some idea how much the gems were worth but didn't dare breathe a word to anyone, including her sons, that she had them. It was bad enough they knew she had the deed to the properties.

She abruptly jumped out of the chair and headed to Mercedes's room. Perhaps she could do a little digging around to see if they could trace the property to the previous owner. Carlita knocked on her daughter's door and then stepped in.

Mercedes quickly closed the computer screen and spun around in her chair.

"What are you doing Mercedes?"

"Oh nothing," Mercedes averted her gaze. "Just a little research on Savannah."

"I was thinking perhaps you could research something else." She picked up the pad of paper and pen next to her daughter's laptop.

Carlita wrote the words. "Find out who owned the Savannah property before your father." She turned the notepad so Mercedes could read the words and her daughter nodded, giving her a thumbs up.

After leaving her daughter's room, Carlita headed to her own bedroom to search for a safe place to put the bag of precious gems. She wandered into the small master bathroom, turned the faucet on and splashed cold water on her face.

She patted her face, draped the hand towel on the towel rack and then gazed at the trashcan sitting next to the toilet. *The trash can...no one would look in the trash, would they?*

Carlita grabbed a couple clean tissues, wrapped the bag of gems inside and carefully set them in the trash.

With the gems safely stashed in the trash, Carlita rambled around the house aimlessly. She dusted the living room and straightened some knick-knacks.

Carlita turned the television on again to watch the local news and finally turned it off. The news was even more depressing than her own life.

She sat quietly in the living room recliner and mulled over what her sons had said. Her husband was dead, possibly "offed" by one of his associates.

Her daughter was turning into a hermit, camping out in her bedroom nearly 'round the clock doing heaven knows what. She had inherited a property that may or may not have been on the up and up, and she was still in her fifties, although pushing mighty close to the big "6-o."

Carlita had promised her husband to get their children away from the "family" and the only prospect was the dump her daughter had shown her. If she were completely honest with herself, the place looked like it needed a bulldozer, not a facelift.

Carlita set the remote on the stand next to her recliner and headed to bed. Her daughter had assured her another day or so of "practice driving" and she would be ready for their road trip. Mercedes may have been almost ready to go, but Carlita wasn't so sure she was.

After brushing her teeth and changing into her pajamas, Carlita crawled into bed and tucked the sheets under her chin. She drifted off to sleep wondering what in the world was waiting for them in Savannah.

***

Carlita woke late the next morning, feeling more rested than she had in days, perhaps even weeks. She wandered into the kitchen to start a fresh pot of coffee and found a note on the counter.

"Hi Ma. I went for a drive. Don't worry about breakfast. I'm going to run by a drive-thru to pick up some breakfast and should be back before ten. Love you. Mercedes."

Carlita glanced at the clock: 9:45.

Screech.

"Sounds like she's home." Carlita crumpled the note and hurried out the back door. The smell of burning rubber filled the air as she watched her daughter ease the Lincoln into the garage. A fresh black spot, tire tracks, marred a chunk of the driveway.

Mercedes, carrying a fast food bag, bounded out of the garage, her face flushed. "I'm gettin' pretty good at driving around and was thinking we can get a head start and hit the open road today."

Carlita pointed at the tire mark. "Yeah, we better get going before we don't have any tread left on the tires." She took the bag from her daughter and followed her into the kitchen. "What are we gonna do for money on this trip?" The thought had just occurred to her and she had no clue how much gas it would take to drive to Savannah and back, not to mention the cost of hotels or meals for several days.

"We need to figure out how to pump gas," Carlita said.

"Got it covered. I stopped at a station a block over and this nice man showed me how to fill up. It was a piece of cake." Mercedes set her purse on the counter, grabbed a Coke from the fridge and slid into an empty chair at the kitchen table. "I figured we could hit a..."

Carlita put a finger to her lips and using her other hand, pointed to her ear. "Let's eat out at the picnic table."

Mercedes hopped out of the chair and snatched her Coke from the table as the women headed to the backyard. "You think the house is bugged?" she said as she swung her legs over the side of the picnic bench.

"I wouldn't put it past anyone." Carlita opened the food bag, reached inside and pulled out two sausage biscuits and two crispy hash browns.

Mercedes took one of each from her mother, unwrapped the sandwich and placed the hash brown on the paper. "I was gonna say, we can find a pawnshop on the way and pawn one of the smaller gems to cover expenses. There's still a stack of cash in the safe but I don't think there's enough to cover everything."

Mercedes dipped a hash brown in catsup and popped it in her mouth. "I think we should leave today. The boys were here last night. They won't stop by for another day or so. If we leave today, we'll get a good head start."

Carlita started to shake her head. She hadn't yet mentally prepared for the trip. Not only that, she wasn't 100% convinced her daughter was up for the drive, although she seemed confident.

Mercedes could see her mother was on the fence. "Nothing is stopping us. I mapped the route this morning. It will take a little more than thirteen hours to get to Savannah. We can stop halfway. Tomorrow morning we can get up bright and early and finish the drive."

Mercedes looked so excited, so hopeful, Carlita didn't have the heart to tell her no. Not only that, at least she would know the gems were safe...

"Okay." Carlita bit into her sandwich and chewed thoughtfully. "But I'll need at least an hour to pack."

The women agreed to bring enough clothes for an entire week, although Carlita hoped they wouldn't be gone that long. The sole purpose of the trip would be to scope the place out and get a feel for how many repairs the properties would need.

Carlita swallowed her last bite of food, crumpled her empty wrapper, tossed it into the empty bag and eased off the picnic bench. "I guess I better start packing."

Chapter 7

Mercedes eased the big black sedan onto I-95 southbound with nary a glitch, if you didn't count almost sideswiping a tractor-trailer, running a four-wheel drive pick-up off the road and nearly rear ending a minivan, whose occupant opened the driver's side window and waved his middle finger at them.

"That was easy," Mercedes said as she tightened her grip on the steering wheel.

Her mother tugged on her seatbelt and nodded. "Piece of cake."

"You got the gems?" Mercedes asked.

Carlita patted her purse. "They're in here."

The drive was a little smoother once they were cruising down the highway. Mercedes rattled off the details of the trip, right down to where she planned to stop for the night, which was somewhere in the State of Virginia and in a place Carlita had never heard of.

The plan was to pull off a little early and Carlita was proud her daughter had thought to research the pawnshops near their exit. As the afternoon wore on,

Carlita began to relax a little. She stopped glancing in the rearview mirror to see if they were being followed.

She wondered what her sons would think when they discovered Mercedes and she had gone off on their own and then reminded herself she was not only the parent but also an adult. Carlita could do as she darn well pleased, even if it meant driving halfway across the country with a daughter who had limited, almost non-existent, driving skills, with only a little cash to a place they had never been before.

Carlita knew her sons would freak out. At least she had asked if they wanted to come along. She knew they would never dream that Mercedes and she would strike out on their own, but Carlita was certain her Vinnie was watching over them. She had also prayed about it, convinced God was with them.

After several long hours of riding, with only a couple quick stops to fill the car, which they quickly realized was a gas-guzzler, they pulled off the highway and into the small town of Pinckney, Virginia.

The first order of business was to stop at the pawnshop Mercedes had found online. The plan was for Carlita to wait in the car while Mercedes tried to pawn the smallest of the gems she figured was worth an estimated four thousand dollars. It would be more than enough cash to fund the trip and maybe even enough to bring a little home with them.

Carlita kept one eye on Mercedes through the storefront window and the other eye on the glove box where she had placed her loaded handgun. She had a sneaky suspicion it was illegal to carry a loaded firearm in the glove box and across state lines, but her concern over their safety won out over obeying a possible law, so the gun was in the glove box.

Mercedes waved her hands frantically at the male clerk behind the counter and turned to go when he rounded the counter and grabbed her arm to stop her.

Carlita leaned forward as she reached for the glove box.

The store clerk and Mercedes talked animatedly for several moments before Mercedes followed the man away from the counter and out of sight.

It seemed like an eternity before Mercedes emerged from the pawnshop, grinning from ear to ear. She climbed into the driver's side seat and reached for the seatbelt. "Four thousand five hundred in cold, hard cash. He wanted to give me thirty-two hundred and when I started to walk, he started to panic and grabbed my arm."

She glanced in the rearview mirror and shifted the car in reverse. "The money should tide us over for the trip plus some."

Mercedes crept to the stop sign, looked both ways and turned left. "The hotel, Wander Inn, is on the other side of the highway and it should be on the left."

Carlita spotted the hotel first, its bright red and green sign flashing. "Over there."

Mercedes turned into the parking lot and eased to a stop under the portico. "I'll be right back." She didn't wait for a reply as she grabbed her purse, climbed out of the car and hurried through the front entrance. She returned a few moments later. "Our room is straight ahead and on the second floor."

By the time Carlita and Mercedes carried their bags to the room and looked around, Carlita was ready to kick off her shoes and close her eyes. It had been a harrowing day and she had never been this far from home and had never traveled without Vinnie.

Carlita wondered if her sons had tried to call. She pulled her cell phone from her purse, turned it over and switched it to on. "One missed call," she told her daughter as she pressed the phone icon. "Paulie called." Carlita tapped out the access code, switched the phone to speaker so Mercedes could hear and then turned up the volume.

"Hi Ma. It's me, Paulie. I tried calling the house phone but no one answered. I figured maybe you and Mercedes went out for dinner or somethin' since you started driving Pop's car around. Call me when you can." Paulie told his mother he loved her and then the line went dead.

Mercedes, who sat perched on the edge of the other bed, stood. "Well, at least we're halfway to Savannah and they haven't caught on yet."

No one knew they were gone, not even Father Dadore, who had called while Carlita was packing and asked if he could meet with her the following day.

Carlita made half a dozen excuses and was finally able to put him off indefinitely.

The women watched a little television and then decided to call it a night. It was late and they planned to hit the road early so they would arrive in Savannah while it was still daylight.

As Carlita drifted off to sleep, she wondered what her sons would say when they found out their mother and sister had left town without consulting them.

During the night, Carlita tossed and turned, her dreams filled with visions of her ramshackle inheritance. In one of the dreams, they made their way into one of the buildings, only to find the entire interior of the building trashed. The dream had seemed so real, it woke her.

It took hours for her to fall back asleep and when she did, it seemed like only minutes before Mercedes was leaning over her, shaking her awake. "Time to hit the road."

Chapter 8

Whatever Carlita Garlucci had pictured historic Savannah, Georgia to be like, what she found wasn't even close. It was quaint. It was charming. The people were warm and welcoming. Even the workers at the gas station, just outside of town, were friendly, asking if they were in the area visiting and offering advice. In other words, Savannah was the complete opposite of Queens, New York.

They were also full of information. When Mercedes told the clerk behind the counter at the gas station that they were looking for 210 Mulberry Street in Savannah, he gave her an odd look. "You sure about that?"

"Positive," Mercedes nodded. "We recently inherited the property and drove down from New York to check it out."

"That place is haunted," the young man blurted out.

The hairs on the back of Carlita's neck prickled. "Why do you say that?"

"Everybody in town knows it. Some old man died there a few years back. If you drive by there after dark you can see lights on, and someone walking around inside."

Carlita thanked him for the information and they stepped out of the store, making their way back to the car.

Mercedes opened the driver's side door and gazed at her mother over the roof. "You think Pop knocked somebody off?"

There was a strong possibility the property had mafia ties, which meant the business may have been a cover for drugs or money laundering - the possibilities were endless.

"Could be," Carlita said and eased into the passenger seat. "We still have no idea how your father ended up with the deed to the properties." She could only guess.

The drive from the gas station to the property was a short five minutes, tops, and it was exactly as Mercedes had described. 210 Mulberry Street was in the historic district, not far from the river.

They circled the block three times before Mercedes spotted an alley behind the larger of the two buildings. She eased into the alley, shifted the car into park and eyed the back of the building warily.

"This is it." Mercedes turned the engine off and reached for the door handle. "We should bring the gun."

Mercedes may as well have saved her breath since her mother was already reaching inside the glove box for the loaded weapon.

There were no keys to the property, which meant the women would have to break in somehow and then perhaps, if it was even worth it, arrange for a locksmith to meet them the following day to install new locks.

Carlita gently placed the loaded weapon inside her purse and exited the car, quietly closing the door behind her. The alley was empty, at least it appeared to be empty, and mother and daughter tiptoed to the sidewalk.

Across the street from the property was a tidy row of stores, including a gift shop, an ice cream parlor, a tattoo parlor, which looked out of place, and finally, a real estate office.

The women turned right and studied the side of the building as they walked. There was a large wooden door leading to a side entrance. Farther down the sidewalk were several glass block windows as well as basement windows. Black wrought iron bars covered the basement windows.

"Let's try this door." Mercedes climbed the two steps to the side entrance, grasped the metal doorknob and turned. "It's locked." She hopped off the steps. "We'll have to try the front."

The women hurried to the end of the sidewalk and then turned right so that they stood facing the front.

"Looks like an old grocery store and possibly a restaurant," Carlita said. She shuffled close to the front window, the only one that wasn't boarded up, cupped her hands to the glass and peered inside. Her heart sank. The inside was a disaster, and in worse shape than the outside. "Oh no!"

Mercedes joined her mother and looked inside. "It doesn't look that bad." She tugged on Carlita's arm. "C'mon. Let's go check it out." On the other side of the window was the front entrance door.

Mercedes grasped the thumb latch and pushed down. The door creaked open and she jumped back. "It's unlocked."

Her mother reached inside her purse and gripped the gun. "I'll go first." She eased past her daughter and slipped inside the building.

The overpowering stench of moldy, rotting wood and stale cigarette smoke filled the air. She took another tentative step forward, her ear tuned to the sounds of the abandoned building. "Hello?"

Nothing.

Mercedes bumped into the back of her mother, gripping the edge of her blouse. "This place is creepy. Maybe we shouldn't be here."

Carlita shifted her gaze to her daughter. "We just drove almost a thousand miles and now you want to leave?" She crept forward taking another step, the wooden floor creaking beneath her weight.

The women continued to walk slowly as they inched toward the back. Rusting metal racks with chunks of peeling paint lined the walls. A vintage cash register sat on top of what once had been a checkout counter.

Behind the checkout counter were small shelves lining the walls. Empty liquor bottles dotted the shelves. To the left of the checkout counter and shelves was another door. "I wonder what's back there," Carlita said.

The women crept to the back door. Carlita shifted the gun to her other hand and reached for the door handle. The door was locked.

Mercedes bent forward and peered through the skeleton keyhole. "Looks like a storage area," she whispered. "I guess we've seen enough." She turned to go.

"Not so fast," Carlita grabbed her daughter's arm and lifted her gaze. "There has to be a key around here somewhere. Drag that chair over." With her free hand, she pointed to a lime green vinyl chair tucked under one of the wire shelves.

Mercedes reluctantly did as she was told and brought the chair to the door.

"Hop up there and feel along the edge of the trim piece to see if there's a key."

Mercedes frowned at her mother but obeyed as she lifted her hand and ran it along the top. "No key." She dusted her hands off and hopped down. "Now can we go?"

Carlita studied the locked door. "We could kick it open," she said. "Here. Hold this." She handed the gun to her daughter, lifted her leg, arched her back and with as much force as possible, kicked the door with the heel of her shoe.

A sharp pain bolted from Carlita's kneecap to her hip. "Ouch," she groaned.

"Let me try," Mercedes lifted her leg and kicked the door.

"What's going on in here?" An angry male voice echoed from the doorway.

Chapter 9

Carlita's eyes darted to the looming figure that filled the door. The menacing figure, who was holding what appeared to be a gun, stepped inside.

Mercedes flung herself in front of her mother, brandishing her weapon. "We own this place. Who are *you*?" she retorted.

The figure relaxed his stance slightly and lowered the weapon, just a tad. "Steve Winter. I own the tattoo shop across the street and I came by to check on the place. I had to run off some riff raff the other day, a squatter who decided to set up camp in here."

The man strode across the dark room, and as he drew closer, Carlita could see he was young. Thirtyish, red hair, short and on the pudgy side. "I thought he might have come back."

Mercedes extended her free hand. "I'm Mercedes Garlucci and this is my mother, Carlita. We inherited this property and drove down from New York to check it out."

Steve Winter switched the weapon to his other hand and then shook Mercedes's hand, a small smile crossing

70

his face. "Pleasure to meet you Mercedes. You can call me Steve-O."

"It's nice to meet you...Steve-O." Mercedes grinned.

Carlita glanced at the "gun" in the man's hand. She had seen her share of weapons in her lifetime and was certain Steve was holding a BB gun. "And you can call me Mrs. Garlucci." She pointed to the BB gun. "That's not a real gun."

Steve-O turned the weapon over and smiled. "You're right. It's not, but on first glance you can't tell."

"True," she admitted.

Steve's expression grew serious. "Like I said, someone has been camping out in here off and on for a few months now. This place has been vacant since old George Delmario died a few years back."

He shifted his gaze and eyed them suspiciously. "I thought Mrs. Delmario owned this property."

"Nope." Mercedes shook her head. "Not anymore. It belongs to us."

"I see." Steve-O changed the subject and pointed at the back door Mercedes and Carlita had attempted to kick open. "I have a tool over at my place that will pick the door lock if you'd like me to go get it."

"That would be great," Carlita said.

"Be right back." Steve-O strode out of the store and they watched him pass by the front window.

After he disappeared from sight, Carlita stepped close to her daughter. "Don't tell him too much," she whispered. "We don't know if he's on the up and up. What if he's the one who has been staying here?"

Mercedes wrinkled her nose. "You think so? We'll ask to see his tattoo shop after we're done inspecting the place."

Carlita's bullcrap radar shot up. She zeroed in on Steve, who was carrying a large pick, as soon as he returned. "So why don't you carry a real gun?"

Steve tightened his grip on the pick. "Had a little run in with the law years ago, back when I was young and foolish." He shrugged. "Anyway, I tried getting a concealed weapons permit but with my background, it's a no-go."

Carlita rolled her eyes. She was in Savannah to get *away* from the criminal element and the first person Mercedes and she met had a criminal record!

Steve could tell Carlita didn't care for the answer and quickly changed the subject. "Let's see if we can get the door unlocked." He sauntered over to the door and with a couple quick jabs of the pick inside the keyhole, the lock clicked and he swung the door open.

"Let me guess. They got you for breaking and entering," Carlita said, only half kidding.

Steve didn't reply, which Carlita took for an admission of guilt, but let it slide.

Mercedes walked into the back room first. Steve followed behind Mercedes and Carlita brought up the rear, still not 100% certain he was on the up and up.

Steve was right about one thing - someone had been staying there. On the back wall was a compact kitchenette. A metal, two-burner hot plate sat on top of the counter. Next to the hot plate was a small cooler and on the floor in front of the cupboard was a sleeping bag and pillow.

"You got a squatter, for sure," Steve said. "I've had to get rid of a couple myself." He glanced around the room and at another door off to one side. "Been a long time since I've been back here."

He pointed at the door. "The Delmarios lived in an apartment above this place. If my memory serves me right, there are a couple other units up there, too."

Mercedes turned to her mother. "We should check it out."

The door leading to the upper level was unlocked and Steve seemed disappointed he wouldn't have to pick it. The women followed him up the steep stairs, which opened onto a large landing.

The color of the hall walls was a dullish gray and scattered along the edge of the floor were chunks of paint that had peeled off. The wooden floors appeared to be in decent shape except for one spot where it looked like there was an active roof leak and water had dripped onto the floor.

Carlita shifted her gaze and studied the doors. There were two on the left and two on the right. She walked to the first door on the right, turned the knob and opened the door.

She took a tentative step into what appeared to be the living room. The room sported the same wooden floors and dull, peeling paint.

Mercedes slowly walked to the center of the room. "I wonder why the squatter is staying downstairs instead of up here."

"Quick getaway," Steve answered. "If the cops show up, it would be easier to escape if you're downstairs."

Mercedes and Carlita headed to the other side of the room. To the left was a small dining area and on the other side was a compact kitchen, complete with chipped Formica countertops, a vintage 1960's single door refrigerator and matching gas stove.

"This place needs a lot of work," Carlita frowned. "A lot."

They finished inspecting the apartment. There were two surprisingly large bedrooms. A spacious bath, complete with claw foot tub, separated the bedrooms.

"I love it," Mercedes gushed and clasped her hands as she gazed at the pink and black ceramic tile covering the bathroom walls. This place has so much potential."

Carlita, not wanting to burst her daughter's bubble, remained silent.

The trio retraced their steps and made their way out into the hall. They scoped out the other apartments, which were mirror images of the first one in both size, layout and the same deplorable dilapidated condition.

They headed back down to the first floor and finished their inspection of the grocery store before heading next door to the second building.

On the way to the second building, Carlita noticed a black wrought iron fence and gate that connected the properties. She stepped to the gate and peered between the bars.

Beyond the gate was a cobblestone walkway. Overgrown bushes and shrubs obscured the view. She tilted her head so that she could see past the greenery. "There's a small courtyard back there," she said excitedly.

Carlita pushed on the gate but it wouldn't budge. "It's locked."

Steve pulled the pick from his pocket and waved it in front of Carlita's face. "Not for long."

She stepped to the side and watched as Steve inserted the key in the keyhole, and wiggled it around. After a couple twists back and forth, the gate creaked open.

Steve pushed it all the way open and stepped inside with the women following close behind. "It looks like there's a bigger space up ahead."

Carlita, followed by Mercedes, carefully tiptoed down the uneven steps and into a small clearing. "This is magnificent," she gushed.

Although the courtyard had suffered from years of neglect, it had the potential to become a serene oasis.

The brick walls gave way to a circular paved area. Near the rear wall was a fountain, a statue of a woman tilting a vase toward a round pool circling her feet.

To the left of the fountain were a rusty bistro table and two chairs. At one time, it had been white, but years of neglect and exposure to the elements had transformed it into a thick layer of rusty brown.

"This place is magical." Mercedes spun around in a slow circle. "We could clean this place up; hang twinkling lights from the trees."

With a little elbow grease, it could become a special place, an oasis from the hustle and bustle of a busy city. "This is like finding a lost treasure." Carlita turned to Steve. "What a wonderful surprise. I'm glad we found it."

They headed back out and Steve pulled the gate shut behind them, using his handy dandy tool to lock it before the trio walked to the other building.

"This was a diner," Steve explained as he followed them inside. "Denny's Deluxe Diner." He patted his pudgy potbelly. "Denny used to serve up some of *the* best greasy cheeseburgers this side of the Mississippi."

"I could..." Carlita's voice trailed off.

"You could open a restaurant," Mercedes interrupted. She turned to Steve. "My ma is one of the best Italian cooks in the world."

Steve smiled. "I love Italian food. I would be your best customer," he promised.

The restaurant was in the same dilapidated state of disrepair as the other properties. The place needed a gut job, but it had possibilities. It would also take a lot of money.

Carlita voiced her concerns. "I wonder how much it would cost to get this place whipped into shape – the restaurant, the grocery store not to mention fixing the apartments so they were habitable," she mused.

"We would only have to worry about one apartment for now," Mercedes pointed out. "If Vinnie and Tony decide to move down, we could finish the rest."

"Or we could fix them up and rent them out," Carlita said.

"I have a buddy who's a handyman. He's not a general contractor, but he owns his own business and does top notch work." Steve pinched his index finger and thumb together to form a circle. "He lives here in Savannah."

"Perfect," Mercedes said. "We should give him a call."

Steve led them out of the restaurant and they stood on the sidewalk while Carlita pulled the door shut behind them. "If you want my buddy's number, I have his card over at my shop."

Carlita had never been inside a tattoo parlor. "That would be great." They passed by the properties, hurried across the street and over to the tattoo parlor.

She followed Steve and Mercedes inside the small shop and stood off to one side as she studied the interior. A variety of pictures dotted the walls; images Carlita could only speculate were examples of art Steve offered to tattoo on customers' bodies.

He stepped behind the counter, opened a drawer and fumbled around inside, pulling out a business card. He handed it to Carlita, who glanced at the front and then dropped it into her purse. "Thanks."

"Bob Lowman is his name. If you decide to call him, tell him Steve-O sentcha."

"I will." Carlita gazed at her daughter. "We should get going. We still have to find our hotel and it's getting late."

"Will you be back tomorrow?" Steve gazed at Mercedes, who turned to her mother.

"Yes. We drove all the way down here. It wouldn't hurt to have a few people give us estimates on repairs," Carlita said.

Steve nodded. "When you come back tomorrow, just be careful. The place has been vacant since old George was murdered and his body found in the alley behind the restaurant."

Chapter 10

Mercedes's mouth dropped open. Steve had mentioned the previous owner had died. He never said he had been murdered. "Murdered?"

"Yep." Steve gazed out his front window at the side of their building. "Someone stabbed him in the neck with a butcher knife. His wife found his body over by the dumpster. According to the police, he had been dead for several hours before she found him."

He went on. "Course there was a rumor circulating the missus had done him in, even though they never charged anyone. I mean, they lived in one of the apartments upstairs. You would think she would've known that someone had killed her husband the night before."

Carlita made a mental note to have Mercedes do an on-line search for George Delmario after they checked into the hotel. They thanked Steve for his information before leaving.

Neither of them spoke until they were safely inside the car, the doors locked. "What do you think?" Carlita asked her daughter.

"You don't think Pop had anything to do with Mr. Delario's murder, do you?"

"I don't know what to think," Carlita admitted. "When we get to the hotel, you should search the internet to see if you can dig something up on the owner's death." The last thing they needed was to walk straight into some decades-old mafia feud.

With the small windfall from the sale of the ruby, the women splurged on an upscale hotel in the center of the historic district. Mercedes had booked two nights and after a full day tomorrow, the women would decide if they needed to extend their visit.

Mercedes, nervous about maneuvering around the parking garage, was relieved when her mother suggested they spring for valet parking. The fact that they had arrived in one piece with nary a fender bender was a small miracle.

It looked as if they might stay longer, especially if they planned to set up appointments for quotes. Carlita had already scheduled an appointment the following morning with a local attorney to review the property papers.

They decided that next on the list would be to line up a locksmith to re-key all of the doors and secure all of the windows, hoping it would deter the current squatter from returning.

Carlita headed to the shower to rinse the grime and grit from the long drive not to mention the ramshackle properties. She showered for a long time and emerged wearing one of the hotel's terrycloth robes, her hair in a turban.

Mercedes was sitting at the small table near the window, pounding on the keyboard. She quickly closed the screen when her mother emerged.

"Why is it every time I see you working on your computer, as soon as I get close, you close the lid?" Carlita unwound the towel from around her head and began drying her shoulder length hair.

"I'm working on a small...project." Mercedes still wasn't ready to tell her mother she was cruising right along on her story about life as a mobster's daughter. The trip had given her some great fodder for her stories and after tweaking a few of the details and names, including Steve-O's, the ideas were practically exploding from her fingertips and she was burning up her keyboard.

Carlita draped her towel on back of a nearby chair and plucked at her hair with her fingers. "Have you had a chance to research local locksmiths?"

"Yep." Mercedes waved a sheet of paper she had taken from the small notepad she found on the bedside stand. "I called three. No one answered since it's after hours but I left messages for them to call me back as soon as possible."

She abruptly stood. "I should shower too. After I finish, maybe we can head to the restaurant downstairs for dinner. I'm starving." The last time either of them had eaten was hours ago, right before stopping at the gas station on their way into town.

"Sounds good," Carlita said. "Can I use your computer to search for construction companies while you clean up?"

"Sure." Mercedes slipped back into her chair, lifted the lid on the laptop, clicked a few keys and then hopped back out of the chair. "It's all yours."

Carlita waited until her daughter was in the bathroom and the door closed behind her before wandering over to the laptop. She settled into the chair and studied the icons on the screen, all of which looked innocent enough, including her daughter's email icon and a picture folder.

Carlita was just about to click back on the search bar when one of the icons, "Murder, Mayhem and the Mafia," caught her eye.

"I wonder what this is." Carlita double clicked on the icon and a security passcode button popped up. "Shoot." She could hear Mercedes banging around in the bathroom and quickly clicked away, returning to the search screen.

By the time Mercedes emerged, ready to go, Carlita had contacted four local contractors, including the one Steve had recommended, and left messages for them to call her cell phone, deciding Mercedes would have her hands full trying to line someone up to install new locks.

"I haven't had time to dress." Carlita picked up the first outfit inside her suitcase and headed to the bathroom.

Mercedes was sitting on the edge of the bed, waiting for her mother when she emerged. "Vinnie called my cell phone. He tried calling the house all day and when you didn't answer, he drove by there and discovered we weren't home."

Carlita rummaged around inside her purse and pulled out her cell phone. "I see he called a couple of times. I must have turned the volume down." She glanced at her daughter. "What did he say?"

"I figured there was no point in lying so I told him we were in Savannah checking out the property," Mercedes said.

"And?" Carlita prompted, certain she already knew what her eldest son's reaction would be.

"He was madder than a wet hornet and insisted we drive home. Tonight."

Carlita wrinkled her nose. "That's absurd." She waved her hand in the air. "I'll call him back in the morning, once he has a chance to cool off. In the meantime, let's go eat. I'm starving."

In the back of her mind, Carlita knew her son was more than just a tad angry. He was probably home spitting bullets and had already called his other brothers to tell them their irresponsible mother and errant sister had run off to Georgia.

The more she thought about it, the more aggravated she became. She was a grown woman, and his mother to boot. Who was he to tell her what she could and couldn't do?

With renewed determination, Carlita Garlucci decided that tomorrow morning she would set the record straight. She would calmly, but firmly, inform her children she was perfectly capable of making her own decisions.

She also decided she was going to fix up the Savannah properties and sell them once they were renovated or – as she promised her Vinnie – she would move to Savannah and hopefully they would follow her there.

The decision gave Carlita a boost of self-confidence she had never known in her life. In the past, there had always been a man around to take care of her. She glanced across the table at her only daughter. Mercedes was living the same sheltered life, following in her mother's footsteps, and it was wrong.

They needed to be strong women, to be able to care for themselves because one day, perhaps Mercedes would marry but the last thing Carlita wanted was for her daughter to depend on a man.

The menu was pub fare and included not only wraps, but also sandwiches and burgers.

Carlita had eaten her share of burgers and fries during the trip so she decided on a grilled shrimp salad with a side of chicken wings after the server assured her they were the best buffalo-style wings in all of Savannah.

Mercedes ordered a grilled steak wrap with a side of macaroni and cheese.

When the food arrived, the women devoured the tasty dishes, each declaring theirs one of the best they had ever had.

After eating, they explored the hotel, stumbling upon a magnificently landscaped outdoor pool, a large fitness room, a business center and a bar area that served more burgers and sandwiches.

It had been a long day, and with their stomachs full and their brains fried, the women quickly fell asleep. Tomorrow was shaping up to be another long day.

Chapter 11

Carlita's eyes flew open and she stared at the ceiling. It took a minute for her to figure out where she was and then realized her cell phone was beeping.

She reached over the side of the bed and glanced at the alarm clock before reaching for the phone. It was 8:15 a.m. and the number showing up on the screen, unknown.

It was one of the construction companies she had left a message with the previous evening. An hour later, she had three companies lined up to meet her at the property.

In the meantime, Mercedes had taken a couple calls from local locksmiths. Thankfully, one of them was able to fit them into his schedule and they set a time to meet at the property as well.

Pleased with the morning's progress, Carlita headed to the bathroom to dress. After she emerged, it was Mercedes's turn.

"We need to get a move on," Carlita said. "We have an appointment with the attorney at ten." She started to slip on a pair of sneakers when her cell phone rang again.

Carlita grabbed the phone, not bothering to look at the screen before answering. "Hello?"

"Ma. It's me - Vinnie. You got me worried sick. Are you on your way home?"

"No. I'm sitting in a hotel room, waiting for your sister to get ready. We're meeting with an attorney before heading to the property to meet construction crews to get repair estimates on fixing up our investment," she patiently explained to her eldest child.

He let loose a string of expletives before launching into a verbal tirade of why mother and daughter should never have embarked on the trip.

Finally, he calmed down long enough for his mother to get a word in edgewise. "As I said before, Mercedes and I are here. We're also meeting a locksmith to change the locks since a squatter has taken up residence in one of the buildings..."

"Squatter!" Vinnie exploded again.

Carlita interrupted her son. "It's fine. I have a gun with me for protection."

"You took a gun with you?" her son roared.

Apparently, her explanation was only making matters worse. "We may start for home tomorrow. It depends on what happens today."

She let her son rant while her mind wandered. "Have you ever heard of George Delmario?" She quickly asked when her son took a breather.

"Yeah. That was Frank's pop. He lived in..." Vinnie grew quiet, the wheels turning. "Are you saying George Delmario owned the Savannah property before it was deeded to Pop?"

"It looks that way and from what Steve-O said yesterday, he may have been murdered," Carlita said.

"Who is Steve-O?" Vinnie asked.

Mercedes wandered into the room, making a slicing motion across her neck. "Look, son. We can talk later. Mercedes and I need to head out or we'll be late for our first meeting."

Carlita could hear her son still talking as she disconnected the line and dropped her cell phone into her purse. "Well, that went well," she said with a hint of sarcasm and then turned her attention to her daughter. "We better get going before we're late."

The first order of business was the appointment they had scheduled for mid-morning with Attorney Gurley, a local probate attorney.

They had emailed a copy of the papers ahead of time so Mr. Gurley and his firm could verify the validity of the papers. The appointment was to settle payment and confirm Carlita was the rightful owner of the properties.

Two hundred and fifty dollars and half an hour later, they walked out of the attorney's office and climbed into the car.

Carlita reached for her seatbelt. "I have a feeling this is going to be an expensive day."

Three of the four people Carlita had contacted for quotes showed up. They all took notes, measurements and even photos of the property but none of them gave a clue as to what it would cost for the needed upgrades, repairs and general updates, each insisting it would take some time to prepare an estimate and explaining to Carlita there was no way they could give her a ballpark figure.

Steve stopped by close to lunchtime and chatted with Mercedes.

After he left, Mercedes hurried to her mother's side. "Steve-O invited us to dinner and I told him I needed to check with you." She quickly continued. "He said they have a fabulous Italian restaurant a short walk from here and I figured since you were thinking of opening an Italian restaurant, it wouldn't hurt to check out the competition."

"Sounds like a great idea," Carlita told her daughter. Befriending Steve had its advantages. Not only could she glean a little more information on historic Savannah, it wouldn't hurt to have someone nearby to keep an eye on the place after they left.

Thankfully, the locksmith arrived a short time later and installed new locks on each of the doors, both front and back. Not only that, the nice young man who showed up secured the windows, pounding nails into the corners of the wood so the windows wouldn't open and intruders wouldn't be able to sneak in.

After they all left, Carlita looked...really looked around the restaurant with new eyes. Hope began to swell in her. She could do this. She could move to Savannah and start a new life.

Now all she had to do was convince her sons she hadn't lost her mind.

***

Mercedes, Steve and Carlita walked from the tattoo shop toward another "square" as Steve called them. From the small square they walked through, Carlita was able to catch a glimpse of the beauty of the architecture, the unique shops and restaurants that filled every available inch of space. She was looking forward to being able to explore the area.

Carlita glanced at her daughter. They could explore when they had more time, but first they had to have somewhere to live, somewhere safe.

The construction supervisors promised to forward rough estimates to Mercedes's email the following day with more detailed quotes to follow. The women decided to spend at least one more night in Savannah in hopes of being able to settle on a construction crew before heading back to New York.

They would also need to work out a timeline and then set up an account at a local bank so they could sell another gem from their stash and then deposit the money from the sale into the new account. There were many little steps that needed to be taken, but each step brought them closer to their goal.

As they strolled down the sidewalk, Carlita gazed at the majestic homes. A déjà vu moment washed over her, although she had never stepped in Savannah before.

Home. Carlita was beginning to believe Savannah could be her home.

Now all they needed to do was steer clear of trouble and hopefully figure out who was breaking into her house.

Carlita was convinced the person or persons breaking into her house were searching for the gems. If the small ruby they had just sold pulled in several thousand dollars, she wondered how much the other, larger gems might be worth.

"...so I got my sister, Autumn, a part-time job over at the Savannah Evening News. She has a nose for sniffin' stuff out."

Mercedes perked up. "Working at a newspaper sounds fascinating." She almost slipped and told Steve-O that she was writing a book about mafia life, but caught herself in the nick of time.

Steve gave her a sideways glance. "I'll give her a call, see if she has time to stop by. Maybe tomorrow."

"We're going to stay one more night to wrap things up before heading back home," Carlita said.

"But we'll be coming back soon," Mercedes reassured Steve.

If my sons don't lock us in the house. Carlita nodded. "That is the plan."

Steve stopped abruptly in front of a massive double door. "This is it," he announced. The sign on the awning read, "Russo Brothers Italian Eatery."

He held the door while Mercedes, followed by her mother, stepped inside.

Carlita scanned the room, stopping when she spotted the open kitchen in the back. The clatter of dishes echoed from behind a partitioned wall. The smell of garlic and grilled chicken caused Carlita's stomach to growl. It had been hours since Mercedes and she had eaten.

"Follow me." Steve zigzagged past several tables. "Mike always saves a table for me in the back." He waved to several of the diners as he made his way to the rear of the restaurant where they settled into a small round table not far from the kitchen area.

Steve reached for the basket of garlic rolls sitting in the center of the table and then offered the basket to Mercedes. "I can take you around for an evening out when you come back, you know, show you some of the local pubs and clubs."

Mercedes gave her mother a quick glance. "I..."

"Mercedes would love to, Steve," Carlita said. The last thing she wanted was for her daughter to be concerned over her mother's welfare. They would settle into their new life and she would be busy with the businesses. It was a relief to have someone who knew the area and could steer them in the right direction.

The waiter arrived moments later to bring glasses of ice water and take their order. Carlita let Steve order for them and he selected a family meal where they shared several dishes.

She waited until the waiter left before asking the one question that was burning in the back of her mind. "The man, Mr. Delmario, do you have a theory of what happened to him?"

Steve glanced around the restaurant, lowered his head and leaned in. "You're never gonna believe this one."

Somehow, Carlita was quite certain she was going to believe it.

Chapter 12

"Mr. Delmario, George, was an odd duck. Kept pretty much to himself, him and his wife." Steve reached for a garlic roll. "They had a thriving business there, between the grocery store and restaurant. George and Louise lived upstairs in one of the apartments. Their sons lived there, too, on and off, but for the most part it was just the two of them."

Steve continued. "I always tried to tell George he could make some extra money if he rented out those apartments but he never seemed interested."

"Why do you think that is?" Carlita asked as she reached for her glass of ice water.

Steve drummed his fingertips on the tabletop. "Well..."

"Drugs?" Carlita prompted.

"Could be," Steve shrugged. "Or maybe something else. The tattoo business, we stay open kind of late, later than say, a grocery store or mom and pop restaurant. They had cars parked there...not just any cars, but expensive cars. They came and went at all hours."

Carlita was convinced George Delmario and Frank Delmario were related. She remembered several "business trips" Vinnie had taken, never telling her exactly where he was going. She had a hunch that at least one of those trips included a visit to 210 Mulberry Street.

Had her husband killed George Delmario and, because he held the deed, once George died, Vinnie had inherited the properties?

Carlita's mind reeled at the thought. Perhaps whoever was breaking into her house wasn't searching for the gems after all, but looking for the deed to the properties, which meant they wouldn't be safe, not even in Savannah.

Thankfully, the food arrived, giving Carlita a chance to digest that tidbit of information. The manicotti was baked to perfection, but the lasagna dry and tasteless, and the chicken parmesan nothing to write home about.

Carlita was certain she could run circles around this restaurant, but didn't tell Steve that. Instead, she complimented the food and wondered how Russo Brothers Italian Eatery would feel about a little competition only a couple blocks away.

After dinner, which Steve insisted he buy, the trio headed back to Mulberry Street and Carlita pretended to study the local architecture while Steve chatted with Mercedes.

Steve walked them to their car and Carlita thanked him again for the lovely dinner before climbing into the passenger seat to wait for her daughter.

Mercedes and Steve chatted for a couple minutes and then Mercedes opened the driver's side door and slid behind the wheel.

Carlita set her purse on the floor and turned to her daughter. "Steve likes you."

Mercedes smiled and stuck the key in the ignition. "He likes you too."

"No." Carlita shook her head. "I mean he *likes* you."

Mercedes blushed and shook her head. "That's crazy. He's not my type."

"Exactly," her mother said. "You know the saying...opposites attract."

She didn't tease her daughter anymore and instead gazed out the window as they crept past the property. Carlita didn't want to believe her husband was capable of killing another human being, but if she were being honest with herself, he probably had. More than once, perhaps even using the same gun she now kept in her purse for protection.

When they reached their hotel, Mercedes eased the car into the hotel's valet area, turned the keys over to the parking attendant and they headed indoors and to the bank of elevators.

Mercedes pressed the "eight" button and the doors closed. "Only one more day, Mercedes. Then it's time to head home."

"I'm sure we're gonna get an earful when we get there." Mercedes grinned and patted her mother's arm. "I'm proud of you, Ma, for sticking up to Vinnie and Tony. If they had their way, we'd be spinsters, sitting at home, cooking Sunday dinner and watching life pass us by."

Mercedes's words rang true. Carlita didn't want that for her daughter, she wanted more. She wanted her to be independent, to think for herself, not be under her brothers' thumbs, the way she had lived under her husband's thumb for so many years.

When she got home, Carlita would sit her sons down and calmly, but firmly, inform them she appreciated their concern, but she would be moving to Savannah – with or without them.

***

Carlita slept fitfully, her dreams of her husband, still alive. In one dream, she was inside the restaurant when Vinnie snuck up behind her and surprised her. She dropped the broom she'd been using to sweep the floor, burst into tears and fell into her husband's open arms. "I thought you were dead," she sobbed.

"Ma." Mercedes gently shook her mother's shoulder. "You're having a bad dream."

Carlita's eyes flew open. Rays of early morning light peeked in through the side of the curtain and she could see the outline of her daughter's concerned face. "I'm okay. What time is it?"

"Six fifteen," Mercedes said. "I'll make us a pot of coffee. I didn't sleep well, either. I guess I'm all wound up about leaving and facing the music back home," she confessed.

"Don't worry about that, Mercedes." Carlita flung the covers back, swung her legs over the side of the bed and slipped her feet into her slippers. "I'll take care of your brothers."

The women quickly got ready for their final day in Savannah, dressing in sweats and t-shirts since they planned to clean the place up before they had to head home.

Mercedes stopped at a fast food drive thru for breakfast and then a convenience store to purchase some cleaning supplies before heading to the property.

They passed by "Shades of Ink," Steve Winter's tattoo shop. The shop was closed, the place dark. "I guess they don't open until later."

Mercedes parked the car behind the grocery store and they climbed out. The women hurried from the vehicle and darted to the front.

Key in hand, Mercedes quickly unlocked the door to the grocery store. She held the door and her mother, carrying their breakfast and the bag of cleaning supplies, stepped inside.

Carlita flipped the wall switch and bright light illuminated the dark interior. She had paid an extra fee for expedited service to get the power and water turned on the day before, and it was worth every penny.

She gazed around with a new appreciation for the place. It would take some work, but she was certain they could whip the place into shape, with a little help from a competent construction crew.

The girls gobbled their bacon, egg and cheese croissants and tater tot hash browns, finished their coffee and got to work, emptying shelves, sweeping floors and filling several garbage bags full of trash.

They worked hard all day, in between meeting construction supervisors. Steve stopped by during the lunch hour to check on their progress and offered to bring tacos around the dinner hour.

"There's a great place around the corner, Taco Viva, and they deliver." He told them his sister, Autumn, would be by later to meet them.

Carlita told Steve she was looking forward to meeting his sister and dinner, but insisted on buying the food since he had paid for their dinners the evening before.

By the time late afternoon rolled around, Carlita's back ached, her feet were swollen and her knees complained every time she attempted to bend down. She grabbed a bistro chair she found in the corner and eased into it.

Mercedes gazed at her mother. "Don't overdo it Ma. All this will still be here next time." She waved her hand around the room.

"Bite your tongue," Carlita said. "This place better look a lot different the next time I see it." The women discussed the tentative bids they had gotten and Carlita was leaning toward hiring Bob Lowman, the man Steve had recommended. Mercedes agreed.

With a decision made, Carlita called Bob to tell him they wanted to hire him and he promised to stop by later so that they could sign some papers. She explained that as soon as they arrived home she would wire the money and was relieved when Bob said that was not a problem.

She disconnected the cell phone and looked at her daughter. "We need to sell another gem to pay for the first phase of construction."

"I'll get on it as soon as we get home," Mercedes assured her mother and then glanced at her watch. "I'm going to run over to Steve's place to see how long before we should order dinner." The breakfast sandwiches had worn off long ago, and all of the hard work had made both women hungry.

Carlita wandered next door to lock up the old restaurant while she waited for Mercedes to return. She stepped inside and studied the interior. The place needed a ton of work. She only hoped they would have enough money to pay for all the repairs to not only the restaurant and the grocery store, but also remodel one of the upstairs apartments.

The thought crossed her mind that perhaps they had taken on more than they could handle but she quickly shoved the thought aside. This place was her future...Mercedes's future. She could feel it in her bones.

Carlita retraced her steps, locking the front door behind her when she spotted a small business card lying on the front stoop. She bent down to pick it up.

"Watch out!" A female voice screeched.

Whoomp! Carlita teetered to the side before toppling over, landing on her hands and knees. A sharp pain shot up her left arm.

"Oh my gosh. I am so sorry."

Carlita shifted onto her rear and gazed up at a petite young woman who was hovering over her. The woman yanked a helmet off her head and waves of blonde hair tumbled over her shoulders. "Are you okay?"

Carlita shifted to her knees and rubbed the dirt off the palms of her hands. "I-I think so. What happened?" She glanced at the apparatus that had attacked her.

"I'm so sorry," the girl apologized. "My Segway careened out of control. I'm still learning how to use it."

"Autumn." Steve Winter hustled down the sidewalk. Mercedes was right behind him. "I told you to practice using that contraption on the back alley, not on the sidewalk."

The young woman clutched the helmet she was holding. "I have been, but you told me to meet you out front so here I am."

Mercedes raced over and helped her mother to her feet before turning to the young woman. "You must be Steve's sister."

Autumn's eyes darted from mother to daughter. "Don't tell me I just bowled over Steve's new neighbor."

"I'm sorry for Autumn's behavior," Steve apologized. "I'd like to say that she's usually not accident prone but that would be a lie. She's a train wreck for the most part." His voice was teasing.

"I hope you're okay." He turned to Carlita, who was on her feet now.

"No harm done."

"I sure know how to make a lasting first impression." The young woman, a warm smile on her face and a mischievous twinkle in her blue eyes, extended her hand. "Steve has told me so much about you, Mrs. Garlucci. You and Mercedes."

Carlita studied the young woman, who looked nothing like her brother. "Steve told me you're going to fix the place up and move down here from New York."

"Yes, that's the plan." Carlita nodded and then gazed at the card she held in her hand. "I found this shoved in the door." She turned the card over and read the front. "Savannah Architectural Society. Please contact us at your earliest convenience."

"Oh no," Steve groaned. "Not the SAS."

Chapter 13

"Who?" Mercedes asked.

"The SAS, short for Savannah Architectural Society," Steve explained.

"More like PITA," Autumn Winter shook her head. "Pain in the -."

Steve abruptly cut his sister off. "Autumn," he warned and then fixed his gaze on Carlita. "It's a bunch of nosy old biddies who think they have the power to run all of historic Savannah by telling you what you can and cannot do."

"In other words, they stick their noses in where they don't belong," Autumn finished.

Carlita frowned. "Great. All I need is one more person telling me what I can and cannot do."

"If I were you, I'd give them a call before they decide to come back. Maybe you can head them off at the pass," Steve said.

"Thanks. I'll do that." Carlita tucked the card in her back pocket and made a mental note to call SAS later that evening.

Autumn reached for the handle of her Segway and gazed at the boarded up building. "I have to warn you this place is haunted," Autumn Winter said solemnly.

"We've heard that before," Carlita admitted.

"How exciting." Mercedes clasped her hands, all the while thinking it would make a great plot line for her next mafia novel.

Autumn went on to tell them that since she'd started working at the Savannah Evening News, she had done some research on her brother's tattoo shop. While she was snooping around, she had run across an old article on the grocery store, how it had originally been used as a casket making factory and the skeleton crew who worked the graveyard shift regularly complained there were odd noises, foggy silhouettes and cold spots inside the building, especially in the back.

Carlita eyed the old grocery store warily. The last thing she needed was a ghost. The living creatures stalking her were bad enough. "Great. Just what we need."

She changed the subject. "We should order the food."

"I already did, over at Steve's place," Mercedes told her mother.

Autumn started to climb back on the Segway when her brother grabbed the handlebars. "Oh no you don't." He guided the Segway through the front door of the store and eased it off to the side.

"I would love to learn to drive a Segway." Mercedes followed Steve and Autumn into the grocery store. She stepped over to the Segway and ran a light hand over the steering bar. "Can you teach me next time we're here?"

"Sure. If you teach me how to drive a car," Autumn bargained. "Steve bought me the Segway to get around town a few weeks ago but I'm still learning."

Carlita was going to point out that Mercedes was still a newbie at driving herself, but decided to keep quiet.

The tacos arrived a short time later and Mercedes had thought to ask them to throw in a few napkins and paper plates.

While they ate, Autumn entertained them with stories of her job at the newspaper. For a petite little thing, she had a huge appetite. Carlita was still working on her first taco while Autumn was reaching for her third.

"I'm looking for a place to live, closer to downtown so if you get one of those other apartments fixed up, I'd love to rent it out."

A tenant already. "We'll put you at the top of the list," Carlita promised.

Autumn chattered nonstop, talking about how she had broken off a recent engagement after finding out her betrothed had been cheating on her with her best friend. She reached for a packet of hot sauce, snapped it with her finger and then tore the corner off before spreading the contents on top of her taco. "You should have seen the look on ole Monica's face when I caught her and my ex, Jason, cozying it up in the Pink Pony Pub."

Autumn squeezed the last of the hot sauce on her finger and licked it. "I called Darren, Monica's boyfriend, to tell him that I caught the two of them together."

She tossed her head, blonde strands of hair falling off her shoulder. "Boy, Darren was spitting mad! He barged into the restaurant." A small grin played on the corner of Autumn's lips. "He knocked Jason out cold with one blow and then poured the tramp, Monica's, fancy schmancy martini on top of her head before the bouncer got to him and threw him out."

She popped the top on a can of Diet Coke and took a big swig. "I swore I was done with men, at least for another year or so. Darren keeps inviting me out so maybe we can hang out as friends."

As the meal wore on, Carlita decided that Steve had his hands full with his younger sister. She gathered from what Autumn said that her parents were lenient with their only daughter and the only one with any sort of control was big brother.

Carlita glanced at her daughter out of the corner of her eye. Mercedes was eating up every word that came out of Autumn's mouth and the warning bells went off in her head. Mercedes had led a sheltered life while Autumn seemed a little on the wild side.

"We will be busy when we return, getting everything up and running," Carlita warned.

Mercedes and Carlita planned to leave early the next morning to start the drive back to New York. They had a lot to take care of now that mother and daughter had made the decision they were moving to Savannah.

For years, Carlita had been promising Vinnie she would clean out the attic, the basement and the garage after decades of collecting junk. Vinnie had teased her they lived in "The Packrat Palace."

Not only did Mercedes and she have the major task of cleaning, packing and moving, they would have to manage the renovation/construction project from hundreds of miles away.

All of that paled in comparison to her thoughts of her "Vinnie" and his unexpected death. She also worried about their safety. Who was breaking into her home and what were they after?

Carlita remembered Steve telling them that George Delmario had been murdered, his body discovered in the alley out back. She dropped an uneaten piece of taco shell inside her napkin and tossed it in the trash. "I'm whupped."

She was also more than a little sore, not only from all of the cleaning Mercedes and she had done, but from her run-in with Autumn's Segway, which had given her a couple extra aches and pains.

Mercedes threw her empty wrappers inside the bag and stood. "We should get going. We have a long day ahead of us tomorrow."

Steve and Autumn followed them out the front and they parted ways, but not before Carlita gave Steve a key to the property. "Please keep an eye on it while we're gone."

Steve lifted his hand in salute. "Will do."

On the way back to the hotel, Mercedes stopped by a local drugstore to pick up a bottle of ibuprofen to take the edge off her mother's aches and pains.

Carlita's mind was in neutral for part of the ride, which Mercedes didn't seem to notice as she chattered excitedly about Autumn, Steve and the thought that the grocery store might actually be haunted.

Back at the hotel, Mercedes headed to the balcony to check in with her girlfriends and let them know she was on her way home. Both Mercedes and Carlita had agreed not to call Vinnie, Tony or Paulie, certain they would have to endure another lecture, which Carlita wasn't ready for.

While Mercedes talked to her friends, Carlita headed to the bathroom for a hot shower. The shower, along with a couple of ibuprofens eased her aches and pains and she was ready to hit the hay. Thankfully, she fell asleep as soon as her head hit the pillow and if she did dream, she didn't remember any of them.

They rose early the next morning and drove all day, making a couple quick pit stops for gas. By early evening, they were ready to call it a day and decided to spend the night at the same hotel they had stayed at on the way down.

After they checked in, Carlita told Mercedes to get ready for bed first and decided to check her cell phone.

There was a voice mail from Tony, her middle son, asking her to call as soon as she got the message. She waited until Mercedes emerged from the bathroom. "Tony asked me to call him."

She dialed her son's cell phone number and pressed the speaker button so both Mercedes and she could hear. "Hi Ma. I know you said you were on your way back today, but I thought I better give you a heads up before you got here."

"We're halfway home," Carlita said. "We should be back around six tomorrow night. What's going on?"

"Well, me 'n Vinnie stopped by the house this morning to check on it. Looks like someone tried to torch the place."

Chapter 14

Carlita pressed the side button to turn the volume. "You mean tried as in didn't succeed?"

"Yeah. Some of the vinyl siding on the back of the house near the bathroom window melted but the inside of the house wasn't damaged. Pop musta ticked somebody off but good."

And left a big mess behind for me to deal with. Carlita closed her eyes briefly. "Did they get inside the house again?"

"Nope, thanks to the locks Vinnie and I put on last week."

Her son continued. "We were talkin'...someone is bent on some sort of revenge. We was thinking one of us should come stay with you 'til we can figure out who's behind all this."

The last thing Carlita wanted was to have her sons underfoot. She had a construction project to manage, a house to sell, although she certainly couldn't put the house on the market with a big black burn mark on the back.

"I appreciate that, but Mercedes and I feel safe enough with the guns now that we know how to shoot." Carlita wasn't 100% sure they were that confident. She made a mental note to schedule another shooting lesson with Bud over at *Shoot Great*.

"I thought you was gonna say that so I'm gonna loan Rambo to you for protection."

Carlita wrinkled her nose. "You don't have to do that."

"It's either me or Rambo," Tony insisted. "Take your pick."

"Rambo," Mercedes and Carlita said in unison.

"That's what I figured. I'll stay at the house here tonight with Rambo to make sure no one else tries to mess around." Carlita thanked her son and disconnected the line.

Mercedes flopped on the bed and flung her arm across her face. "We may be sorry we opted for Rambo."

Rambo was a mutt, a stray that Tony had found on the streets a couple years back. He was part German shepherd, part Doberman and part clown. He looked scary for about the first thirty seconds until he tried to lick you to death. In other words, he was a big baby, although still a good watchdog.

Carlita's husband, Vinnie, had never cared for the dog. Vinnie hadn't cared for animals period. Carlita, on the other hand, had always secretly loved dogs...and cats.

"This will be a good test. Maybe if Rambo works out, we should consider getting a dog of our own," Carlita told her daughter.

"True." Mercedes abruptly sat up. "We better get to bed. Rambo and Tony are waiting for us."

***

The final leg of their trip was anything but smooth. They managed to run into several accidents on the highway, a detour around construction, and finally arrived at the house close to seven.

Tony's sports car was parked out front when they pulled in the drive.

"Better not pull into the garage," Carlita reminded her daughter. "We have to unload."

"You're right." Mercedes stopped in the drive, shifted the car to park and shut the engine off.

Tony and Rambo emerged from the house and met Carlita on the passenger side of the car. "I was beginning to worry." He kissed his mother's cheek and then headed to the trunk where he reached inside and grabbed a couple suitcases. "I hope you got this whole Savannah thing out of your system."

Carlita didn't answer. She was too tired to fight tonight. Tomorrow would be another day. The traffic and long hours on the road had frayed her nerves. All she wanted to do was kick back in her recliner, turn on the television and pretend she didn't have a million and one things to do.

Mercedes and she had set a deadline. They had exactly a month to get to Savannah, which was when Bob Lowman, the construction supervisor, had told them the apartment would be ready. As soon as the apartment renovations were complete, Bob and his crew would start working on the grocery store, which they planned to get up and running first.

After they had a firm handle on running the grocery store and cash flow coming in, they would start fixing up the restaurant.

The women had also discussed possible suspects, trying to figure out who was breaking into their home not to mention vandalizing it.

There was Frank Delmario, George Delmario's son. According to both Steve and Autumn, George Delmario's killer had never been apprehended.

Still, Frank, the son, was a crumb, a non-mafia, so they put him at the bottom of the list of suspects.

Next was Vito Castellini, who was at the top of the list of suspects. Carlita was certain Vito was anxious to get the bag of gems back and Carlita was just as anxious not to let him have them.

They needed to sell the gems to raise enough cash to renovate the Savannah property. She tossed around the idea of bargaining with Vito, that they would keep the gems and pay him back when the businesses were turning a profit, but mafia men made the rules, not mafia wives, so they quickly nixed the idea.

Next on the list was Carmine Tonesci, whom one of her sons suspected was involved.

Tony stayed for a short time. Rambo never moved a muscle when Tony patted his head and told him good-bye. He barely even blinked as Tony walked out the front door.

"Don't you want to go home?" Carlita asked the pooch.

Rambo thumped his tail, rolled over and flung his paws in the air as he wiggled back and forth on the living room carpet.

Tony had left behind a large bag of dog food, not to mention a doggie bed, a small box of stuffed toys and container of doggie treats. "I guess you're here for the long haul," Carlita said as she grabbed Rambo's front paw and shook it. "You'll have to let me know when you need to go out."

Rambo rolled over, shot to his feet and trotted to the dining room sliding glass door that led to the backyard.

"I guess that means now." Carlita wiggled out of the recliner and met Rambo at the door. She unlocked the slider and they stepped out onto the back deck.

Years ago, Vinnie had fenced in the entire backyard and Carlita was grateful for the fence as she watched Rambo patrol the perimeter.

Summer was right around the corner and every spring Carlita planted flowers on both sides of the deck and another flowerbed near a bench that sat under a large oak tree in the corner of the yard.

Rambo watered the tree, sniffed the overgrown weeds that lined the fence and then made his way back to where she was waiting. "Not a very exciting yard, huh?" She patted his head and they stepped back inside. "I'm ready for bed if you are."

The dog eyed her sadly and then looked longingly down the hall, at least that's what she thought as she tried to read his expressions. She wasn't much up on doggie body language.

"What?" Carlita pointed to his doggie bed. "Your bed is over there."

Rambo let out a low whine.

Carlita thrust her hand on her hip. "Let me guess. You want to sleep in my room." She picked up the doggie bed and carried it to the back with Rambo trotting along behind her.

Carlita placed the bed in the corner of her room, next to her vanity. Rambo climbed on top, circled a couple times, flopped down and closed his eyes.

He was still in his bed, fast asleep, when Carlita emerged from the bathroom a short time later. She slipped between the sheets, pulled them to her chin and closed her eyes, ready for the day to end.

Yap. Yap.

Carlita's eyes flew open. Her first thought was that someone was trying to break in, and then she heard it again.

Yap. Yap. A soft whine followed the yap. It was Rambo.

Small rays of daylight poked through the blinds and Carlita glanced at the clock next to her bed. Six ten in the morning. "You're kidding," she grumbled and flung back the covers.

"Let's go." Rambo and Carlita shuffled down the hall and to the slider where Carlita opened it a crack to let Rambo out for a morning break before heading to the kitchen to brew a pot of coffee.

After starting a pot of coffee, Carlita filled Rambo's water dish, added more dog food to his dish and then let him back in.

Rambo drank some water, turned his nose up at the dog food and plopped down in the center of the kitchen floor to watch her every move.

Carlita scrambled some eggs, popped a couple slices of bread in the toaster and when everything finished cooking, she carried the cooked eggs and toast to the kitchen table.

Rambo followed her to the table.

"Do you like eggs?" Carlita scooped a large spoonful and then carefully made her way over to Rambo's doggie dish where she sprinkled the eggs on top of his uneaten food. He promptly gobbled the eggs and crunched on a few bites of dog food before flopping down in the center of the floor.

Carlita ate her breakfast, sipped her coffee and read the morning paper, enjoying a few quiet moments. She had finished her last sip of coffee when she heard a knock on her back door.

She made her way over to the door where she spotted a familiar face looking in through the glass pane. It was Vinnie. Carlita opened the door and stood off to the side to let him into the house. "I was wondering how long it would take you to show up."

"I'm meetin' my buddy, Leo, here shortly. He's gonna fix the torched siding on the back of the house." Rambo wandered over and Vinnie patted his head. "Nobody mess with the house last night?"

"Nope," Carlita shook her head. "I'm glad you're getting the siding fixed because I'm calling my cousin, Marty, the real estate agent, to put the house on the market."

"Y-you can't sell this place," Vinnie blustered. "Where you gonna live?"

Vinnie answered his own question. "You still think you're gonna up and move to some backwoods bumpkin town in the south?"

"Savannah is not backwoods. It's a lovely, historic town not far from the ocean, and, no, I'm not thinking about it, I'm going to do it. Mercedes is going with me."

"That's right." Mercedes, hearing Vinnie's booming voice, made her way into the kitchen and stood next to her mother. "We've already lined up a contractor to fix the apartment above the grocery store. As soon as it's ready, we're moving."

Vinnie shook his head. "You're makin' a big mistake. You'll be back," he warned.

Carlita changed the subject. Vinnie was not going to win the battle. "We still need to find out who is breaking in and vandalizing the house."

"Yeah, I figured while Leo is surveying the damage, I'm gonna install motion lights out back. I'm surprised Pop never did it. I got the stuff in my car." Her son headed back to his car and Rambo followed him out.

Carlita waited until the door closed. "They are going to fight us tooth and nail on this move."

Mercedes strode across the room, reached inside the kitchen cupboard for a coffee mug. "Short of keeping us prisoner inside this house, there's not much they can do." She grabbed the coffee pot and filled her cup. "The motion lights might help in catching a glimpse of who is breaking in and setting fire to the house, but I have a better idea."

"What's that?" Carlita asked.

Mercedes motioned her mother out onto the deck and closed the door behind them. "Set a trap. You know, like the police, some sort of sting," Mercedes said.

Carlita frowned. "Isn't that dangerous?"

Her daughter shrugged. "It's dangerous driving down the street or walking down the sidewalk." Mercedes could see her mother on the fence. "Wouldn't it be nice to start our new lives fresh, without always having to look over our shoulder?"

She had a point. It would be nice not to have to worry about someone coming after either the property or the gems. It would be safer to flush out whoever it was while her sons were still close by and able to help, if needed. "So what's the plan?"

Chapter 15

Carlita wiped her sweaty palms on the top of her slacks. Visions of the sting going awry and being shot, or worse yet, someone shooting her daughter, filled her head. They weren't dealing with a two-bit thug who might spend a week or two in the county jail for stealing lottery tickets from a grocery store.

They were dealing with professional hit men, career criminals, the cream of the criminal crop, so to speak. In other words, they were asking for trouble.

Carlita smoothed her hair. "All I need to do is tell them I'm searching for something your father mentioned on his deathbed, a packet or package of something he stashed that I think might be in the garage."

"Yep." Mercedes nodded. The women had placed a roll of bills in a bag and stuck it in an empty paint can before they left the house. Never mind that it was only a roll of dollar bills – a grand total of seventy-five bucks.

They had decided to spread the rumor in an attempt to reach the people they considered prime suspects...Carmine Tonesci, Frank Delmario and Vito Castellini.

Carlita had even added Sal from Sal's Market. Vinnie and Sal had been pals and had hung out on a regular basis.

Mercedes and Carlita started at Sal's place, spreading the rumor, before heading to Carmine Tonesci's wife, Luciana's, nail salon.

Their last stop was Vito Castellini's hangout, East Side Pawn Shop, where Vito's girlfriend, Sandra, worked. Everyone knew about Vito's girlfriend, even Vito's wife, which surprised Carlita since Francesca Castellini was as formidable a character as Vito himself. Carlita had a sneaky suspicion the gems Vito had given Vinnie to drop were somehow tied to the pawnshop.

Carlita grabbed the door handle and for a brief moment, almost changed her mind.

"We can do this." Mercedes propelled her mother forward with a gentle shove and they entered the store.

"We can." Carlita sucked in a breath and studied the store. She spotted Sandra, "Sandy" behind the jewelry counter, her bright red beehive hairdo towering on top of her head. She glanced up when the women stepped inside.

"Hello Carlita." Sandy nodded to Mercedes. "Mercedes."

She folded her hands on top of the glass display case. "How're you doin' Carlita?"

"Ohh..kay." Carlita blinked back unexpected tears.

Sandy tilted her head. "I'm sorry. It's a tough spot."

Carlita sucked in a breath and nodded as she tried to control her emotions. "We just put the house on the market this morning," Carlita said. "Mercedes and I want to make a clean start somewhere new."

"Where ya' goin?" Sandy asked.

Mercedes and Carlita had agreed to keep mum about Savannah. Word would spread soon enough. For now, they wanted to keep that information close to the vest.

"We're not sure," Mercedes said. "First we gotta see if we can sell the house."

She went on. "Which is why we're here. We might have some stuff to sell and wanted to find out what kind of merchandise you might be interested in."

"The usual." Sandy ticked off the list. "Jewelry, antiques, old coins."

Sandy patted the top of her beehive hairdo. "I can always move jewelry, precious gems like rubies, sapphires, emeralds and of course, diamonds."

A cold chill ran down Carlita's spine and she nodded. "Great. We'll be bringing some stuff by in the next week or so. We're startin' with the garage since Vinnie mentioned having some things he stored in there he was anxious to get out."

"The place is a mess." Mercedes rolled her eyes. "I never knew Pop was such a packrat." She turned to her mother. "Then there's the package or packet Pops told you about we haven't been able to find yet."

Carlita shook her head and gave her daughter a dark look. "Mercedes..."

Mercedes frowned. "Sorry." She turned to Sandy. "It was nothing...I guess."

They chatted a few more minutes before exiting the store and stepping out onto the sidewalk.

Carlita waited until they were a safe distance away. "I hate fibbing." They were only a few blocks from the house and the women had decided to walk versus taking the car out for the short ride.

"A necessary evil," Mercedes said. "What about Frank Delmario?"

"Sandy will take care of that. He'll hear about it before the day ends," Carlita predicted as she shaded her eyes and gazed down the street at her church, Saints Peter and Paul Catholic Church. "I should stop by for a quick confession. I haven't been to church since before our trip to Savannah."

Carlita and Mercedes headed up the cement steps and quietly slipped inside. Their shoes echoed on the massive tile floor as they passed through the vestibule and entered the church.

There was no one in sight and the women tiptoed to the front, toward the confessional on the left.

"I'll be back in a minute." Carlita left Mercedes near the front of the church and made her way over to the confessional. She opened the door and eased into the small space, closing the door behind her.

She stepped out a few moments later and joined Mercedes near the front. "I feel better, getting everything off my chest, although I don't think Father Dadore was there."

For years, Carlita had avoided going to church, feeling hypocritical that her family's suspected crimes distanced her from God. Now that Vinnie was gone, Carlita had started attending Mass.

The church had been her sanctuary, saving her sanity, and giving her peace and a sense of calm since her husband's death.

"God still heard your confession," Mercedes assured her mother as they retraced their steps and made their way out of the church.

When they got home, Rambo was waiting for them at the back door. He snuck out when they walked in, trotting down the drive and making a beeline for the street out front.

"Rambo! No!" Carlita chased after the errant pooch.

"I'll be inside." Mercedes shook her head and hollered after her mother as Carlita charged down the sidewalk in hot pursuit of Rambo.

Carlita snagged Rambo mere seconds before he trampled the neighbor, Mrs. Gillespie's, freshly planted flowers.

She grabbed his collar and led him back across the drive. "Naughty Rambo," Carlita scolded. "Tony will never forgive me if something happens to you. Not only that, Mrs. Gillespie will have your hide."

When they reached the back of the house, Carlita opened the side gate. "Now you can run around." She released her grip on Rambo's collar and he sauntered into the backyard.

She watched Rambo inspect the backyard and wondered how long it would take for word to spread that not only was Carlita moving, but there may be something of interest inside her garage.

Carlita also wondered how long it would take her sons to find out that Mercedes and she were spreading the rumor.

Rambo finished his romp and the two of them headed back to the driveway and in through the side door, where Mercedes was in the kitchen waiting for them.

She was holding a small device in her hand. "Steve-O loaned me this mini camera to put in the rental properties but I forgot all about it until I found it in the bottom of my purse. I'm going to put it inside the garage, right in front of the door so we can get a visual on anyone breaking in."

"Can't we just leave the door unlocked?" Carlita was all for damage control, literally. She was already going to have to pay to have the back of her house fixed, not to mention the properties in Savannah.

"I wish one of the boys had gone into construction. They could save me a small fortune," she said wryly.

"We can't leave the door unlocked," Mercedes patiently explained. "Think about it. That would be a red flag."

"Okay." Carlita's shoulders sagged. "What's one more repair," she sighed.

Mercedes headed for the back door and Carlita started to follow.

"It'll look suspicious if we both go out there." Mercedes reached for the door handle.

"True." Carlita hovered in the doorway and watched as her daughter stepped through the side door.

Mercedes emerged a few moments later and walked back into the house. "Now all I have to do is make sure I can use the phone app." She pulled her cell phone from her back pocket, switched it on and tapped the screen. "It's a little dark. We'll have to see what happens."

Carlita attempted a pep talk with Rambo to keep him on guard for intruders or people sneaking around outside. He didn't seem at all interested in patrolling the inside of the house like he did the outside.

The women ate dinner, watched television for a couple hours and then finally, after the eleven o'clock news, Carlita gave up on waiting for an intruder to break into the garage and decided to go to bed. "I can't stay awake all night waiting." She lifted both hands above her head and arched her back.

Mercedes shot her mother a glance. "I'll stay up a little while longer, but you're right." She shifted her gaze to Rambo, who was sprawled out on the kitchen floor napping. "What about Rambo? Do you think he'll alert us if he hears a noise?"

Carlita snorted. "So far he doesn't seem interested. We can leave him out here tonight to see if he hears anything." Rambo, hearing his name, lifted his head, yawned and then laid it back down.

She gave her daughter a quick hug and retreated to her bedroom. Carlita started to change into her nightgown and then decided on sweatpants and a t-shirt in case something happened. She didn't want to have to run outdoors and confront a thug in her pajamas.

"Ma."

Carlita walked around the side of her bed and opened her bedroom door. "Yes dear."

Mercedes stood on the other side, rubbing her eyes. "I'm going to bed, too."

"Okay. Make sure all the doors are locked and that you have your gun next to the bed."

"They are. I will."

If Vinnie were still alive, they wouldn't have to worry about safety. He had always taken the job of protecting his family seriously.

The night passed uneventfully and early the next morning, Rambo pawed at her door, waking her.

Carlita crawled out of bed and opened the door. "What? Time to go out already?" She followed the dog down the hall and opened the slider.

Her gaze shifted to the fence where she could barely make out the top of the garage door. Nothing looked out of place and the door wasn't busted open. Perhaps the culprit hadn't heard the word on the street yet.

She headed back into the kitchen, leaving the slider open far enough for Rambo to come back in, before starting a pot of coffee. Carlita mentally ticked off her list of things that needed to be done.

The first thing on the list was calling Bob Lowman, the construction supervisor in Savannah. Mercedes had suggested having him email pictures of the project's progress and even though they had just started, she couldn't wait to see the changes.

Next on the list was a trip to the grocery store, not Sal's around the corner, but the large super store a few miles away.

Mercedes had offered to drive versus calling a taxi and Carlita agreed it made sense. It would also give her daughter a little more practice before they hit the road again in a few weeks.

She also needed to work on becoming better organized with everything that was going on. Mercedes had offered to help, but it was still overwhelming.

Carlita couldn't wait until the house sold and they were in Savannah, where she hoped things would calm down.

The construction workers showed up right around eight to start replacing the torched siding on the back of the house. Carlita led them around back and then headed inside to call Bob Lowman.

She dialed Bob's number and he answered right away. "I was just getting ready to give you a call. We have a small problem."

Chapter 16

"A problem? What kind of problem?" Carlita didn't need any more problems, especially if they were going to cost money.

"Bats. There's a bat infestation in the attic above the apartments."

Carlita's skin started to crawl as visions of black creatures with flapping wings and beady eyes popped into her head. She had heard squeaky and creaking noises when she'd been alone in the property cleaning but chalked it up to being an old building that was settling.

"Do you want me to call an exterminator? I can text you once I get a quote. For now, work in the apartment is at a standstill until we can get rid of the infestation," Bob said.

Carlita began to pace the floor. "Yes. Please. How did they get in?"

"Through the fireplace. There was no screen on the top to keep them out. We got it covered now. It'll be a nice fireplace once it's fixed up. The good news is this place is solid. My guys found some stuff in the attic that you might want to take a look at, unless you want me to toss it."

Carlita's interest was piqued. "No. Please keep whatever you find." She thanked Bob for being on top of things. The news of bats in the attic was both good and bad. Perhaps the place wasn't haunted like Autumn had told them, but instead inhabited by disgusting living creatures.

After she hung up, Carlita changed into some old gardening clothes. Mercedes emerged from her room a short time later and the two of them headed to the attic.

While they were cleaning, Mercedes convinced her mother a garage sale was in order, arguing they could not only make some much-needed quick cash, they could get rid of a lot of stuff they wouldn't be able to fit in the tow-behind U-Haul they planned to rent when they moved to Savannah.

Anything they couldn't sell at the garage sale, they would donate to the Salvation Army. Carlita reluctantly agreed it was a good plan and mentally added a garage sale to her growing list.

The women worked hard all day and cleaned out not only the attic, but also the spare bedrooms and all of the closets. They called it quits when they reached the kitchen. They still needed to tackle the basement but it would have to wait until the following day.

Vinnie arrived as they carried a scuffed coffee table, minus one leg, to the side of the street. He pulled alongside the curb, climbed out of his car and surveyed the pile of odds and ends waiting to be picked up. "What's all this junk?"

"Just that. Junk," Mercedes quipped. "Useless crap we aren't taking to Savannah."

"You still on the moving-to-Savannah kick?"

"It's not a kick," Mercedes insisted. "It's a well thought out plan. We're moving by the end of the month." She pointed to the "For Sale" sign the real estate agent had placed in the front yard. "The agent texted half an hour ago to let us know she has already lined up two showings for tomorrow with several more in the works."

"It might be even sooner," Mercedes added.

Carlita didn't think so, since the contractor now had a bat infestation to deal with. He had promised to text her as soon as he had the quote, although she had already told him to go ahead and have it taken care of.

She hadn't mentioned the bats to Mercedes, who had an aversion to anything creepy, crawling, slimy or smelly.

"Huh." Vinnie changed the subject. "Word on the street is Pop told you he left something in the garage but you haven't been able to find it."

Carlita had wondered how long it would take before the rumor reached her sons. "Yep. Maybe it's a deed to more property."

Vinnie rolled his eyes. "That's just what we need. Maybe Pop owned somethin' in Vegas. Now that might be worth checking out." He rubbed his hands together and then eyed the garage. "Mind if I take a look around?"

"Be my guest." Carlita waved a hand toward the garage. "Good luck finding anything in all the piles of stuff we stuck in there for the garage sale." The women had managed to fill every nook and cranny, carving out a narrow path to maneuver around.

Mercedes watched her brother disappear inside the garage. "You think he'll find the rolled up bills?"

Carlita shrugged. "Maybe. Maybe he'll find some stuff to take home while he's at it. In fact, that's a great idea. Call your brothers and tell them to come by one day this week to see if they want anything before the sale Saturday."

Vinnie was still rifling around in the garage when Mercedes and Carlita, accompanied by a rambunctious Rambo, headed back inside.

The dog had kept them company as they sorted through the boxes and bags, and Carlita had even stumbled upon a few old stuffed animals she gave him.

Mercedes texted her brothers while Carlita inspected the contents of the refrigerator, searching for something quick to fix. She decided on grilled cheese and tomato soup, and it was almost ready when Vinnie wandered inside. "There's nothing but a bunch of old junk out there. If Pop left something behind, he hid it real good."

Vinnie held up an antique pocket watch. "This is the only thing I found. I remember Poppa always carried this in his front pocket." Poppa was Vinnie's grandfather and Carlita's father-in-law.

Carlita's eyes squinted and she studied the watch. "You're right. I guess I was in such a hurry to go through everything, I missed it." She vowed to pay closer attention when Mercedes and she organized the sale items. "Do you have time to eat a sandwich and some soup with us? It'll be ready in a minute."

Vinnie started to shake his head no and changed his mind. He nodded. "Sure, if it's not too much trouble."

He pulled out the kitchen chair and watched his mother as she slid the frying pan back on top of the stove and grabbed a couple more slices of bread. "You're serious about moving to Savannah?"

They were alone in the kitchen, just the two of them. Mercedes had gone to her room.

Carlita half-turned and faced her oldest child. Noting the serious expression on his face, she shifted all the way around to give him her full attention. "Yes, Vinnie, I am. Mercedes is, too. We'd like you to come with us."

Vinnie had been married once, years ago, to Michele, a woman that Carlita had liked. She wasn't part of the "family," but rather an outsider. They had married young, right out of high school.

Carlita had heard rumors her parents were dead set against their oldest daughter marrying Vinnie, but the young couple was in love and determined to wed. For the first couple of years, things had been good.

It took some time for the honeymoon to wear off and Michele's eyes opened to Vinnie's "career." Vinnie had confessed to his mother that Michele wanted him out of the "business," and Vinnie insisted he had tried to warn her before they married but Michele either hadn't wanted or refused to accept who - and what - her husband was.

144

What had once been "okay" was no longer tolerable. Michele refused to bring children into a criminal atmosphere. Vinnie refused to leave it. After three short years of marriage, they divorced.

The last Carlita had heard, Michele had married a lawyer and they lived in upstate New York with their two children. It had been heartbreaking for Carlita. Vinnie had deeply loved Michele.

Since then, Vinnie had dated on and off, but never gotten serious about another woman. Michele had been his one true love and Carlita was convinced he never wanted to go through the heartbreak of divorce again.

Vinnie ran a hand through slicked hair. "There's nothin' there for me, Ma. My friends...my work...it's here. What would I do down there?"

"Plenty," Carlita argued. "We're going to open a grocery store and restaurant." She tapped her spatula thoughtfully on the edge of the pan. "What would you like to do? There's a third building I haven't even thought about, let alone looked at yet. We could turn it into whatever you want."

The third, smaller business was located on a side street, connected to the others by a breezeway. Carlita had been so overwhelmed by the grocery store and the restaurant, not to mention the apartment units; she had refused to look at it.

Mercedes had gone in and after a quick glance around, told her mother it was best left alone until they had a handle on the rest of the construction projects.

Vinnie was already shaking his head. He couldn't picture himself living anywhere but New York.

Carlita smeared a thick layer of butter on two slices of bread, placed one slice of bread, butter side down in the pan and then sprinkled a generous handful of sharp cheddar cheese on top. She carefully placed the second piece of buttered bread on top.

"You could follow us down there, take a look for yourself." Perhaps once he got there, Vinnie would change his mind.

Vinnie tilted his head to the side and studied his mother. "Yeah. I been thinkin' maybe I should go to, you know, check it out."

Mercedes popped into the kitchen, having overheard the conversation. She snuck up behind her brother and gave him a quick hug. "Yay. You're a good brother. I don't care what Tony says."

Vinnie chuckled and hugged his little sister before releasing his grip. "I may live to regret my decision, but yeah, I'll follow you down there."

Chapter 17

Vinnie left not long after they finished eating, and since Carlita had made the meal, Mercedes insisted her mother let her clean up. Carlita was happy to let her daughter help. She was whupped after a long day.

They hadn't even had time to drive to the grocery store, but decided to go first thing in the morning before they tackled the basement.

Carlita awoke early the next morning to the now familiar thump – Rambo's signal it was time to go out. She was getting used to her early morning wakeup call, and in fact, was growing attached to the pooch. It would be a sad day when they had to leave him behind.

Tony was gone a lot "taking care of business" and she knew Rambo was alone in Tony's small condo for hours on end. At least here, he had a yard to run around in and she was home most of the time.

Carlita let Rambo out through the slider before heading to the bathroom to get ready for the day. She jumped in the shower for a quick scrub down.

When she finished, she towel dried her hair and then ran her fingers through it. For years, Vinnie insisted she wear her hair long. Finally, she grew tired of messing with it and impulsively stopped at a nearby salon and had the girl chop it all off.

It was a flattering style and one that was easy to manage, although with everything going on, it had been awhile and her hair was now almost shoulder length.

Mercedes wore her hair long and straight, like her mother had for years. Her daughter was a striking woman and Carlita was secretly surprised she was still single.

Carlita slipped into a pair of jeans, a plain gray blouse and a pair of tennis shoes before heading to the slider to let Rambo back in. She slid the door open and cupped her hands to her mouth. "Rambo!"

When he didn't come, she stuck her head out and gazed around. Her heart sank when she noticed the side gate was wide open. Carlita had checked to make sure it was shut before she had let him out for his morning romp,

"Good heavens." She darted out onto the deck, down the steps and ran toward the gate, all the while yelling the dog's name. "Rambo!"

By the time she reached the drive, she had shifted into full panic mode. The dog was nowhere in sight. Carlita shouted his name as she raced down the sidewalk.

She circled the block before retracing her steps to the backyard. When she reached the gate, she noticed the side garage door was ajar. Carlita hurried to the door and pushed it open. "Rambo?"

A black shadowy figure catapulted over a stack of boxes. Carlita quickly backed up. She tripped over a pile of garbage bags and landed on top of them.

The shadowy figure pounced on top of her and licked the side of her face. It was Rambo. "What in the world?" She turned her face to the side and pushed him away as she scrambled to her feet. "How did you get in here? Better yet, how did you get out of the backyard?"

"I had no idea you knew how to open doors." Carlita held onto Rambo's collar and led him out of the garage when she spotted an unfamiliar car in the drive. Parked behind the car was a police car.

She opened the side door and shooed Rambo inside before wandering down the drive.

Father Dadore and a uniformed officer made their way up the drive. She waited until the men were close. "Hello Father Dadore."

"Good morning, Carlita. I'm sorry to bother you." The priest clasped his hands in front of him. "I wonder if we might have a minute of your time."

She shifted her eyes and gazed at the detective. "Yes, of course." Carlita led them through the backyard, across the deck and into through the rear slider. "Would you care for a cup of coffee?"

"No. We won't be long," Father Dadore said and pointed at the officer. "This is Detective Striker. Your husband, Vincent...Vinnie stopped by to chat with me a few days before he was admitted to the hospital. He had a confession to make and I believe it may have had something to do with his death."

"Looking back, I should've said something sooner," the priest confessed.

Carlita took a few steps backward and leaned against the kitchen cabinet. "What are you talking about?"

The detective shifted uneasily. "It concerns something that happened not long before your husband died."

Chapter 18

Father Dadore continued. "We were wondering if he may have mentioned a...problem concerning his job."

"No. He didn't. What would that have to do with his death?" Carlita's mind reeled. She had always known the hazards of being a made man, that there was always the chance someone would "off" Vinnie, or any of her sons for that matter, not to mention Mercedes or even her.

"Have you ever heard of a man by the name of Vito Castellini?" Father Dadore asked.

"Yes, of course. Vito is..." Carlita's voice trailed off.

"The head of the organization," the detective interrupted. "We've had our eye on Mr. Castellini for years and know for a fact your husband, Vincent, met with Mr. Castellini a couple days before he was hospitalized."

He went on. "Vinnie was working on a big drop for Vito, but before we could get to your husband, he died. We think Vinnie may have had the goods with him or on him at the time of his death. In other words, if others think your husband still possessed the goods Vito gave him, your life may be in danger."

Carlita pushed away from the kitchen counter and began pacing the floor. *Had Vinnie told Father Dadore about the gems or the property deed?*

"Someone broke into the house the day I was at the hospital, the day Vinnie died," Carlita confessed. "We've had another break in since then."

She didn't dare say more, not trusting anyone. She gave the detective and Father Dadore a quick glance. Not even them.

Detective Striker could see Carlita Garlucci was becoming agitated, a sign she was hiding something. "You have no idea what your husband may have been holding onto?"

Carlita stopped pacing. "Like I said, Vinnie never talked business with me. I'm sure you know the drill. Wives are kept in the dark for our own safety," she explained. That much was true. Surely, the detective would know that.

"Ma. You'll never guess what." Mercedes burst into the kitchen. She stopped abruptly as her eyes shifted to the priest and then to the detective. "Hello."

"Mercedes, Father Dadore and Detective Striker think that your father had something in his possession just before he died that may have been tied to his death."

"What..." Mercedes's voice trailed off. "You mean Pop didn't die from lung disease?" Her lower lip began to tremble and Carlita wrapped an arm around her daughter's waist.

"I'm sorry dear. I'm as shocked as you are," Carlita said in a low voice. She gave her daughter a hard stare. "Can you recall your father saying anything odd to you before he became ill?"

"Pop never talked business." Mercedes said almost the exact same thing her mother had. "I have no idea."

Detective Striker gazed from daughter to mother. "If you think of anything, anything at all." He pulled a card from his front pocket and held it out. "Please give me a call."

Carlita walked the detective and Father Dadore to the door. She waited until the men had reached their vehicles before turning to face her daughter. "Do you think they're onto us?"

"It's hard telling." Mercedes tucked a stray strand of hair behind her ear. "It seems like everyone is after us."

"Which means we need to step things up," Carlita said. "By the way, did you leave the gate and garage door open? Rambo got loose again."

"No. I haven't left my room all morning." Mercedes said. "Maybe someone finally broke into the garage."

"If so, we missed catching the culprit again," Carlita groaned.

"That sucks."

"What if Rambo saw the person? If only we could get him to talk." Carlita shrugged. "Well, there's nothing we can do about it now. I'm glad Rambo is safe." She changed the subject. "Are we still grocery shopping this morning?"

"Yep." Mercedes tightened her ponytail and tugged on the ends. "I'll go get ready."

"I think I need more coffee." Carlita poured a fresh cup of coffee before heading to the kitchen table, where she plopped down in a chair and reached for yesterday's newspaper, all the while mulling over what the detective and Father Dadore had said.

Rambo settled in at her feet and they stayed put until Mercedes emerged from the bathroom. "Ready when you are."

Carlita downed the last drop of coffee, folded the newspaper and then carried the cup to the sink were she rinsed it out and set it inside the dishwasher. "We should grab a bite to eat while we're out since there's nothing here to eat."

Carlita had faithfully checked her bank account every day. Vinnie had left behind a small retirement account and they had a joint savings account with a good chunk of money they had accumulated over the years, but it wasn't enough to live on for the rest of Carlita's life. If she were lucky, it would last long enough to get the Savannah businesses up and running.

The gems were their ticket to fund everything else except day-to-day expenses. There was no mortgage on the house and once the house sold, she would breathe easier, which reminded her that the real estate agent, her cousin, had scheduled several showings for that day.

Carlita prayed they would find the right buyer, someone who would love and care for the home, maybe even a young family who could grow in it. It had been a good home for many years and she would miss it.

Financially, she was in good shape and not saddled with tons of bills. It was a shame Vinnie and she had never had a chance to do all the things they always talked about doing. Carlita had always wanted to drive to Florida to visit family and fly to Vegas, although Vinnie had been there many times without her.

They had even discussed taking a cruise. It seemed that life had gotten in the way and they never got around to all of the adventures they had talked about doing. Now it was too late.

When they reached the grocery store, Mercedes pulled into an empty spot and Carlita reached for the door handle. "I don't want to lollygag so let's get in, grab the goods and get out."

"Sounds good." Mercedes agreed. The women were on a mission as they zipped up and down the aisles grabbing everything on their list, plus more. Carlita was shocked the grocery bill hit the $200 mark and hoped they had purchased enough food to last until they moved.

The women quickly filled every square inch of the trunk and then climbed back into the car. When they reached the house, Carlita spotted Tony's car parked out front and the garage door was wide open.

Tony emerged from the garage when he saw his father's car pull into the drive and he met Mercedes and Carlita near the trunk.

Tony gave his mother a quick hug before reaching for a bag of groceries. "I wondered where you went. I've been going through the junk in the garage."

The three of them made quick work of carrying the groceries inside before Tony resumed his inspection of the garage contents.

Carlita had grabbed a rotisserie chicken on the way out of the grocery store, along with a side of coleslaw and potato salad. It was almost lunchtime and she invited Tony to join them.

After they settled in at the table, Tony reached for a drumstick. "Heard Vinnie is gonna follow you down to Savannah since we can't talk sense into either of you."

Mercedes scooped a large spoonful of coleslaw onto her plate and passed the container to her brother. "I'm sure Ma would be happy to see you go, too."

"Nah." Tony shrugged. "Seems like a big waste of time. You'll be back," he predicted.

Carlita arched a brow. "What if we're not? Will you come visit us?"

Rambo trotted over to the table and nudged Tony's leg. He tore a small piece of meat from the drumstick and fed it to the dog. "Yeah. If you don't come back in six months, I'll come visit."

He changed the subject. "Anything else happenin' 'round here?"

Carlita told her son of the morning incident where Rambo got loose and she found him in the garage, although she was certain that the fence gate had been secure and the garage door locked.

"Anything missing from the garage?" Tony chuckled at his question. "Not that you could make heads or tails what with all the stuff out there."

"Not that I'm aware of. I haven't had a chance to look around," Carlita admitted. She went on to tell her son that the repair crew had finished fixing the scorched siding on the back of the house and Mercedes and she were going to make themselves scarce after lunch so that the real estate agent could show the home to prospective buyers.

Tony replaced the lid on the potato salad and carried it to the fridge. "How is Rambo? Has he been doin' his job?"

"He's a great dog," Carlita smiled.

"So you wanna keep him?" Tony asked.

"I..." Carlita didn't want to take her son's dog from him.

"He's a good dog." Tony placed the potato salad on the refrigerator shelf and closed the door. He reached down and patted Rambo's head. "I'm not home much. I think he gets lonely."

"Well, if you're offering, then yes, I'll keep Rambo. He's going to Savannah, though," she warned.

"You'll be back," Tony repeated.

Carlita finished straightening the kitchen and then the three of them, along with Rambo, headed outside. The real estate agent and potential buyers were scheduled to arrive soon. She had given the agent a key to the house and the agent had told Carlita she planned to put a lockbox on the front door.

"I better get out of here." Tony hugged his mother, patted Rambo's head and climbed into his car. "I'll call you later."

The women waited until Tony's car disappeared around the corner before heading to the breezeway to grab the boxes of stuff they planned to take to the pawnshop.

"Let's walk to the pawnshop." Carlita clipped a leash to Rambo's collar and balanced one small box under her arm while Mercedes carried the larger one.

A gust of wind blew the door wide open and Carlita studied the storm clouds, which were starting to gather.

"I think we're in for a good one," she said as she eyed the sky warily.

The women hurried down the sidewalk, arriving in front of the pawnshop a short time later. Mercedes held the door for her mom and Rambo.

Carlita wasn't sure pets were allowed so she waited just inside the door while Mercedes carried the boxes to the counter.

Sandra was working the counter and she waved Carlita and Rambo over. "As long as he doesn't bite, you can bring him in," she said.

"Bite – no. Lick you to death – probably," Carlita joked. She pointed to the boxes Mercedes had placed on the counter. "We brought a few things we thought you might be interested in buying."

Sandra unfolded the top of the smaller box and peeked inside. She pulled out a collection of baseball cards that once belonged to Paulie, a couple old oil paintings Carlita deemed hideous and a set of china that had belonged to Vinnie's mom.

Carlita had asked Mercedes if she wanted the china set, but her daughter told her no. Not only that, there would be limited space inside the U-Haul and precious little space for sentimental items, although now that

Vinnie was following them to Savannah, they would be able to pack a few extras into his car.

"You ever figure out what Vinnie had in the garage?" Sandra asked as she opened a jewelry box and studied an emerald bracelet inside. It wasn't a real emerald. At least, Carlita assumed it wasn't real. The way Sandra was eyeballing it, she wasn't so sure anymore...

"Nope." Carlita shook her head.

"We have tons of crap in there now. It's hard to find anything," Mercedes joked.

Carlita gave her a dark look.

"Uh-huh." Sandra shifted her gaze from Mercedes to Carlita. "Vito said Vinnie bailed on a drop right before he died," she said bluntly. "In fact, he mentioned stopping by the house today to talk to you, to ask if Vinnie mentioned it."

Carlita's eyelid started to twitch. No one ever wanted Vito Castellini to "pay" a visit.

She shifted her feet and blinked rapidly, willing the twitch to stop. "I see."

Mercedes took the news in stride and shrugged. "We got a real estate agent showing the house right now but

162

we should be home later." She turned to her mother. "Right Ma?"

Carlita turned deer-in-the-headlight eyes on her daughter. "Y-yes," she stuttered. "We'll be home later."

Sandra offered to take the baseball cards off her hands, along with some of the jewelry, including the emerald, the ugly paintings and a couple old posters Carlita had almost dumped in the trash, all for the princely sum of four hundred-fifty dollars.

Sandra counted out the money, and all the while, the only thing going through Carlita's mind was, if Vito didn't like her answers, she might not need the money after all.

Chapter 19

Carlita's steps dragged during the walk home. Filled with a sense of impending doom, she wondered when, exactly, Vito Castellini would show up on her doorstep. She also wondered if he would be by himself or if he would bring some of his "associates."

When they reached their place, she glanced around uneasily before unlocking the front door and letting her daughter in first. "I want you to head over to Gia's place to hang out." Gia was one of Mercedes's close friends.

Mercedes shook her head. "No way, Ma. I'm not gonna leave you alone with Vito Castellini. I'd be worried the entire time."

"I don't want you here," Carlita insisted, but Mercedes refused to leave the house. Her mother and she were in this together, through thick and thin, life or death. Hopefully not the death part.

Finally, Carlita gave up trying to convince her daughter to leave and instead they reached a compromise. Mercedes promised as soon as Vito showed up, she would head to her bedroom and if anything happened, she would dial 911.

Mercedes patted Rambo's head. "Rambo will protect you and bite Vito if he comes after you."

"Rambo is a big baby." Rambo, hearing his name, demonstrated his fierceness by flopping down on the living room floor and rubbing the side of his face on the carpet.

Carlita stepped over him and headed to the kitchen. "We can wait for Vito to show up or take our minds off it by starting on the basement," she said as she placed her purse on the kitchen counter and her keys on the hook by the back door.

The women opted to tackle their last big project, and after changing into old clothes, headed to the basement.

Carlita flipped the light switch on the wall and descended the steps, making her way into the laundry area where the washer and dryer sat off to one side.

She glanced at the small, rectangular windows above the appliances, which desperately needed a good cleaning but not today. "Maybe we can add a laundry area to the apartment units that isn't in the basement."

Mercedes tilted her head and studied the washer. "Is there a basement in Savannah?" If there had been one, she hadn't noticed it. She shuddered and rubbed the sides of her arms. "It's probably creepy...creepier than this one."

Beyond the laundry area were three other rooms, all of them crammed full of discarded furniture, stacks of yellowed paperback books, vintage clothes and some toys.

Mercedes and Carlita quickly decided to toss the boxes of old clothes since they smelled damp and musty from years of being stored in the basement.

They created three piles: toss, keep and either donate or try to sell at the garage sale. The largest pile by far was the "toss" pile, followed by the garage sale/donation pile. The smallest was the "keep" pile.

Some of the stuff hadn't seen the light of day in decades and Carlita didn't even recognize several of the boxes. She opened one of the unfamiliar boxes, pulled out a long strip of furry cloth and held it up. "What in the world is this?"

"I know what it is." Mercedes snatched it from her mother's hand, flung it around her neck, tilted her head and batted her eyes. "A mink stole motha." She added the fake accent for emphasis.

Carlita grinned. "It's all yours," she shook her head. "It must have belonged to your Grandmother Garlucci."

She reached inside the box and pulled out a rectangular jewelry box.

Carlita flipped the clasp and opened the lid. She tilted the box toward the bare bulb overhead for a closer inspection. "I had no idea this box was in here," she said as she reached inside and pulled out a strand of pearls. "These are the real deal."

Mercedes adjusted her newfound mink stole and held out her other hand. "Let me see."

Carlita dropped the necklace in the palm of her daughter's hand. "Cool. We don't have to sell these, do we?"

"You can keep whatever catches your eye," her mother assured her as she began digging around inside the jewelry box. In addition to the strand of pearls, there was a matching broach and a pair of clip-on earrings.

They dug through the rest of the open box and found an album full of old photographs. Carlita added the pictures to the "keep" pile.

Hidden behind the boxes was an old filing cabinet that had been in the basement for as long as Carlita could remember. She had never looked inside. The cabinet had belonged to her husband.

Carlita straddled a stray box, shifted to the side and grabbed the filing cabinet door handle. "It's locked."

"Pick the lock," Mercedes suggested.

"How?"

"I'll do it. Hang on." Mercedes hurried across the basement floor and darted up the stairs. She returned moments later with a bobby pin, a butter knife and a pair of small scissors.

Carlita stepped to the side and watched as Mercedes attempted to pick the lock using the butter knife first. The end of the knife was too large.

She tried using the bobby pin, which was too small. She handed the butter knife and bobby pin to her mother. "Hold these." Mercedes leaned forward, stuck the tip of the scissors into the lock and wiggled.

Pop.

"Sweet." Mercedes removed the scissors, twisted the metal handle and opened the door. "What on earth?"

Shelves lined the interior of the metal cabinet. On top of the shelves were what looked like mini bales of hay, covered in yellow plastic wrap.

Mercedes reached inside and pulled one out. "I...what..."

Carlita reached around Mercedes and picked one up, turning it over in her hand. "Drugs," she whispered. "I think this cabinet is full of drugs."

"What kind?" Mercedes lifted the package close to her face and sniffed the corner.

"I don't know." Carlita's mind reeled. If these plastic packets were what she thought they were, it was no wonder people were breaking into her house. *Had Vinnie been a drug dealer to boot?*

"I can take one upstairs, try to do a little research online to see what exactly these are," Mercedes suggested.

Ding-dong.

Carlita's eye widened and she stared at the stairs. "The doorbell."

Chapter 20

Carlita quickly slammed the cabinet doors shut and hopped over a stack of boxes. "We better find out who that is." Her heart began to pound in her chest as she headed for the stairs, certain beyond a shadow of a doubt Vito Castellini was standing on her front step.

Mercedes followed her mother up the stairs. When they reached the hall, Carlita signaled her daughter to go to her room and to take the plastic brick she was holding with her.

"Vinnie Garlucci, I can't believe you left me with such a mess," Carlita muttered under her breath as she hurried down the hall. She hadn't formulated a plan on what she would say to Vito. Maybe he was after the drugs..., the gems..., or the property. At this point, it was hard telling. Maybe all three.

At the end of the hall, she turned right and stepped into the living room where she spotted the silhouette of someone standing on her stoop. One figure. One person. She let out the breath she'd been holding. It looked as if Vito was alone.

Carlita opened the front door and peered out. "Hello Mr. Castellini." She wasn't sure if she should call him by his first name. Better to err on the side of caution.

Vito Castellini was a tall man, in his mid-60's with shocking white hair, and his clothing a little on the unkempt side. He stooped at a slight angle as he reached up, snatched his hat off his head and held it in his hand. "Hello Carlita. I'm sorry to bother you, but wondered if I might have a minute of your time."

Carlita unlocked the screen door and pushed it open, letting Vito Castellini, the head of the mafia, into her house. "Would you like a cup of coffee? A glass of water? Can I take your hat?" She knew she was rambling but couldn't stop herself.

He followed her to the kitchen.

Rambo was asleep in his bed. He lifted his head to study the newcomer and then laid it back down, closing his eyes. *Great watchdog.*

"Would you like to have a seat?" Carlita pulled out a kitchen chair for him to sit.

"Thank you. I won't take much of your time," he said as he eased his large frame into the chair.

Carlita pulled out another chair, leaving an empty one between them, and faced her husband's ex-boss.

"I'm sorry about Vinnie."

Carlita nodded. "Thank you. I-uh. His death was a shock." So far, so good. She began to relax, which turned out to be a big mistake on her part.

"I'll get right to the point. Vinnie was supposed to make a drop for me the day before he was hospitalized. My...customer...said the goods were never delivered." Vito paused, letting the words sink in. "Vinnie didn't happen to mention anything to you in the hospital about where my goods might be?"

"No." Carlita shook her head. Vinnie *hadn't* told her about the safe deposit key in his pocket, or the safe deposit box, which held the deed to the Savannah property and the gems...or the cabinet full of plastic-coated bricks. "He went so fast, by the time I got to the hospital, he couldn't talk, couldn't breathe." Sudden tears burned the back of her eyes and she blinked rapidly, steeling herself to remain composed.

"Sandra mentioned somethin' about Vinnie might have left somethin' in the garage."

Carlita had almost forgotten about the "sting"...Mercedes and her attempt to try to draw out whoever was breaking into her house. "Yeah. You're free to look around, Vi- Mr. Castellini," Carlita corrected herself. "My boys have already looked. The garage is full of junk I plan to sell at a garage sale this weekend." She went on. "I'm selling the house and moving."

Vito nodded. "I saw the sign." He leaned in, his eyes piercing into hers. "So you don't know nothin' about a package?"

Carlita steeled her gaze, never wavering from his. She had once heard if you break a stare, it's a sure sign you're lying. "No sir. I don't have a package." *Just a bag of gems and deeds to crap holes in Savannah that need tons of repairs, not to mention a cabinet full of drugs - maybe.*

Vito nodded slightly, satisfied Carlita was telling the truth, which she was. If he had come right out and asked about a bag of gems, she would have had to confess.

It was also possible the gems weren't the "drop." Maybe Vito was after the drugs. Her heart skipped a beat and she began to feel lightheaded. She was living in a drug house.

Before the swoon turned into a full on faint, she abruptly stood. "Would you like me to show you the garage?"

Vito followed her lead and slowly got to his feet, pushing the kitchen chair back. "If you don't mind." He followed Carlita out of the kitchen, down the steps, across the driveway and in the side garage door.

She flipped the light switch. "Like I said, we're selling our stuff and moving so I'm sorry for the mess," she apologized.

Vito grunted and shuffled into the garage, gazing at the walls, the rafters, the boxes. He made a half-hearted attempt at reaching Vinnie's workbench, which was under the small garage window and then gave up. He shook his head. "I don't think Vinnie was stupid enough to leave anything of value in here," he said bluntly.

Carlita nodded. *Just the basement.*

"If you tell me what you're looking for, I'll keep an eye out for it," Carlita offered.

Vito shoved his hands in his pockets, rocked back on his heels and gazed at her thoughtfully. "Sure. I put word out on the street that it was some rocks, but it's more like bricks. Six bricks of coke."

He headed for the door. "If you happen to run across them." He waved his hand at the piles of junk. "Give me a call." He pulled a business card from his front pocket and handed it to Carlita.

"This is between us, right?"

Carlita took the card, glanced at the front and then looked at Vito. "Yes. Of course. Just between us," she repeated.

Carlita closed the garage door, followed him to the end of the driveway and then watched as he strode across the front lawn. His driver, one of his henchmen, was standing by the rear passenger door.

He held the door open and Carlita watched as Vito eased into the backseat. The driver closed the door before scowling at her and slowly walking to the driver's side and climbing in.

If what Mercedes and she had found in the basement cabinet were blocks of cocaine, there were a lot more than six. There were dozens. If Vito Castellini was only looking for six, who did the others belong to?

Chapter 21

Carlita tapped on Mercedes's bedroom door, and then held a finger to her lips, motioning her to follow her outside.

When they reached the backyard, she explained to her daughter that Vito wasn't looking for gems, but six "bricks" of cocaine. "Were you able to research what we found?"

"No." Mercedes shook her head. "I was afraid Vito would burst into my room and I would be caught red handed with the goods."

Carlita hadn't thought about that. She had lived on the fringes of criminal activity but now that she had been thrown into the center of it, there were so many things to worry about. "The good news is no one is looking for the gems, or the deed to the Savannah property."

"That we know of. The bad news is we've got a cabinet full of illegal drugs in our basement and someone out there has to be looking for them," Mercedes said.

"Besides Vito," Carlita added. There was no one they could trust, no one they could tell...not even her own sons. They could go to the police, but what if they determined Carlita and Mercedes were involved and decided to arrest them and charge them with drug possession? "I could call that nice Detective Striker who stopped by with Father Dadore."

"Are you nuts?" Mercedes gasped. "If Vito catches wind we found his drugs and turned them over to the cops, we're as good as dead."

"So you think we should return the drugs to Vito and do what with the rest?" Carlita's stomach began to churn. They were in a real catch-22. "What if someone else is missing their drugs and they come after us?"

"Before we do anything, we need to find out what we've got," Mercedes said as she pressed the palm of her hand to her forehead.

The women headed back inside the house with Rambo following behind.

The situation was worse than Carlita could ever have imagined. What if they returned the drugs to Vito, he suspected they were in on it and decided to take them out? People disappeared off the face of the earth if there was even a hint of disloyalty to the family, especially the godfather.

Carlita paced the kitchen floor. "Baking. I need to start making something." She pulled a mixing bowl, some graham crackers, chocolate chips, shredded coconut and nuts from the cupboard and placed all of the ingredients on the counter.

She reached inside the fridge for a stick of butter and placed it next to the other ingredients. It was time to make one of her all-time favorite desserts, dream bars.

She pressed the crumbled graham cracker crust, mixed with melted butter, in the bottom of the baking dish before layering the other ingredients on top and placing the dish inside the preheated oven.

Mercedes walked into the kitchen as her mother was closing the oven door. She waved her to the slider and the women stepped outside. "Our hunch was right on. We're sitting on a boatload of cocaine."

Carlita tugged on the strings of her apron. "I had a feeling you were going to say that. Now what do we do?"

The women discussed their limited options, and there were only two – call Vito to pick up the cocaine or call the police. More than anything, Mercedes wished they had not found the cocaine.

It was a difficult situation either way. Carlita ran a hand through her hair and stared out into the backyard. "I say for now, we pretend we don't know it's there. We'll have to decide what to do with the cabinet before we move. Where is the...block?"

"On my desk," Mercedes said.

"Let's put it back inside the filing cabinet, lock it and deal with it later." Carlita reached for the door handle. "I hate to say this, but I almost hope someone breaks into the house again, finds the cocaine and steals it."

Mercedes snapped her fingers. "That's it. What a great idea. We move it into the garage and hope someone breaks in, finds it and steals it. Word on the street is something is in the garage. Maybe we'll get lucky and the cops will catch wind, get a search warrant for the garage or the house and take this hot mess off our hands."

"Let's start loading them up," Carlita nodded. "We'll put the bricks in boxes and carry them out to the garage and then move the empty storage cabinet."

Carlita and Mercedes stepped back inside to wait for the dream bars to finish baking.

The timer chimed and Carlita carefully pulled the decadent dessert from the oven and set them on top of the stove before heading to the basement to carry their first two boxes of "bricks" to the garage. It took four trips in all to empty the filing cabinet.

Every time they carried a box out of the house and across the drive, Carlita's eyelid started to twitch. She was certain that at any moment, cops would careen into the driveway, guns blazing, ready to arrest them, but it didn't happen and when the last box was stacked in the corner, she breathed a sigh of relief.

Carlita placed her fisted hands on her hips and gazed at the last box she'd set on top of the stack. "We shouldn't have too much trouble moving the cabinet. Let's take a quick break, sample a dream bar and grab a glass of cold milk to calm our nerves."

Mercedes followed her mother out of the garage, closing the door behind them and they headed back inside.

The gooey chocolate coconut bars were still warm. Carlita sliced two large pieces, placed them on small dessert plates and carried them to the kitchen table while Mercedes poured two glasses of cold milk, grabbing a couple paper towels on her way to the table.

She placed a paper towel next to her mother's plate and handed her a glass of milk. "A toast."

Carlita lifted her glass. "To what?"

"A toast to a successful break in," she whispered as she lightly clinked her glass to her mother's glass.

Carlita shook her head and took a sip before reaching for the warm gooey treat. "I never thought I would agree but since your father died, life has been anything but normal." She took a big bite of the dream bar. The graham cracker crust along with melted chocolate, bits of crunchy walnut and toasted coconut, melted in her mouth. "This is so good," she mumbled between savory bites.

Mercedes nibbled the edge of hers before breaking off a large piece and popping it into her mouth. "Mmm. You haven't made these in years." She quickly gobbled the rest of hers before making her way to the stove for second piece. "Do you want another one?"

"No thanks." Carlita licked the tips of her fingers, picked up her napkin and dabbed at the corners of her mouth. "Tomorrow we'll start organizing for Saturday's garage sale."

Mercedes settled into the chair again and picked up her glass of milk. "Maybe we'll have less to get rid of." She winked at her mom.

"True." Carlita crumpled her napkin. "Why don't we move the last cabinet into the garage, the one we found in the basement?" Carlita raised her voice so she was almost yelling. "The one Vinnie kept locked in the basement that he never let us go near. Maybe one of the boys can run by tomorrow to try to open it."

Mercedes opened her mouth to say something and then circled her thumb and forefinger to signal an "okay" sign. "Yeah. He must have had something pretty important locked inside for him to never allow anyone near it."

"I wish we had a key," Carlita said. She hopped out of her chair, tossed her crumpled napkin in the trash and carried her empty plate and glass to the kitchen sink.

When they finished taking care of the dishes, they headed back downstairs and over to the cabinet.

Mercedes wrinkled her nose and stared at the cabinet. "How we gonna get this up the steep steps?"

"I thought I saw a handcart around here somewhere." Her mother began poking around the last section of boxes and spied a metal handcart in the far corner, hidden behind the water heater. "Aha!"

Carlita dragged it from the corner and steered it to the front of the cabinet. "You tip it back and I'll slide the bottom underneath."

Mercedes squeezed behind the cabinet, grasped both sides and tipped it back. Her mother slipped the bottom of the cart underneath. "You can let it back down."

The women tugged, pushed and pulled the cabinet, finally succeeding in wheeling it to the bottom of the basement steps.

Mercedes gazed from the cabinet to the steps. "There's not enough clearance. We'll have to slide it up. You push, I'll pull."

Carlita grabbed hold of the bottom and began pushing. "Maybe we should leave the...stuff...in the boxes," she gasped.

Finally, they managed to maneuver the bulky cabinet up the steps, shift it sideways and out the back door. It was easier dragging the cabinet into the garage than it had been up the stairs.

They stopped to take a brief break when they reached the garage. Carlita brushed her hands together. "Piece of cake," she grimaced. "Now where do we put it?"

"There," Mercedes pointed to an empty spot near the door.

"Perfect." Carlita and Mercedes shifted the cabinet into place before carrying the boxes of bricks to the front and placing the contents back inside.

After they finished, the women stood back and admired their brilliant plan. Now all they had to do was wait for someone to break in and take it, lock, stock and barrel.

Mercedes wiped her hands on the front of her pants before tossing the last empty box on top of the pile. "I think we worked hard today and deserve a nice steak dinner," she announced. "Not only that, we need to skedaddle to give someone a chance to break in."

Carlita couldn't have agreed more. It had been a stressful day, a stressful week...stressful months. If she dwelled on it too long, she knew she would fall apart. She was heartbroken over her husband's death, she was angry with him for not only leaving her, but also leaving her in this predicament, and if she were completely honest with herself, she was overwhelmed.

Carlita gave Mercedes a quick hug. Her daughter needed her. Her sons needed her, too. They just didn't know it yet. "What a wonderful idea. Let's go."

Chapter 22

Bellafonte's Steakhouse was the nicest steak restaurant in all of Queens and possibly all of New York. Vinnie and Carlita had eaten there every so often, on special occasions such as birthdays and anniversaries.

Today was a special occasion. On the way out the door, the real estate agent had called to let Carlita know that not only had they gotten a full price offer on the house, they had gotten two. The agent told her she would send the offers over via email that evening and Carlita promised to look them over the next morning.

Bellafonte's was packed, which wasn't a surprise, and Mercedes circled the block twice before finding an empty parking spot a block away.

Carlita waited on the curb for her daughter to climb out of the driver's side and make her way to the sidewalk. The two of them had decided to spiff up and unknowingly chose to wear almost identical black skirts. Mercedes wore a sleeveless red silk blouse while Carlita opted for a gray button down. She was still mourning her husband and decided bright colors weren't appropriate.

Although the restaurant was packed, they were seated almost immediately, at a table for two, located smack dab in the center of the restaurant. It was a high traffic area and servers buzzed by as they flitted from table to table. Carlita didn't mind. It was the perfect spot to people watch.

Carlita ordered a ribeye steak while Mercedes decided on a porterhouse. "I want leftovers," she explained.

Her mother raised an eyebrow. "Uh-huh. Or maybe you want to make sure you have leftovers for Rambo," she teased.

Mercedes and Rambo were beginning to bond, which may have been an understatement. Rambo followed Mercedes everywhere...to the kitchen, the living room, her bedroom. He even tried to follow her into the bathroom, but she drew the line and Rambo waited patiently outside the door each time she went in.

"Yeah. He's a stinker. He loves to paw my closet door open, crawl inside and chew on my shoes." Rambo hadn't bothered Carlita's shoes, which may have been because Mercedes's were a lot flashier with more bling.

Dinner was a leisurely affair and by the time Carlita had eaten all of her salad, part of her steak and a couple bites of her baked potato, she was stuffed. They both ended up with to-go boxes.

After paying the bill and leaving a generous tip for excellent service, mother and daughter wandered out of the restaurant and strolled the short distance to the car.

Carlita climbed in the passenger seat and set the containers of leftovers on the seat between them before reaching for her seatbelt. "I wonder if the goods are gone."

Mercedes stuck the key in the ignition and started the car. "Me too. I never thought I would say this, but I hope someone robbed us."

"You know, Mercedes, I've been thinking about it. We need to do the right thing. I'm going to call Detective Striker tomorrow and tell him what we've got. We'll let the chips fall where they may." She silently added she hoped that by the time Vito Castellini discovered they had turned the drugs over to authorities, they would be long gone.

The first thing Carlita did when they pulled into the drive was head to the side garage door. It was closed. She opened the door, flipped the light switch on, her eyes automatically honing in on the filing cabinet. Carlita's heart sank when she saw the cabinet was still there.

Mercedes waited for her near the back door, leftovers in hand. "Well?"

"Still there," Carlita reported as she turned the light off and slowly pulled the door shut. "Maybe we'll get lucky and they'll break in while we're sleeping."

***

The illicit drugs were still inside the cabinet when the women wandered into the garage the next morning to start organizing and pricing the items they planned to sell.

Carlita shoved aside her worries over the cabinet and its contents and focused her attention on the task at hand.

Mother and daughter worked all morning, taking a short lunch break around noon, and finally finished later that afternoon. Bob Lowman, the construction supervisor in Savannah, called to tell Carlita the coast was clear, the bats were gone and they were moving full steam ahead with the repairs.

Mercedes had forwarded a few suggestions, changing the layout of their apartment so it flowed better and Carlita was proud of her. They decided if the changes worked for them, they would rearrange the floorplans of the other units, as well.

Bob told them he was working on installing new kitchen cabinets, countertops, a breakfast bar, updating the electric and plumbing, as well as updating the apartment's only bathroom. They had decided to remove the old claw foot tub and replace it with a shower/tub combo, something much more practical.

Carlita felt a twinge of guilt over taking out some of the unique details of the apartment, but practicality won out. They needed a functioning home, one that was completely modernized if they planned to focus their energies on running both a grocery store and restaurant.

She still secretly hoped her sons would move to Savannah, not only to keep her promise to Vinnie, but because Mercedes and she would need all hands on deck to run the businesses.

They rearranged the last card table and loaded it with household appliances Carlita rarely used and had no desire to drag halfway across the country. The goodies to go included a waffle maker, a popcorn popper, snow cone machine and a rice cube.

Mercedes grabbed the rice cube and held it up. "You're not gonna get rid of this, are you?"

Carlita frowned. "I have no idea what it is."

"It's a rice cube. You know, to make the perfect sushi square."

Her mother shrugged. "Keep it if you want. It won't take up too much space."

When they finally finished rearranging the sale items, Carlita closed the overhead garage door and they headed to the kitchen. She shuffled over to a kitchen chair, eased into it and then kicked off her Crocs. "I don't feel like cooking," she announced to Mercedes, who had reached inside the fridge to grab an ice water.

They had devoured their leftovers from the night before at lunchtime and Carlita's stomach began grumbling. "I say we order pizza."

"Or Chinese," Mercedes said. "Seeing the rice cube has me craving sushi."

"Squishy," Carlita teased as she eased out of the chair. "I could go for some crab Rangoon and lo mein." She opened the silverware drawer, lifted the edge of the silverware tray and reached underneath to grab the small stack of take-out menus.

She rifled through the pile until she found the one for *Hungry Wok.* "I hope they're still in business." It had been several years since she'd ordered Chinese. Vinnie had never been a fan of Asian food.

They were in luck and the restaurant was still in business. Mercedes showered while her mother ordered and afterwards, Carlita headed to her bathroom for a hot shower, rinsing away the day's grit, grime and sweat. As she showered, she wondered how Mercedes and she would manage sharing a single bathroom.

Carlita had forgotten how quick Chinese deliveries were and by the time she emerged from the bathroom, the delivery driver was standing at her back door.

The young man with dark hair and olive-colored skin handed Carlita the bags of food. "You have package on front door," he said after she handed him a generous tip.

"I do? Thank you." She waited for the young man to leave before placing the food on the table.

"The food is already here?" Mercedes wandered into the kitchen.

"Yes and the delivery driver said we have a package on the front porch," Carlita said. "Did you order something?"

Mercedes frowned and shook her head. "No. I wonder what it is."

Carlita headed to the front door, pulled it open and stepped out onto the stoop. There wasn't a "package," but more of a large brown envelope. She reached down, picked it up and turned it over. The front of the envelope was blank. There was no return address, no postage stamp. "That's odd. There's no name or address on it."

Mercedes peeked around the side of the door. "Someone walked up here and put this on our front porch?"

Carlita turned it over, ran her hand over the seal and peeled it open before peering inside. "It looks like a photograph." She reached inside and pulled it out.

"What is it?' Mercedes asked.

"I can't believe this." The photo slipped from Carlita's fingers and fell to the ground, right before she passed out.

Chapter 23

Mercedes dragged her mother inside the house and rolled her onto the sofa. She grabbed a couple pillows from the end of the sofa and propped her mother's feet up. "Ma."

It took a few moments before Carlita's eyelids started to flutter and she slowly opened her eyes. "Mercedes? What happened?"

"You fainted," Mercedes said. "I'll be right back." She darted out the front door, returning moments later with the photo and envelope in hand.

Mercedes studied the photo. It was a picture of her father and another woman, who looked vaguely familiar. They were locked in a loving embrace, their lips mere inches apart. She could tell the photo wasn't very old, judging by her father's gray hair and receding hairline. The woman was younger, maybe in her mid-40's, with bleach blonde hair, the dark roots starting to show.

Her face was round, her cheeks plump. It was a head shot so Mercedes couldn't see anything beyond the woman's neck. The look on the woman's face was what caught Mercedes's attention. It was the look of a woman in love...with her father.

Carlita struggled to sit up, her face pale and her hand trembling as she tugged on the edge of her blouse.

"Whoever did this is a cruel person," Mercedes gritted through her clenched jaw. "I'd like to find out who would do such a heartless thing."

"Bonnie Bimbo."

"Huh?"

"Bonnie Bimbo." Carlita placed both hands on the sofa cushion and pushed herself off. "That's the name of the woman in the picture. Bonnie. Not the bimbo part. I don't know her last name."

"Bimbo is fitting," Mercedes muttered. She tapped the edge of the photograph on the palm of her hand. "I can't believe Pops was running around on you."

Carlita couldn't either. It was one of those things that happened to someone else, not her...not Vinnie. She glanced at the clock on the wall. "I've had about all I can take today. I'll see you in the morning."

Her shoulders slumped and she hugged her daughter briefly before stumbling to her room. It was bad enough Carlita had lost her husband and that he had left her with a cabinet full of illegal drugs. The final straw was the other woman.

Mercedes watched her mother disappear around the corner and then glared at the offensive photo. If her father had still been alive, she would've given him a piece of her mind. She waited until her mother's bedroom door closed and then headed to her own room to track down her cell phone, vowing to uncover exactly "who" Bonnie Bimbo was.

***

"I don't know who you're talking about," Tony told his sister. "I don't know no Bonnie and I don't know no Bimbo."

"She's cross eyed, with frizzy blonde hair and a crappy dye job with three inch black roots showing. There's a gap between her two front teeth with enough room for a hockey puck and she has a dark, bushy unibrow."

Tony snorted. "She sounds like a real beaut, Mercedes. I can't believe Pops was messin' around on Ma, neither."

"We have a picture to prove it," his sister insisted.

"I'm comin' by tomorrow. I'll take a look at the picture then."

Mercedes hung up the phone and dialed her brother, Vinnie. He didn't pick up so she left a message. Her last call was her brother, Paulie. Paulie claimed he had no idea either, which may have been the truth since Paulie knew few people from Queens or the "family."

He said he would swing by tomorrow afternoon, too. After disconnecting the line, Mercedes slid the envelope and picture into her top dresser drawer and then headed to the bathroom to get ready for bed. Tomorrow was going to be a very long day.

When she passed by her mother's bedroom, she heard muffled sobs and lifted her hand to knock, but changed her mind. There was nothing Mercedes could say - or do - to mend her mother's broken heart.

***

Carlita woke early the next morning. It had taken hours to fall asleep, and when she did, her dreams were jumbled scenes of her husband and the other woman. She dreamt he wasn't dead after all, but had run off with "Bonnie."

She was exhausted and wanted nothing more than to escape into a dreamless abyss, but it was no use so Carlita finally crawled out of bed and headed to the bathroom. As she brushed her teeth, she wondered how long her husband had been having an affair and how many other people knew.

Carlita wondered if she was the laughingstock of the neighborhood and if people were talking about "poor Carlita" behind her back. She couldn't wait to move, to put this last, bitter chapter of her life behind her.

With renewed determination, she spent extra time fixing her makeup and hair before heading to the kitchen. Daylight was at least an hour away. It was going to be a long day and a big breakfast was in order, even though she wasn't hungry.

Carlita fried enough bacon and eggs for both Mercedes and her, and even threw in a couple extra pieces of meat for Rambo. Next, she warmed a side of fried potatoes in the microwave and then toasted some wheat bread.

"What's up with all the racket out here?" Mercedes wandered into the kitchen and over to her mother, kissing her on the cheek and then surveying the mess. "I love you, Ma. Today will be a better day."

"I love you too, Mercedes, and you're right. Today will be a better day." Carlita attempted a smile.

After they finished cooking breakfast, they headed to the table where Mercedes crumbled a slice of bacon and dropped it into Rambo's dish. He gobbled his treat and eyed her hungrily.

"You can have some eggs, too." She scooped a couple heaping spoons into his doggie dish and then slid her plate onto the table. "Did you get any sleep?"

"Not much." Carlita picked up her fork and stabbed a potato wedge. "I'll be glad when this is all over, which reminds me I need to sign and send back the offer on the property."

The women had carefully inspected the offers on the house and at the real estate agent's suggestion; Carlita accepted the full price offer with no contingencies. As long as the buyer's financing didn't fall through, the closing was three short weeks away...not soon enough in Carlita's opinion.

Mother and daughter discussed the garage sale, the move and the "cabinet" but carefully avoided the elephant in the room – the picture of Vinnie and the other woman.

They finished their breakfast and Mercedes made quick work of cleaning up the breakfast dishes while Carlita signed the offer and sent it back to the agent. "Ready to check on our garage sale stuff?"

"As ready as I'll ever be." Mercedes hung the kitchen towel on the refrigerator door handle and followed her mother to the garage.

When they got there, Carlita opened the overhead door and gazed at the metal cabinet, right where they had left it. "I don't get it. We don't want someone to break in, they do. We want someone to break in, they won't."

"Maybe we should set the cabinet on the curb with a sign that says 'free,'" Mercedes joked.

"Or maybe we should take it to the city landfill and get rid of it," Carlita said. "I'll put the garage sale sign out front."

Carlita returned moments later and a car followed her into the drive. It was their first customer. The day flew by and there were only a couple lulls when they didn't have someone stopping by, shopping for bargains.

Tony arrived late afternoon and Mercedes dragged him into the house to show him the photo. He swore up and down he had no idea who the woman was.

Paulie came by a short time later and told his sister the same thing. He had no idea who the woman in the picture was.

Vinnie was the last to arrive and claimed he didn't know who the woman was either, but he wouldn't look Mercedes in the eye and she knew he was hiding something. She tried to get him to confess but Vinnie was like his father had been – tight-lipped.

By late afternoon, it was time to pull the sign from the yard and pack it in so Carlita's sons headed to the garage to sift through what was left. She followed them inside while Mercedes manned the money table situated outside the door.

Vinnie was the first to spot the cabinet. "You dragged this out of the basement?" He reached for the handle.

Carlita lunged forward to stop him. "You don't want to open that!"

"It's locked." Vinnie twisted the handle hard and popped the lock before swinging the door wide open.

The cabinet was empty.

Chapter 24

"It's empty." Carlita stared at the cabinet in disbelief.

"Yeah." Vinnie nodded. "I could use this in my garage."

"Take it." Carlita blinked rapidly and studied the empty shelves.

Mercedes hopped out of her seat and ran over when she saw her mother and brother in front of the cabinet, the doors wide open. "It's empty."

Vinnie cast a puzzled gaze at his sister. "Yeah. Empty." He leaned forward. "Why? Was there somethin' in it?"

A movement caught Carlita's eye. "We have another customer..." Her voice trailed off and her expression grew grim.

Mercedes followed her mother's gaze. She could've sworn the customer was the woman in the photo with her father but as she got closer, she could see that it was not. "Not her Ma," she said in a low voice.

The woman smiled. "I'm looking for baby clothes. I have a new grandson."

Carlita briefly closed her eyes and shook her head. "I'm sorry, we don't have any." They chatted briefly about the weather, the neighborhood. The woman perused the nearly empty tables and then walked away without purchasing a single item.

"I think it's time to shut this party down." Mercedes patted Carlita's arm, noting the haggard expression on her mother's face.

While Carlita and her sons packed the remaining items into boxes, Mercedes snuck into the house to call Father Dadore, to ask if he could swing by to talk to her mother. The priest told her he had an errand to run but would be there within the hour.

The priest arrived right after Carlita's sons departed. "You called Father Dadore?"

Mercedes squeezed her mother's arm. "It has been a long couple days. I thought you might need someone to talk to." She left her mother and the priest in the kitchen and headed to her room.

Mercedes paced her bedroom floor as she worried about her mother. Finally, she slipped into the hall to listen in. She tilted her head but was only able to catch a word or two.

Convinced her mother was in good hands, she began to tiptoe back to her room when something the Father said caught her attention. "...the gems..."

She slowly backed into her bedroom, leaving the door open a crack before hurrying to her bedroom window to keep an eye on Father Dadore's sedan.

A short time later, the priest climbed into his car and drove off.

Mercedes darted into the kitchen. "Father Dadore has been breaking into our house. He's looking for the gems."

In a tumble of words, she told her mother that looking back, they had never told Detective Striker or Father Dadore what was in the safe...the gems. There was no way for him to know.

Carlita, who was still seated at the kitchen table, folded her hands in her lap and listened in disbelief.

"Remember when Father Dadore called just before we left for Savannah? He wanted to stop by here but you put him off. He must have realized we were out of town," Mercedes said. "Right after that, Vinnie told us someone broke into the house and set the back of the house on fire."

A cold chill ran through Carlita's veins. "Your father must have told him something during his Last Rites."

"Or maybe he knew all along. Do you still have Detective Striker's card?" Mercedes asked.

"I think so." Carlita slid out of the kitchen chair, walked over to the kitchen counter and opened her purse, reaching into a side pocket and pulling out a small business card.

"Here it is." She grabbed the home phone and dialed the number on the front of the card. "Yes. Detective Striker? This is Carlita Garlucci. You stopped by my house not long ago with Father Dadore. I'm calling to tell you I think I may have some new information for you."

After hanging up, Carlita and Mercedes stepped outside to wait for Detective Striker to arrive. Thankfully, he arrived a short time later, pulling his unmarked police car into the drive and climbing out. "You're in luck. I happened to be in the neighborhood. Whatcha got?"

Carlita turned to her daughter. "You tell him."

Mercedes nodded. "Father Dadore stopped by a short time ago to visit with my mother. He made an odd comment, something about a cache of gems. I don't recall anyone ever mentioning gems."

Detective Striker rubbed his chin thoughtfully. "Anything else?"

"Yes," Carlita said. "My daughter and I recently left town. I think Father Dadore somehow knew we were out of town. We didn't even tell my sons we had left. While we were gone, someone broke into my home and vandalized it."

Carlita suddenly realized how the priest had known. She turned to Mercedes. "Remember that day we stopped by the church and I went to confession? I blurted out everything. I mentioned the trip to Savannah, the gems."

"It all makes sense now," Mercedes nodded and looked at the detective. "You never told us that day, what Pops was supposed to deliver, but Father Dadore said gems. How would he know what it was?"

Detective Striker stared at Mercedes and then shifted his gaze to Carlita. "I appreciate the call. You may be onto something. I'll head over to have a chat with Father Dadore." He promised he would contact them if anything came of his visit with the priest.

Carlita and Mercedes walked the detective to his car and watched as he climbed behind the wheel and backed out of the drive. "Do you think Father Dadore took the cocaine, too?"

Carlita shrugged. "I don't know what to think anymore."

They headed back inside to wait. Carlita hoped Detective Striker would call to let them know what happened, but they never got the call so they finally gave up and headed to bed.

Carlita slept better than she had the night before. Perhaps it was because she knew she was one day closer to closing a painful chapter of her life and starting a new one.

Later that morning, mother and daughter left the house to run errands and when they returned, they found Detective Striker's card tucked in the crack of the door. On the back were the handwritten words, "Call me."

"I can't wait to find out what happened." Carlita's fingers trembled as she dialed his number. When the detective answered, he told them that Father Dadore had confessed to breaking into their home and searching for the gems Vinnie had mentioned to him on his deathbed.

Rumor had it that certain "goods" had not been delivered and Father Dadore assumed it was the gems and that they had been in Vinnie's possession when he died. He had broken into the house but been unable to find them.

"That's because they were in Savannah – with us," Mercedes whispered under her breath.

"You never know about someone." Carlita shook her head.

Detective Striker continued. "He should have gotten a slap on the wrist for breaking and entering. We obtained a search warrant for his home and lo and behold, the man had enough cocaine in his hall closet to buy a small island."

Carlita gasped and clamped a hand over her mouth. "You don't say," she finally blurted out. "Did he admit to setting the back of my house on fire?"

"No. He swore up and down he didn't vandalize your home, but then he could be lying."

After the conversation ended, Carlita disconnected the line and turned to her daughter. "It was him. One hundred percent. He must've snuck into the garage, looking for the gems. Instead, he found the drugs."

Mercedes frowned. "And he was still after the gems, too? What a scum."

Vinnie called a short time later to check on his mother. Paulie was the next to call, and Tony was the last. "Father Dadore ever show up last night?" her son asked.

"Yes, he sure did," Carlita said.

"Word on the street is he's in jail. Somethin' about some cocaine bricks the cops busted him with," Tony said. "Hope he stays put in jail cuz Vito has a mark on him now. That coke came up missing a few months back and Vito was on the line for it. Now the cops got it."

Tony paused to let the words sink in. "Carmine told me Vito thought Pop had it. Imagine that. Pop. He was a shylock for sure, but a drug dealer? Can you believe that?"

Carlita closed her eyes for a brief moment. She nodded her head but told her son that, "No." She couldn't believe it and silently added, *Had she not seen it with her very own eyes.*

After she hung up, she turned to her daughter. "I hope Savannah is a lot more peaceful than this place."

Mercedes rolled her eyes. "So do I, Ma. So do I."

Chapter 25

"Well, that's the last of it." Carlita taped the box shut and set the tape gun on top. "Good thing Vinnie is following us to Savannah tomorrow morning."

Mercedes nodded. "Right? I'll load this in the car." She went out the door and Rambo followed her out.

The women had filled not only the car, but also the back seat and trunk of Vinnie's sedan not to mention a small U-Haul trailer. There wasn't an extra square inch of space.

The past few weeks had been a whirlwind of packing, getting their affairs in order for the big move and worrying that they wouldn't get it all done in time, but they had.

A small knot had formed in the pit of Carlita's stomach and had been there for two days solid. The finality of the move had finally sank in. She was leaving the only life she'd ever known behind. She was leaving two of her children behind, not to mention her grandchildren.

There were brief moments when sheer panic had set in and she'd almost changed her mind, but Mercedes had kept her on track and deep down, she knew she needed to do this for not only herself, but for her daughter, too.

There had been no more break ins at the house and Father Dadore's face was all over the evening news. Apparently, he had a sketchy background and every evening police uncovered additional evidence linking the priest to mafia crimes.

The last day in the house flew by, and bright and early the next morning, Mercedes and Rambo headed to the car, itching to start the long drive south.

Carlita lingered a little longer as she wandered through the empty rooms of what had been her home for so many years. She gazed into each of the rooms as memories filled her mind. She had had a good life, and she'd forgiven Vinnie for his indiscretions, determined not to let them ruin her...their happy memories.

She knew it was time to go, time to move on. She had to do this for her family. She had to do this for her sanity, and most of all, she had to do this for herself.

Carlita wandered to the patio slider, overlooking the back yard. She smiled as she gazed at the bright yellow daisies she had impulsively decided to plant as a housewarming gift to the new owners.

She hoped the new family would love the home and make as many wonderful memories as she and her own family had.

Carlita slowly walked to the kitchen counter, placed the house keys on top and made her way out the front door, pulling the door closed behind her.

The end.

If you enjoyed reading this book, please take a moment to leave a review. It would be greatly appreciated! Thank you!

Wonder Cookie Bars Recipe

Ingredients

1-1/2 cups graham cracker crumbs

½ cup melted butter

1 (14 oz) can of sweetened condensed milk

2 cups (12 oz package) semi-sweet chocolate chips or butterscotch chips

1-1/3 cup flaked coconut

1 cup chopped walnut or pecans

Directions

Preheat oven to 350 degrees.

Coat a 13x9 inch glass baking dish with no-stick cooking spray

Mix graham cracker crumbs and melted butter. Press into the bottom of the greased baking dish.

Pour sweetened condensed milk over top of graham cracker mixture, making sure to cover evenly.

Sprinkle chocolate chips over graham cracker crust.

Sprinkle coconut over chocolate chips.

Sprinkle chopped nuts over coconut.

Press lightly with fork.

Bake 25 – 30 minutes or until lightly browned.

2-Road to Savannah

Made in Savannah
Cozy Mystery Series Book Two

Hope Callaghan

hopecallaghan.com
Copyright © 2016
All rights reserved.

Visit my website for new releases and special offers:
hopecallaghan.com

Thank you, Peggy H., Cindi G., Jean P., Wanda D. and Rosmarie H. for taking the time to preview *Road to Savannah,* for the extra sets of eyes and for catching all my mistakes.

A special thanks to my reader review team: Alice, Amary, Barbara, Becky, Becky B, Brinda, Cassie, Christina, Cyndi, Debbie, Denota, Devan, Francine, Grace, Jo-Ann, Joeline, Joyce, Jean K., Jean M., Kathy, Lynne, Megan, Melda, Kat, Linda, Lynne, Pat, Patsy, Renate, Rita, Rita P, Shelba, Tamara and Vicki

Chapter 1

"You okay Ma?" Mercedes Garlucci kept one eye on the highway and glanced at her mother.

"Yeah, I'm okay." Carlita Garlucci tugged on the edge of her seatbelt and stared out the window. "I was wondering if we made a huge mistake."

That "huge mistake" was selling everything they owned, including the home Carlita and her husband, Vinnie, had owned for the past thirty plus years, where they had raised their four children.

Carlita had promised her husband on his deathbed that she would get her children out of Queens, New York...and out of the "family." Cosa Nostra – the mafia. She had been somewhat successful. Her daughter, twenty-five year old, Mercedes, was moving with her.

"No, we didn't." Mercedes reached over to pat her mother's arm. "You've just got a case of cold feet."

Carlita glanced in the rearview mirror and caught a glimpse of the familiar sedan following close behind - her eldest son, Vinnie. Although Vinnie, a made man, swore he wasn't going to move out of Queens, he had volunteered to follow his mother and sister to their new home in Savannah, Georgia so he could "check it out."

She hadn't chosen Savannah. Savannah had chosen her, or maybe her husband had chosen it. After Carlita promised Vinnie she would get their sons out of the "business," she had discovered a key in one of his jacket pockets.

Vinnie had been wearing the jacket when he'd been admitted to the hospital, where he'd died a short time later. The key opened a bank safe deposit box, which contained a deed to property in Savannah, Georgia.

To say Carlita was surprised would have been an understatement. She had no idea Vinnie had ever visited Savannah, Georgia, let alone owned property in the historic city.

It was all hers now...lock, stock and barrel, and in need of a lot of repairs. Carlita planned to turn one of the Savannah businesses into a grocery store. The money from the sale of the home would give mother and daughter a small cushion to get by on until they were turning a profit.

In addition to the property deed, Carlita had also discovered a cache of gemstones inside the safe deposit box, but that was another story.

Rambo stuck his head over the front seat and licked the side of Carlita's face. She reached back to pat her pooch's head. "We're almost there," she promised. Rambo, part German shepherd, part Doberman and part goofball circled the backseat and then plopped down to wait.

"This is our exit," Mercedes announced as she veered off the highway and drove under the "Savannah 16 East" sign. After exiting the highway, she steered their 1977 Lincoln town car into the nearest gas station and alongside one of the gas pumps.

Vinnie pulled his newer sedan to a set of pumps opposite their vehicle and climbed out of his car. "I hope we're almost there," he grumbled as he reached for the nozzle. "We're almost to Florida."

"Only a few more miles east," Mercedes promised as she leaned her hip against the back of the car and studied her brother. "Fifteen minutes, tops, and we'll be there."

Vinnie continued to grumble under his breath as he pumped gas. "All the crap you loaded into my car is weighing it down and ruining my gas mileage."

Mercedes rolled her eyes and ignored her brother's comments. He wasn't complaining nearly as much today as he had the previous day. To hear him talk, his mother and sister were forcing him on this journey when, in fact, he had made the decision to follow them to their new home.

She knew her mother secretly hoped Savannah would grow on Vinnie and he would decide to move to Georgia, too, but Mercedes had her doubts. It was almost unheard of for a member to "leave the family." Most men who left the family, aka the mafia, left in a box.

One of Mercedes's other brothers, Tony, the second oldest in the family, was also a made man. He had refused to make the trip to Savannah, telling his sister and mother that if they were still living in Savannah in six months, he *might* come visit.

Mercedes's only other sibling was Paulie. Mercedes was the youngest and Paulie just over a year older than she was.

Paulie lived in Clifton Falls, New York, with his wife, Gina, and their three young children. Paulie had nothing to do with the family business. Instead, after a brief dabble in the "family business," he had taken the straight and narrow path, and was current mayor of the small town of Clifton Falls.

The gas pump clicked off and Mercedes removed the nozzle, set it back in the holder and screwed the gas cap on before grabbing the receipt.

Her mother and Rambo, who had headed out for a potty break, returned and they all climbed back into the car to finish the final leg of the trip.

Carlita reached for her seatbelt. "What was Vinnie griping about?"

Mercedes started the car and shifted into drive, careful to keep the car, and the U-Haul trailer they were towing, a safe distance from the pumps. "The usual. The distance, the extra stuff we packed in his car, blah, blah, blah." Mercedes grinned. "He wasn't nearly as long-winded as yesterday so I think he's coming around."

Carlita nodded. "I called Bob Lowman while I was walking Rambo, to let him know we were getting close." Bob Lowman was the construction project supervisor who was handling their Savannah property repairs.

Because their property was located in Savannah's historic district, there were extra committees and permits needed to approve the repairs and renovations, and all the extra approvals had slowed the construction crew down.

When they reached historic downtown, Mercedes turned the car onto Mulberry Street and Carlita leaned forward in an attempt to catch her first glimpse of the properties. Her heart sank when she noticed the store's exterior looked the same as the last time she'd seen it. "Oh."

"Nothing changed," Mercedes said. She turned onto the side street and then into the alley out back, pulling far enough ahead so that Vinnie could pull in behind them.

"At least this is an improvement." Carlita studied the outside of the building, lifting her gaze to the upper floor where she spied a new wooden deck near the top. She pointed up. "Look. Bob added a deck," she said excitedly as she flung the car door open and hopped out.

Rambo was right behind her as he vaulted over the front seat and scrambled out of the car.

Vinnie climbed out of his car and joined them in the alley. "This is where you're gonna live? This place is a dump!"

Chapter 2

"All you're seeing is the back alley," Mercedes argued. "You haven't even seen the inside yet."

"It's not a dump," Carlita added. "At least not all of it." She clipped Rambo's leash to his collar and gently tugged, leading her children and dog out of the alley, around the side of the building and to the front.

"This just keeps gettin' better and better," Vinnie said as he walked alongside his sister and inspected the exterior of the building.

The front door to what would be the grocery store was open and the sounds of hammering and saws echoed from within.

Carlita made her way in first. The smell of sawdust and fresh paint filled the cavernous space. Although the outside hadn't changed, the interior had been completely transformed. All of the old shelving, checkout counter, cash register and refrigerator / freezer cases were gone.

Workers had painted the walls and ceiling, and it appeared they were getting ready to strip layers of old varnish off the narrow plank wooden floors.

A tall man with light brown hair spotted them and made his way over. It was Bob Lowman. "Hello Mrs. Garlucci." He nodded at Mercedes and Vinnie. "Well? What do you think?"

"It looks much better and even bigger than before. You and your men are doing a great job," Carlita complimented.

"We're gonna start stripping the floors today. After we finish the floors, we'll replace all the broken windows. The last big project will be moving new freezer and refrigerator units in. Have you had a chance to take a look at the information I emailed to you?"

Bob had sent over several recommendations for companies who sold not only stocking shelves and refrigerator / freezer units, but also state-of-the-art checkout lanes and cash registers.

Carlita couldn't make heads or tails of what would work best for them and decided she needed to consult someone who knew a lot more about running a grocery store than she did, which was a big fat nothing. "I was hoping you might be able to suggest someone who is already in the grocery store business."

"Not right off hand." Bob shoved his hands in his front pockets and rocked back on his heels. "I'll talk to some of my buddies. Maybe they can recommend someone."

"What about Sal?" Vinnie asked. "Sal" was Sal Necchi, a family friend. Sal also owned Sal's Market back in Queens, New York.

"Good idea," Carlita said. "I'll give him a call later."

The group toured the rest of the grocery store while Bob explained the progress they had made and the work they had done. He told Carlita they were roughly a week away from her being able to order supplies so they could start setting up shop.

After they toured the grocery store, Bob motioned them through the back and to the stairs that led to the second floor and the apartments.

The vintage oak banister was still in place and true to his word, Bob had restored it to its original charm, stripping off the dark stain and refinishing it in a lighter, brighter shade of golden oak.

Carlita placed the palm of her hand on top of the newel post. "You did a great job, Bob. I can hardly wait to see the apartment."

Bob had told them he'd spent almost all of the money from the first draw she had paid and he would need another forty-thousand dollars to finish outside repairs, purchase the necessary equipment and then start working on the building Carlita owned next door - an old restaurant.

The idea of opening a grocery store had seemed like a great idea, but Carlita was beginning to have second thoughts.

Mercedes had done a great deal of online research and words like foot traffic and pedestrian counts kept popping up. What if they opened the grocery store and no one showed up to shop there?

It would be a total bust and a waste of precious time and money, not to mention heartbreaking. Carlita pushed her anxious thoughts aside and followed the others to the second level.

Bob and his crew had transformed the second floor as well. The hall walls were a bright, cheery off-white and the wood floors were almost too pristine to walk on.

The upper floor contained four apartments in all - two on the left and two on the right. During their previous visit, mother and daughter had decided to take the front apartment on the right.

It was identical in both shape and size to the other three apartments but Carlita and Mercedes both agreed it would not only be quieter, since it was farther from the street, but it was also closer to the stairs, an added bonus for Rambo.

Bob opened the door to their unit and stepped to the side to let Mercedes, Vinnie, Carlita and Rambo enter first.

Carlita's eyes grew wide. "This looks fabulous." She had given Bob the go-ahead to rip out walls and open up the space so that the living room, dining room and kitchen were one large room. The entire outside wall, which had been covered in a layer of peeling, water-stained plaster, was now a wall of exposed red brick.

Workers had ripped the ceilings out and the apartment now sported large wooden beams that ran the length of the space.

At one end was a large, spacious kitchen that covered the back wall. A dining area separated the kitchen from the living room. Similar to the other areas of the building, the oak floors had been stripped and refinished.

Centered on one of the living room walls was a large, marble fireplace.

Carlita squeezed in next to Bob and gazed at the open rafters. "That's one way to get rid of the flapping varmints," she joked.

"Flapping varmints?" Mercedes flicked her jet-black locks over her shoulder and turned to her mother.

"It's nothing dear." Carlita winked at Bob, having already alerted him to the fact Mercedes would freak out if she knew their new apartment had once been occupied by furry flying creatures of the night.

Mercedes sauntered to the center of the room, her tennis shoes squeaking on the gleaming wood floor. "This is perfect."

Carlita unhooked Rambo's collar so he could explore his new home while the women and Vinnie wandered into the bedrooms. The bedroom walls were painted in the same shade of light beige as the main living area. The rooms also sported one wall of exposed brick. The workers had added a spacious closet to each bedroom and a row of leaded glass transom windows above the door completed the look. It was elegant. It was unique. It was perfect.

They finished the tour in the bathroom, which was as small as Carlita had remembered, but tastefully updated.

She ran a hand over a white cabinet door. "This will work."

They retraced their steps, returning to the living room where Bob was waiting. Carlita patted his arm. "You've done an amazing job. Mercedes and I should be able to pay you the next draw tomorrow or the next day," she told him.

Vinnie opened his mouth and then quickly clamped it shut. Carlita knew her son was going to ask her where she was coming up with the money to pay for repairs. She had not told her sons that, along with the deed to the property, their father had left behind a small pouch of precious gemstones.

Chirp. "My cell phone." Mercedes pulled her phone from her back pocket, flipped it over and studied the screen. "Autumn is downstairs waiting for us." Mercedes darted out of the apartment and down the steps, disappearing from sight.

"Who is Autumn?" Vinnie turned to his mother.

"Steve's sister," Carlita replied.

Vinnie frowned. "Who is Steve?"

"He owns the tattoo shop across the street," Bob and Carlita said in unison.

"It's a long story," Carlita added. "He's a nice guy." She eyed her son closely. "And his sister, Autumn, is adorable." She didn't wait for a reply as she followed Mercedes out of the apartment, down the hall and then descended the steps to the lower level.

Carlita passed the construction crew, who was hard at work, as she made her way out onto the sidewalk where Mercedes stood talking to an attractive blonde woman with mischievous blue eyes.

Autumn hopped off her Segway when she spotted Carlita. She unclipped the clasp that secured her helmet and slipped it off, her long blonde locks tumbling around her shoulders. "I'm so excited you're finally back." She patted the handle of her Segway. "I'm getting much better at handling my Segway, Mrs. Garlucci. I haven't run anyone over in almost a week now."

"That's great news," Carlita smiled. "I'm sure your brother is happy to hear that."

"Steve wanted me to stop by to ask if you are free for dinner either tonight or tomorrow night." She glanced at a sour faced Vinnie, who had followed his mother outside and now stood next to Carlita.

"If you want..."

Carlita elbowed her son, a warning to straighten up, the smile still firmly planted on her face. "We would love to, Autumn. Perhaps not tonight since we've been driving all day and are tired. Tomorrow sounds good."

Autumn smiled back. "I'll let him know." She pointed at the store. "I hope you don't mind, but I've been stopping by to check on the progress. Your apartment is fabulous."

"We love it," Mercedes piped up. "After the construction crew finishes working on the grocery store, maybe they can start on another apartment for you...if you're still interested in renting one."

"Absolutely." Autumn nodded excitedly and then started to slip her helmet on her head. "I should let you get going. Oh. When I drove by, I noticed the door to the old restaurant was ajar so I pulled it shut."

Carlita frowned. "That's odd. Bob told me his men hadn't touched the other building. In fact, he mentioned he hadn't gone inside since the last time we were here. I wonder if the squatter we had in the grocery store moved to the restaurant."

Carlita hurried to the building next to the grocery store, grasped the doorknob and turned the handle. The door wasn't locked.

"Let me go in first Ma." Vinnie eased past his mother, pushed the door open and stepped inside. "Uh-oh."

He quickly turned, blocking the view of the inside. "I don't think you want to go in there."

Chapter 3

"Why not?" Mercedes sidestepped her brother as she barged into the building. "Oh my gosh."

Carlita, anxious to see what was going on, followed her daughter inside and almost tripped over a woman, lying just inside the doorway, face down.

Vinnie leaned over the woman and gently nudged her. "Hey." The woman was unresponsive so Vinnie rolled her over, exposing an angry dark line, along with a smaller, round mark, around the woman's neck. "Looks like somebody burned her, literally and figuratively."

"We need to call the cops," Mercedes pulled her cell phone from her back pocket, turned it on and started to dial 911.

Vinnie snatched the phone from his sister's hand. "Wait a minute. We need to think things through before we go callin' the cops." He began to pace back and forth while Carlita averted her gaze and offered a silent prayer.

"We have a dead woman lying on our floor," Mercedes argued. "What is there to discuss?"

"Murder Mercedes," Vinnie explained patiently. "You're not thinkin'. The first ones the police are going to suspect will be you and Ma, the property owners."

Carlita quickly glanced at the body and then focused her attention on Vinnie again. "It appears she has been...gone for some time now," although she couldn't be certain. It wasn't every day she saw a dead body.

"Which means *we* weren't around when it happened," Mercedes said.

Vinnie ignored his sister's comment as he began casing the joint, searching for clues. "Somebody dropped the body, but how did they get in here? You said the doors were locked and the construction guy and his crew haven't touched the place." He walked over to the nearest window and tugged on the sash. "Locked."

Vinnie moved to the next window, making his rounds as he checked every window. All of the windows were locked. "Where's the back entrance?"

Carlita motioned to her son. "This way." They walked around the server station, past the cash register and into the kitchen area where the old fryers and grills were located. She pointed to the left. "There."

Vinnie strode over to the door and grabbed the doorknob. "It's locked." He unlocked the door and stepped outside.

Carlita followed him into the alley, not far from where they had parked their vehicles.

"Could be they jimmied the back lock, dropped the body and slipped back out through the alley, locking the door behind them." He gazed past the cars. "This would be a good spot to dump a body. Easy in, easy out. Especially if they knew the place was vacant."

Carlita stepped back into the kitchen. Vinnie followed her in and then closed and locked the door. "Who knows how long the woman has been inside here rotting."

Carlita's stomach churned at the thought. She pushed the unpleasant visual of the woman's body from her mind and focused on the facts. "Autumn said the front door was ajar."

Vinnie didn't have time to answer as Mercedes burst into the room. "The cops are here."

"Mercedes," Vinnie said.

"I swear. I didn't call them."

Carlita followed her son and daughter into the front of the restaurant where two uniformed police officers knelt over the body. Autumn stood off to the side, a hand covering her eyes.

At the sound of their footsteps, one of the officers looked up. "Are you the one who called 911?"

Carlita stepped forward. "I-I..."

"I did," Autumn volunteered. "The door was ajar and when we opened it, we found this woman lying on the floor."

Autumn must have followed them in and Carlita hadn't noticed. It was too late now. "We haven't touched anything," she told the officers and then turned to her children. "We should wait in the other building."

One of the officers stood. "Don't go far. You'll need to answer some questions."

Carlita nodded. "Of course." She was the last one out of the building, and she let Autumn and Mercedes step back inside the grocery store before grabbing Vinnie's arm. "Maybe you should get out of here, son. Head over to the hotel."

As far as Carlita knew, her eldest child didn't have a 'rap sheet', although he'd had a few minor brushes with the law. If there was more, she wasn't aware of it. Still, it was better to be safe than sorry.

Vinnie nodded. "That's a good idea. I have the address here on my phone."

"We'll call you when we're on our way." She watched as Vinnie strode down the sidewalk and disappeared into the alley before heading inside the grocery store.

"Where's Vinnie?" Mercedes asked.

"He's going on ahead to the hotel." Carlita gave her daughter a dark look and Mercedes lifted a brow. "Oh...kay."

Bob Lowman, who had been standing on a ladder in the back, climbed down and made his way over. "I ran next door when I saw the cop cars pull up and was able to catch a glimpse of the body through the doorway. I've seen that woman before."

Autumn nodded. "Me too." She looked over her shoulder and then leaned in. "It's Norma Jean Cleaver, one of those SAS members."

"SAS...SAS." Carlita rubbed her forehead. "I've heard the name before."

"Savannah Architectural Society," Bob said. "The nut jobs who think they control Savannah with their ridiculous architectural guidelines."

"I remember now." Carlita snapped her fingers. Right before she'd left Savannah to return to New York, she had found a business card with Savannah Architectural Society's name on the front tucked in the door of her store. On the back of the business card was a handwritten note, asking her to call them.

Steve Winter, the owner of Shades of Ink tattoo parlor, had advised Carlita to call SAS and head them off at the pass or they would be breathing down her neck, harassing the construction workers and being a general nuisance.

She'd forgotten all about them...until now. "Oh boy. I hope the rest of the SAS posse doesn't shut down construction once they catch wind one of their own was found dead inside my restaurant," Carlita fretted.

Autumn peered over Carlita's shoulder toward the entrance door. "You won't have to wonder for long. Their ringleader, Betty Graybill, is standing out front."

Chapter 4

Carlita whirled around. A uniformed officer was standing on the sidewalk talking to a tall, thin woman, not the least bit vertically challenged. Her back was ramrod straight, her mouth moving ninety miles an hour as she glared at the officer.

Carlita took a step forward and Bob Lowman grabbed her arm. "You might not want to do that," he warned. "I've had a few run-ins with Betty and all I can say is the less contact you have with her, the better."

"Maybe she'll leave soon," Mercedes added hopefully.

"Or maybe not," Autumn groaned as the head of SAS dismissed the officer with the wave of a hand and marched into the building, her stern gaze honing in on the group.

Bob slunk away, and Autumn and Mercedes quickly hurried to the other side of the room leaving Carlita to face Betty Graybill alone. She shifted her feet so her stance was firm, in an attempt to show no fear.

The woman stopped abruptly in front of Carlita, peering down at her. "I'm looking for the owner of this eyesore."

Carlita should have taken offense at the rude statement, but had to admit on some level, the woman was correct. "I'm the owner of this establishment," she answered in a firm, even voice. "How can I help you?"

"My name is Betty Graybill, President of the Savannah Architectural Society. I sent one of my associates, Norma Jean Cleaver, here a few days ago to discuss the construction and design elements of your properties." Betty leaned closer, hovering over the top of Carlita. "It appears she made it here and then someone murdered her, leaving her body next door."

Carlita shook her head. "I arrived in town today. I have never met your...associate, Norma Jean, and I certainly have no idea how her body ended up on my property."

"Humpf!" Betty adjusted the purse on her shoulder and frowned. "We'll just see about that. In the meantime, I'm on my way to the code enforcement office to shut this mess down."

"On what grounds?" Carlita lifted her chin in defiance.

"The front entrance is not up to code," Betty said. "Not only that, you have ignored our attempts to contact you."

Carlita tried to explain the building was still in the process of renovations and she hadn't been in the area but her explanation fell on deaf ears.

Betty Graybill cut Carlita off. "It's too late now." She turned on her heel and marched out of the building, disappearing from sight.

Bob Lowman hurried over. "I heard what the old bat said and I'll run down to the permit department to try to head her off at the pass. I have a buddy who works down there." He touched Carlita's arm. "Don't worry. Betty is mostly hot air but it won't hurt to stop her in her tracks."

"Thank you," Carlita said gratefully.

She watched Bob exit through the front door while an officer made his way inside. Carlita hadn't been in Savannah more than a couple hours and there was already a dead body, and someone was threatening to shut down her construction project. She was beginning to think the place was cursed and couldn't imagine it getting any worse.

The officer approached Carlita. "Mrs. Garlucci?"

Carlita nodded and watched as he reached in his front pocket, pulling out a small notepad and pen. "I'd like to ask you a few questions about Norma Jean Cleaver."

He flipped the cover on the notepad. "Tell me what happened, from the moment you found Ms. Cleaver's body."

Carlita explained to the officer how they had arrived a short time ago, had spoken with the construction supervisor and then Autumn, a friend, had stopped by to say hello. "We were out front and Autumn mentioned the door to the building next door was ajar so she closed it. I went over to check on it and discovered it was unlocked. When we stepped inside the building, we found Ms. Cleaver lying on the floor." Carlita didn't mention Vinnie was the first person to spot the body.

The officer jotted notes on the pad and then paused, tapping his pen on top of the notepad. "There was another gentleman here when we arrived. He was tall, with dark hair."

The officer was describing Vinnie. Carlita feigned ignorance. "I'm not sure I know who you're talking about."

Autumn, who had been listening in on the conversation, piped up. "Your son, Vinnie." She glanced around. "Where'd he go?"

Carlita's eyes widened. "He, uh, he left."

The officer rubbed his chin and nodded. "Uh-huh. We'll need him to come back here to give a statement."

"Of course," Carlita said.

"I'll call him," Mercedes offered before stepping to the back of the building.

"I'd like to talk to your daughter." The officer didn't wait for an answer as he headed toward the back and Mercedes.

"I'm sorry Mrs. Garlucci. I should've kept my mouth shut," Autumn whispered in a low voice. "I wasn't thinking."

"It's okay Autumn." There was no sense getting upset. The damage was done. "We have nothing to hide."

Steve Winter, Autumn's brother, arrived moments later, and he and Autumn huddled off to one side, talking in low voices.

Carlita wandered to the window and gazed out. Autumn was the one who had told Carlita and the others the door to the restaurant was ajar. She was also the one who had called the police and had tipped the officer off to Vinnie's identity.

Carlita narrowed her eyes and studied the young blonde. Was Autumn setting them up? She seemed quite familiar with the Savannah Architectural Society.

She shifted her gaze to Steve. Perhaps Steve had set them up, knowing they were out of town. Had he killed Norma Jean Cleaver and then dumped her body inside the abandoned building?

"Something smells fishy," Carlita muttered under her breath. She had been exposed to enough criminal activity to know the person you least suspected should be your number one suspect. Perhaps the members of SAS had it in for the tattoo shop. She vowed to keep an eye on the siblings until the police identified the woman's killer.

The officer finished talking to Mercedes and then stopped to chat with Bob while Mercedes made her way over to her mother. "That cop is a jerk," Mercedes hissed.

Carlita was only half-listening as she watched Bob and the officer chat. Was Bob the killer? He had a key to the empty restaurant and there had been no signs of forced entry.

She shifted her gaze to Steve, still talking to Autumn. Steve had a key, too.

"I overhead someone say the woman from the Savannah Architectural Society threatened Steve-O, too."

Mercedes had her mother's full attention now. "You mean the society was harassing Steve, as well?" Had they been duped into thinking Steve and Autumn were trying to befriend them, all the while the scheming siblings has set them up to take the fall for the murder?

The officer finished talking to Bob and made his way over. "I'll be leaving as soon as I interview your son."

"My brother will be here any minute," Mercedes said. "I have no idea why you need to talk to him since we can prove we only arrived in Savannah a couple hours ago."

The officer tapped the tip of his pen on his notepad. "You're telling me you can prove your whereabouts yesterday and the day before?"

"I have receipts in my purse," Carlita said. "Hotel receipts, gas receipts."

"And your son, as well?"

"Of course," Carlita nodded, although that wasn't entirely true. She had insisted on paying in cash for gas and food since she was still paranoid someone from their past, from New York, was stalking her, following her and her children to Savannah.

The only receipt with their name on it was the hotel receipt and she had put that in Mercedes's name, believing that if someone were hot on their trail, they wouldn't think to search for Mercedes.

Vinnie arrived moments later and once again, the officer insisted on interviewing him separately.

Mercedes waved her mother to the other side of the building, out of earshot. "We don't have receipts Mom. You paid cash for everything except for the hotel, which was in my name."

A tight knot formed in Carlita's stomach. She'd thought she was playing it safe, staying under the radar. Little had she known she would have to prove she'd been in another state when someone had been murdered and the body found on her property.

Chapter 5

The investigating officer finally left. Steve and Autumn left shortly thereafter and promised to stop by later, after the construction crew had gone home for the day.

Vinnie, Mercedes and Carlita headed to the vacant restaurant only to discover investigators had covered the entire front of the building with crime scene tape.

Carlita shifted to the window, cupped her hands to her face and peered inside. From where she stood, she could see the chalk line where investigators had marked the spot where the woman's body had been found.

Vinnie was the first to speak. "They think one of us had something to do with the broad's death."

"And other than a receipt for a hotel in Virginia with Mercedes's name on it, we can't prove we weren't here when it happened," Carlita said.

Vinnie adjusted the gold chain around his neck. "They can't tie the dame to us. She was a complete stranger."

"No, Vinnie. They can tie her to us. The woman was part of Savannah Architectural Society. She was here to discuss concerns the society had over the building repairs and upgrades."

"They think you offed her over some paint colors?" he asked incredulously. "What about your buddy there, the tattoo artist?"

"I would think he's also a suspect," Carlita said. "Not only him, but his sister and the construction foreman. There are also a slew of construction workers who might have had access to the key."

"You can't be serious in thinking it might be Steve-O or Autumn?" Mercedes gasped. "They're our friends."

"Frenemies," Vinnie said. "Trust no one, not even flesh and blood. That's my motto."

Mercedes glared at her brother and clamped her mouth shut, refusing to believe either Steve or Autumn had killed the woman and set them up.

Carlita was on the fence. She didn't want to believe it, but someone had murdered the poor woman and it would be up to them to try to figure out who had it in for her. "We need to find out everything we can about SAS and its members, including Betty Graybill. I don't trust her."

"Maybe she set us up," Mercedes suggested.

The list of suspects was growing by the minute. Bob Lowman, the construction crew, Steve, Autumn, Betty Graybill. Carlita's head was spinning. It was as if crime was a black cloud following her no matter where she went.

Mercedes shifted into detective mode. There was a sliver of a silver lining to the current dilemma. She could use parts of the investigation for the mafia-style, daughter-of-a-mobster book she was writing. She'd put her writing on the back burner the last couple of weeks as she and her mother prepared for the move, but now that they were in Savannah, she planned to kick it into high gear and a real murder investigation was perfect. "We need to search for clues."

"That will be a little tough since they put enough crime scene tape around the place to tape off the whole City of Savannah." Vinnie pointed at the tape.

The trio circled the building, searching for clues that weren't there, ending up in the same place where they started.

"That was a waste of time. I guess I can start digging around in the victim's background and also the suspects' backgrounds," Mercedes said. She plucked her cell phone from her back pocket, switched it on and tapped the screen. "The Savannah Architectural Society is only a couple blocks from here. I say we scope it out on our way to the hotel."

It had been a long day and Carlita was exhausted. Not only was she exhausted from two harrowing days of riding with her daughter, the speed demon, the last few hours had been nerve wracking. She was ready to relax and unwind. The last thing she wanted to do was drive around town.

Mercedes dangled the car keys in front of her mother. "We can swing by there on our way to the hotel."

"I'll take Rambo with me and we'll meet you at the hotel." Vinnie and Rambo headed to his car while Mercedes and Carlita headed next door to tell Bob they were leaving for the day and that he could reach them on their cell phones if anything came up.

She was going to suggest Mercedes run over to Shades of Ink, Steve's tattoo shop, to let him know they were leaving, but decided it was best they just head out and blame their quick exit on the day's events. Carlita didn't know what to think of the siblings. There were too many clues pointing in their direction.

After they climbed into the car, Mercedes punched SAS's address into the GPS and sped out of the alley and onto the side street.

Carlita kept an eye on the U-Haul, still hooked to the back of the car. She'd hoped they would have time to unload it but with everything that had happened, decided to put it off until the following day. She was too tired to deal with it.

The car crept along the busy streets of downtown Savannah as the women searched for Savannah Architectural Society's headquarters. After missing the street during the first drive by and then nearly turning the wrong way down a one-way street, they finally found 155 Stalwart Street.

Mercedes eased the car into an empty spot in front of the building and shifted into park.

Carlita craned her neck and peered out the window. "Huh. Not what I expected."

"Me either," Mercedes agreed.

The building was narrow, which may have been a major understatement. Carlita was certain if she stood at the center of the building and extended both arms, she would easily be able to touch both front corners.

The blood red entrance door was tall and thin, a perfect match for the structure. It made the building look even narrower since it took up half the front. On both sides of the door were tall narrow windows with miniature wrought iron planter boxes under each window.

Long, thin stems stuck out of the flower boxes and at the top of the stems, pale, almost translucent, flowers hung precariously, as if a good gust of wind would blow them away. The tips of the flowers were black.

"Those look like the flowers of death," Mercedes whispered.

Carlita shivered. They were creepy. "You're right. Now what?"

"We watch," Mercedes said.

"Watch what?"

"Keep an eye peeled for suspects, anyone who comes out." Mercedes picked up her cell phone and switched it on. "My battery is almost dead. Let me borrow your phone."

Carlita reached for her purse, sitting on the floor near her feet. "Why do you need my phone?"

"To take pictures of suspects," Mercedes patiently explained.

"Why don't we go inside, tell them someone left a note on the door of the restaurant and then offer our condolences over Ms. Cleaver's untimely demise," her mother suggested.

"This is much more exciting," Mercedes argued, but quickly changed her mind after the look her mother gave her. "Okay. You win." She reached for the door handle. "How boring."

Carlita pushed the passenger side door open and slid out of the car, waiting for her daughter to join her on the sidewalk.

Mercedes waved at the entrance. "This was your idea. You go first."

Carlita sucked in a deep breath, grasped the door handle and turned the knob.

The inside of the building was even smaller than the outside. There were two small desks crammed against one wall. A narrow path connected the front to the back.

What the interior lacked in width, it more than made up for in depth. Beyond the desks was a small kitchenette, a water cooler, a coat tree and then beyond that another door, which was closed.

"Can I help you?"

Carlita spun around. She had been so mesmerized by the tiny space she hadn't noticed the dark-haired woman sitting behind one of the desks. "Yes. I uh…" Her voice trailed off.

Mercedes took over. "I'm Mercedes Garlucci. This is my mother Carlita. We're here to offer our condolences on the loss of your...co-worker, Norma Jean."

The chair scraped across the wood floor as the woman pushed it back and then stood.

She was even shorter than Carlita's 4'10" frame. On closer inspection, she was an attractive woman with a pixie face, short dark hair she wore swept off to one side and enormous green eyes, which appeared larger than life, perhaps because the rest of her was so compact. "I'm Glenda Fox. I heard about poor Norma Jean. I didn't know her all that well, but she seemed to have a troubled life."

"Glenda," A sharp voice echoed from the back of the building, causing Glenda to jump.

"Sorry." Her shoulders hunched and she took a step back as she gazed fearfully toward the rear of the building.

Carlita watched as a woman with bright red hair and matching red lips marched to the front of the store. "I'll handle this. You get back to work."

Glenda nodded, backed into her seat and then spun around so that her back was to them.

Poor thing. Carlita crossed her arms and faced the redhead.

"So you're the troublemaking twosome? You have been in town less than a day and you're already violating our building codes and killing people."

Carlita could feel the tips of her ears burn and her blood began to boil. She took a step forward as she prepared to take the woman down a notch or two.

Mercedes recognized the look and stepped directly in front of her mother in an attempt to diffuse a tense situation. "We stopped by to offer our condolences. This is the first we've heard of a code violation so you can stop with the flapping of the gums unless you have something to show us."

The woman's jaw dropped at Mercedes's rebuttal and she quickly clamped it shut.

A tinkle of laughter erupted from Glenda. Her shoulders began to shake as she burst out laughing. She spun around in the chair and wiped at the corner of her eyes. "She told you now, didn't she Carol Weatherbee? Serves you right."

Carol glared at the woman in the chair, which made Glenda laugh even harder. In that instant, Carlita liked Glenda Fox. A lot.

"I wouldn't be so quick to side with them," Carol growled. "These two might be killers, here to take us out next."

For a brief moment, Carlita had a crazy urge to pull her concealed weapon from her purse and wave it in the air. She even went as far as to open the clasp and reach inside, but common sense and fear of an imminent arrest stopped her.

"We're also here to discuss whatever issues you may have with our properties before we continue with our renovation projects," Mercedes explained.

Carol sniffed. "I'll go get your file." She gave Glenda a warning look, turned on her heel and headed to the rear of the building, glancing back once, as if to reassure herself they hadn't left the building.

"Her bark is worse than her bite," Glenda whispered. "I think she likes you," she added.

Carlita snorted. "You coulda fooled me."

Carol returned moments later, file folder in hand. She stopped near the empty desk, set the folder on top, flipped it open and grabbed the paper on top, lifting it close to her face. Her eyes scanned the sheet and she cleared her throat. "There are enough violations here to shut your construction project down."

Chapter 6

"Shut us down!" Mercedes roared. "You can't do that."

It was Carlita's turn to be calm. "Can I see the list?"

Carol handed the sheet to Carlita and glared at Mercedes.

Carlita studied the list of offenses. Most of the items listed were minor and nothing Carlita hadn't already planned to fix. She handed the list to Mercedes. "Most of those items are on our to-do list. I can have Bob Lowman, the construction supervisor, forward a detailed list of scheduled repairs."

Carol's expression softened. "That would be helpful."

"If you'd like, you can meet us at the property first thing tomorrow morning and we can go over your list of concerns," Carlita's voice soothed.

"What time?" Carol asked suspiciously.

"Not too early," Glenda quipped.

Carol glared at Glenda and then turned to Carlita. "Ten would work for me. That will give you time to go over the list with the construction foreman before I get there."

"Perfect," Carlita beamed. "We'll see you at ten." She turned to Glenda. "Are you coming too?"

"Why sure." Glenda hopped out of her chair, ignoring the scowl on Carol's face. "I heard the old place on Mulberry is haunted." She rubbed her hands together. "I love haunted houses."

"Me too," Mercedes said. "That and a good mystery." The smile vanished. "I hope the police can figure out who killed your friend, Norma Jean."

"Friend," Carol snorted. "Norma Jean had more enemies than Savannah has trolley cars."

Finally. They were getting somewhere. "Like who?" Mercedes asked.

"Coulda been her newly-minted ex, Harold Stetson. She kicked him outta her place a couple weeks ago. He kept hanging around, but the more he tried to get back into Norma Jean's good graces, the crueler she was to him."

"Carol is right," Glenda said. "One day she's screaming at him on the phone, calling him a lying cheat. Next thing I know, Norma Jean let him move into the apartment above her garage because he told her he didn't have a place to live, but from what she said, she was having a grand old time making his life miserable."

She continued. "Betty didn't care for her either."

"Glenda." Carol cut her off. "Betty wouldn't harm a fly."

Carlita didn't get a warm and fuzzy for the hulking woman she had met earlier. Perhaps she was like Carol, the more you got to know her, the better you liked her.

The thought quickly dissipated at Carol's next comment.

"Don't forget these two are prime suspects." Carol eyed them warily. "For all we know, Norma Jean threatened them, and in a fit of rage they strangled her."

Carlita couldn't argue the point, and it sounded reasonable except that she hadn't killed Norma Jean Cleaver. "Like I said, we just arrived in town. I'm sure the police will uncover the real killer." She changed the subject. "I'll see you both at ten tomorrow morning." She nodded at Carol and Glenda, and then motioned her daughter to follow.

They stepped out of the building and made their way to the car. Carlita waited until they climbed in and the doors shut before turning to her daughter. "Maybe we need to check out this Harold Stetson fellow."

Mercedes buckled her seatbelt and stuck the key in the ignition. "I think they're all suspects. Glenda, Carol, Betty, Harold."

"Steve, Autumn, Bob..." Carlita added.

Mercedes glanced in the side mirror and then pulled out onto the street. "I'll bet a year's worth of house cleaning it's not Steve or Autumn."

"What about Bob?" Carlita asked.

"I dunno. There are too many suspects and I can't think clearly right now," Mercedes admitted. "We have to put our sleuthing caps on. Motive and opportunity."

They rode to the hotel in silence, both mulling over the growing list of suspects. Carlita had considered installing motion lights and an alarm system before returning to New York, but had nixed the idea. There was nothing inside the properties worth stealing.

If only she'd known she hadn't had to worry about thieves, but killers. "We need to install motion detectors and an alarm system."

"We'll talk to Mr. Lowman about it tomorrow," Mercedes agreed.

When they reached the corner, they turned left, heading toward a quieter section of town. They had opted to stay at a cheap hotel, located on the outer edge of the historic district, opposite the river, in an attempt to save a little money.

Tomorrow was going to be a busy day. Not only did they have to unload all of their belongings, they needed to shop for household necessities...beds, lamps and living room furniture.

Carlita hoped they would be able to spend the following night in their new home and that Vinnie would hang around long enough to help.

The unexpected death would likely set them back, along with the SAS meeting in the morning.

Mercedes pulled into the hotel parking lot and drove to the back where she parked the car and U-Haul in an empty area with plenty of room to navigate.

Carlita had called Vinnie to let him know they were pulling in. Vinnie and Rambo met them in the back of the lot and waited for them to exit the car.

Vinnie handed Mercedes Rambo's leash and headed to the trunk for the women's suitcases. "You sure do know how to make an entrance. If I didn't know better, I'd think someone offed a world leader instead of some nobody in a rinky dink town," he grumbled.

"This isn't a rinky dink town," Carlita argued. "Why do you say that?"

"Cuz it's all over the local news down here. It seems this Norma Jean lady was well known in the area."

Carlita's heart thumped in her chest and she could feel the heat of Johnny Law starting to breathe down her neck. Why couldn't it have been someone less infamous? They didn't need this sort of publicity.

"That's not cool," Mercedes groaned. "Hopefully it'll blow over by morning and the locals will forget about it."

"I doubt it." Vinnie squeezed the button on the luggage handle to extend it. "They were showin' a bunch of nosy reporters standing out in front of the restaurant, filming. They even showed a head shot of Ma. Not a good one either. Not sure where they got it from."

"I looked bad?" Carlita ran a hand through her hair and smoothed the ends.

"You got the deer-in-the-headlights look." Vinnie shrugged.

Carlita scowled. "Maybe it had something to do with the fact we found a body in our building. Maybe that had something to do with it."

"Calm down. I was kiddin'. You looked great." Vinnie patted her back and began to walk toward the hotel entrance. Carlita followed her son, and Mercedes and Rambo brought up the rear.

"We're on the third floor in Room 308." Vinnie led the way to the elevator and waited until they had all crowded inside before pushing the button. "They might replay it on the channel I was watchin'. Seems to be the hot topic of the day."

"If not, I could find the news station on my laptop and search for the story," Mercedes suggested.

"I can't wait to see it," Carlita mumbled. When they reached their floor, the door silently opened and she marched out of the elevator and to their room. "I guess I better stay out of sight in case someone recognizes me."

The motel room was more suite than room, with a small living area, a kitchenette in the corner and two queen beds in a separate room. A bath connected the bedroom and the front entry hall.

Vinnie rolled the suitcases into the bedroom and placed them between the beds. "I'll sleep on the sofa," he offered.

Carlita sank onto the sofa, grabbed a pillow and leaned her head back. "Thanks Vinnie and I'm sorry for snapping at you," she apologized.

"It's okay Ma. We've had a long day," he said as he plopped down on the other end of the sofa.

Vinnie hadn't given Carlita a timeframe on how long he planned to stay in Savannah and she didn't want him to head back home early, thinking she was being ungrateful. He was only trying to help. It wasn't his fault they had found a body in the dilapidated restaurant and the local news had managed to catch Carlita on camera.

She lifted her head and gazed at her children. "What do you want for dinner? I don't feel like going anywhere."

"Pizza will be fine." Mercedes plucked a hotel guidebook off the table, flipped it open and studied the pages. "This one looks good." She grabbed her cell phone from her pocket, switched it on and dialed the number. After ordering the pizza, she disconnected the call and set the phone back on top of the table.

"I'll try to find the news story while we're waiting." Mercedes shrugged off the backpack she'd carried inside, placed it on the floor next to her and unzipped the front. She placed the laptop on the desk, and pressed the power button, waiting for it to warm up. "What station were you watching?" she asked her brother.

"I don't remember." Vinnie grabbed the remote off the coffee table and turned the television on. "It was this station. Channel 9 News."

"Thanks." Mercedes turned her attention to the computer and tapped the keys. "I think I found it."

Carlita hopped off the couch and made her way over to her daughter, hovering over her shoulder to peer at the screen.

Mercedes turned the volume all the way up and pressed the play button. The news story was brief, less than a minute long. It showed a young man, standing in front of the vacant restaurant, holding a microphone. The camera panned the front of the building, zoomed in on the entrance and then zoomed back out before scanning the sidewalk and showing a shot of the street out front.

All the while, the reporter's monotone voice described how the new owners, who allegedly had been out of town when the death occurred, had found the body.

"Allegedly!" Carlita exploded. "Allegedly?"

"Shh." Mercedes pressed the pause button and placed a finger to her lips.

Carlita clenched her jaw and glared at the screen while Mercedes pressed the play button.

The reporter continued by identifying the victim as Norma Jean Cleaver, and explaining to viewers she was a member of the Savannah Architectural Society. He also mentioned that Ms. Cleaver had been sent to the property to discuss violations with the owner.

"He's making it sound..." Carlita interrupted again. She couldn't help herself. Someone was trying to frame her.

Mercedes paused the video again.

"I'm sorry. I'm just ticked off," Carlita muttered and then waved her hand. "Keep going. My lips are sealed." She made a zipping motion across her mouth.

The video ended shortly after, with a quick head shot of Carlita. She asked her daughter to play it back one more time.

Near the end of the video, the camera scanned the sidewalk and something caught Mercedes's eye. "Wait. Did you see that?"

Chapter 7

Mercedes hit the pause button, tapping the tip of her finger on the computer screen. "Her. That's what's-her-name, Betty Graybill. She was there right after it happened."

"She talked to me right after it happened," Carlita reminded her daughter.

Vinnie set the remote on the arm of the sofa. "There were a lot of people there. A death must be big news in this one horse town. In Queens, this wouldn't even have made the news, which is another reason I don't like this place. We stand out like sore thumbs."

Vinnie was right. They were different, a lot different. If the fine, upstanding citizens of Savannah had an inkling of their background, they would run them out of town.

"Which is why we need to keep our previous life history on the down low," Mercedes said. "No one needs to know." She gazed at her mother. "We gotta make up a past life, something so utterly boring no one would take notice."

Carlita began to pace back and forth in front of the window. "You're right. I never thought about it. If the police catch wind of our past, they'll throw us in jail and charge us with this poor woman's death."

"Librarian," Vinnie suggested.

Carlita quickly nixed the idea. "They don't make enough money."

"True." Mercedes drummed her fingers on the desktop thoughtfully. "Where would we have come up with the money to fix the properties? We have to be wealthy *and* boring."

"Accountant," Mercedes wrinkled her nose. "They're duller than a box of rocks."

"I've got it."Carlita slapped the palms of her hands together. "I was a housekeeper for a wealthy old gentleman and when he kicked the bucket, he left his worldly possessions to me."

"That'll work," Mercedes nodded.

"Problem solved," Vinnie said as someone tapped on the outer door of the hotel room. "Just in time for dinner." He hopped off the sofa and headed to the door where a delivery person stood on the other side. "Do I need to pay for this?"

"Nope. I put it on my credit card," Mercedes replied.

"Huh." Vinnie turned his attention to the pizza delivery person, signed the receipt and then waited for the door to close before moseying into the living room. "Where'd you get a credit card?"

Carlita took the drinks from her son while he set the pizza box on the small table. "The same place I got mine."

Vinnie lifted the top on the pizza and stared at his mother. "You got one too? Why'd you go and do that?"

Mercedes pushed her chair back. "Because we needed them. We can't carry cash everywhere we go. Look where that got us."

"True," Vinnie shrugged.

"Can you save the video clip?" Carlita asked as she cleared the small table to make room for the food.

"Sure." Mercedes sank back down in the chair, tapped the keyboard and then shut the lid. "Done." She dragged her chair to the small table, eased in next to her mother and reached for a paper napkin. "We also set up a bank account with debit cards."

"Next you'll be telling me you're gonna carry guns and go shooting them off at the gun range."

Mercedes grabbed a piece of pizza and bit the end. "We did some practice shooting before we left," she mumbled between chews.

Vinnie grunted and reached for a slice of pepperoni pizza. "I guess I never thought about it. Pop always took care of you."

"Pop is not here," Carlita said quietly. "You're leaving soon so it will only be Mercedes and me. We need to be able to take care of ourselves." She reached for a slice of pizza, tore off a piece of crust and slowly chewed. "Shame on me for sitting back all of those years and letting your father take care of everything."

She nodded toward Mercedes. "I vowed to myself after your father died that this would not happen to your sister and I intend to keep my promise."

Vinnie hated to admit it, but his mother was right. She would be on her own, although it wasn't his fault she had gotten the hair-brained idea to move halfway across the country. "I would take care of both of you."

Carlita squeezed her son's arm. "You have your own life, Vinnie, just like your brothers, Tony and Paulie. I thought maybe if you came down here and took a look around you would see the potential, the potential to leave the mob life and start over, to start fresh and maybe even meet someone and settle down. You could live a life where you wouldn't have to look over your shoulder every minute of the day, waiting for someone to take you down."

A tear rolled down Carlita's cheek at the thought of what could be for her children, all of her children. It broke her heart to know that one day, there was a good chance they would end up like their father, gone too soon or maybe even ending up in prison.

Mercedes twirled her drink straw and then took a sip of Coke. "You can lead a horse to water, but you can't make them drink."

"Are you sayin' I'm an animal?" Vinnie roared.

Mercedes grinned. "Yeah. A stubborn mule."

"Or horse." Carlita swiped at her damp cheek and smiled. Vinnie was not only the spitting image of his father in his younger years with his jet-black hair and dark brooding eyes, he had his father's personality...stubborn and bullheaded.

Carlita changed the subject and they began to discuss the repairs to the property. Vinnie grudgingly admitted he was impressed with what he'd seen and appeared slightly interested in the third property, the empty building Carlita hadn't even looked at yet. She reached for another slice of pizza. "We'll run over there tomorrow and take a look around."

Vinnie shrugged nonchalantly. "Might as well while I'm here."

"The first thing we need to do is buy some furniture," Mercedes said. "Or we'll be sleeping on the floor."

The trio decided Vinnie and Mercedes would drop Carlita off at the properties the following morning so that she could meet with the SAS members. The siblings would then drive to a wholesale furniture warehouse Mercedes had found online, to try to find not only beds and dressers, but also living room and dining room furniture.

Mercedes had sold one of the emeralds their father had left in a safe deposit box before they left New York and then deposited the money in their new checking account.

Vinnie had asked where the money had come from and Carlita had told him it was from the sale of the family home, which was partially true. They were living on the money from the sale, along with a small retirement account and savings Vinnie had accumulated over the years.

They were using the sale of the gems to fund the construction projects.

It was late by the time they finished eating and Vinnie and Rambo headed outside for a bathroom break. A short time later, they bolted back into the hotel room. "I caught someone trying to break into our U-Haul trailer!"

Chapter 8

Mercedes popped out of the bathroom. "Did they steal anything?"

"Nah." Vinnie grinned. "I scared 'em off with this." He pulled a handgun from the waistband of his jeans and waved it in the air. "The two punks took one look at my gun and ran off."

"You didn't." Carlita's eyes grew wide.

"You pulled a gun on them?" Mercedes asked. "Way to go, big bro. I'm sure that's helping us blend in," she wisecracked.

"I know how to handle my weapons." Vinnie shoved the gun in the waistband of his slacks and pulled his t-shirt over the top. "That'll teach them to mess with Vinnie Garlucci's goods."

"And you were worried about me carrying a loaded gun in the glove box, crossing state lines," Carlita said.

"True." Vinnie unclipped Rambo's leash, sauntered over to the sofa and flopped down, putting his feet on the coffee table, before leaning back. "This place ain't as boring and humdrum as I thought. I guess it's worth takin' a look at the extra space tomorrow."

Carlita slowly nodded her head. "Sounds good." She was almost glad Vinnie had to chase off potential thieves if it helped assure her son that Savannah could be an exciting place to live. "We'll check it out tomorrow."

After they finished getting ready for bed and the excitement of the would-be thieves wore off, Carlita climbed into bed. Mercedes closed the bi-fold doors that separated the living room and sleeper sofa where Vinnie was sleeping.

Carlita pointed toward the closed door, giving her daughter thumbs up before shutting the light off.

Despite the discovery of a body inside the restaurant, things were starting to look up for Carlita.

***

Vinnie, Mercedes and Carlita made quick work of unloading the U-Haul and the trunks of both vehicles the next morning. It took several trips to carry everything up the stairs and into the apartment.

Carlita loved their new home and couldn't wait to get settled so she and her daughter could focus their attention on getting the businesses up and running. Not only that, she was thrilled Vinnie was showing some interest in the properties. "Let's take a look at the third building and then Mercedes and you can head out to do some furniture shopping," she told her son.

Vinnie led the way. "Yeah. Let's see whatcha' got."

Mercedes and Carlita followed him downstairs, past the construction crew who was already hard at work, and then out onto the front sidewalk.

"It's over here." Carlita waved a hand and the trio walked past the restaurant, still shrouded in police tape, to a small door on the other side. She stuck a key in the lock, turned it this way and that until the door finally creaked open.

It was a dismal space, not large enough for anything other than storage and it was crammed full of boxes and bags Carlita was in no mood to sort through. She'd done enough of that back in New York.

"This isn't going to work." Vinnie shook his head and pulled the door shut. "In fact, it oughta be condemned."

"Don't let the SAS hear you say that," Mercedes joked.

The trio slowly walked back toward the construction site and stood out front, studying the street.

Carlita stared at the store thoughtfully. Bob had told her yesterday the crew was almost finished with the interior building repairs and would soon begin work on the front exterior.

It would be up to Carlita to select the shelving, freezers and refrigerators and other equipment. "I was thinking, the only reason we decided to open a grocery store was because that's what had been here before," she said.

"Yeah," Mercedes agreed. "We don't know anything about running a grocery store."

"What about a pawnshop, Vinnie?" Carlita turned to her son.

"You mean movin' fenced goods?" he asked. "It's a thought."

"Not fenced goods. I'm talking about a legitimate business, where you can make an honest living."

Vinnie rubbed the back of his neck. "I dunno Ma."

Carlita didn't answer. Instead, she headed inside to study the interior. There was plenty of room. They could increase the size of the back for storage, add a long counter, similar to the one she'd noticed at East Side Pawn, the pawnshop she'd recently visited in Queens when she sold some of her old possessions before the move.

"This would be the perfect spot for a pawnshop," she said. They could add rows of shelves for merchandise. "It would be a lot easier than trying to sell food, which spoils or expires if you don't sell it."

Vinnie held up a hand. "Now don't go gettin' crazy ideas Ma. I said I might *think* about it." He turned to his sister. "Let's get outta here before she hires me," he teased.

"You really need to give it some thought, Vinnie," Carlita said as she followed her son to the rear of the store. "I can have the construction crew start working on one of the other apartments for you."

Mercedes followed her brother out the back and turned around once to wink at her mother as she mouthed the words. "It's working."

Carlita waited for them to leave before closing the back door. She hummed a catchy tune as she headed upstairs to start unpacking boxes and to wait for the SAS to show up. If she could smooth things over with the Architectural Society members, all she'd have left to worry about was Norma Jean Cleaver's murder.

She started in her bedroom closet, hanging clothes and arranging boxes before moving to the kitchen.

Carlita paused to admire her surroundings. Everything was brand spanking new. The cupboards were new. The counters were new. Even the appliances were new. She quickly unloaded the kitchen boxes, arranging dishes, silverware and the small household appliances she'd brought with her.

"Well, they did a decent job on this place," a shrill voice called from the doorway.

Carlita set the toaster on the kitchen counter and hurried to the living room where Betty Graybill stood hovering between the hall and Carlita's living room. "It almost looks habitable," she sniffed.

"I hope so," Carlita said. "We're moving in."

Betty tugged on the edge of her blouse and took a step inside. "The other society members are downstairs talking to your construction supervisor, Will Bowman."

"Bob Lowman," Carlita corrected.

"Bowman, Lowman." Betty waved a dismissive hand. "What exactly are your plans for this property?"

"We originally intended to re-open a corner grocery store but that may change," Carlita replied. "If my son decides to move here, we may open a pawnshop instead."

"Pawnshop!" Betty's hand flew to her throat. "You can't open a pawnshop. It would be a magnet for criminals." *If she only knew.*

"It would be a service to the community, helping those in need of fast cash while offering bargains for the budget-conscious." Carlita wasn't sure where that had come from but it sounded good.

"I-we'll fight it," Betty sputtered.

Carlita stuck a fisted hand on her hip. "Go right ahead, lady. I'll fight back. This is my property and I'll do as I darn well please."

Betty Graybill stomped her foot, turned on her heel and marched across the hall, her heels making a loud rapping noise on the stair treads as she headed down the stairs.

Carlita stuck her tongue out at the empty doorway. "I guess I better have Mercedes do a little research to find out how much power these women actually wield." She slowly followed behind, closing the door to the apartment before descending the steps where she found the women huddled in the corner, their heads close together.

"They're fit to be tied," Bob whispered as she walked past. "I dunno what you said to the ringleader, but she's throwing a temper tantrum."

Carlita nodded and continued walking until she reached the outer circle. "Can I answer any questions for you *ladies*?"

The conversation ceased and the others turned to Betty Graybill. "We've taken notes and will forward our recommendations later today," she said stiffly.

"Recommendations?" Carlita lifted a brow.

"We can't technically force you to do anything." Glenda Fox spoke up. Carlita gave her a small smile.

"But we can make your life miserable," Carol Weatherbee quipped.

"Even more than it already is," Betty snickered. "I heard the police are getting ready to make an arrest in Norma Jean's murder."

Chapter 9

The blood drained from Carlita's face. She began to feel lightheaded and started to sway.

Glenda reached out to steady her. "Are you okay?"

"Of course she's not," Betty snapped. "She's about to be charged with murder."

A woman Carlita had not noticed took a step closer. "That's the first I heard of an arrest, Betty. I talked to Sharon Stine who works at the Savannah-Burnham Police Department and she said Detective Wayne Polivich, who is in charge of the investigation, was still following up on leads."

She went on. "He said Norma Jean had more enemies than Savannah has churches."

Betty clamped her hand around the woman's wrist and squeezed. "Vicki Munroe - that is outright gossip."

"Ouch!" Vicki wrenched free from Betty's tight grip and rubbed her wrist. "How do you know?"

Betty gave Vicki a warning look and turned to Carlita. "I need your email address so I can send the recommendations later today."

Carlita rattled off her email address, while Betty typed it into her cell phone and then slid the phone into her purse. "I hope you're not serious about the pawnshop," she warned.

"I love pawnshops. You can find some great deals," Carol clapped her hands and then dropped them to her side when Betty cleared her throat.

The ringleader gave Carlita a hard stare, turned on her heel and strode out of the store with the others following behind like sheeple.

Glenda was the last to leave. She turned back, gave a small wave and then followed the others.

Carlita waited until they had passed by the front picture window before relaxing her stance.

After the women left, Bob made his way over. "Don't let the woman get under your skin. She's mostly hot air with a miniscule amount of authority. Vicki Munroe has the real pull in their posse."

"You mean the woman with the black bob?"

Bob nodded. "Yep. Vicki is Mayor Clarence Puckett's sister. They're a colorful family, for sure." He went on. "Course Vicki, she's a real sweetheart. Kind of evens out Betty Graybill's nasty disposition."

"The women, with the exception of Betty, seem reasonable. I'm on the fence about Carol," Carlita said.

"Carol is an odd duck. She worships the ground Betty walks on," Bob said. "I don't know too much about the woman. I've had a few run-ins with the society over the years and if my memory serves me, she has only been a member for about a year now."

Bob returned to work and Carlita headed upstairs to the apartments. Two of the three apartments were in decent shape while the third was in rough condition and would need the most work.

She vowed to have Vinnie take a closer look at the units in case he decided to make the move. Carlita tried not to get her hopes up because Vinnie had been dead set against moving south, but the thought of having two of her four children close by was exciting.

Rambo wandered around with her and after the two of them finished inspecting the apartments, headed back to their unit. She knew her pooch was going to miss having the backyard he'd had in Queens. Carlita hoped the small deck would suffice.

From what she remembered from the last time Mercedes and she had visited Savannah, there were a lot of common areas, or "squares" as Steve had called them, in Savannah's historic district, which would be perfect for taking Rambo for long walks.

She opened the slider door and Rambo trotted out, making his way to the railing where he stared down into the alley.

Carlita had almost forgotten about the courtyard Mercedes and she had found during their last visit. She patted Rambo's head. "We'll scope out the courtyard later. I'm sure once we whip it into shape, you're gonna love it," she promised him.

By the time Carlita finished unpacking the boxes and dragging Mercedes's belongings into her bedroom, her children had returned from their shopping trip.

They had hit the jackpot, purchasing the majority of furniture needed at the wholesale warehouse and gotten great deals on almost everything.

Bob and his crew helped carry the mattresses, the living room sofa, two bedroom dressers and a dining room table up the steep steps.

The sofa, a blue chintz fabric, fit the room to a "T." The siblings had also found two end tables and a coffee table with only minor imperfections. If Vinnie hadn't pointed out the flaws, Carlita never would have noticed.

The small oak dining room table was the perfect size for the space and included four matching chairs, which would be plenty of seating for mother and daughter plus a couple extra guests.

The only thing missing was patio furniture for their new deck but that would have to wait.

Carlita placed a silk floral arrangement in the center of the dining room table and stood back to admire it while Vinnie slid the chairs around the table. "I want you to take a look at the other apartments, Vinnie, just in case you decide you're going to move down. That way, I can have Bob work on the unit you like next."

Mercedes flopped down on the new sofa and curled her legs underneath her. She ran her hand along the arm of the sofa. "This is super comfy." She patted the arm. "You should try it."

Carlita joined her daughter on the sofa, agreeing it was comfortable.

Vinnie eased into the recliner, one of the few pieces of furniture Carlita had insisted she bring with her from New York. "I see the look in your eye, Ma. I'm not sure I wanna move, you know?"

"I know. No pressure," she assured him. Carlita lifted the edge of the sofa cushion. "I hope this is a sleeper sofa." They had decided to purchase a sleeper sofa for company, and Vinnie would be the first to try it.

"Of course." Mercedes hopped off the sofa and waved her hand at her brother. "We should go check out your unit. I wonder if Autumn still wants to rent one of them, too."

"I completely forgot about Autumn," Carlita said. "Maybe we should finish up the store downstairs and then have Bob and his workers begin work on the other units. It would give us some quick cash flow."

The trio wandered out of the apartment. Mercedes and Carlita waited in the hall while Vinnie inspected all three units. After finishing a brief tour, he joined them in the hall. "The one across from yours is a mess. The others aren't too bad, though," he admitted. "I guess if I was gonna have to pick one, it would be the one behind yours."

Mercedes clapped her hands. "Awesome. We'll have Bob build a deck on yours too. What do you think about the layout of ours? I changed it around so it flows better."

"It looks great, Mercedes," Vinnie said. "You did a good job."

Mercedes turned to her mother. "How did it go with the SAS meeting?"

Carlita rolled her eyes. "The ringleader, Betty, almost blew a gasket when she found out we were thinking about turning the store into a pawnshop instead of grocery store."

"Why?" Vinnie asked.

"She said it will bring in the criminal element," Carlita said. "Then she told me the police were getting close to making an arrest and charging someone with Norma Jean Cleaver's murder, hinting that it was probably going to be me."

"That's absurd," Mercedes sputtered. "We weren't even in Savannah when the woman was murdered."

"But we can't prove it," Carlita said quietly. "The only thing we have is a hotel receipt with your name on it, Mercedes."

"The hotel clerks saw you," her daughter argued.

"Did they? I never stepped foot inside the lobby. The entrance to our room was through an outdoor balcony. I didn't go into the lobby to check in. Neither did Vinnie."

"True." Mercedes stomped her foot. "Why us? Why couldn't they have dumped the body somewhere else?"

"Because they knew the place was empty," Carlita theorized.

"Once we have internet, I'm gonna do some research on the deceased."

"I forgot all about internet," Carlita sighed. "We need to find someone to come out and install that and cable."

Mercedes headed to her bedroom to get her phone while Vinnie and Carlita made their way out onto the deck where Rambo was napping.

Vinnie stared across the alley at the back of another building. "This is an ugly view."

Carlita had to admit he was right. There wasn't much to look at, but it was outdoor space for Rambo. "There's a small courtyard separating the two buildings. Mercedes and I plan to clean it up."

A small movement caught Carlita's eyes. She leaned over the railing and peered out at the road, just in time to see a small figure zip down the alley on a Segway, blonde hair flying from beneath the helmet. It was Autumn.

Carlita shifted her gaze and stared at the large pothole Autumn and her Segway were headed right toward. She cupped her hands to her mouth. "Watch out for the hole!"

Chapter 10

It was too late. Autumn hit the pothole dead center. The sudden impact caused Autumn to lose her balance.

The Segway went one way while Autumn went the other, landing flat on her back and then rolling to the side.

The passenger-less Segway continued its forward motion for several seconds before finally rolling to a stop near the back door of the restaurant.

"Oh my gosh. I hope she's not hurt." Carlita straddled the railing and hopped over to the fire escape before swinging half circle and scampering down the ladder.

Carlita rushed to Autumn's side and dropped to her knees. "Autumn. Are you okay?"

Autumn's eyes fluttered and then opened. "I-uh." She tried to lift her head.

"Don't move."

Vinnie arrived moments later. He knelt on one knee and studied her motionless body. "The helmet saved her noggin. I'm not sure about the rest of her. Does anything hurt?"

"My pride," Autumn groaned and then pulled her hands from behind her back. "I tried to break my fall." She lifted both arms for inspection and Carlita noticed her pinky finger jutted out at an odd angle. "I think you may have broken your finger. What about your legs?"

Autumn bent her knees. "They seem to be all right."

"Can you try to sit up?" Vinnie asked as he reached a strong arm behind her back and gently lifted her to a sitting position.

Autumn's face turned bright pink and her eyes widened as she gazed at Vinnie. "I-Thank you..."

"Vinnie," he said, his voice deepening.

"What happened?" Mercedes raced out of the building and came to an abrupt halt next to her mother. "I heard Mom yelling."

"Autumn took a tumble," Carlita explained.

"I wasn't paying attention to where I was going and the Segway and I had a run in with your pothole." Autumn held up her hand and pointed to her pinky. "I think my finger is broken."

"We should get her to the nearest emergency clinic to have it looked at," Vinnie said.

"I have no idea where that would be," Carlita said.

"It's not far." Autumn shifted to the side. "I can drive my Segway."

Vinnie cut her off. "No way. I think someone should go with you. Mercedes and I can go," he said.

Carlita stood and brushed the debris from her knees. "I think that's a great idea. Vinnie can drive you in his car. In the meantime, I'll take the Segway inside for safekeeping."

Despite Autumn's protests, Vinnie insisted they accompany her to the nearest emergency clinic.

Vinnie escorted Autumn to the passenger side of his sedan and waited for her to climb in before he made his way to the driver's side.

Mercedes hopped in the back seat but not before winking at her mother and pointing at her brother and Autumn in the front seat.

Carlita had also caught a spark between Vinnie and Autumn. Her oldest son, a confirmed bachelor, was once again interested in a woman.

***

Carlita paced the alley before deciding there was nothing she could do so she headed indoors to get Rambo.

When she reached the apartment, she pulled the slider door shut and locked it before hooking Rambo's leash to his collar and heading downstairs.

Bob Lowman was standing in the corner, talking on his cell phone. She and Rambo waited off to the side for Bob to finish his conversation.

"I'll look into it. Good-bye." Bob pressed the "end call" button and frowned at the phone before slipping it into his front pocket. "I have no idea what you said to get on Betty Graybill's bad side, but she is down at the building inspections office demanding they shut this project down due to a conflict in city interest."

"What conflict in city interest?" Carlita asked.

"Apparently, you mentioned to SAS that you were thinking of opening a pawnshop instead of a grocery store."

"I did. In fact, I'm here to talk to you about it to get your thoughts."

Bob rocked back on his heels and crossed his arms in front of him. "It'll save you a boatload in start-up expenses. You won't need freezers and refrigerators. It will save on electric, not to mention all the perishable goods. Yeah. You'd probably be better off with a pawnshop."

He rubbed his chin and gazed at Carlita thoughtfully. "That kind of business brings in a..."

"Criminal element?" Carlita suggested.

"Yeah. You sure you and your daughter can handle it?"

"It wouldn't be me," Carlita said. "My son, Vinnie, is thinking of moving down here. He would run the business."

"He would have to be prepared for some rough customers." *That will be the least of my worries.* Carlita thought silently. *If he only knew.* "Vinnie can take care of himself," she said aloud.

She went on. "Just in case he does, I would like your crew to start working on the apartment behind mine."

"You still plan on opening a restaurant?" Bob asked.

"Yes. Absolutely. I was kinda iffy on the grocery store, but a restaurant would be a piece of cake." At least Carlita hoped it would be a piece of cake. She'd never run a restaurant, let alone a business. There would be a learning curve. Perhaps she could hire a manager to help, someone who was familiar with the restaurant business.

"If you want me to start on the apartments, it would be just as easy to gut and remodel all three at once," Bob told her. "We can get the mess and noise over all at once."

Carlita hadn't thought of that and quickly gave him the go ahead to work on all three.

Rambo began tugging on his leash.

"I better take Rambo out." She turned to go.

"Oh. Carlita, one more thing."

Carlita turned back.

"I have a box of stuff I found up in the attic. It's over on the counter of the small kitchen area here in the back."

Carlita followed Bob to the back and he pointed to a cardboard box sitting on top. She quickly sifted through the contents. There were some old newspapers, an avocado green rotary dial telephone, a yellowed book of stamps and a small stack of postcards. At the very bottom of the box was a skeleton key. She snagged the key from the bottom of the box and held it up. "I wonder if this opens the courtyard gate."

Bob leaned in and studied the key. "Looks like it might. If not, I can get one of my guys to unlock it for you."

"Thanks." Carlita slipped the key in her pocket. "I'll give it a try and let you know if it doesn't work."

She let Rambo lead her from the building. They strolled down the sidewalk, or more like "trotted." Rambo pulled hard and seemed to know exactly where he was going, which was to the end of the block, across a busy intersection and to a park on the opposite side of the street, next to a river.

When they reached the other side, Rambo slowed and began sniffing the meticulously manicured grass while Carlita gazed at a large statue of a woman. She was holding something, waving it in the air. It looked like a piece of cloth.

"What's this?" Carlita led Rambo to the statue of a woman. Standing next to the woman was a statue of a dog. It looked like a collie.

"Check that out Rambo. She's waving to the ships." Carlita shifted her gaze to the river and watched a freighter glide past. She impulsively lifted her hand, giving it a shake and one of the crew on deck waved back.

They waited until the ship was out of sight before meandering down the brick walkway, passing several park benches. They made it as far as the shopping and eating district before turning back.

Carlita studied her surroundings as they walked. Her properties were located in a prime spot and she could only guess that fixed up they would be worth a pretty penny, not that she planned to sell them.

When they got back to their neighborhood, they stopped at the wrought iron gate in front of the courtyard. Carlita pulled the key from her pocket and inserted it in the lock. It was a perfect fit. She turned the key and the gate creaked open.

Carlita nudged the gate with the tip of her shoe. "I think we're gonna love this place," she told Rambo as they stepped inside. It was exactly as Carlita had remembered.

Rambo darted down the cobblestone walkway and Carlita brought up the rear. With a lot of elbow grease, the peaceful oasis would shine. She could hardly wait to get started as she reached down and pulled a weed from the edge of the walkway.

She absentmindedly began pulling weeds as she mulled over the death of Norma Jean Cleaver. As soon as Mercedes was able to access the internet, Carlita would have her daughter research the woman's past. She ticked off a list of things to research including the Savannah Architectural Society.

Carlita also made a mental note to study the news station's video footage to see if she could glean any clues from the scene. It had been so chaotic, Carlita hadn't been thinking clearly and she may have missed something.

She also wanted to chat with the other Savannah Architectural Society members, including Carol Weatherbee, Glenda Fox and Vicki Munroe. Vicki was a talker. Maybe she could start with her. The woman also had connections.

Glenda Fox would be next. Carlita liked her. She seemed like such a sweet person, which made her wonder why on earth she put up with Betty Graybill. Last, but not least would be Carol Weatherbee. Carlita wasn't quite sure what to make of the woman.

She also wondered about the construction crew. Carlita wanted to believe Bob Lowman and his men had nothing to do with Norma Jean's murder. The fact there was no sign of forced entry was a clue.

Carlita reluctantly added Autumn and Steve to the list of suspects. Steve had a key to the property, too. Carlita had given it to him before returning to New York a few short weeks ago.

Autumn was the one who had discovered the unlocked door and then called the police, which placed her smack dab on the suspect list. It was hard to believe the young woman could be capable of murder, but Carlita had been a mafia wife for most of her life. Anyone was capable of murder under the right circumstances.

Rambo began chewing on a low hanging vine. "No Rambo! That's poison ivy."

Rambo stopped chomping on the leaf and hung his head.

"Let's head back to the apartment for some water and a treat." The two of them retraced their steps and Carlita gazed back one last time before opening the gate and stepping onto the sidewalk where a woman, close to her age with straight brown hair, thick black glasses and a serious expression stood on the other side.

Carlita smiled as she pulled the gate shut. "Can I help you?"

"Yes, uh," the woman said in a soft voice. "I'm Annie Dowton and I own the real estate office across the street. I wanted to stop by to introduce myself." She handed Carlita a business card.

Carlita took the card and glanced at the front. *Riverfront Real Estate.* She held out her hand. "I'm Carlita Garlucci. My daughter and I inherited this property. We moved down from New York."

The woman nodded. "That's what I heard. Are you going to keep the properties?" she inquired.

"That's our plan." Carlita wrinkled her nose. "Of course, it may change after we try our hand at entrepreneurship," she joked.

Annie nodded. "I also heard Betty Graybill is giving you a hard time. She's a real trip."

Carlita grinned. "You can say that again. I think I started out on the wrong foot with Ms. Graybill."

"She doesn't have a right foot." Annie smiled. "It's nothing personal. Those members of the SAS regularly terrorize the local business owners so don't let her get under your skin."

"Thanks for the warning."

Rambo began nudging Annie's hand. "What a pretty dog," she said as she patted Rambo's head.

"Thanks. He's a character," Carlita said. "Would you like to come upstairs for a cup of tea?"

"No." Annie glanced at her watch. "I have to head out for a showing, but wanted to pop over and introduce myself and welcome you to the neighborhood. We're a tight knit group here on Walton Square. Like family. You'll like it here."

Carlita grinned at her choice of words. Hopefully it wasn't *that* kind of family. "I appreciate it, Annie. It was nice to meet you."

Annie turned to go and then spun back around. "One more thing. That woman who was murdered, Norma Jean Cleaver...I noticed her hanging around here the past few weeks. About a week ago, I noticed she was trying to get into your courtyard so I decided to approach her, try to figure out who she was and what she was doing. She freaked out and started screaming that the SAS was going to shut my real estate business down."

"I recognized her face from the picture on the front of the Savannah Evening News."

Chapter 11

Carlita took a step forward. "Did you call the police?"

Annie nodded. "I did and told them the same thing I told you."

"Maybe the society sent her over on a recon mission, you know, to snoop around."

"True. That's what I thought." Annie shrugged. "I thought it was odd she kept hanging around and it was the same time every day, like she was waiting for someone."

Carlita glanced over Annie's shoulder and lowered her voice. "Was it after the construction people left for the day or were they still here?"

"It was always around 5:30, right around the time I leave my office and there's never anyone over here working that late. The only one I noticed was the woman, Norma Jean."

Annie Dowton had just given Carlita her first solid clue. "Thank you so much for telling me that, Annie. I have a feeling somehow, her hanging around here had something to do with her death."

"Me too. The police didn't seem particularly interested, though." She glanced at her watch a second time. "I gotta run. Nice to meet you."

Carlita and Rambo watched as Annie hurried to the end of the sidewalk before looking both ways and crossing the street where she climbed into a silver convertible, the top down. She fastened her seatbelt after starting the car, and with a small wave in Carlita's direction, sped off down the street.

With nothing left to do but wait for Vinnie, Mercedes and Autumn to return, Carlita headed upstairs to try out her new kitchen.

She decided to surprise Vinnie and Mercedes with one of their favorite Italian dishes, stuffed shells, but first, she had to find the nearest grocery store, one that she could walk to. She stopped by her bedroom for her purse before heading out.

Rambo was waiting by the door. "Sorry Rambo. I can't take you this time." He lowered his head and plopped down on the living room floor to pout.

She headed down the steps, out the back door and into the alley. At the end of the alley, she made a quick left and hurried across the street to Shades of Ink, Steve Winter's tattoo shop.

Steve was behind the counter, talking to a customer when Carlita stepped inside. He waved her to hold on for a minute and after the customer paid, the woman passed Carlita as she exited the store, sporting a shiny new tattoo on the side of her arm. Surrounding the tattoo were angry red splotches.

Carlita took a closer look. It was a rainbow-colored butterfly and she had to admit he'd done a great job. She made her way to the counter and placed her purse on top. "Nice tattoo. Very colorful," she complimented.

"Thanks." Steve grinned. "You want one? I think you'd look good with a small rose or maybe a cross. You go to church?"

An image of Father Dadore, her family's former priest, flashed through her mind. "Yes. We're Catholic."

"You're in luck. There's a huge Catholic cathedral within walking distance. Cathedral of Saint John the Baptist. It's over on Norris Street. She's a beaut."

"Thanks for the info. I would love to check it out. In the meantime, I'm trying to find a local grocery store I can walk to," she said.

"That would be Colby's Corner Store. Go to the end of this block, turn right and it's on the right."

"Thanks." Carlita reached for her purse and then paused. "I'm breaking in the new kitchen, fixing a big Italian dinner. Would you and Autumn like to join my children and me? We'll be eating around six."

Steve patted his stomach. "I'm not one to turn down a home-cooked meal, especially authentic Italian. Can I bring anything?"

"You can bring a dessert if you like," Carlita suggested.

"I will, and a jug of sweet tea," Steve added. "Have you ever tasted sweet tea?"

"No." Carlita shook her head.

"You're in for a real treat." Steve rapped his knuckles on the counter. "The cops any closer to figuring out how the nosy broad, Norma something's body ended up in your place?"

"No. The rest of the society stopped by the store earlier. They were fit to be tied when I told them I was considering opening a pawnshop instead of a grocery store," she admitted.

"I bet they were. Did they threaten to shut you down?"

"How did you know?"

"They did the same thing to me when I applied for a permit to open this tattoo parlor. They tried everything short of burning the place to the ground." Steve chuckled. "In the end, those old gals didn't have a leg to stand on."

"That's good to know." Carlita said. "I'm sure you heard about Autumn's little accident on the Segway?"

Steve rolled his eyes and stepped around the side of the counter as he walked Carlita to the door. "The girl is the most accident-prone person I know. I think she has broken both legs and one arm, not to mention her nose."

"Is Autumn younger than you?"

"Yes. I'll be twenty seven this year and she's twenty two, although sometimes it seems more like fifteen. Autumn sometimes doesn't think things through and she can be impulsive." Steve sighed deeply.

"So can Mercedes."

"Yep. We had better keep a close eye on them. I think they could get into a lot of trouble."

Carlita nodded her agreement. She'd been thinking the exact same thing, but more of Autumn getting Mercedes into trouble, not the other way around. She thanked Steve for the directions, told him she would see him at six and then stepped out onto the sidewalk.

The neighborhood...her neighborhood with its tree-lined streets, was charming. Circling each of the trees was an array of peonies and daffodils.

Savannah was smack dab in the dog days of summer, and despite the ample shade from the trees, it was hot. By the time Carlita reached the bright blue awning of Colby's Corner Store, beads of perspiration covered her brow.

She pulled a small packet of tissues from her purse, plucked one out and dabbed at her forehead before shoving the tissue in her pocket and stepping inside the store.

The cool of the air conditioning was a welcome relief from the oppressive heat and Carlita pushed her damp bangs off to the side as she studied the inside of the grocery store. It was larger than it appeared on the outside. A deli counter spanned the entire left hand side of the grocery store.

Toward the back was a cozy restaurant with small booths, separated by bright yellow Formica countertops. The smell of fried foods drifted in the air and Carlita realized she'd skipped breakfast.

"Can I help you?" A young woman, in her late teens or early twenties, smiled at Carlita as she approached the food counter.

"I have some groceries to pick up but it smells so good in here, I think I might grab something to go." She thought about her children and Autumn. Surely, they would be hungry by now. "The chili dogs sound good."

"They're the best. My favorite is the Rockford. It's made with chili sauce, a dash of mustard, a sprinkle of red onions and a dill pickle spear. If you order the special, it comes with two hotdogs, French fries and a small side of coleslaw."

"That sounds perfect. I'll take four specials to-go and will stop back to pick them up after I finish shopping."

"I'll get right on it."

Carlita wandered around the spacious store before grabbing a hand basket, which she promptly filled with a box of pasta shells, shredded cheeses, a carton of cottage cheese and a dozen eggs. She had already unpacked her Italian seasonings she'd brought from New York. Carlita was particular about her seasonings and she hoped she would be able to find comparable seasonings in Savannah.

She picked up her to-go orders just as the girl finished bagging them and then headed to the checkout near the front. Carlita set the basket on the counter and lowered the handles before sliding it forward.

The man behind the checkout counter, Ken, according to his nametag, reached for the bags of food first. "These are the best," he said. "The chili sauce is a secret family recipe my grandmother passed down."

Carlita shifted to the side. "Do you own this store?"

"Yep," Ken nodded. "We've been here since 1982. You're new to the neighborhood?"

"Yes. I'm Carlita Garlucci," she said.

"Ah." Ken nodded. "You're the new owner of the old grocery store and Denny's Diner down on Mulberry."

"Yep. That's me," she said. "My daughter and I just moved here from New York."

"Welcome to Walton Square. You'll like it here."

He went on. "I see you're working on the old buildings. They sure needed it." Ken reached for the carton of eggs. "You gonna open up the old grocery store again?"

"Maybe. Maybe not. I'm leaning toward opening a pawnshop. It depends on whether I can convince my eldest son, Vinnie, to stay and run it for me."

"Sounds like a solid plan. Old George Delmario gave the place a good run, but you can only have so many grocery stores, you know? Now a pawnshop." Ken shook his head. "I bet old Betty Graybill and the Savannah Architectural Society wasn't too keen on the idea."

"Not at all." Carlita smiled as she remembered the look on Betty's face. The smile vanished when she remembered Betty informed her that the police were close to making an arrest. "I don't think she likes me."

Ken finished scanning Carlita's purchases and placed them in a plastic bag before reaching for a second bag. "She doesn't like anyone." He opened the empty bag and placed the full one inside. "I'm gonna double bag these so they don't break while you're carrying them."

"I appreciate it," Carlita reached for the bag. "You have a great store here. Thanks for the warm welcome."

She exited the store and began the short walk back to the apartment. The noonday sun was beating straight down. Carlita picked up the pace; quickly deciding the southern heat was something that would take some getting used to.

New York was hot in the summer, but not this hot.

Carlita spotted Vinnie's car parked in the alley as she slipped inside the back door and headed up the stairs.

Vinnie, Autumn and Mercedes were seated at the dining room table when she opened the door.

The conversation abruptly ceased as Carlita closed the door behind her. She walked through the living room and into the kitchen, placing the bag of groceries on the counter. All eyes were on her as she carried the hotdogs to the table. "What?"

"A Detective Polivich just left," Vinnie said. "He was looking for you."

Chapter 12

Carlita's heart skipped a beat. "Did he say why?"

"Nope." Mercedes shook her head. "We tried to find out. He asked when you were coming back and since we had no idea where you'd gone, we told him we didn't know."

"He mumbled something about swinging back by later this afternoon," Autumn added.

Vinnie shifted in the chair and faced his mother. "We need to figure out who offed that lady so we can get the cops off our backs."

"I agree," Mercedes said. "I scheduled an appointment for cable and internet installation and the technician should be here within the hour. As soon as he hooks us up and I can access my computer, I'll start my research. I've already put together a list."

Carlita tugged on the edge of her blouse and turned her attention to Autumn. "What about you, young lady? Did the doctor find anything other than a broken finger?"

Autumn held up her hand to show Carlita the splinter on her pinky. "I got lucky. It's only a fracture."

"No concussion or head injury?" Carlita prompted.

"Nope." Autumn lightly tapped on the side of her forehead. "Harder than a rock up there."

"Not to mention she was wearing a helmet, thank goodness," Mercedes said. "Maybe I don't want Autumn to teach me how to ride a Segway," she teased her friend.

Carlita pointed to the brown bag. "I found a local grocery store with a small restaurant in the back so I picked up their lunch special." She rattled off the special. "It's two chili dogs, French fries and a small side of coleslaw."

Autumn rubbed her hands together. "You found Colby's place," she guessed.

"Yep." Carlita headed to the kitchen. "You set the table while I put the groceries away." She reached for one of the bags. "I'm going to make stuffed pasta shells for dinner and stopped by the tattoo shop to invite Steve and of course, Autumn."

Vinnie pushed back his chair and headed to the kitchen. "Ma makes *the* best stuffed shells ever. You're in for a real treat," he told Autumn.

"I picked up some spicy Italian ground turkey to mix with the sauce," Carlita said as she placed the packages of cheese and other ingredients inside the fridge. "Steve promised to bring dessert and sweet tea."

Mercedes arranged the hotdogs on the table while Autumn distributed the fries and coleslaw. "You all are gonna make me fat," Autumn groaned.

"You could stand to gain a few pounds," Vinnie said.

Carlita gazed at her son and lifted a brow.

"What? She can." Vinnie shook his head and carried the silverware and napkins to the table.

Carlita settled into an empty chair, between her two children and unwrapped her hotdogs. She dumped the crinkle cut French fries next to the hotdogs and popped the top on the coleslaw before reaching for her fork. She turned to Autumn. "Mr. Colby seems like a nice man," she said.

"Yes. He is. I've never seen a Mrs. Colby but his daughter, Faith, works with him in the snack shop. You probably met her. She's about my size, with curly blondish hair."

"Yep. Friendly young lady," Carlita picked up her hotdog and bit the end, savoring the spicy chili and tangy dill pickle. "Delicious."

"I agree." Mercedes nibbled the end of her hotdog before taking a big bite. "Da best," she mumbled between chews.

Vinnie gobbled his food, wiped his mouth and threw the napkin on top before crumpling the wrapper and tossing it into the empty bag. "I'm gonna head downstairs to see if I can lend a hand to the construction guys, maybe get a feel for the area business market." He shoved his chair back and stood. "You need me for anything?"

Carlita shook her head, unable to hide her ear-to-ear grin.

"Now I haven't promised nothin' Ma."

"I know." Carlita continued to smile as she watched her eldest child stroll out of the apartment, closing the door behind him. She picked up a French fry and dunked it in her mound of catsup. "I think he's gonna move here."

"Me too," Mercedes said. "But you know Vinnie. If he thinks you're trying to convince him to do something, he'll do the opposite."

"True." Mercedes was right. Vinnie was bullheaded. Carlita turned her attention to Autumn. "I took Rambo for a walk over to the park in front of the river. The name of it was More something."

"Morrell Park," Autumn said. "It's a great place for pooches and people." She reached down and patted

Rambo's head before feeding him one of her fries. "There are some awesome restaurants and shops at the other end."

"I found them, too," Carlita said. "After walking in the park, Rambo and I were checking out our courtyard when Annie Dowton, the woman who owns the real estate office across the street, stopped by to introduce herself."

Autumn, who was reaching for her second hotdog, stopped midair. "She did? What did she say?"

"It was mostly small talk. I guess she was trying to drum up business because she asked what I planned to do with the properties once we finished the renovations. Maybe she wanted to list them." Carlita shrugged.

"When you mentioned her name, it reminded me of something," Autumn said, right before she shoved her hotdog in her mouth, biting off half and then chewing noisily.

Carlita watched as Autumn devoured half the dog in four large bites, swallowed it all at once and then reached for her Coke. "She asked about Norma Jean Cleaver, if the police had updated me on the investigation and I told her not yet but that Betty Graybill had told me they were close to making an arrest."

"That's what I was gonna say," Autumn said. "The woman who died, I remember seeing her and Annie fighting out front."

"Fighting, as in yelling at each other?" Mercedes asked.

"That and they were shoving each other," Autumn said.

Chapter 13

"That's odd," Carlita murmured. "She told me the SAS terrorized business owners, that she'd noticed Norma Jean hanging around and asked her what she was doing when she caught her trying to break into our courtyard. Annie never said a peep about a physical altercation with her. She did say she'd talked to the police."

"Yeah," Autumn flipped her blonde locks over her shoulder and then sipped her Coke. "I don't think they saw me. I'm stealthy on my Segway."

"Unless you're getting thrown off," Mercedes joked.

"True." Autumn inhaled the last half of her hotdog, shoved a fry in next to the hotdog and chewed with chipmunk cheeks. "I'm getting better. You should get that pothole fixed Mrs. G."

Carlita grinned at the "Mrs. G" and nodded. "You're right Autumn. I definitely need to do that." A knock on the outside door interrupted the conversation.

"I'll get it. It's probably the cable guy." Mercedes bolted from the table and hurried to the door.

While Mercedes chatted with the technician, Autumn helped Carlita clear the table. "Thank you for lunch and for dinner tonight. I owe you two meals now." She downed the rest of her Coke and then tossed the empty can in the trash. "I make a mean peanut butter and jelly sandwich."

Carlita carried her half-empty Diet Coke to the kitchen. "That sounds horrid," she said. "Maybe I should give you some cooking lessons."

"I'd like that." Autumn glanced at her watch. "I better check in with Steve-O so he knows I survived my Segway spill with only minor injuries." She impulsively hugged Carlita and then skipped to the hall door. "See you later."

"Bye Autumn," Mercedes called out. "See you at six."

Carlita turned her attention to the task at hand – preparing the best stuffed shell dish possible. As she gathered her spices from the spice rack, she mulled over the possible suspects. All of the Savannah Architectural Society members were suspect, along with Bob Lowman, and both Steve and Autumn, although Carlita hated to add them to the list.

She also added Annie from the real estate office. The fact the woman hadn't mentioned a physical altercation with the deceased mere days before her death was suspect.

Finally, yet importantly, was Bob's construction crew, who may have had access to the vacant building. Perhaps Bob had placed the keys somewhere and one of his men had found them. Still, there had to be a motive.

What motive could one of the SAS members possibly have had? Had one of them set Norma Jean up, killed her and then attempted to frame an innocent business owner? The thought made Carlita's blood boil.

She had not moved hundreds of miles from home in an attempt to escape the criminal element just to be erroneously charged with the murder of a woman she had never met. Carlita slammed the spices on the counter so hard, she jumped.

The society had their share of enemies including Steve Winter. Had the members of the SAS harassed Steve and he became so fed up with them, he killed one of them in a fit of rage?

She would have to figure out a way to get close to one of the members, perhaps one on one. Carlita's best bet would be either Glenda Fox, the nice one, or Vicki Munroe, the chatterbox. She crossed Betty Graybill and Carol Weatherbee off the list.

After the pot of water began to boil, Carlita dumped the box of jumbo pasta shells in the water, added a few shakes of salt and waited for it to begin boiling again. She mixed the sauce ingredients and set them off to the side before she started browning the Italian ground turkey.

By the time the shells were al dente, Carlita removed them from the heat, drained them in a strainer and then ran cold water over the top to cool them.

While the shells cooled, Carlita mixed the spices, cheeses, eggs and garlic powder together. She spread a third of the spaghetti sauce in the bottom of the baking dish, stuffed the shells and placed them open side up, in the dish. The last step was to spread the remaining sauce on top and sprinkle more parmesan cheese, adding a little extra since Carlita loved gooey melted cheese.

She opened the oven door and a blast of heat along with the lingering odor of electrical hit her in the face. She wrinkled her nose. "New oven smell. Yuck." Carlita slid the dish inside the preheated oven, closed the oven door and set the timer.

The internet/cable technician was in the living room, installing cable boxes. He turned when he heard Carlita approach. "You got this place lookin' sharp." He nodded his head toward the hall that connected the other units. "Your daughter said you got other units in the building. You gonna fix 'em up and rent them out?"

"I...yes." Carlita nodded. "I have one – two units not yet spoken for." *Depending on whether or not Autumn or Vinnie decide to take them.*

"I'm lookin' for a place closer to downtown." The technician dropped the cable wire on top of Carlita's television, reached in his front pocket and pulled out a business card. "I might still be in the market, depending on when the unit will be available. This is my cell phone."

Carlita took the card and glanced at the front. *Bernie Feldman, Service Technician.*

"I'm guessing the units are the same size as this one, two bedrooms, one bath," Bernie said. "You know how much you're gonna charge for rent?"

"No. I haven't gotten that far yet," Carlita said. "I'll have to do a little research to figure out the going rate."

Bernie reached for the cable, shifted the box and stuck the end in before picking up the remote and turning the television on. An image appeared on the screen and he began clicking through the channels. "You're in business." He set the remote on top of the television. "I already hooked up the internet."

He nodded toward the small hall and the bedrooms in the back. "As soon as the internet was up, your daughter was on her laptop." Bernie shook his head. "Kids. Why back in the day, we didn't care about all these fancy contraptions. Give us some fresh air, bikes and a park and we were happy campers."

Carlita nodded. "True. Of course, we came from the city and you can't let your kids roam free." *Especially if their family is in the mafia,* she silently added.

Bernie picked up his clipboard and pen, scribbled on the front, ripped off the top sheet and handed it to Carlita. "I'll need to collect the hook up fee for today's visit."

"How much do I owe you?" Carlita headed to her bedroom where she'd left her purse.

"My usual charge is a hundred bucks, but I'm gonna give you a discount so it'll only be seventy five."

Carlita quickly wrote a check, tore it from the check register and carried it into the living room where Bernie was packing up his tools. "Thank you for the discount," she said sincerely. "I appreciate it."

"You're welcome. Don't forget to give me a call if you decide to rent out the units."

Having an electronics whiz for a neighbor would have its benefits. Carlita thanked him again and then held the door as she waited for him to leave. She closed the door behind him and then made her way to Mercedes's room where she lightly tapped on the door.

The door flew open and a startled Carlita took a step back.

"It's you."

"Of course it's me," Carlita said.

Mercedes swung the door open and waved her mother inside.

"It looks nice in here." Carlita admired the tidiness of the interior. She loved the exposed brick wall where Mercedes had placed her headboard. Her small desk filled one corner and one of the large five-drawer dressers the siblings had purchased earlier took up the other corner.

Carlita carefully inched her way to the bedroom window, lifted the blind and peeked out at the alley. "We don't have much of a view."

"Yeah," Mercedes gazed over her mother's shoulder. "Looking back, we should have taken the units overlooking the courtyard."

"I hadn't thought about that. We might want to move once one of the courtyard units has been renovated," Carlita said.

"But we'll give up the deck," Mercedes pointed out.

It was true. If they took one of the apartments across the hall, they would gain a courtyard view but lose the balcony. Carlita thought about Rambo.

"It's something to think about. We should hold off on a decision until we see how they turn out." Carlita turned her attention to Mercedes's laptop. "Any luck researching Norma Jean?"

"Whew." Mercedes blew air through thinned lips. "I wasn't able to find much out about the woman, but man, there is a boatload of info on the internet about the Savannah Architectural Society. Let's just say the group has a lot more enemies than friends."

Mercedes sat on the edge of her daughter's bed and crossed her ankles. "What have you found?"

"They have their noses in everyone's business. Business owners have filed numerous complaints, but the one with the most publicity happened about a year ago when SAS picketed in front of the Girl Scout's first headquarters because they weren't happy with the color of the shutter trim."

"What color was it?"

"They had painted it navy blue and the SAS wanted it painted black," Mercedes reported.

"Who won?"

"The shutters are black," her daughter answered. "Anyhoo, a bunch of business owners in the historic district banded together to oust the SAS leader, Betty Graybill. According to one of the articles I read, she was almost out the door until she hired Vicki Munroe as her second in command. Vicki is the Vice President of the Savannah Architectural Society."

"And Vicki is the mayor's sister." Carlita scratched the tip of her nose. "So we're stuck with these women."

"It would appear so, which leads me back to my main point. Any number of people could have done poor Norma Jean in," Mercedes said. "I say we pull one or two of the members aside to try to get the insider scoop on the society's inner-workings."

"That's what I was thinking and we should start with the nice one," Carlita said. "Glenda Fox."

The timer on the oven beeped a reminder that Carlita's stuffed shells needed attention. "I need to take the cover off the stuffed shells."

"You already made dinner?" Mercedes asked. "I thought we weren't eating until six."

"We aren't," Carlita said, "but I wanted to make it ahead of time. I can throw it back in the oven while the garlic bread bakes. In the meantime, I'm going to head down to the courtyard and work on sprucing the place up. Rambo is going to love it."

"I'll help." Mercedes swiveled in her chair. "I need to finish working on a couple things. I'll meet you in the courtyard in about half an hour."

Mercedes was a little more than halfway through working on the first draft of her secret novel, *Murder, Mayhem and the Mafia, A Mob Daughter's Confessions.*

Mercedes had always had a passion for writing and shortly before her father's sudden death, had started the novel. After his death, she had put the project on the back burner, preparing for the move to Savannah, but now that they were settling into their new home, she planned to begin working on it again.

She had started the project as a biography but had switched to fiction with all of the mystery and intrigue that had recently occurred. In other words, she had plenty of material to work with.

Mercedes's brothers alone could give her plenty of fiction fodder if she decided to write a sequel to the first book.

While Mercedes finished working on her computer, Carlita quickly changed into old paint splattered gardening clothes. Rambo was waiting for her by the door. The crazy dog somehow knew they were going somewhere.

"Are you ready to head to our yard?" Carlita asked as she patted his head.

She opened the door and let Rambo lead the way as they headed into the hall and down the stairs. Rambo tugged on his leash and darted into the front of the store where the workers were sanding the floors.

Carlita exited the building, rounded the corner and nearly collided with a man dressed in a pale blue button-down shirt and gray slacks. "Mrs. Garlucci?"

Carlita nodded. "Yes, that's me."

The man reached in his front pocket, pulled out a badge and flashed it in her face. "I'm Detective Wayne Polivich."

Chapter 14

Carlita shifted Rambo's leash from one hand to the other. "H-how can I help you?"

"I have a few questions I'd like to ask." Detective Polivich glanced at the construction workers just inside the store. "I wondered if there was somewhere we could talk privately."

She fleetingly thought about offering the detective a cup of coffee, but hoped he would make his visit brief so she opted for the courtyard instead. "I was on my way to the courtyard." Carlita didn't wait for a reply and began walking toward the entrance with Rambo trotting along beside her.

The detective followed behind and they walked in silence.

When they reached the courtyard gate, Carlita pulled the key from her pocket, inserted it in the lock and then twisted the key as she pushed on the heavy gate. "I think this will be my favorite part of the property once I clean it up," she said as she swung the gate open.

"Savannah is famous for their courtyards," the detective said as he looked around. "This one is bigger than it looks from the street." He shifted his gaze to Carlita. "Rumor has it you're tossing around the idea of opening a pawnshop instead of a grocery store."

Carlita closed the gate behind them and then unleashed Rambo so he could explore. "Yes and I can only guess where you heard that." She immediately thought of Betty Graybill.

Detective Polivich nodded. "I paid a visit to the SAS office this morning. They weren't particularly forthcoming about Norma Jean Cleaver. It appears she managed to ruffle a few feathers down at the society."

Carlita lifted a brow. "You don't say. Perhaps one of the members took out Ms. Cleaver."

"We're still in the early stages of the investigation. I'm here to ask a few questions, to find out if you recall any suspicious activity in the vicinity, odd occurrences or noticed unusual visitors."

"No," Carlita said. "As I told the officer yesterday, my family and I just arrived. We drove straight from New York to the property and that is when we found...Ms. Cleaver's body on the floor of the old restaurant."

She went on. "Actually Autumn Winter, the tattoo shop owner's sister, was the one who noticed the front door was ajar." Carlita didn't want to throw Autumn under the bus, but she was telling the truth. "She told me the door was unlocked and when we got to the property, we discovered not only was the door unlocked, but Ms. Cleaver was lying on the floor."

"Who had access to the property?" the detective asked.

"Bob Lowman, the construction supervisor, Steve Winter, the owner of Shades of Ink down the street," Carlita ticked off the list.

Detective Polivich interrupted. "Mr. Winter had a key?"

"Yes. We gave him a key over a month ago, during our first visit to the property," Carlita explained, although now that she thought about it, she wondered how wise she had been to give someone she had only known a couple days, access to the properties.

In her defense, there hadn't been much to steal or take. The property had been vacant and vagrants had broken in and taken up residence. It had seemed like a good idea at the time.

Carlita didn't want to believe Steve or Autumn were involved in Ms. Cleaver's death. She remembered her conversation with Annie Dowton, the real estate agent, and what Autumn had said. "Have you spoken with the owner of the real estate office across the street? She told me earlier she noticed Ms. Cleaver hanging around the area on several occasions, just days before her demise."

Detective Polivich nodded. "Yes, I've already spoken to Ms. Dowton."

She was about to mention the argument Autumn had told her about but kept silent. Technically, it was hearsay and it didn't mean Annie was the killer. In fact, the way the rest of the SAS members ran around threatening local business owners, Carlita probably would've done the same thing.

The detective asked a few more questions regarding the timeline of when Carlita and her children had arrived in town before thanking her for her time and exiting through the gate.

Carlita waited until he was out of sight before releasing the breath she'd been holding. It had gone well, at least she thought it had. Looking back, perhaps she should've mentioned the incident with the deceased and Annie Dowton.

Mercedes joined Carlita in the courtyard a short time later. Carlita began trimming trees and overgrown bushes while Mercedes pulled weeds and swept the cobblestone walkway.

When they finished, they began working on the fountain as they cleaned the debris from the pool, and wiped the dirt and grime from the figurine.

After the exterior was semi-clean, Mercedes crawled around back, near the statue's foot, where she found a switch to turn the water on. On the other side of the fountain, near the base was a power switch. Moments later, the vase the female figurine held began spewing water, which turned into a steady stream, cascading into the circular pool at the base.

Carlita clapped her hands as she watched the fountain begin to fill.

Rambo, who had been sitting at Carlita's feet, trotted to the edge of the circular base, stuck his head over the side and began lapping up the water.

"Rambo!" Carlita reached for his collar. The first spurts of water that poured out were rusty and not fit for consumption. "We need to scrub this first, then drain the dirty water and add fresh water."

She tugged gently on Rambo's ear. "Then you can drink it," she promised.

Mercedes shut off the water and pulled the drain plug before brushing her hands on the front of her shorts. "This is great. I can hardly wait to refurbish the bistro table, add some twinkling lights to the trees and other outdoor furniture so we can start entertaining."

Carlita had trimmed all of the overhead trees but left enough branches hanging so there were several shady spots, perfect for escaping the brutal summer heat, which was bearing down on them, even in the late afternoon.

Carlita wiped her sweaty forehead with the back of her arm. "I've had enough for today."

"Me too." Mercedes nodded. "We still have to clean up before dinner." The women wandered down the walk and exited the courtyard. Carlita pulled the gate shut, making sure it latched before they headed back inside the store.

Bob Lowman's crew was packing up for the day. They had finished stripping the thick layers of old varnish off the floors and one of the workers began sweeping up when Bob Lowman walked over. "Tomorrow we'll stain the floors. We still have some paint and other detail work to finish on the outside, but after that we'll be done with this project."

Carlita glanced around. "What happened to my son, Vinnie?"

"He helped out for a while and then mentioned something about having some errands to run. That was a couple hours ago."

He went on. "You decide where we're going from here boss?" he asked.

"I think I mentioned before moving back upstairs to work on the apartments. I may already have two tenants lined up."

Bob nodded. "Sounds good. They'll be quicker and cheaper to finish than the restaurant, plus you can get some quick cash flow."

Carlita and Mercedes said their good-byes and then headed upstairs.

Vinnie wasn't inside the apartment and Carlita stepped over to the slider, gazing out. His car was gone. "I wonder where he wandered off to," she mumbled.

"You want to shower first?" Mercedes was standing in the hall, towel in hand.

"No. You go first. I have a couple phone calls to make," Carlita told her.

Mercedes disappeared inside the bathroom, closing the door behind her while Carlita headed to her room. Her first call was Vinnie's cell phone and it went right to voice mail so she left him a message.

Her second call was to the Savannah Architectural Society where she left a message for Glenda Fox to call her back. Carlita's plan was to invite the woman over for tea the following day and perhaps glean a little information about Glenda's co-workers.

By the time Carlita downed a bottle of water, Mercedes had finished showering.

"All yours," Mercedes chirped merrily and then disappeared into her room.

Carlita stopped by her bedroom to grab a pair of khaki shorts and sleeveless blouse before heading to the bathroom.

The workers had removed the original claw foot tub and in its place was a spacious tiled shower with decorative trim and a frameless glass door for easy cleaning.

She stepped inside, turned the dial to full blast and adjusted the temperature to just shy of lukewarm. The cool water pelted Carlita's body and she reached for the shampoo bottle, squirting a generous glob in her hand before lathering her hair.

As she showered, Carlita pondered the predicament. Detective Polivich seemed both capable and thorough. Surely, he would discover Carlita and her children had nothing to do with Ms. Cleaver's death. They had never even met her.

Carlita rinsed the shampoo from her hair and picked up the bottle of lilac scented body wash, her favorite one.

Her thoughts turned to Steve and Autumn Winter. Despite the fact several clues pointed to them, Carlita was almost 100% certain they weren't the killers.

It could have been one of the construction workers, someone who "borrowed" Bob's key and then returned it with him not even realizing it had been missing.

Carlita finished rinsing, turned the shower off and reached for her towel. One thing was certain, someone was attempting to frame her and she vowed to do whatever she could to help find the real killer.

She quickly dressed and then headed back to the kitchen, glad that she had made the stuffed shells ahead of time since it was already after five. On her way to the kitchen, she spied her eldest, Vinnie, out on the deck, sitting in a chair.

He was facing the alley and Rambo was sprawled out next to him.

"Where did you get the furniture?" Carlita stuck her head out the open slider.

Vinnie shifted in his chair and grinned at his mother. "It's a housewarming gift. I picked it up at Paradise Pawn, a pawnshop over near the city market."

Carlita stepped out onto the deck and ran her hand over the top of a chaise lounge. "It looks brand new," she said. "Thank you." She impulsively leaned over and hugged her son. "How thoughtful." She straightened her back. "So what did you think?"

"About what?"

"About the competition, Paradise Pawn Shop," she said. "That's what you were doing, right?"

"Yeah," Vinnie admitted. "I was checkin' it out. Those guys are makin' a killing over there. I talked to one of the owners and he said they're the only game in town. Can you believe it?"

"So there's room for one more," Carlita said.

"Yeah." Vinnie shifted his gaze to the alley. "I need to go home and think about it. It sounds good while I'm here but I dunno."

Carlita knew her eldest son and she knew it was time to back off. She shrugged nonchalantly. "That's your decision. I can't force you to move here." She switched subjects. "I told Bob we'll be starting on the other

336

apartments since he's almost done downstairs. I might already have a couple of the units rented."

"You gonna rent one to Autumn?"

"Maybe. The cable guy seemed interested. It looks like we're in a hot rental market," Carlita said. "Now all I have to do is figure out how much we can get for each unit."

She remembered Annie, the real estate agent. Maybe she could help Carlita figure out how much they could charge per month and perhaps even help them with the rental agreements, for a fee.

"I'm going to check with Annie over at Riverfront Real Estate." Carlita glanced at her watch. "I better get dinner warmed up. Our guests will be arriving shortly."

She headed back inside, leaving Rambo and Vinnie on the deck.

Carlita worked alone in the kitchen while her daughter remained holed up in her room and Vinnie relaxed out on the deck. She knew he was deep in thought. At least he had choices. Even if he decided to stay in New York, the door would always be open for him, for all her children.

She switched the television on and turned up the volume to listen to local news. Carlita half-listened to the local weather report and had just popped the garlic bread into the oven when something the news anchor said caught her attention.

"Police have just made an arrest in connection with the murder of Savannah Architectural Society member, Norma Jean Cleaver."

Chapter 15

Carlita raced to the living room television set and watched as a uniformed police officer led Glenda Fox out the front door of the SAS office and to a police car parked out front. "Oh my gosh."

"Oh my gosh what?" Mercedes emerged from her room.

"The police arrested Glenda Fox for Norma Jean Cleaver's murder."

"Well, I guess we're off the hook. We don't have to talk to Glenda Fox and we don't have to worry about being charged with the murder," Mercedes said.

"But..." Carlita's head was spinning. She never would've pegged Glenda as the killer. She had seemed so sweet, so innocent. "I don't think she did it."

Vinnie overheard the commotion and made his way inside, picking up the tail end of the conversation. "It's not your problem Ma. You should be glad they're charging her and not you."

"True." Still, Carlita's gut told her it wasn't Glenda. "I don't think it was her." She left her children in the living room, high fiving over the police charging someone else and returned to the kitchen to finish dinner.

While the pasta warmed and the bread baked, Carlita mixed a salad. Steve and Autumn arrived at six o'clock on the dot, carrying a peach pie, the top dusted with a thin layer of confectioner's sugar and the promised jug of sweet tea.

Mercedes held the door, took the pie and sniffed the top. "Yummy. Come on in. You're just in time for the celebration."

Autumn reached down and patted Rambo's head. "What celebration?"

"The police arrested Glenda Fox, a member of SAS, and charged her with Norma Jean's murder."

Autumn blinked rapidly. "That's shocking. She was the last person I would've suspected."

"Which would make her the perfect killer," Vinnie pointed out.

Carlita headed to the dining area to finish setting the table while the others chatted about the new developments in the case. "Dinner is ready."

"This looks delicious." Steve eyed the dish of pasta hungrily. "I've been saving my appetite."

"Guests first," Carlita said as everyone settled into a chair.

Vinnie carried one of the new patio chairs to the table, squeezing in between his mother and sister.

Autumn spooned two large stuffed shells onto her plate and then passed the dish to her brother, who scooped three onto his. The dish made its rounds and ended at Carlita, who took only one pasta shell, scooped a spoon full of sauce on top and then reached for the garlic bread.

While they ate, the group discussed the case and murder charge. The others agreed it was cause for celebration, but not Carlita. She sensed a set up. Poor Glenda was not the killer. She wondered what evidence the police had obtained to charge Glenda and where they had gotten it.

After dinner, Carlita refilled everyone's iced tea glass, sliced the pie and they all headed to the deck to enjoy the cool evening air and the delicious dessert.

Carlita cut a piece off the end and popped it into her mouth, savoring the sweet and tart as the flaky piecrust melted in her mouth. She turned to Steve. "Did you make this?"

"Yep." Steve nodded.

"Liar. You did not," Autumn chuckled. "He bought it at the farmer's market this morning on his way to work."

"Farmer's market?" Carlita was all ears. She would love to visit a farmer's market.

Autumn explained that the market was open several mornings a week and told her where it was located.

After everyone finished their dessert, they carried their dirty dishes to the kitchen where Carlita rinsed them off and placed them in the dishwasher.

"I hate to eat and run, Mrs. G., but big brother won't let me ride my Segway alone after dark," Autumn said as she hugged Carlita, thanking her for a delicious dinner.

"I better make sure she's on her way. Thank you for the scrumptious dinner." Steve patted his stomach. "It was delicious."

Carlita walked them to the door, closing it behind them before joining her children out on the deck. "I never thought I would enjoy a deck overlooking an alley as much as I do." She sank into the chaise lounge, tipped her head back and closed her eyes.

She thought about Glenda, sitting in a dark, dank jail cell. "I think I'm going to visit Glenda tomorrow, if I can," she told her children when she lifted her head and opened her eyes. "Something isn't sitting right and Glenda isn't getting a fair shake."

Her children argued she should stay out of it and let the police handle the case but Carlita was determined to talk to the poor woman. They argued back and forth but Carlita wouldn't budge.

The first thing she was going to do when she got up the next morning was visit the Savannah-Burnham Police Department.

Chapter 16

Carlita tossed and turned all night, unsure of whether it was from being in a new place, from too much sugar or carbs or if it was the fact that she suspected an innocent woman was sitting in jail.

She woke early the next morning and crawled out of bed as the first rays of daylight peeked in through her bedroom window.

After brushing her teeth and splashing cold water on her face, she headed to the kitchen to brew a pot of coffee.

Rambo tromped to the front door, a reminder he needed to go out.

"I forgot all about you," Carlita groaned and then darted to her bedroom to grab her bathrobe.

They made their way out the back door, down the alley and to a grassy patch Rambo and Carlita had stumbled upon the previous day.

Rambo inspected the overgrown weeds, sniffed some discarded trash and finally took care of business. Carlita picked up the trash and led him back inside. "I'll take you to the park again later today," she promised as she opened the apartment door.

The coffee had finished brewing. Carlita poured a cup and headed to the deck to savor her first cup as she mulled over the recent events.

Vinnie had hinted he would be leaving that day and Carlita had told him they would miss him after he was gone.

She glanced through the open slider at her son, still fast asleep on the sleeper sofa. It would be sad to see him go but maybe he would be back. She hoped so. She also hoped he would bring his younger brother, Tony, with him.

Carlita knew her youngest son, Paulie, would never move from Clifton Falls, New York. Paulie was mayor of Clifton Falls. He and his wife, Gina, and their three children lived a quiet, suburban life in the charming town. Carlita didn't worry about him nearly as much as she did her other two sons.

While Paulie was not a part of "the family," Vinnie and Tony were the exact opposite. Mafia was everything.

Carlita hoped Vinnie could see there was life beyond Queens, that he could live in Savannah and not feel as if he was "missing out" on something.

Vinnie stirred as Carlita tiptoed through the living room to her bedroom to dress. It was still early, too early to make a trip to the Savannah-Burnham Police Department.

She was restless. Not wanting to wake Vinnie since he had a long drive ahead of him, she decided to take a closer look at the other apartment units, her new project. Carlita wondered how long she should wait before moving forward with the store plans.

When she reached the unit across the hall, Carlita flipped the light switch, casting long shadows into the dark corners. She stepped over to the window and gazed down at the courtyard. It looked so much nicer since Mercedes and she had cleaned it up.

A sudden movement caught Carlita's eye and she shifted her gaze. The lights inside the real estate office across the street were on.

Carlita gazed at her watch: 7:20 a.m. She wondered if Annie was at work already and then glanced at Rambo, who stood next to her, staring out the window. "Do you want to visit Annie?"

Rambo turned in a circle. Carlita took that for a yes so they hurried from the apartment and headed downstairs and out the back door.

As they passed the large picture window and the gold lettered sign that read "Riverfront Real Estate," she caught a glimpse of a dark head bent over a desk. It was Annie.

Carlita lightly tapped on the door and Annie's head shot up, an unreadable expression on her face until she recognized Carlita and strode to the door to unlock it. "Good morning Mrs. Garlucci." She patted Rambo's head. "Good morning to you. I can't remember his name."

"Rambo," Carlita said. "I'm sorry to bother you, but I saw the light on and wanted to stop by to ask you a quick question."

"Sure." Annie waved her inside and then closed the door, locking it behind them.

"It's still early," Annie explained as she clicked the lock. "Don't want someone wandering in and catching us off guard."

"Like me," Carlita joked.

"Nah." Annie waved a hand. "Have a seat."

Carlita settled in a nearby chair and Rambo sniffed the chair before plopping down next to her. "I've decided to have the construction crew work on the upstairs apartments to get them rent ready. I was hoping you could help with the rental process. I don't need tenants," she explained. "I think I may already have them rented."

Annie picked up a pen and began tapping it lightly on the desktop. "You're in a great area. What would you like me to do?"

"There are a couple things." Carlita shifted in her chair. "I need to figure out how much rent per month I could get on a two bedroom, one bath unit and I also need help with rental agreements."

Annie nodded. "I think they could easily rent for over a thousand. Let's take a look." She turned her attention to her laptop as she lifted the lid. She tapped the keys, clicked the mouse and then slowly nodded. "Ah. Well, a two bedroom, one bath remodeled loft apartment." She turned to Carlita, peering at her over the rim of her thick glasses. "Is it a loft?"

Carlita grinned. "When I tear the ceiling out it will be."

"You should easily be able to rent a unit out for around $1,100 - $1,300 per month, maybe even close to $1,500 per month."

Carlita's pulse raced. If Annie's calculations were correct, the apartments had the potential to bring in over four thousand dollars a month. Unless, of course, Vinnie moved into one of the units, then she might be able to squeeze out $3,000. Still, it was a nice chunk of change. "That's great news. I'll let you know when I get closer to having them rent ready so you can help me with the agreements, for a fee, of course."

"Sounds good. I appreciate the business." Annie stood.

Carlita, taking her cue, stood. "I guess I'll have to figure out the parking."

"Isn't there a small, open area out back?" Annie asked.

Annie was talking about the grassy area Rambo was using for potty breaks. "Yes. I guess we could clean it up and pave it."

Annie walked Carlita to the door. "Tenants will need parking. Of course there is street parking, but the apartment would be more appealing to potential tenants if there were designated parking spots."

Carlita nodded, her head swimming. She was on information overload. These were all things she'd never had to worry about. Still, the thought of money coming in was great news and something Mercedes and she could use.

After leaving the real estate office, Rambo and Carlita stopped by the courtyard but didn't go in since she hadn't brought the key with her. They continued past the store where several workers were inside, staining the store's freshly sanded floors.

They made their way to the rear entrance and up the steps to the apartment. Vinnie was awake and packing his suitcase.

"Leaving already?"

Vinnie paused, shirt in hand. "Yeah. I gotta hit the road. I've got a long drive ahead of me."

"Thanks for following us down here, Vinnie," Carlita said as she settled onto the edge of a nearby chair. "You were a big help."

"You're welcome." With the last of his clothes packed, Vinnie dropped the lid on the suitcase and zipped the side. "I feel better now that I've seen the place. You and Mercedes will be fine." He nodded toward the door. "Where'd you sneak off to so early?"

"Riverfront Real Estate," Carlita said. "The agent, Annie, gave me a ballpark figure on what I could rent the units for once they're fixed up. She said I could get $1,200 to $1,500 per month for each unit."

"That's great Ma."

Carlita nodded. "I think so too. Even if you take one unit, we'll still have well over two thousand a month coming in," she hinted.

"Ma," Vinnie warned and Carlita held up a hand. "I know, I know."

She stood as Vinnie headed toward the door. "I noticed the lights on over there when I took a walk last night."

"A smoke break?" she asked. Vinnie was an occasional smoker, something Carlita didn't agree with, but couldn't stop her adult son from doing.

"Yeah. Anyways. The lights were on. Had to be after eleven."

Warning bells went off in Carlita's head. Annie had been in her office after eleven and then returned early the next morning? Perhaps she had spent the night. Was that how Annie had known Norma Jean Cleaver was hanging around? She remembered how Autumn had told her that Norma Jean and Annie had been fighting in front of the courtyard.

"Tell Mercedes I said good-bye and to behave herself." Vinnie gave his mother a hug, kissed her cheek and then patted Rambo's head.

"I will. Be careful. Call me later." Carlita held the door as Vinnie pulled his suitcase over the threshold. She swallowed the lump in her throat as she watched her son descend the steps and disappear from sight.

It was hard not knowing when she would see him again. She was tempted to dart over to the slider and onto the deck overlooking the alley, but she couldn't bear to watch him drive off.

Instead, she headed to the kitchen to warm a cup of coffee and munch on a piece of the peach pie Steve had left behind. Sweets soothed Carlita's nerves and she warmed the piece in the microwave before heading to the deck.

By the time she slipped out onto the deck with her coffee and pie, Vinnie - and his car - were gone.

Chapter 17

At eight a.m. on the dot, Carlita dialed the number on the card Detective Polivich had given her.

"Detective Wayne Polivich speaking."

"Hello officer, I mean Detective Polivich. This is Carlita Garlucci. I...heard on the news last night you made an arrest in the death of Norma Jean Cleaver."

"Yes. Glenda Fox, one of Ms. Cleaver's co-workers at SAS, has been charged," he confirmed.

"I...I don't think it was her," Carlita blurted out.

There was a brief silence on the other end before Detective Polivich spoke. "Why do you say that, Mrs. Garlucci? Do you have evidence pointing to someone else?"

"No. I don't. It's just that she doesn't seem like the killing kind."

Carlita could hear the strain in the detective's voice as he answered. "Mrs. Garlucci, I appreciate your concern, but a hunch is not evidence. Some of the worst criminals ever apprehended have been someone's neighbor down the street or the girl next door. Appearances can be deceiving."

Carlita couldn't argue with that. In fact, she'd seen it many times living in Queens with her shylock / mafia husband. Looks could be deceiving, but Carlita's gut told her something wasn't right. She changed tactics. "Is Ms. Fox being held at a local jail?"

"Yes. She has a hearing at ten o'clock and we expect her bond, if there is one, will be paid, making her a free woman, for the time being."

"What kind of bond?" Carlita was curious.

"I'm guessing, with this particular judge and the severity of the crime, it will be right around a million dollars," the detective replied.

"A million dollars!" Carlita gasped. "Glenda Fox has a million bucks sitting around?"

The detective explained only a percentage of the bond would need to be paid, but even that would be a hefty chunk of change, which only deepened the mystery surrounding Glenda Fox.

"Thank you, Detective Polivich. I appreciate your time," Carlita said.

Before the detective hung up, he left Carlita with a word of warning. "I would stay out of this if I were you, Mrs. Garlucci. You'll only end up making more enemies."

Carlita thanked the detective for taking her call and disconnected the line, staring at the phone in her hand. Had Detective Polivich just threatened her?

"You can't save the world Ma." Mercedes was standing in the hall, leaning against the doorway. "We already have enough on our plate."

Mercedes was right. They did have their hands full, but something was nagging Carlita. "Glenda Fox is loaded. Detective Polivich didn't come out and say that but who could afford to post a million dollar bond if they didn't have some serious cash?"

"Can I borrow your computer?" she asked her daughter.

"Of course, but I think we need to get you your own," Mercedes said.

Carlita started to argue, but knew her daughter was right. She had always fought modern day technology but she was warming to the idea of getting a laptop. It would come in handy to research stuff on her own, find new recipes when she opened her restaurant, and possibly research goods for the pawnshop.

Mercedes had convinced her not to install a home phone and instead, had taught her mother all the ins and outs of her cell phone. Carlita was surprised she hadn't even missed the home phone and it was nice not having the extra payment.

"I heard Vinnie leave." Mercedes lifted both hands over her head and arched her back. "I was up early and thought about coming out but I'm not fond of good-byes."

"Me either. It was sad," Carlita said.

Mercedes moseyed to the kitchen where she poured coffee in a clean mug and then warmed it in the microwave before following her mother to her room.

"I want to pay another visit to SAS and then maybe to Glenda Fox," Carlita said as she settled in front of her daughter's computer. "Do you want to go with me?"

Mercedes started to shake her head, but changed her mind when she saw the look on her mother's face. Carlita was looking for trouble and Mercedes was determined to make sure she didn't find it. "Of course. I'll go get ready."

While Mercedes headed to the bathroom, Carlita began researching Glenda Fox's name. She typed in "Glenda Fox, Savannah, Georgia" and several search results popped up on the screen.

Carlita read with interest that Glenda was the daughter of a wealthy real estate developer. She had married one of her father's investment partners, Mark Fox, a wealthy man in his own right.

Glenda and her husband, Mark, had never had children, instead choosing to focus their energy on preserving historic Savannah. Glenda had been added to the staff at SAS as an unpaid volunteer three years ago.

It was apparent the writer did not care for Glenda and Mark Fox, and his view slanted as he alluded to the fact the only reason Savannah Architectural Society accepted Glenda as a member was for her money and possible connections.

The article also suggested the only reason she'd applied for the position was so that her husband and father would have an inside track on what was happening in not only historic Savannah, but the entire county.

One of the articles showed a picture of a younger Glenda, although she was easily recognizable with her dainty pixie features, enormous green eyes and dark hair swept off to the side. She didn't strike Carlita as a killer.

Neither did Annie. Carlita remembered how Vinnie had mentioned the fact the lights at the real estate office had been burning late into the night.

Carlita opened a new screen and typed in "Riverfront Real Estate, Savannah, Georgia."

357

She clicked on the first article and read how Annie Dowton had opened the office several years ago. She had several agents working under her, including someone by the name of Lillian Cleaver.

Carlita wasn't able to find much more than that. She hopped out of the chair and began to pace back and forth. "You'll wear the varnish off my floor," Mercedes joked as she stepped into her room.

"I'm beginning to wonder about Annie Dowton, the real estate agent across the street." She reminded Mercedes how Autumn had said she spotted Norma Jean and Annie fighting in front of the courtyard.

Carlita told her daughter how Vinnie had mentioned the lights were burning bright last night and then again early this morning at the real estate office. "Last, but not least, she has an employee by the name of Lillian Cleaver. I'm wondering if this Lillian was somehow related to Norma Jean."

"Maybe you should tell the police," Mercedes said as she reached inside her closet and grabbed a pair of sandals.

"I already talked to Detective Polivich this morning and he warned me to mind my own business, that I already had enough enemies."

"What does that mean - you already have enough enemies?" Mercedes asked. "Is he talking about the SAS? They're enemies with most of the business owners in Savannah."

Carlita strode into the hall. "I'm marching right over to Riverfront Real Estate and get to the bottom of this. I think someone is framing poor Glenda, maybe even Annie, but either way, someone knows something."

"Wait for me!" Mercedes snatched her purse off her dresser and chased after her mother, who was already opening the front door. "You can't storm in there, accusing people of murder," her daughter reasoned.

Carlita paused and Mercedes pressed on. "We need a plan. Maybe set some sort of trap to get a confession out of the killer."

"A red herring," Mercedes said, warming to the idea. "Remember how we set a trap back at the old house, to catch the perp who kept breaking in?"

"Which was a major fail," Carlita pointed out. "Your sharp ear and attention to detail is what brought the thug down."

"True," Mercedes said. "But there has to be a way." She snapped her fingers. "What about the television footage from the other morning? Most criminals return to the scene of the crime. Now that we know some of the suspects, maybe we'll catch a glimpse of them on the tape."

"Great idea."

Mercedes returned to her room, slid into her computer chair and lifted the lid on her laptop. She searched her files and when she got to the one labeled, "News footage of Ma," she double clicked on the file and the video screen popped up. Mercedes hit the play button and mother and daughter leaned in to study the small screen.

For the most part, no one looked familiar, except for a shot of Betty Graybill, who had arrived that morning to talk to Carlita regarding her building plans and discovered one of her staff had been murdered.

There was another person who kept hovering in the background. It was a bald-headed man. Carlita jabbed her finger on the computer screen. "That man. He's acting odd."

Chapter 18

Mercedes paused the video and they studied the image. "There were a lot of people hanging around that morning, but I have to admit he's acting kinda sketchy."

"You don't think..."

"Wait a minute," Mercedes interrupted. "Didn't someone tell us Norma Jean had kicked her boyfriend to the curb? You don't suppose that was him – and that he killed Norma Jean and then returned to the scene of the crime."

"His name is on the tip of my tongue." Carlita snapped her fingers. "Harold something."

"Harold could be anything," Mercedes groaned. "Autumn is working down at the newspaper today. Maybe she has a connection, someone tight with the Savannah PD who can track down the ex's last name."

Mercedes pulled her phone from her back pocket, switched it on and tapped the screen as she typed a text message. She hit send and then shoved her phone back inside her pocket. "We'll see if Autumn can help us out."

The women finished watching the news clip, replayed it a second time and both agreed the man in the background appeared agitated as he paced back and forth behind the camera crew.

Autumn texted back moments later, telling Mercedes she was on it.

Knock. Knock.

"That must be Bob." Carlita hurried to the door, peeked through the peephole and then flung the door open.

"My guys are finishing the last section of floor."

"Great." Carlita said. "Let's take a look at the other apartment units."

Bob, Carlita and Rambo inspected each of the apartments as they discussed renovations. They decided to gut the apartments, making them exactly like Carlita and Mercedes's apartment.

Mercedes was still in her room when Carlita walked back inside the apartment. She hovered in the doorway. "Rambo and I are going to take a walk around the riverfront park if you'd like to join us."

"No...yes." Mercedes closed the lid on her computer and hopped out of the chair. "I can take care of this later."

Although it was hot outside, there was only a hint of humidity as they headed down the sidewalk, across the major intersection and to the park on the other side.

It was getting close to lunchtime and Carlita's stomach growled as they passed by several gift shops and restaurants. They stopped in front of a tavern and grill to peruse the menu on the outside wall. "Those deli sandwiches look delish," Mercedes said.

"They have outdoor seating." Carlita glanced around. "We deserve a treat. Let's have lunch."

Carlita settled on the *Smokin' Georgia Brown,* smoked turkey and ham on Texas toast. The description included not only hickory-smoked ham and smoked turkey, but also a layer of melted cheddar cheese, tomatoes and strips of smoked bacon.

"We better order a hamburger, plain and no bun for Rambo," Carlita told her daughter before she disappeared inside the restaurant to place their order.

Carlita eased into an empty chair to people watch. It was turning out to be another glorious day as rays of sunshine danced off the Savannah River.

A paddleboat drifted by and the occupants standing on the decks waved to the people walking along the riverfront. "That looks like fun," she told Rambo.

There was so much of Savannah they hadn't even explored, it would take years to see it all.

Mercedes returned a short time later, carrying a paper bag and two large soft drinks. "The place was packed but the inside smells heavenly."

She placed the bag of food on the table and slid the drinks next to it. "If this food tastes half as good as it smells, we're going to have a new favorite restaurant."

Carlita peered into the bag and pulled out the first container. It was her open-faced sandwich. Next to her sandwich and centered on top of a thick pile of fries was Rambo's hamburger. She tore off the top half of her food container, broke the hamburger into bite size pieces and placed the container next to her chair where Rambo promptly gobbled his snack.

She turned her attention to the sandwich and the aroma of smoked meat made her mouth water. Carlita lifted the first half of her sandwich and took a big bite as melted cheese dripped down her chin.

The combination of smoky turkey, salty ham and crisp bacon was scrumptious. She quickly ate the first half before tearing off a piece of ham and turkey to share with Rambo, who begged for more.

The fries were tasty but Carlita secretly thought the ones they had gotten from Colby's were slightly tastier. "This food is so good."

"I agree." Mercedes had chosen a grilled Mahi sandwich and declared it one of the best fish sandwiches she'd ever tasted. "I almost forgot. Autumn was able to get the last name of that Harold guy. His name is Harold Stetson."

"Stetson, Stetson." Carlita repeated it several times. "Yeah. That's the one. So he was Norma Jean's ex-boyfriend."

"Returning to the scene of the crime if I had to guess, although we can't be certain that was him," Mercedes pointed out as she reached for her soda. "Motive and opportunity. He was a spurned lover who followed Norma Jean to an empty building and strangled her, knowing no one was around and then tried to frame us."

Carlita jabbed her straw into her drink and sipped. It was possible, but how angry was this Harold at Norma Jean for tossing him out? Was he angry enough to kill her?

Why their place? Why not somewhere else? Something wasn't adding up.

"I would still like to pay a visit to SAS and talk to Glenda Fox." Carlita finished her last bite of food and placed the empty container in the bag before picking up Rambo's empty container and placing it on top.

"If you don't want to go, I understand," she told her daughter.

"Oh, I'm going, too." Mercedes picked up the bag and tossed it in the nearby trashcan. "I say we start with Glenda Fox."

"Me too." Carlita nodded. "Let's stop back at the house. Maybe you can get on your handy dandy computer and find out if she's been released from jail and if so, where she lives."

***

It didn't take long for Mercedes to track down Glenda's home address using a combination of the property appraiser's website and a search of Savannah's white pages.

Carlita peered over her daughter's shoulder and watched in amazement. "I had no idea you could find that kind of information on the internet. Maybe you should get into the private investigator business."

"It's fun," Mercedes admitted. "Yup. Here we go."

Glenda and her husband, Mark, lived not far from downtown, on the edge of the riverfront district, but at the exact opposite end of Carlita's properties.

"We can walk there," Carlita suggested as she headed out of Mercedes's bedroom.

"What are we going to say?" Mercedes followed her mother from the room. "We don't think you killed your co-worker? What can we do to help?"

"It's a start." Carlita shrugged. She wasn't sure what she would say to Glenda or if Glenda would even talk to them. There was a chance she would slam the door in their face, if she were even home.

The quickest way across town was to take the main road, which ran along the riverfront. According to the directions Mercedes had mapped out on her phone, when they reached the other end, Glenda's street would be right around the corner.

The humidity was starting to kick in and Carlita was glad they had left Rambo at home in the air-conditioned apartment. As they walked, the women chatted excitedly about the property's rental potential.

They also discussed the odds of Vinnie returning to open a pawnshop, each giving it a 50/50 chance. "I think he's interested in Autumn," Mercedes said. "He was giving her googly eyes."

Carlita had detected a hint of something, too. "I think you're right."

"You shoulda seen how he hovered over her at the clinic while we waited for them to call Autumn back to check out her pinky. You would've thought she was incapacitated the way he was waiting on her, bringing her a soda, trying to do everything for her." Mercedes rolled her eyes.

The women abruptly stopped in front of a square, brick four-story home. Several rows of tall windows lined the front and curved steps on both sides of the entrance flowed down to the sidewalk. At the very top of the building were three compact dormer windows and on each side of the windows, tall chimney stacks.

"This is quite the place." Carlita shaded her eyes and lifted her gaze.

"I've been checking out some of the historic homes online," Mercedes said. "This one is a Federal-style home, built in the early to mid-1800's I'm guessing." She pointed at the two sets of curved steps, leading to the front door. "See the double steps? Back in the day, women wore only dresses and to avoid scandal, the women would use one staircase and men the other. If a man were to catch a glimpse of an unmarried woman's bare skin, even her ankle, it was considered scandalous."

"Interesting," Carlita said. "We should take one of those historic tours to learn more about Savannah's fascinating history."

Mercedes nodded. "That's what I was thinking. I say we take one of those trolley tours we noticed last time we were here."

The women made their way up the steps on the left hand side and Mercedes grasped the large round iron knocker in the center of the massive wooden door. "Here goes nothing."

Chapter 19

The front door of Glenda Fox's stately home opened abruptly and a gray haired man wearing a black suit coat appeared in the doorway. Underneath the black jacket was a crisp, white button down shirt, covered by a gray vest and matching gray tie.

He stood ramrod straight and gazed down his nose. "May I help you?" He spoke in a clipped tone with a hint of a British accent.

"Yes. Uh. We were wondering if Glenda Fox is available," Mercedes said.

His eyes narrowed. "Ms. Fox is *not* available. Would you care to leave a message?"

"Yes, uh, please tell her Carlita Garlucci stopped by. I wanted to discuss..." Carlita's voice trailed off.

"Her current predicament," Mercedes piped up. "We think we may have some information regarding her unfortunate quandary."

"I'll pass your message along."

"Thank you..." Carlita was hoping for a name to put with the stuffy man.

"Reginald. Higgins."

"Thank you Reginald." The door shut as abruptly as it had opened and Mercedes began to giggle. "Reginald Higgins," she mimicked in a deep gravelly voice.

They hurried down the steps and Carlita glanced back at the magnificent estate. "I can't imagine having a butler."

"I can," Mercedes said. "He could fix us afternoon tea, make those fancy finger sandwiches." She tapped her mother's arm. "We need an invite to this place. I would love to see the inside."

Carlita would, too, wondering if the interior was half as impressive as the exterior.

At the end of the block, they stopped and stared across the street at the Savannah River. "Now what?"

"We could stop by the SAS to see if we can get a feel for the other society members' take on Glenda's arrest," Carlita said.

They were only roughly two blocks from the Architectural Society's headquarters, if you could even call the small structure that.

"Let's go." Mercedes motioned them forward and they picked up the pace as they walked to 155 Stalwart Street.

When they reached the narrow building, Carlita grasped the doorknob and sucked in a breath. "This should be interesting." They stepped inside the front door and the overhead bell tinkled, announcing their presence.

Carol Weatherbee emerged from the back. She frowned when she spotted mother and daughter. "You two again. I thought you'd leave well enough alone now that you managed to get Glenda arrested and charged for Norma Jean's murder," she spat out, fire in her eyes.

"I managed?" Carlita splayed an open palm against her throat. "I did no such thing," she said stiffly. "If you and your band of merry troublemakers would mind your own business, perhaps you would have a few more friends and a lot less enemies."

"What's going on out here?" Betty Graybill followed Carol out of the back room and stopped abruptly behind Carol as she glared at Carlita.

Betty sidestepped her co-worker and wagged her index finger at Carlita and Mercedes. "If I didn't know better, I would think that you two are looking for trouble. First, you murder one of our society members, plant clues so it looks as if poor Glenda was the killer and now you have the nerve to show your faces here."

"Calling yourself a grieving widow, who is trying to start over again my foot," Betty screeched. "More like black widow. I have half a mind to hire a private investigator to check you out," she threatened.

A cold chill ran down Carlita's spine. The last thing she needed was to have someone start digging up dirt on her poor Vinnie, not to mention her sons.

"I came by to tell you how sorry I was that police arrested Glenda," Carlita whispered, "but I guess I should have saved the trip." She inched backward and reached for the door handle. "I am sorry," she said before opening the door and stepping onto the sidewalk.

"You two are a couple of witches!" Mercedes yelled before following her mother out onto the sidewalk and slamming the door behind them. "I have half a mind to write them into my book as crazed killers," she muttered.

"Huh?" Carlita had only half-listened, her ears still ringing from the accusations she had killed her husband. What kind of cruel person would say something like that?

Mother and daughter silently walked back to the apartment. Carlita was shocked someone would say such a thing, and Mercedes?

Mercedes was fuming, silently concocting a plan to get even with Carol Weatherbee and Betty Graybill.

When they reached the apartment, Carlita warmed some leftover coffee in the microwave and sank into a dining room chair.

Mercedes's heart broke as she watched her mother's shoulders droop. She knew the callous words Betty Graybill spoke had hurt her.

Carlita ran her finger around the rim of her coffee cup. "I think Rambo and I will head down to the courtyard to start working on that old rusty bistro table."

"That's a great idea Mom. Don't worry about the nasty old sourpuss. She'll get hers." *If I can help it,* Mercedes silently added.

Mercedes needed a partner in crime and Autumn was the first person who came to mind. "I think I'll run over to the Savannah Evening News to check it out."

She whipped her cell phone from her back pocket, clicked the message icon and tapped out a message to Autumn. She hit send and seconds later, Autumn replied she would be at work for a couple more hours.

She shoved the phone back in her pocket. "We should take that trolley tour we've been talking about. Why don't we go tomorrow?"

"That sounds lovely." Carlita sipped her coffee and studied her daughter over the rim.

Carlita stared sightlessly out the slider then abruptly stood. "Time to get to work." She downed the last of the coffee, rinsed the cup and placed it inside the dishwasher. "Tell Autumn hello for me."

Rambo and Carlita headed out first. Mercedes followed them down the steps. She watched as her mother and mutt headed to the courtyard, vowing to pay Betty Graybill back if it was the last thing she did.

***

Mercedes stepped inside the front door of the Savannah Evening News and gazed around. The loud hum of voices echoed over the wall partitions that hid the entire back section of the vast space.

She wrinkled her nose at the smell of fresh ink permeating the air. Off to the right was a small desk and a thin, dark-haired woman sitting behind it eyed her curiously. She made her way to the desk. "I'm looking for Autumn Winter."

"You must be Mercedes. Autumn called up here to tell me you were coming." The woman pushed her chair back and stood. "Right this way."

Mercedes followed the woman as they zigzagged around a maze of cubbies and down a short hall before heading to a back corner where Autumn was sitting in a swivel chair, her feet propped up on the desk.

"Hard at work, I see," Mercedes teased.

Autumn swung her feet off the desk and whirled around. "I do my best thinking when I'm 'in the zone.'"

"I'll leave you two." The woman who had led Mercedes to Autumn's cubicle disappeared while Autumn waved her to a nearby chair. "To what do I owe this great honor?" she joked. "I'm guessing it has something to do with SAS and Norma Jean Cleaver."

"I need help." Mercedes explained her mother was adamant that Glenda Fox had not murdered Norma Jean Cleaver and how mother and daughter had gone to Glenda's home to try to speak with her.

Autumn interrupted. "I have to admit I'm just as surprised. Glenda and her husband, Mark, are pillars of Savannah society. I've never heard anything negative about either one."

"Really?" Mercedes asked.

"Yep." Autumn scooched in and began tapping on her computer keyboard. "I already did some research. I mean, think about it. What possible reason could a woman like Glenda Fox have for killing Norma Jean? It doesn't make sense."

"That's what Ma said," Mercedes nodded, "Which was why she wanted to talk to Glenda, but she wasn't home."

"You saw the Fox house? Swank-ee," Autumn let out a low whistle. "They've even got a 'but-lah,'" she added a fake British accent.

"It's a cool house, for sure. I would love to see the inside. Anyway, back to the story. So after we found out Glenda either wasn't home or wasn't taking visitors, we decided to stop by the Savannah Architectural Society office to chat with the other women."

Autumn blew air through thinned lips. "I can see what's coming. It didn't end well," she guessed.

"You could say that." Mercedes ran her hand through her long, dark locks. "Betty Graybill all but accused Mom of being a black widow, killing her husband, then killing Norma Jean and setting up Glenda Fox. She even threatened to hire a private investigator to dig into our backgrounds," Mercedes said.

"So?" Autumn shrugged. "It's not like you have anything to hide."

Mercedes frowned and gave her head a slight shake.

Autumn's eyes widened. "You do have something to hide." She slapped an open palm on the desk. "I knew it! Are you on the lam? Did you break out of prison?" Autumn snapped her fingers. "Maybe you're running from the mob. I hear they're huge up in New York."

Mercedes quickly changed the subject. Autumn was getting too close for comfort. "I'm convinced my mother is right and Glenda was framed. I want to find the real killer, but I need some help."

"I'm in!" Autumn screeched, then looked around and lowered her voice. "We need to jot down a list of suspects and then work on a process of elimination."

"Motive and opportunity," Mercedes said. "We have to focus on motive and opportunity."

Autumn opened the drawer in front of her, pulled out a yellow pad and an ink pen. "I've been thinking about this myself. I have a few suspects. First on the list would be every member of SAS."

She jotted down Betty Graybill, Carol Weatherbee and Vicki Munroe, although she thought both of them were the least likely, seeing how her brother was the mayor of Savannah. Next, they added Annie after Mercedes told Autumn what her mother had said about her hanging

378

around her real estate office day and night. They also added Bob Lowman and his crew because they had access to the building where Norma Jean's body was found.

Autumn chewed her lower lip. "I-I guess Steve and I would be suspects, too. Steve has a key to the property and I was the one who told you the door was unlocked." She lifted both eyebrows. "I swear I didn't do it."

Mercedes held up a hand. "If I thought you were guilty, I wouldn't be sitting here right now," she pointed out.

"True." Autumn clicked the button on the end of the pen. "Can you think of anyone else?'

Mercedes tilted her head and stared at the list, studying the names. "As a matter of fact, there is one more."

Autumn jotted down the name and nodded. "We should start with this one." She pointed to the last name on the list.

Chapter 20

Mercedes stared at the Segway and shook her head. "I dunno about this, Autumn. This looks like an accident waiting to happen." She gazed at her friend's pinky, still in the splint. "What if I crash it?"

"Don't worry." Autumn waved a hand. "My buddy over at Savannah Segway, the one who loaned this baby to me, said it's nearly indestructible." She pointed at her own, the one that had been involved in the recent pothole crash. "Remember the tumble I took on mine? There's not a single scratch on it."

"Just put the helmet on and we'll do a test run around the block." Autumn held out a helmet.

Mercedes frowned at the contraption. It looked dangerous, tippy for lack of a better word. "I'm going to regret this," she predicted as she reluctantly slid the helmet on top of her head before lifting her chin and clipping the buckle. She tugged gently to make sure it was secure.

"Watch closely." Autumn hopped on the borrowed Segway, balancing in the center and then gripped the handles. "All you have to do is tilt forward to move forward, tilt back to move backward and stand upright to stop it."

Mercedes watched Autumn demonstrate the Segway's capabilities. She made it look easy but her friend still wasn't convinced.

Autumn sped to the end of the alley, looped around in a circle and then returned. She stopped abruptly in front of Mercedes. "See? Easy peasy."

The young blonde hopped off, still gripping the handle. "Now you try. Don't lean too far forward because that will make the Segway go faster. Start slow with a slight forward tilt."

"If I break something, you're taking me to the emergency room," Mercedes warned as she reluctantly mounted the Segway and reached for the handles.

Autumn released her grip and took a step back. "Remember, slight tilt forward."

Mercedes studied the handle grips. "Where's the brake?"

"There is no brake. All you have to do is pull the handle straight up to make it stop."

"What if someone darts into my path and I have to make a sudden stop?" Mercedes asked.

"There is no brake," Autumn repeated. "It's one of the Segway flaws. That's what happened when your mother jumped into my path and I mowed her down."

The more Mercedes knew, the less she wanted to try the Segway and started to step off. "This..."

"Uh. Uh." Autumn pressed the small of her friend's back. "You need the Segway for our investigation, remember?"

Mercedes and Autumn had planned a covert spy mission for later that evening with Autumn narrowing down the target's whereabouts. It was on the other side of town and the only access to the location was along a small, narrow alley located behind the property.

Autumn had convinced Mercedes the Segways were the only viable means of transportation and had assured her friend she would love it once she gave it a chance.

"All right. Here goes nothing." Mercedes tilted the handle forward slightly and the Segway abruptly lurched, causing her foot to slip. "Whoa!"

"No worries. I've got you on turtle mode." Autumn studied Mercedes's posture. "You gotta balance," she patiently explained. "Center your body, feet slightly apart and keep your eye on the road."

Mercedes tried again as she eased the bar forward and the Segway began to move. She coasted down the alley at a snail's pace and then centered the handle when she reached the end, stopping it in its tracks.

"So far, so good," she muttered under her breath and then shifted to the side. "How do I turn around?" she yelled behind her.

Autumn lifted her hands and then shifted them to the right. "Tilt the steering bar a little to the right and it will turn."

The instruction sounded simple enough and Mercedes eased the bar to the right. The Segway turned. "That was easy." Feeling a little more confident she was getting the hang of it, Mercedes tilted the handle forward and zipped along the alley, coming to an abrupt halt in front of Autumn.

She grinned. "That was more fun than I thought it would be," Mercedes admitted.

"See? Told ya'." Autumn rubbed her hands together. "Let's take a spin around the block." She popped her helmet on her head, snapped the buckle and jumped on her Segway, which was sitting off to the side.

The women coasted down the alley and stopped at the end before making a sharp left turn. When they reached the corner, they stopped again, making sure there were no pedestrians in sight before cruising down the sidewalk, in front of the properties, passing the restaurant first.

The courtyard gate was open and Mercedes stopped the Segway so she could check on her mother and Rambo.

Autumn steered her Segway into the courtyard but Mercedes, still not completely comfortable with the contraption, walked it inside.

They found Carlita in the back, scraping rust off one of the bistro chairs.

She looked up as the girls approached. "What in the world?"

"Autumn borrowed a Segway so I could take it for a test run. This thing is cool. You should try it."

Carlita frowned and shook her head. "I've already had a close encounter with the Segway. I think I'll take a pass."

"Aw, Mrs. G. I didn't mean to plow you down, I swear," Autumn said.

"I know Autumn. Still, I think it's safer for me to keep both feet on the ground." Carlita changed the subject and turned her attention to her daughter. "Are you thinking of buying one?"

Their tank of a car was too big and bulky for the majority of Savannah's narrow side streets, not to mention all the congestion from other cars, but also the trolleys and the horses and buggies tourists seemed to love to take.

Rambo, who had been inspecting the water inside the fountain, trotted over to sniff the Segway. Mercedes patted his head. "Maybe. It seems like the perfect mode of transportation for Savannah." She unhooked the helmet and slipped it off. "How is it going?"

"Okay. Hot." Carlita wiped her forehead with the back of her hand. "At least we have lots of shade trees." She pointed at the bistro table, stripped of paint and now an ugly rust color. "What do you think?"

"I think it will look great when it's done," Mercedes said. "I should be out here helping you."

"Nah. This is a one woman project," her mother said. "When do you have to return the Segway?"

"Tomorrow," Autumn answered and gave Mercedes a quick look. "We're going to take it out for a longer ride after dinner."

"Yeah. Uh. We thought it would be a little cooler with fewer pedestrians to dodge." Mercedes didn't like fibbing to her mother, but it was only a half fib. They had decided there would be less people to navigate around if they waited until early evening.

The plan was for Autumn to give Mercedes a quick tour of some of Savannah's most popular squares that mother and daughter hadn't explored yet.

After the tour, they would head to their stakeout location on the other side of town. She only hoped it wouldn't be a complete waste of time.

The girls left Carlita to finish her furniture project and headed back out onto the sidewalk. They rode all the way to Morrell Park before returning to their starting point, the alley.

Mercedes hopped off the Segway and removed her helmet. "I'm ready to roll. Now all we have to do is wait for evening."

Chapter 21

The afternoon and dinner hour dragged and Mercedes kept glancing at the clock on the wall. Carlita noticed her daughter's unusual behavior but kept quiet. Mercedes was a grown woman and didn't need her mother questioning her every move.

Not only that, if Autumn had something up her sleeve, Carlita had a sneaky suspicion she didn't want to know what it was.

Dinner was a simple affair, consisting of toasted BLT's and tomato basil soup. Clean up was just as easy and after they finished putting everything away, the girls headed to the deck with a bowl of mint chocolate chip ice cream, Carlita's favorite.

They settled into the deck chairs and Rambo climbed onto the chaise lounge with Carlita and eyed her treat. "Sorry. No ice cream for you," she told the pooch and then handed her bowl of ice cream to her daughter. "Hold this."

She headed back to the kitchen for some doggie treats, returning moments later and placing them in a small pile on the deck. Rambo promptly scrambled to his feet and gobbled his goodies.

The cool minty ice cream was the perfect after-dinner treat. She hadn't had mint chocolate chip ice cream in a long time, not since Vinnie had passed. It had been his favorite ice cream, too.

A brief flicker of sadness crossed Carlita's face and Mercedes noticed the look, correctly guessing what had triggered the expression. "Pop's favorite ice cream," Mercedes said softly.

"Yep." Carlita nodded and blinked back unexpected tears. It had been a long day and Betty Graybill's cruel comment had struck a nerve. She set her spoon inside the bowl and studied her daughter. "Are you having any regrets about moving?"

Mercedes tapped the tip of her spoon on her lower lip and then slowly shook her head. "No. I mean, before we left there were moments of sheer panic when I wondered if we were doing the right thing, but not anymore. I love the apartment, the area. There's so much to see and do, we haven't even begun to explore all that Savannah has to offer."

She scooped a large spoon full of ice cream and savored the morsels of chocolate. Mercedes thought about Steve and Autumn and how much she'd grown to like them. There was so much promise for them in

Savannah with not only the rental income, but also the properties.

The Savannah properties had the potential to ensure Mercedes and Carlita would be able to live comfortably for many years, but there was more to it than that.

It was a feeling of independence, that after all these years of having the men in the family care for them; mother and daughter would be able to take care of themselves. "This was a good move, Ma, and if we ever decide to go back to New York, we can sell it all, like we did before we moved down here."

Carlita's shoulders relaxed at her daughter's words. Although she missed her sons, missed the familiarity of the old neighborhood and city, they were making new friends in their new neighborhood and everyone seemed so friendly. Everyone, that is except for Betty Graybill and Carol Weatherbee.

She scooped the last of the ice cream into her mouth and set the empty bowl on the table. "You're right. It makes me feel better knowing you're happy."

"I'm ecstatic." Mercedes gushed. "No. Seriously. I love it, which reminds me. Are we still going to take the trolley tour tomorrow morning?"

"Absolutely." Carlita nodded. She changed the subject. "I called Vinnie. He's halfway home and made it as far as the northern tip of Virginia."

"Did he say anything about moving down here?" Mercedes asked.

Carlita shook her head. "No and I didn't ask. He'll let me know if and when he's ready." The only problem was that they were in limbo about the business until Vinnie made his decision.

The women carried their empty ice cream bowls to the kitchen, rinsed them and then placed the dirty dishes and spoons inside the dishwasher. "Bob and his crew got most of the apartment demo done if you'd like to take a look."

"Sure." Mercedes dried her hands on the kitchen towel and followed her mother out the front door and down the hall to the apartment directly behind theirs. The door wasn't locked and the two of them stepped inside.

Mercedes slowly studied the open space. "You weren't kidding when you said demo." The workers had ripped everything out. It was a blank canvas, from the exposed rafters to the wooden floorboards. Not a single wall was standing. The only thing left of what had been the kitchen was the ceiling light - a 70's retro fixture, a frosted glass globe trimmed in gold. "It looks so much bigger."

"Tomorrow they start framing the new walls, removing the layers of peeling paint and also ripping out the bathroom fixtures."

The women walked through each of the rooms and finished their inspection near the living room windows that overlooked the alley.

"This apartment will be the mirror image of ours, including the deck." They retraced their steps and exited the apartment. Carlita pulled the door shut. "I'll have to remind Bob to start locking the door once they start installing cabinets, cupboards and fixtures."

They walked back to their apartment and Mercedes caught a glimpse of the borrowed Segway at the bottom of the stairs before glancing at her watch. "I'm going to freshen up and then head over to Steve's tattoo shop to meet Autumn."

"I might walk over and say hello to Steve," Carlita said. "If you don't mind."

"Not at all." The women gathered their keys, their cell phones and Rambo before heading down the steps. Mercedes and the Segway brought up the rear.

"I'll walk it across the street," Mercedes said as they headed down the alley, squeezing past the car. "It's a shame the car has to sit here now that I finally know how to drive." She was warming to the Segway idea and the ease of getting around town.

When they arrived at Shades of Ink, Steve's tattoo shop, she could see Steve leaning over a customer, wearing a pair of black gloves and holding what looked like a small gun. He glanced up when he heard the doorbell chime. "Hello ladies."

"Hi Mrs. G. Did you try out the Segway?" Autumn, who had been sitting behind the small counter, hopped off the chair when she spied Mercedes and Carlita.

"No way." Carlita shook her head.

"It's your fault. You shouldn't have traumatized her," Mercedes joked.

The girls chatted off to one side while Steve finished working on his client.

Carlita glanced at the man's new tattoo, a falcon in flight, as he headed out the door. "It looks painful."

"It's not bad," Autumn said. 'Here. Check this out." She lifted her leg and pointed at a tattoo of a pink Tinker

Bell with baby blue wings fluttering above the mini caricature. "It only hurt a little."

"Depending on where you're tattooed and your pain threshold," Steve added. He turned his attention to Carlita. "I heard these two are going out for an evening tour of the town."

"So they say." Carlita nodded.

"Speaking of that, we should get going." Autumn tugged on Mercedes's arm. "We'll be back in a couple hours."

"You know I don't like you out after dark so be extra careful," Steve called out, right before the door shut behind them.

Steve and Carlita watched through the window as the girls slid the helmets on their heads and then huddled together.

"I think they're up to something," Carlita commented.

Steve nodded. "Me too, but what can we do? They're adults."

"I hope whatever they have up their sleeves doesn't get them in too much trouble."

"So do I," Steve shook his head as the girls hopped on the Segways and disappeared from sight. "So do I."

Chapter 22

Autumn gave Mercedes the grand tour of the Historic District, starting with their own neighborhood, which had recently been renamed Walton Square. They veered onto Bryan Street, which was a straight shot from one end of historic downtown to the other end and close to the city market.

They took a quick tour of the popular touristy strip, passing by busy pubs and restaurants, some with live music blaring from the open doors. They passed by Elmwood Square, a popular family spot with its spacious grassy area and large fountain, complete with sprays of shooting water where children raced through the jets. It looked refreshing.

Autumn guided them back and forth, up and down the streets passing by several more squares, all of them unique with their own personalities.

They finished the tour in front of the Cathedral of St. John the Baptist. The girls stopped at the bottom of the steps leading to the front entrance.

Mercedes hopped off the Segway, her eyes drawn to the magnificent cathedral. "Mom would love this place."

"St. John's has both Saturday and Sunday Mass," Autumn told her. "I went once, just to check it out." She glanced at her watch. "We better head over to our stakeout spot." She eased the handle forward and headed down the sidewalk, moving at a snail's pace in an effort to avoid pedestrians.

Mercedes jumped back on her Segway and followed behind. They zigzagged back and forth, down narrow streets, cutting through alleys before reaching their destination.

Autumn turned down a dark alley and slowed as they traveled over the uneven gravel.

"This is it." She stopped abruptly in front of a hedge of bushes and lowered her voice as she gazed at the garage and the second story. It was the garage apartment where Harold Stetson, Norma Jean Cleaver's ex-boyfriend, lived; at least that was what Autumn's police department informant had told her.

"The lights are on," Mercedes whispered as she hopped off the Segway and removed her helmet. She tiptoed to the edge of the hedge, pulled the greenery to one side and peered at the upper floor window. She could see a figure move back and forth but it was moving too fast to tell if it was a male or female.

"Let's circle around the side," Autumn whispered in Mercedes's ear. The girls maneuvered their Segways behind a cluster of garbage cans.

Autumn reached inside the basket attached to the front of her Segway and grabbed a backpack, slinging it over her left shoulder.

"What's in there?" Mercedes pointed at the backpack.

"I brought a few supplies." Autumn ticked off the list of items inside. "Rubber gloves, a handful of Ziploc baggies, some rope and a garbage bag. I got the idea from watching my favorite movie, *Into the Plight*."

"Are you planning on kidnapping Harold Stetson?" Mercedes asked jokingly.

"No!" Autumn grinned. "Let's move." She waved her hand.

The women crouched down and slunk along the row of hedges. When they reached the corner, they stopped in front of a tall wooden fence.

Mercedes stuck a hand on her hip and frowned at the fence. "Now what?"

Autumn cupped her hands together and made a lifting motion. "Up and over," she whispered.

"Up and over?" Mercedes thumbed her chest. "You want to heave me over the fence?" she gasped.

"Shh." Autumn pressed a finger to her lips. "It's the only way."

Mercedes rolled her eyes. "This is crazy. No. This is trespassing, as in, I'm pretty sure we could get arrested."

"How? The woman who owns this place is dead."

"Her tenant isn't dead." Mercedes jabbed a finger in the direction of the second story lights over the garage.

"You're not chickening out, are you?" Autumn asked. "Don't worry about it. I've got connections."

"With the newspaper," Mercedes argued. "If we get caught, we'll be front page news in the morning."

Autumn ignored the comment and motioned with her hands again.

"All right. This isn't going to end well," Mercedes predicted.

Chapter 23

Mercedes grudgingly stuck her right foot in the palm of her friend's hands, grasped the top of the fence panel with both hands and hoisted herself up onto the fence. She teetered precariously for a long moment before disappearing from sight.

Thump!

Autumn peered through a crack in the fence. "You okay?"

"No."

"Good. I'm on my way." Autumn stuck the tip of her sneaker in a large hole, pulled herself up and using momentum, swung over the other side, landing in a heap next to Mercedes, who was sprawled out on the ground. She flashed her bandaged pinky in the air. "Finger is safe," she reported.

"Welcome to the jungle," Mercedes groaned.

"Jungle?" Autumn jumped up and brushed the leaves and dirt off the front of her jeans. Knee-high weeds surrounded them. A single row of towering oak trees lined the fence. Clumps of moss hung from the branches, eerily drifting back and forth.

"This is some sort of flower garden." Autumn gazed at clusters of wilted flowers, tangled in even thicker weeds.

"Dearly departed at that." Mercedes scrambled to her feet. "My phone took a hit." She pulled it from her back pocket, flipped it on and studied the screen.

"Are you nuts?" Autumn swiped at the phone. "Someone could see the light." She snatched it from Mercedes's hand, quickly switched it off and handed it back.

"Time to move," the blonde said as she tugged on Mercedes's arm. "Let's head this way."

The women crept along the side of the fence as they made their way toward the small dark ranch home. "I hope she doesn't have motion detectors." Autumn said in a low voice.

Mercedes stopped in her tracks. "Did you hear that?"

Autumn stopped. "Hear what?"

"The noise. Listen." Mercedes stood still.

"Yeah," Autumn nodded. "Sounds like a cat. It's probably a stray. Let's keep going."

Leaves crunched under their feet as they tiptoed along the side of the house, rounded the corner and stopped near the outside A/C unit.

"Now what?" Mercedes asked.

"This is my first stakeout," Autumn said. "I guess we keep an eye on the tenant, see if he does anything suspicious." She pointed to a section of fence. "We can watch from over there."

Mercedes scurried to the fence line and pressed her back against the slats before sliding to a sitting position, her knees tucked tight against her abdomen.

Autumn followed suit and they both turned their attention to the upstairs apartment lights. The minutes slowly ticked by.

"This could be a total waste of time." Mercedes shifted to a more comfortable position.

"True. Not much is happening." Autumn sounded disappointed. "I had hoped we were onto something."

They sat silently for what seemed like an eternity and Autumn was ready to admit defeat. "It looks like this stakeout was a bust. Let's go."

The girls eased to a standing position and took a step forward when Mercedes heard the noise again. "I hear a cat meowing. It sounds like it's coming from over there." She pointed to one of the house windows and began following the noise. "I think there's a cat trapped inside the house."

She crept over to the window, cupped her hands to her eyes and peered inside.

Thunk! Something banged against the side of the window. Mercedes jumped back, clutching her chest. "Holy smokes."

Autumn started to giggle. "You're right. It's a cat. He must have heard us."

Mercedes tried pushing on the window frame in an attempt to open the window. "Poor thing. I wonder if he or she has been stuck inside without food or water since Norma Jean's death."

The cat began wailing loudly and pawing frantically at the window as Autumn rubbed her finger against the glass. "He wants out."

"Let's try another window." Mercedes hurried to the next window. It wouldn't budge. "We could break the glass."

"We would get busted for sure. Why don't we place an anonymous call to the police and tell them we were riding by this place and noticed the cat in the window?" Autumn asked.

"Do you think they really care?" Mercedes had her doubts police would bother checking on a cat.

"True. Look, you wait here and I'll circle all the way around the house to see if there's some way we can rescue the poor thing." Autumn didn't wait for an answer as she disappeared around the side of the house.

Mercedes paced back and forth waiting for her friend. She was about to strike out in search of Autumn when she emerged from the darkness and hurried toward her, giving her a thumbs up. "Mission accomplished."

Mercedes opened her mouth to reply when the garage lights came on, illuminating the yard.

Autumn and Mercedes sprinted into the shadow of the house, and Autumn, who was closest, peered around the corner. She watched as the small side door opened and a man wearing a baseball cap, jeans and a t-shirt, stepped onto the stoop and leaned casually against the doorframe.

Moments later, a tall thin figure moving at a fast clip, approached Harold Stetson. It was a woman.

"I can't see the face," Autumn groaned.

"Let me take a look." The women switched places and Mercedes edged forward, peering around the corner. She could make out a woman's silhouette. The woman lit a cigarette, took a drag and then blew the smoke in Harold Stetson's face.

"Nasty habit." Mercedes fumbled to pull her cell phone from her rear pocket. Her fingers trembled as she pressed the button and switched to flash-free camera-mode. She pressed the camera button several times in an attempt to get a clear shot of Harold and the unknown woman.

The woman took a final puff on the cigarette and then flicked the butt of the cigarette into a nearby bush before following Stetson inside the building. The porch light went off.

"I think I got at least one clear picture." Mercedes turned the cell phone off and turned to say something else to Autumn when she came nose-to-nose with a furry, gray face peeking out of the top of the backpack.

Chapter 24

"You-you took the cat," Mercedes sputtered.

"I had to. He looked hungry and I didn't want him to starve. Desperate times call for desperate measures."

"Hey buddy." Mercedes rubbed his head and scratched his ears. The cat began to purr and wiggle in the confined space. "We better get out of here. Hopefully he doesn't mind riding." Her eyes squinted as she looked at the fence. "Vaulting over the side of a fence with a cat in the bag will be interesting."

"No need." Autumn shook her head. "During my cat rescue mission, I discovered all we need to do is walk to the end of the fence, around the corner and to the alley out back."

"You mean we hurtled over the fence for nothing?"

"Nah. It was good practice. Let's go. Spook is getting restless." The women started toward the front sidewalk. "I named the cat Spook cuz he - or she - scared the you-know-what out of me.

Mercedes kept one eye on the cat, which still hadn't made a peep and seemed content.

They walked in silence as Mercedes mulled over the woman they had spotted outside Harold Stetson's place. Something about her was familiar. She hoped the pictures she'd taken would be clear enough to give them some sort of clue to the woman's identity. Still, it didn't mean she – or Harold – had anything to do with Norma Jean's death.

Spook yelped a couple times on the way back to the apartment. The first time was when Autumn stopped abruptly and the other when she made a quick turn after almost missing their street.

Mercedes was secretly enjoying the Segway and was even disappointed when they pulled into the alley behind the apartments.

There was another car parked behind the Lincoln. It was a shiny silver sports sedan.

"That's an alfa Romeo...a hundred thousand dollar car, right there," Autumn said as she set the backpack on the ground, unzipped the sides and gently lifted Spook out of the bag, cradling him to her chest. "You're such a good kitty," she cooed. "Too bad I can't keep you."

"You're not keeping the cat?" Mercedes grabbed the handle of the Segway and steered it through the back door of the building.

Autumn and Spook followed her in. "No can do. I can't have a cat in my dinky apartment."

The sound of voices echoing down the stairs interrupted the exchange.

"We have company," Mercedes said as she tilted her head and gazed up the stairs to their open apartment door.

Autumn tugged her Segway into the building and the women traipsed up the steps and into the apartment where they found Carlita and Glenda Fox sitting in the living room.

Carlita gazed at Autumn. "You have a cat."

Autumn nodded hello and handed the cat to Mercedes. "We rescued this kitty from an abandoned home."

Glenda leaned forward and studied the gray cat. "He looks like Norma Jean's cat, Grayvie. I recognize him from a picture she kept on her desk and the sparkly blue collar. It has his name on it." She pointed to the cat's collar.

Carlita frowned. "Did you...you didn't."

"We did," Autumn admitted. "We were staking out Harold Stetson's place and discovered the poor cat trapped inside the house."

"It was my idea," Mercedes said. "The cat was meowing his head off and Autumn offered to try to let him out. We couldn't just leave him there to starve..." Her voice trailed off.

Grayvie stalked across the floor while Rambo, who had taken notice of the new arrival, scrambled to his feet to investigate.

The two circled each other, sniffing the air cautiously. Grayvie hissed once, which caused Rambo to bark.

After several circles and sniffs, the dog deemed the cat a non-threat and flopped back down on the living room floor.

Grayvie lifted his head and curled his tail as he stalked to the slider.

"He must be hungry and thirsty." Mercedes plucked a small saucer from the cupboard and filled it with water. She placed the saucer on the floor before reaching inside the refrigerator and pulling out a packet of lunchmeat.

She tore a slice of ham into small pieces and placed them on a paper towel. Grayvie promptly lapped up some water and devoured the meat.

"I hate to give him too much in case his poor tummy has shrunk and it makes him sick." Mercedes patted his head and stroked his glossy gray fur. "I'll give you more after I'm certain you're not going to throw up," she promised.

"He doesn't look any worse for the wear." Carlita studied the cat before turning to her daughter. "I hate to condone illegal activity, but were you able to find anything out about Mr. Stetson? I'm sure the police have already talked to him at length."

"Yes and no." Autumn explained to Glenda and Carlita they had waited outside his garage apartment for what seemed like forever. After rescuing Grayvie, they decided to call it a night when someone flipped the porch light on and stepped outdoors. "It was Mr. Stetson. He was hanging around the doorway and we thought maybe he was waiting for someone."

"So we waited to see if anyone showed up and our hunch was right." Mercedes whipped her cell phone out of her back pocket and switched it on. Two of the pictures were blurry, but the third was clear enough where you could make out Harold Stetson's face. The woman was in the photo, too, waving her cigarette in the air.

Mercedes handed the phone to her mother. "This is the clearest shot."

Carlita lowered the phone and squinted at the screen. "That's the guy we saw in the video clip, the one hanging around out front right after Norma Jean's body was discovered!" She handed the phone to Glenda.

"I met Harold Stetson a couple times when Norma Jean brought him by." Glenda lowered the phone and studied the screen. "I know exactly who the woman is. That's Betty Graybill."

"She smokes?" Autumn, Mercedes and Carlita asked in unison.

"Yep." Glenda nodded firmly. "She's a closet smoker. Has been ever since I've known her, course you could never get her to admit it." She handed the phone to Mercedes. "You can always smell a smoker a mile away."

Carlita abruptly stood. "This...the pieces of the puzzle." She turned to Autumn and Mercedes. "Remember the day we found Norma Jean's body? Vinnie said she'd been burned." She turned to Glenda. "Burned is a common term used by the m-."

"Up north," Mercedes cut her mother off. "People in New York use the term burned when they're talking about someone who has been murdered." She gave her mother a quick look.

409

"Yes," Carlita said. "We could tell Norma Jean had been strangled by the mark around her neck."

Mercedes interrupted again. "We watch a lot of investigative crime shows on television," she explained.

"Right." Carlita chose her next words carefully. "Vinnie, my son, pointed out that not only had she been burned, as in murdered, but he also noticed a burn mark on her neck."

Glenda shifted in her chair. "So you think Betty killed Norma Jean, tried to frame you, knowing you weren't around and when that didn't work, turned it on me?"

"It makes perfect sense," Carlita nodded.

"You're right." Glenda sprang from her chair. "Oh my gosh. That day I overheard Norma Jean screaming at Harold, calling him a lying cheat, she must've found out he was cheating on her."

"And the other woman was Betty Graybill," Autumn said.

"My guess is that when Norma Jean confronted Betty, the two argued," Mercedes said. "Betty killed her and then planted her body in the old restaurant."

Carlita picked up. "She tried to frame us by telling authorities the last time she'd seen Norma Jean was when she was on her way to inspect our properties."

"Scum," Mercedes growled. "That's a crappy thing to do to someone you don't even know."

"At least you weren't charged with Norma Jean's murder," Glenda pointed out.

"We need to get on the horn with Detective Polivich." Carlita hurried to the kitchen, grabbed her cell phone and dialed the detective's number, thankful she'd programmed it into her phone. She left a message, telling him they had new information regarding the Norma Jean Cleaver case and then waited.

"If you get me out of this mess, I owe you one," Glenda said.

"Afternoon tea sounds cool," Mercedes said.

"It's a deal. Reginald, our butler, would love it," Glenda winked. "He tries to pretend he's a fuddy-duddy, but he's a big pushover."

They waited for an hour and Carlita was getting ready to call the detective a second time when they heard a loud rap on the downstairs door that led to the alley.

"I'll answer it." Mercedes hurried down the steps and returned moments later with Detective Polivich. "I'm sorry it took so long, but I was in the middle of an interrogation. What have you got?"

The women explained all that had transpired and Detective Polivich listened quietly as they told how Autumn and Mercedes had staked out Norma Jean's place, which was the only time he interrupted, to inform them they had trespassed on private property.

"A necessary risk," Autumn argued.

After telling him all they knew, and showing him the picture Mercedes had taken with her cell phone camera, he told them he would stop by Harold Stetson's place to chat with them, but that they might not hear back until the following morning.

Mercedes forwarded the picture to the detective and then walked him to the door.

Glenda followed behind. "It has been a long day, and I appreciate everything you've done on my behalf," she said gratefully. "None of the SAS members would've done what you did."

When they reached the alley, Carlita gave her a quick hug. "I know how you feel and I only hope what the girls found can help clear your name and that the charges against you are dropped."

Glenda thanked them again before climbing into her sports car. After her car disappeared around the corner, Autumn glanced at her watch. "Steve-O is closing shop right about now so I better head over there."

She slipped her helmet on her head and lifted her hand. "It's time for a high five, girlfriend. Our first cracked case." The women slapped the palms of their hands together and then Autumn switched her Segway on before zipping down the alley and out of sight.

Carlita put her arm around her daughter. "I would love to lecture you on everything you shouldn't have done, but I can't." She squeezed Mercedes's shoulder.

The women stepped inside the building and Carlita locked the door behind them. "And to think Vinnie missed out on all this excitement."

Chapter 25

Carlita boarded the orange trolley and settled into a seat near the window.

Mercedes eased into the spot next to her, placing her purse between them. "I researched each of the trolley tours and I think we'll like this one best," she rubbed her hands together.

"I think you're right." Carlita smiled at her daughter. "I wonder if the trolley will tour Walton Square." She had never noticed a trolley pass by, but then they were virtually the last street before the historic district ended, which was nice in a way...nice and peaceful.

After the passengers boarded, the trolley chugged out of the parking lot, looped around in a circle and passed by the Savannah Visitor's Center. The trolley wove its way back and forth, through each of the squares as the tour guide described the various sights. It was almost too much to take in and when the tour ended, Carlita's head was swimming with all they had seen.

Detective Polivich had called midway through the tour and Carlita had let the call go to voice mail. After they exited the trolley, she dialed her voice mail, pressed the speaker button and the women leaned in to listen.

The detective told them after several hours of interrogation...err, questioning, Betty Graybill confessed to fighting with Norma Jean Cleaver behind the restaurant where she burned her with a lit cigarette, which infuriated Norma Jean.

Norma Jean pushed Betty and the two ended up in a knock down drag out brawl. Betty a much larger, more powerful woman, had strangled Norma Jean with her own necklace.

After realizing she had killed Norma Jean, Betty panicked and dragged her body inside the restaurant.

He finished by telling them that all charges against Glenda Fox had been dropped.

Carlita disconnected the call and slid the cell phone inside her purse. "I still don't understand how Betty got inside the restaurant."

"Unless one of Bob's workers had unlocked the door and forgot to lock it back up, leaving it wide open for who knows how long," Mercedes pointed out.

"True." Carlita had caught the workers leaving doors unlocked several times.

Mercedes linked her arm through her mother's arm and the two strolled through Ormond Square on their way back to the apartment. "And we thought living the life of mafia women was exciting."

Carlita shook her head. "You took the words right out of my mouth. Now what are we going to do about Grayvie?"

The end.

If you enjoyed reading this book, please take a moment to leave a review. It would be greatly appreciated! Thank you!

Italian Stuffed Shells Recipe

Ingredients

1 lb. Italian sausage browned (OPTIONAL)

1 (16 oz.) package of jumbo pasta shells

4 cups small curd cottage cheese (I used 2 cups ricotta +

2 cups small curd cottage cheese)

12 oz. shredded mozzarella cheese

1 cup grated parmesan cheese

2 eggs, lightly beaten

1 tsp. garlic powder

2 tsp. Italian spice mix

1 tsp. salt

½ tsp. pepper

1 (26 oz. jar) spaghetti sauce

½ cup grated parmesan cheese

Directions

Cook shells according to package directions. After
finished cooking, place in cold water and then drain.
Mix together cottage cheese, mozzarella cheese, 1 cup
grated parmesan cheese, eggs, garlic powder, Italian
seasoning, salt and pepper.
Preheat oven to 350 degrees.
In separate bowl, mix spaghetti sauce with (optional)

Italian sausage.

Spread 1/3 of spaghetti sauce in bottom of 13x9 glass baking dish.

Stuff mixture into cooked shells. Place filled shells, open side up, close together, in pan.

Spread remaining spaghetti sauce over top.

Sprinkle remaining ½ cup grated parmesan cheese on top.

Bake at 350 in preheated oven for 20 minutes (covered.) Uncover and bake an additional 15 – 20 minutes.

*This made more than a 13x9 pan, and I ended up using an extra 9x9 baking dish and another ½ jar of spaghetti sauce plus extra grated parmesan cheese for top.

3-Justice in Savannah

Made in Savannah

Cozy Mystery Series Book Three

Hope Callaghan

hopecallaghan.com
Copyright © 2016
All rights reserved.

Visit my website for new releases and special offers: hopecallaghan.com

Thank you to these wonderful ladies who help make my books shine - Peggy H., Cindi G., Jean P., Wanda D. and Rosmarie H. for taking the time to preview *Justice in Savannah,* for the extra sets of eyes and for catching all my mistakes.

A special thanks to my reader review team: Alice, Amary, Barbara, Becky, Becky B, Brinda, Cassie, Christina, Cyndi, Debbie, Denota, Devan, Francine, Grace, Jan, Jo-Ann, Joeline, Joyce, Jean K., Jean M., Kathy, Lynne, Megan, Melda, Kat, Linda, Lynne, Pat, Patsy, Renate, Rita, Rita P, Shelba, Tamara and Vicki

Chapter 1

"I submitted my application almost a month ago," Carlita Garlucci explained to the person on the other end of the line. "Last time I talked to you, you said I would have an answer Monday and it's now Friday."

She listened quietly for a few moments, her shoulders slumping in defeat. "You might not have an answer for me until next week? I don't understand the holdup." Carlita listened again and then spoke. "Okay. I'll try back on Monday. Good-bye."

Mercedes, Carlita's 25-year old daughter, folded her arms. "This is ridiculous," she said. "You would think that we're trying to open a strip club."

"I probably need to go down there and talk to someone in person." Carlita had recently inherited properties in historic Savannah, Georgia and hired a crew of workers to fix up one of the dilapidated properties. Her plan was to open a pawnshop in the newly renovated building. Everything was moving right along, the property was in tiptop shape and ready to go.

There was only one major problem. They didn't have a business license, at least not yet. Carlita was beginning to suspect the Savannah-Burnham District Office was not keen on allowing a pawnshop in the recently renamed Walton Square district.

"It's not fair," Mercedes argued. "What about the pawnshop on the other side of town?"

"Paradise Pawn," Carlita said. "Makes you wonder how they managed to get a license to open shop and we can't."

"Crooked government," Mercedes guessed. "Someone at Paradise Pawn greased someone's palm down at Savannah-Burnham District Offices."

"We should organize a protest and picket in front of their building." Mercedes brightened. "We can ask Autumn to see if the Savannah Evening News will cover the story."

'Autumn' was Autumn Winter, a family friend, who worked part-time at the local newspaper, the Savannah Evening News.

Carlita placed her cell phone on the kitchen counter and faced her daughter. "Picket? Just the two of us?"

"We could ask others in Walton Square to join us. Steve-O, Annie Dowton, maybe even Ken Colby down at Colby's Corner Store."

"Let me think about it," Carlita said. "I'm taking Rambo for a walk." Maybe a little fresh air and sunshine would clear her mind.

Rambo and she stepped into the hall. The sound of hammers and power tools echoed in the hall. Bob Lowman, Carlita's construction supervisor, and his crew were hard at work wrapping up renovations on her apartment units that would soon be ready for tenants.

Carlita was anxious to have them finish the renovations. She needed cash flow coming in, now that the district office was dragging its feet.

Carlita tiptoed to the doorway of the apartment located directly behind hers. The rear unit was the one she hoped her oldest son, Vinnie, would eventually occupy.

Vinnie had helped Carlita and Mercedes move from New York to Savannah, and had shown some interest in the possibility of the pawnshop, but the excitement that one of her three sons might join her in Georgia was quickly fading. There was no reason for Vinnie to move if there was nothing for him to do.

The workers had finished installing all of the kitchen cabinets and appliances, replaced the rotting window frames and removed the ceiling tiles, giving the apartment an open loft feel and making the two-bedroom, one-bath apartment appear even larger.

The smell of fresh paint greeted her and she took a tentative step inside.

Dale, one of the lead workers, smiled when he caught a glimpse of Carlita. "Ms. Garlucci. Come in." He waved her inside, and Rambo and Carlita made their way into what would be the living room. "Well?"

Dale waved his hand. "We're almost done. We'll finish painting the trim today and start working on the floors tomorrow. Then we move onto the next project."

Carlita's heart sank. If she couldn't get a building license, there might be no "next project," but she didn't tell Dale that. "It looks great, Dale. You and your men have done a wonderful job," she complimented.

Rambo and Carlita finished their quick tour of the apartment before stepping into the hall. There were four apartments in all. Carlita and Mercedes occupied the one closest to the stairs. In addition to the unit behind theirs, there were two more across the hall.

The construction workers had almost finished all of them, which was good news. The bad news was wondering where they would go next.

She made a mental note to apply for a restaurant license for the other property she owned, the one the workers hadn't started on yet. Carlita hoped the district office wouldn't drag their feet on the restaurant license since the building had previously been occupied by a restaurant, Denny's Diner.

Rambo tugged on his leash, leading Carlita down the hall and then down the stairs. They stepped out of the building and into the back alley before walking toward the front of the building Carlita hoped would one day soon be their pawnshop.

Perhaps Mercedes was right. Maybe if they brought attention to their dilemma, they could light a fire under the Director of Licensing, Mr. Yates' feet.

Carlita picked up the pace as they passed the front of the building and headed to the corner. She glanced in both directions before crossing the street and then noticed the lights inside Walton Square Souvenirs, a small gift shop, catty-corner to her property, were on.

It was the first time Carlita had seen lights on inside the building. Annie Dowton, the real estate agent who occupied the building next to the souvenir shop, had told her Ruby McKinley owned the building and had been a Walton Square owner for many years. She told Carlita no one had been around for a few months and that Ruby had approached her about possibly selling the business.

Carlita headed toward the small store. She had peeked in the window once before, curious to find out what the inside looked like. It was crammed full of stuff, the usual souvenir store items...postcards, t-shirts, salt and pepper shakers with the word "Savannah" etched on the front.

She twisted the doorknob and the door creaked as it opened. A small, gray-haired woman with dark glasses and shoulder length hair tucked behind her ears, looked up from behind the cash register. She smiled.

Carlita took a step forward. "Mrs. McKinley?"

The woman shifted to the side and stepped out from behind the counter. "Yes?"

"I-I'm Carlita Garlucci. I own the building across the street."

Ruby shuffled to the center of the room. "Yes, I've heard all about you."

"Good I hope," Carlita quipped.

Ruby smiled. "Welcome to Walton Square. You'll love it here, of course, you probably already know that." She pointed out the front window, at the side of Carlita's building. "I thought I saw lights on upstairs. Are you living in one of the apartments?"

Carlita shifted Rambo's leash to her other hand. "Yes. My daughter and I recently moved into one of the front units. We're almost finished with renovations to the other apartments and plan to rent them out."

Ruby nodded. "It's nice to see someone fixing the old place up. It has been vacant since Mr. Delmario's unfortunate demise some time back. I'm sure you heard."

"Yes. Such an unfortunate incident."

"I heard from Ken Colby, who owns Colby's Corner Store, that you were going to open a grocery store, but recently changed your mind."

"That was our original plan," Carlita admitted. "I've applied for a business license to open a pawnshop."

"Won't a pawnshop attract a criminal element to Walton Square?"

Carlita shook her head. It wasn't the first time someone had made a similar comment when they found out she was opening a pawnshop. "Not any more so than a tattoo parlor."

Steve Winter, one of Carlita's friends and another Walton Square business owner, owned Shades of Ink, a tattoo parlor, just down the street.

Ruby shifted her feet and stuck a fisted hand on her hip. "Steve Winter was lucky to get his license. Well, let me know if I can help."

She reached over and patted Rambo's head. "Hey there fella."

"Rambo," Carlita said.

"Rambo. You remind me of my Clifford," she cooed. "What kind of dog is he?"

"Rambo is part Doberman, part German Shepherd and part goofball." The dog licked Ruby's hand.

"We better get out of your hair." Carlita tugged on Rambo's leash and they retraced their steps. "Thanks for the offer. My daughter is considering picketing the district office."

Ruby followed them to the front. She rubbed her hands together. "Ooh...a protest. Sounds like fun. I haven't protested since the 60's, back when we were protesting the Vietnam War."

Carlita took a closer look at Ruby McKinley. She didn't strike Carlita as an activist but appearances could be deceiving. "I'll keep you posted."

They stepped out of the store, passing by the real estate office next door. The lights were on and Carlita slowed her steps, gazing into the window. There was a red-haired woman seated at a desk. It wasn't Annie, the owner, so Carlita kept walking.

Rambo and Carlita headed to one of their favorite spots, Morrell Park. The park was located on the banks of the Savannah River. The meticulously manicured grounds sported meandering paths, which branched out in several different directions, as well as park benches, quiet spots to stop and take a break, to admire the expansive river and watch as the freighters floated by.

Carlita caught a glimpse of the Mystic Queen, the tour boat that carried tourists and visitors up and down the river. The riverboat cruise was on her bucket list of things to do.

After finishing their leisurely stroll through the park, Rambo and Carlita headed back to the apartment and their private courtyard that separated the newly renovated store from the dilapidated restaurant the construction crew hadn't yet started working on.

Carlita stopped abruptly in front of the gate. The frame of the courtyard's wrought iron gate had separated from the cement wall, leaving a large gap. "What in the world?"

Rambo and she eased through the opening and Carlita hurried down the cobblestone walkway, to the back of the courtyard. "Oh no."

Chapter 2

Carlita stared at the smashed figurine, the water fountain Mercedes and she had managed to salvage after years of neglect. It had worked like a top and after a good scrubbing, looked almost new.

She took a step closer. Someone had knocked the figurine's head off and chunks of it were scattered inside the pool of water, surrounding the fountain. The vase the figurine was holding sported a large hole and water was pouring out. A closer inspection showed several hairline cracks in the base.

The leg of one of Carlita's recently refurbished metal bistro chairs jutted out from the base of the statue.

"Who would do such a thing?" Carlita asked Rambo as she gazed at the destruction. Shards of jagged plaster littered the area surrounding the base.

"We better move back." She shooed Rambo away from the broken pieces, not wanting to risk Rambo cutting his paws. "I better go grab a broom and clean the mess."

They retraced their steps. Carlita pulled the damaged gate shut before the two of them made their way back to the apartment to grab a broom, dustpan and garbage bag.

Mercedes wandered out of her room and stared at the broom her mother had just pulled from the hall closet. "Whatcha doing?"

"Someone smashed our garden girl out in the courtyard and I'm going to clean up the mess."

Mercedes followed her mother to the courtyard and watched as Carlita shoved the side of the broken gate open. "Vandals busted our gate."

"Unfortunately." Carlita handed the empty garbage bag to her daughter. "I noticed the broken gate and when I came back here to check on the courtyard, I found this." She pointed at the shattered statue.

Mercedes plucked a piece of the figurine's forehead from the pool of water. "I wonder if this happened last night."

Carlita tried to remember the last time they'd visited the courtyard. It had been a couple of evenings earlier, after dinner, when Mercedes and she had slipped out to enjoy the cooler air and sip glasses of iced tea.

"Should we file a police report?" Mercedes asked.

The figurine held little value, if you didn't count sentimental value. "No. Let's just clean this mess up and make sure the water is turned off so it doesn't flood the place."

The women made quick work of cleaning up the mess and discussed replacing the figurine.

After cleaning, they inspected their cozy oasis and Carlita was relieved to discover nothing else had been vandalized. It was little consolation and more than a little disconcerting. "I'll see if one of Bob's men has time to fix the gate before they leave today."

Mercedes followed her mother out of the courtyard. "Have you given anymore thought to staging a protest? I came up with a slogan.'"

She went on. "I'm going to run down to Savannah Evening News to see what Autumn thinks."

Carlita nodded. "While you do that, I'm going to head over to Colby's Corner Store." Not only did she need to pick up a few groceries, she was going stir-crazy sitting around the apartment, worrying about her business license.

Mercedes tossed the garbage bag inside the dumpster in the alley while Carlita led Rambo up to the apartment, dropped off the dustpan and broom, and then grabbed her purse, along with Mercedes' house keys.

When she reached the alley, Carlita handed the keys to her daughter, who was waiting outside the back door. "Are you still thinking about getting a Segway?"

"Yeah," Mercedes nodded. "I wanted to wait until we had some money coming in before shopping for one."

Historic Savannah was the perfect place for zipping around town on a Segway. Their only mode of transportation, a 1977 Lincoln town car, was too big to maneuver many of the narrow side streets and for the most part, sat parked in the back alley.

Carlita patted her daughter's arm as they began walking. "We have plenty of money in the bank, Mercedes. There's no need to wait."

Mercedes brightened. "Actually, I've been scoping out some different options. A used one would be fine. I don't need a new one. I guess it wouldn't hurt to at least look."

"If Autumn is almost off work, why don't you look at them together?" Carlita asked.

Mercedes smiled. "Okay. You talked me into it." They stopped at the end of the block.

"Tell Autumn I said hello." Carlita waited for her daughter to make her way down the sidewalk before heading to Colby's just up the street.

The bell tinkled as Carlita stepped inside the grocery store. She caught a glimpse of Ken Colby, the store owner. He was standing in the back, talking to a young curly-haired blonde, his daughter, Faith.

Carlita loved the corner grocery. It reminded her of Sal's Market back in Queens. They were both about the same size and offered a large variety of staples.

During her last visit, Carlita discovered Ken was originally from the Bronx, and they chatted about home and what they did and didn't miss about life in the big city.

Ken always talked about his daughter, Faith, but never mentioned being married. Carlita was curious but didn't want to appear nosy so she kept her questions to herself. She'd hinted around to the other neighbors in Walton Square, but no one seemed to know Ken's past.

Faith and Ken turned when they caught a glimpse of Carlita as she grabbed a hand basket.

Ken strolled down the center aisle, a smile on his face. "It's nice to see you Carlita. Haven't seen you around for a few days now. How is the license application going?"

"It's not." Carlita frowned. "The man in charge of issuing licenses, a Mr. Yates, keeps putting me off. They were supposed to reach a decision Monday and when I called again today to check the status, they still weren't giving me an answer."

Ken shook his head. "That's the government for you. You don't think the SAS has anything to do with this?"

The thought had crossed Carlita's mind. The SAS, or Savannah Architectural Society, was a group of women who had limited authority in approval of businesses in Savannah's historic district, which mainly pertained to structural or aesthetic issues, but the women had a reputation for attempting to overextend their authority into other areas – such as licensing. "It's possible. Maybe I should give Glenda Fox a call."

Glenda was a member of SAS, and the only member of the society Carlita considered a friend, which may have been because Carlita and her daughter had helped clear Glenda's name in a recent murder case.

Carlita reached for a bag of wavy potato chips and jar of chip dip. "Mercedes has this brilliant idea we should picket Savannah-Burnham District Office to bring attention to our plight."

Ken chuckled. "It sounds interesting."

"It sounds cool." Faith Colby hurried over. "Walton Square business owners can band together to help you out."

"I..." Carlita looked from Ken to Faith. "Ruby McKinley said she'd join us and picket. I'm sure Steve over at Shades of Ink would help."

"Annie Dowton is a firecracker. She'd be in."

"I guess it wouldn't hurt to try to force the district office to make a decision." Carlita picked up a loaf of bread, a box of beef flavored cat treats for their new pet, Grayvie, and a box of elbow macaroni before heading to the checkout counter.

Faith had returned to the small restaurant in the back to wait on a customer while Ken met Carlita in the front of the store. He reached inside her basket and pulled out the bag of chips. "Let us know if you decide to picket. That would be the most exciting thing I've done since fighting a parking ticket last December."

Carlita thanked Ken for his offer and told him she would keep him posted. She carried her groceries out of the store and began walking back to the apartment. Picketing was something Carlita never would've considered, but maybe they did things differently here in the South.

The apartment was empty when Carlita stepped inside. It was going to be a quiet afternoon with Mercedes gone.

After unloading the groceries, she stopped by the other apartments, searching for Bob Lowman. She found him installing a section of trim in the unit across the hall.

He began discussing renovations and Carlita's mind wandered as she gazed out at the courtyard and spotted the broken figurine.

"...when we finish staining the floors?" Bob looked at her expectantly.

Carlita's mind had drifted to the vandalism and she shook her head. "I'm sorry Bob. I missed what you said."

"We're almost done and I was asking about your license approval."

Carlita told him what she'd told everyone else, how the licensing department was dragging their feet and that Mercedes was gearing up to stage a protest.

"It sounds interesting." Bob grinned. "Boy, that oughta get the employees down at the district office fired up. Let me know if you decide to protest so I can stop by and show my support."

"Or join us," Carlita teased. She switched the subject and told him about the busted water figurine fountain.

Bob tilted his head and gazed out the window. "I'll have one of my guys get on it right now. My guess is some old crumbling concrete gave way. School's still out." He shrugged. "Could be just a bunch of kids messing around."

"You're probably right," Carlita agreed. "I'd be forever grateful if one of your men could take a look at it."

Carlita's cell phone began to beep and she pulled it out of her pocket. It was Mercedes. "If you'll excuse me." She headed back to her apartment before answering.

"Where are you?" Mercedes asked when her mother answered.

"I'm touring the apartments with Bob."

"Meet me in the alley. I have a surprise."

Chapter 3

Carlita was tempted to peek out the living room window that overlooked the alley to catch a glimpse of the "surprise," but was almost afraid to. "I'll be right there."

She grabbed her apartment key before locking the door and heading down the stairs and out the back door.

Mercedes and her friend, Autumn, were standing behind the car.

Mercedes motioned her mother over.

Carlita rounded the side of the car and almost tripped over Mercedes' surprise. It was a scooter. "You bought a scooter?"

Mercedes patted the handlebar. "Not yet. I'm taking it for a test drive. Check out the sidecar." She pointed to the small, bullet shaped metal car attached to the scooter.

"A sidecar?"

"For you, Mrs. G," Autumn said. "Now you can travel around town with us."

Carlita's eyes grew wide. "My feet work just fine."

"Mother," Mercedes rolled her eyes. "At least try it out before you say no."

Visions of Mercedes racing down side streets and alleys with Carlita hanging onto the sides of the bullet for dear life raced through her mind.

Her daughter's driving skills were marginal, at best. At least in their car, Carlita had a shot at surviving if, heaven forbid, they were to get into an accident.

An open sidecar was a different story. She started to shake her head but Mercedes persisted. "I brought it all the way over here just so you could try it out." She reached inside the sidecar and pulled out a helmet. "Put this on and we can take it for a spin."

Carlita was about to put her foot down until she noted the look on her daughter's face. Mercedes was trying to do something good and Carlita didn't have the heart to tell her "no," so she took the helmet and wiggled it onto her head.

Autumn burst out laughing, plucked her cell phone from her back pocket and snapped a picture. "Priceless," she chuckled.

"What?" Carlita ran the palm of her hand down the side of the helmet to the ends of her hair, which were sticking straight out like a tufted rooster.

"Here, let me help." Mercedes smoothed her mother's hair and then flipped the face shield down.

440

"Do I really need this?" Carlita's eyes narrowed as she stared through the clear shield.

"Bugs." Mercedes and Autumn answered in unison.

Mercedes slipped her helmet on and fastened the clasp before motioning her mother to the sidecar. "It's a little snug but I think you'll still be comfy."

When Carlita was safely inside the contraption, Mercedes swung her right leg over the seat of the scooter and then started the motor.

Autumn climbed on her Segway and led the way out of the alley and down the side street. They circled the block so that Mercedes could practice driving with a passenger before heading toward the center of town. "We're going to scope out Savannah-Burnham District Office," Mercedes yelled over her shoulder.

Carlita cupped her hands to her mouth. "Okay. Just watch where you're going," she hollered back, moments before they hit a bump and Carlita flew off the seat. She gripped both sides of the bullet, closed her eyes and began to pray. "Dear Heavenly Father..."

There was only one incident where Mercedes screeched to a halt, causing Carlita a mild case of whiplash, before they reached the front of the district office.

Mercedes hopped off the scooter and ran over to help her mother exit the sidecar. Carlita was a little stiff from the excursion, the jolt and the screeching halt, but no worse for the wear after she was standing upright with both feet on solid ground.

Passersby eyed Carlita curiously and she realized she was still wearing the helmet.

She yanked it off and fluffed her hair.

"Well? What did you think?" Mercedes asked.

"Not as bad as I thought it would be," Carlita grudgingly admitted. "It beats walking this far." She turned her attention to the concrete steps leading to the entrance. Savannah-Burnham District Office was an impressive structure.

Autumn hopped off her Segway and stood next to Carlita as she studied their surroundings. "This would be the perfect place to picket, right here on the corner of this busy intersection. I'm going to try to line up a camera crew to cover the story."

Carlita shifted to the side and then looked across the street at another official-looking building. "What's that?"

"It's the customs house." Autumn shrugged. "It has something to do with imports."

Carlita was still on the fence about the whole picket thing. "What if the police arrest us?"

"Every U.S. citizen is entitled to freedom of speech, Mrs. G. I did a little research," Autumn said. "We can picket on the sidewalk as long as we don't impede foot traffic or disrupt businesses."

"Think about it. We've already got our picketers lined up," Mercedes argued. "Autumn, Steve, you, me."

"Mrs. McKinley, who owns the souvenir shop, volunteered, and so did Ken and Faith Colby," Carlita said. "Do you think it will work?"

"It's worth a try. Autumn and I thought Monday would be the best day. This weekend won't work since the district office will be closed."

The trio hopped back on their modes of transportation and began the scenic drive back toward Walton Square. They passed by Stalwart Street, the street where the Savannah Architectural Society's office was located.

Carlita had tossed around the idea of asking Glenda Fox to put in a good word for them and decided, depending on how Monday's picket turned out, she might still contact her friend.

The girls steered the Segway and scooter into the alley, parking near the rear of the car before hopping off.

Carlita removed the helmet and handed it to her daughter.

"So what do you think about the scooter?" Mercedes asked as she took the helmet.

"Although I think the scooter and sidecar are a novel idea, I would rather walk. The money would be better spent if you bought a Segway instead," Carlita said.

"Okay," Mercedes shoulders slumped. "I'll return it. I did have my eye on an i2 that's reasonably priced."

The girls headed out via Segway and scooter, and Carlita headed to the courtyard to check on the gate repairs.

When she reached the courtyard gate, Carlita could see where workers had patched the posts, using fresh cement to anchor the sides of the gate to the concrete.

Carlita retraced her steps as she started to head to the street corner when she spotted Annie Dowton's convertible parked in front of Riverfront Real Estate, Annie's real estate office.

With a quick glance around, Carlita hurried across the street and entered the front door of the small office.

Annie was the only one inside and she looked up when Carlita stepped inside. "Hello Carlita."

"Hi Annie. You got a minute?"

"Yes ma'am. Have a seat." Annie waved to a chair in front of the desk. "You look troubled."

Carlita sucked in her breath. "I am." She poured out her frustration over the building license and her daughter's idea to picket in front of the district office.

Annie smiled. "We Walton Square residents stick together. I'd love to lend a hand or a leg to help picket."

"Are you sure? The plan is to start Monday at noon," Carlita said. "We'll bring the signs."

"Yes. Absolutely." Annie slapped an open palm on the desk. "I can't wait to see the look on Calvin Burell, the Savannah-Burnham District Office Manager's face when we show up."

Carlita had never heard of Calvin Burell. "It should be exciting." Carlita changed the subject. "The apartments are almost rent ready. I'm not sure if Autumn Winter is still interested, but I have at least one unit available."

Carlita had left a voice message for Bernie Feldman, the cable repair guy who had showed an interest when he'd visited her apartment and hooked up the cable and internet, but he never called back.

"Funny you should say that." Annie pushed her glasses up and stared at her laptop screen. "I just got an inquiry, someone who is looking for an apartment in the historic district. Would you like me to schedule a showing?"

"Yes, the sooner the better." Carlita rattled off the times that would work best before hopping out of her chair. "It would be great if we can work on getting the apartments occupied."

Annie walked Carlita to the door and opened it. "I'll send a text if and when I have an appointment. In the meantime, I'll see you Monday at noon with my tennis shoes on."

Carlita strolled back to the apartment, a spring in her step. Things were starting to look up. She was grateful her neighbors were rallying around her to help get her business up and going. Not only that, the apartments were ready to roll and the cash flow on the way.

Chapter 4

"Well? What do you think?" Mercedes turned the large white sign with black letters around so Carlita could read the words:

"Unfair in Walton Square."

"Catchy," Carlita said. "How many signs have you made?"

"Ten. I have enough for everyone plus a couple extra." Mercedes rattled off the names. "We have Ken and Faith Colby, Autumn and Steve Winter, Ruby McKinley, Annie Dowton and us for a total of eight picketers. That should be enough to get some attention."

"Hopefully not arrested," Carlita groaned as she picked up one of the signs. "I can't wait to see what Monday brings."

***

The weekend passed uneventfully, and even seemed to drag as Carlita waited for Monday's protest. She woke early Monday morning, anxious to do something, anything to move her business aspirations forward.

By eleven, she was raring to go, and so was Mercedes, who was sitting at the dining room table, doodling on the corner of one of the picket signs.

"We should pack some bottled waters to distribute to our volunteers." Carlita said as she made her way to the hall closet to grab an empty backpack before heading to the kitchen where she filled it with not only bottled waters, but also a handful of energy bars and a bottle of sunscreen.

At 11:40 on the dot, Carlita carried the backpack and Mercedes carried the signs downstairs.

Bob Lowman was in the store, working in the backroom when the women reached the bottom of the steps. "Let me help." He took the backpack from Carlita and the signs from Mercedes. "You're picketing after all?"

"We'll be out there at noon," Mercedes announced.

"I'll be there to cheer you on," Bob grinned as he shook his head. He followed the women into the alley and waited while Mercedes opened the trunk of the car. He placed the signs in the bottom and the backpack on top before slamming the trunk shut. "I can't wait to see the expression on old Calvin's face."

"Thanks for the hand," Carlita said. "You sure you don't want to join us?"

"Nah. I think you'll ruffle enough feathers without my boots on the ground." Bob saluted the women and then turned on his heel and headed back inside.

Mother and daughter were the first to arrive on scene and parked the car on a side street. Autumn and Steve arrived not long after, followed by Ken and Faith Colby. Ruby McKinley and Annie Dowton were the last to arrive.

The group quickly decided to let Ruby take the lead since she was the only one who had ever picketed before, although she claimed it had been decades ago. They decided a single file march and chant were in order to draw attention to Carlita's cause.

Autumn assured them she had lined up a news crew, who would show up around 12:20 for some quick footage that would make the six o'clock evening news.

Carlita's palms began to sweat as she followed the others around the side of the building and onto the sidewalk out front.

For a brief moment, she wondered how in the world she had let her daughter talk her into picketing, but Mercedes had a way with her mother. She remembered the sidecar. It wasn't all bad. Mercedes had some great ideas.

The volunteers, along with mother and daughter, lifted their signs high in the air, marching down the sidewalk chanting, "Unfair in Walton Square," and "Support Local Business."

They drew a fair amount of attention, and many of the cars that passed by honked and the passengers waved or gave a thumbs up. A few of them even pulled off to the side to ask if they needed more volunteers and several of the pedestrians hovered near the curb to take their picture.

The Savannah Evening News reporter, along with a Channel 9 News crew, showed up right on time and a young reporter interviewed Mercedes, who did an excellent job of stating their grievance and asking viewers to contact the district office to demand they issue the pawnshop license. She even remembered to mention another pawnshop was located in the historic district.

The news crew wrapped up the interview and headed out while the protesters continued the march.

Things were going smoothly and they'd even had time to take a quick break before the front doors of Savannah-Burnham District Office flew open and a flurry of police officers marched down the steps. They lined both sides of the steps and glared at Carlita and the protesters.

A man dressed in a dark suit, with curly black hair and a frown on his face descended the steps. He stopped on the bottom step. "What is going on here?" he roared.

"We're picketing," Mercedes stepped closer to the building. "My mother and I applied for a business license almost a month ago and a Mr. Yates, who works in your licensing department, is blowing us off."

A small man with a receding hairline scurried down the steps and hovered behind the man in the dark suit. "I can explain Mr. Burell. A Ms. Garlucci applied for a pawnshop license in the Walton Square district."

"And?" Calvin Burell turned his attention to the man. "What's the holdup Mr. Yates?"

"I-I was just getting ready to submit the permit application last week when I received an anonymous letter about an unlawful drug ring operating out of that location."

Carlita was so stunned; she dropped her sign, the tip of it stabbing her big toe. "Ouch."

"We have not." Mercedes pointed her sign at the man. "That's absurd."

Mr. Yates puffed up his chest. "I assure you we are thoroughly investigating the matter."

It was the first time Carlita had heard such a thing, which meant the district couldn't have been doing that thorough of an investigation if the "investigatee" hadn't even been contacted.

Just then, a strong gust of wind whipped around the side of the building and blew Carlita's bangs into her eyes, causing her momentary blindness.

Carlita swept her hair to the side and attempted to tuck the strands behind her ear. She wasn't the only one who was having their hair tossed in the wind.

The front of Mr. Yates' hair flipped up and began flapping up and down.

"Oh my gosh." Carlita held onto her hair with one hand and covered her mouth with her other.

Mr. Yates was unaware his hair was bobbing up and down, but Ruby noticed and she lifted the bullhorn to her lips. "Your rug is making a run for it."

The Walton Square picketers began to snicker and all eyes were on Mr. Yates. He hadn't heard what Ruby had said as he began huffing and puffing about protocol and following procedure.

The district office manager, realizing all eyes were no longer on him but on Mr. Yates, shifted his gaze. He lifted a hand to point at his employee's head when the toupee peeled back, flew off and landed on the cement step behind him.

Yates must've felt a cool breeze on his smooth head as he lifted his hand and patted the top. His eyes widened and he spun around before snatching his toupee off the steps and racing toward the building. He flung the front door open and disappeared inside.

Calvin Burell turned to face the protestors, his eyes scanning the crowd. "Mrs. Garlucci."

Carlita raised her hand and took a step forward. "Here."

The district office manager took a step down. "I wasn't apprised of your situation, but rest assured I will get to the bottom of your license application status."

Carlita thanked Mr. Burell before he turned on his heel and made his way back inside the building. The formation of police officers followed behind.

"I guess we've done everything we can possibly do," Carlita told the group of protesters. "I appreciate your time, but we can pack it up and head home."

The group carried their signs to their vehicles.

"Yates is blowing smoke," Steve said as he took the signs from the protesters and threw them in the back of his pick-up truck.

"Sounds like a disgruntled business owner." Ruby tapped her bullhorn on the palm of her hand. "Where is the other pawnshop Mercedes mentioned?"

"Paradise Pawn," Ken Colby nodded. "They're not far from City Market."

Carlita remembered how, during his recent visit, her oldest son, Vinnie, had visited Paradise Pawn to scope out their business and even talked to one of the owners. "But how would he know we were applying for a pawnshop business license?"

"It's public information," Annie said. "Or maybe the owners know someone who works at the district office."

"Let's hope Calvin Burell will follow through with his promise and you'll get your license," Ken Colby said.

The group disbanded and each of the Walton Square owners told Carlita to let them know if there was anything else, they could do to help.

Mercedes and Carlita walked to their car, which was parked nearby.

Carlita slid into the passenger seat and smoothed her hair. "I'm not sure if the protest made our situation better or worse."

"Me either." Mercedes started the car and mother and daughter drove home, mission thus far, unaccomplished.

Chapter 5

Mercedes and Carlita tuned to Channel 9 and the six o'clock news, hoping to catch a glimpse of their protest in front of the district office, but there was only a brief mention with the news anchor telling viewers they would have the complete story on the eleven o'clock news.

"I'm not going to be able to stay awake until eleven." Carlita was exhausted.

"I'll record it." Mercedes grabbed the remote, clicked a few buttons and then turned the television off. "All set."

Holding onto a glimmer of hope the news coverage would nudge the officials into issuing her pawnshop license, Carlita headed to bed.

***

Carlita woke to someone pounding on the outside of her bedroom door. Her eyes flew to the bedside clock. It was 8:15 in the morning, an hour past her usual wake up time.

She threw the covers back and crawled out, hurrying to open the door.

Mercedes was standing in the hall. "Autumn called me a few minutes ago. Steve just got to the tattoo shop.

Someone busted out his back window and spray painted the floor of his shop."

"You're kidding." Carlita said. "Let me get dressed and we'll run over there to see if we can help." She threw on the first outfit she saw, quickly brushed her teeth and splashed cold water on her face.

Mercedes was pacing the living room floor. "Something is going on. First someone breaks into our courtyard and destroys the water fountain and now this."

"I'll be right back." Rambo still needed his morning bathroom break so Carlita led him down the steps and out the door.

The smell of fresh asphalt filled the alley. Carlita took a quick glance to the side. "It looks like Bob's crew finally filled our pothole."

The pothole in the alley was an accident that had already happened...Autumn's Segway accident to be exact. There was a smaller pothole near the other end of the alley and when Carlita got close, she was relieved to see that one patched, as well.

Bob had also finished clearing the brush from the small tenant parking lot off to the side and she made a mental note to thank him before leading Rambo back upstairs.

Mercedes was waiting in the outer hall. Rambo trotted into the apartment and the women headed out and across the street to Steve's tattoo shop.

Carlita slowly pushed open the front door of the shop and stuck her head inside. Angry splotches of black paint dotted the floor. The front of the cash register and counter looked as if a two year old had gotten hold of a paintball gun and gone to town.

"Oh no," Carlita gasped.

"Oh yes." Steve stepped from behind the counter and held up a hand. "Don't walk over here. I'm not sure if it's even dry."

Carlita took a step back. "This is crazy. Someone is targeting our neighborhood."

Steve grimaced. "What a mess. You didn't happen to see anything unusual or notice anyone hanging around last night?"

Carlita shook her head. Although her place was only a stone's throw from the tattoo shop, none of the windows faced Steve's shop. "I'm sorry. I didn't see anything, Steve."

"I don't know if I should bother calling the cops." Steve shook his head in disgust. "A couple coats of paint and

458

it'll look like new. At least the floor is concrete. It's a pain, but a lot quicker than filling out a police report."

"Mercedes and I will help," Carlita offered. "The three of us can have a fresh coat of paint down in no time."

"Thanks," Steve said. "I appreciate it."

Carlita and Mercedes headed home to change into work clothes while Steve ran to the nearest hardware store to purchase several gallons of gray paint and some rollers.

They met back at the shop and the trio worked efficiently, covering the shop floor in a fresh coat of gray paint within the hour.

After applying the first coat, they took a break to wait for the floor to dry and walked to a nearby coffee shop to grab breakfast sandwiches and coffee. By the time they returned, the first coat was dry and they began applying a second coat as well as painting and cleaning the cash register and counter.

The morning flew by and the trio finished the task around noon. "Thanks for the help ladies. I think it'll be dry by the time my first appointment shows up at three."

"You're welcome," Carlita said. They stood in the small hall leading to the storage area in the rear of the store. "Do you have any idea how they got in?" she asked.

"They busted out the bathroom window," Steve said. "This is the first time in the four years I've been here that I've had a break in."

Mercedes turned to her mother. "Do you think this has anything to do with what happened in the courtyard?"

"What happened in the courtyard?" Steve asked.

Carlita explained how she had found her courtyard gate busted and upon investigating, discovered someone had destroyed their fountain, knocking the figurine's head off, and cracking the base. "They may very well be related."

"Not to mention the anonymous note sent to the district office, telling them we're dealing drugs," Mercedes pointed out. "We should warn the others."

"Good idea," Carlita agreed. "I'm sorry this happened to you, Steve."

The women left a few minutes later, making their way through the back alley and down the sidewalk. "Let's stop by Ruby's place first to warn her," Carlita said.

Ruby wasn't there, so they headed to Annie's real estate office. The place was locked tight so the women headed back across the street to their apartment.

When they got inside, Carlita reached for her phone to text Annie but much to her surprise, Annie had already sent her a message. "Good news. I have someone who would like to take a look at the apartment later today."

Carlita replied to Annie's text to confirm the appointment and told her she'd decided to rent the apartment directly across the hall first. She pressed the send button on the screen and placed it on the kitchen counter.

Mercedes wandered into the kitchen and over to the fridge where she reached inside and pulled out a bottled water. "I asked Autumn if she was still interested in moving into one of the units."

Carlita nodded. On the one hand, if Autumn decided to move in, she would not have to run a background check on her, but on the other, she wasn't sure she wanted Autumn living in close proximity to Mercedes.

Mercedes unscrewed the top on the water bottle and took a big gulp. "She said she just signed another year's lease on the place that she's in." It was apparent Mercedes had given the situation some thought. "It's probably best that Autumn not live here. I mean, if she didn't pay her rent, how could you evict your friend?"

Carlita hadn't thought of that angle. "Good point. It looks like we'll go ahead and rent both units across the hall." She was still holding out hope that her son, Vinnie, would join them and move into the apartment directly behind Carlita and Mercedes.

The women took turns in the bathroom and after Carlita cleaned up and dressed, she grabbed her cell phone off the kitchen counter. It was time to have a chat with Rodney Yates, to get to the bottom of the mysterious letter stating Carlita was dealing drugs.

He didn't answer so Carlita left a message. She poured a glass of iced tea and stepped out onto the deck with Rambo. The air was stifling and the day was going to be another scorcher.

She took a sip of tea and then set the glass on the small table before walking over to the tomato plants she had placed along the edge of the deck. There was just enough noonday sun for the plants to thrive. Several of the tomatoes were ripe and ready to pick so she plucked them from the vine and set them on the small patio table, next to her tea.

Carlita had also planted a pot of basil. She snipped several pieces off and set them next to the tomatoes.

Soon, she would have more tomatoes than she could eat, but for now, she had enough to make one of her favorite summer dishes, gazpacho soup.

Carlita and Rambo settled into the chaise lounge. At first, Carlita thought she would never use the apartment's deck, since there wasn't much of a view and it overlooked the alley, but the more time she spent using it, the more she liked it.

The alley had a life of its own. The squirrels had created a path across the electrical wires that connected her building to the one across the alley. Two cardinals had built a nest on the roof of the neighboring building.

After finishing her tea, she headed to the kitchen where she lifted her apron from the hook and slipped it over her head before tying it in the back.

The gazpacho would need a few hours to chill so she decided to make a big batch now and then Mercedes and she could eat it for dinner.

Carlita preferred her gazpacho pureed so she pulled her food processor from the cupboard before chopping chunks of green bell pepper, onion and tomatoes and placing them inside.

She added small pieces of fresh garlic before turning the food processor on.

Once the vegetables were minced, and the green onion and cucumber chopped, she added the other ingredients, blending each of the ingredients in a large Tupperware bowl and then placing the mixture inside the fridge.

Carlita's phone chirped. It was Annie, letting her know she and the potential tenant were across the hall.

Carlita had decided to let Annie handle the showing and asked her to send another text when they had finished the tour.

She darted over to the peephole and peeked out, catching a glimpse of the back of Annie's head. Standing next to her was petite woman holding the hand of a young child. They disappeared inside the apartment and the door shut.

Mercedes' bedroom door flew open and she darted into the living room. "I think I might be getting a job."

Chapter 6

Carlita straightened her back. "A job? What kind of job?"

"It's a temporary, part-time job working as a receptionist at the newspaper with Autumn."

"I didn't know you were looking for a job. What about the pawnshop and restaurant?"

"It could take months for us to get up and running," Mercedes said. "In the meantime, I can work to make a little extra cash to help cover our expenses."

Carlita's heart sank. She slowly stepped over to her daughter as tears welled in her eyes. "I love you Mercedes, and it's so sweet that you're worried about money and us, but remember, we still have several gems left to sell, not to mention I still have part of the money from the sale of the house in Queens."

"I want to help." Mercedes clasped her hands beneath her chin. "Plus it will keep me busy and out of trouble."

Carlita had her doubts about the second half of that statement. Working with Autumn might put her smack dab in the middle of trouble.

"You're an adult, Mercedes," Carlita said. "I can't stop you."

She went on. "When would you start?"

"I go in for my interview with Autumn's boss this afternoon, which means I better get ready." Mercedes disappeared inside her room and Carlita could hear her banging around in her closet.

Perhaps a job wasn't such a bad idea after all. Mercedes could make some new friends; it would get her out of the house and give her something to do. Not only that, she seemed so excited.

Carlita's cell phone rang and she picked it up. It was her middle son, Tony. "How you doin' ma?"

"I'm good, but frustrated," Carlita admitted. "We're still waiting on the district office to issue a license for the pawnshop."

"Do I need to come down there and knock a few heads together?" Tony asked.

Carlita smiled at the vision of Tony knocking Calvin Burrell and Mr. Yates's heads together. "I'm not sure that would help."

"Well, the reason I called, other than to see how you and Mercedes were doing, is I was thinking about coming down for a visit, you know scope the place out."

"We would love for you to visit. I'm sure Rambo would be thrilled to see you too." Rambo had been Tony's dog before he had given him to his mother for protection. "When?"

"I got some business dealings to wrap up but I was thinkin' I could hit the road toward the end of next week and be there Saturday or Sunday."

That would give Carlita enough time to clean house and plan some things for the three of them to do. "We can hardly wait to see you. Mercedes has a job interview later today."

"A job? What kinda job? You need some money?"

"No." Carlita shook her head. "I think she's bored. This may be a good thing and a way for her to make friends."

The two of them talked for a few more minutes and Tony promised to give his mother a call later in the week to update her on his plans.

The news of her son's upcoming visit cheered Carlita and with a spring in her step, she and Rambo headed down the steps and to the courtyard. When she spotted the busted fountain, her mood shifted.

Someone was targeting not only her, but Steve Winters, as well. Who would contact the licensing department and tell them she was a drug dealer? It was absurd. Still, the thought of having the government digging around in her past, in her husband's past, was a little unnerving.

Carlita wasn't sure exactly what they would find. She had nothing to hide, but her deceased husband, and her sons, Vinnie and Tony...that was another story.

"Knock. Knock." Carlita turned her attention to the gate where Annie stood on the other side.

Carlita stepped over to the gate and opened it.

"I saw you out my front office window and thought I'd run over. The showing went well," Annie said. "I do have something to discuss, if you have a minute."

"Of course," Carlita waved Annie to one of the bistro chairs. "Have a seat."

Annie eased into a seat while Carlita sat across from her. "What's up?"

"It's about the potential tenant. Her name is Shelby Towns. She has a four-year old daughter, Violet."

"Pretty names," Carlita commented.

"They're sweet as can be. Why her little girl is adorable." Annie rubbed her index finger across the bistro table, swiping at a small spot of dirt. "I think they would make wonderful tenants."

"Great."

"There are a couple things I need to tell you before I start working on the paperwork or running the background check."

Something in the tone of Annie's voice...whatever it was, was serious. "Shelby and Violet are living in a local women's shelter. The shelter is helping Shelby and her daughter to get back on their feet by paying the deposit and first month's rent."

"Oh my." Carlita frowned. "She's homeless."

"Yes. I don't know the circumstances. Shelby didn't offer and I can't ask, but I can tell you that she told me she has just accepted a part-time position at the local post office and hopes to move into a full-time position. She is only able to afford eight-hundred dollars a month for rent."

Annie continued. "The going rate for your apartment is almost double that. I didn't promise Shelby anything

469

and she said she understood, but what she can afford, well, it's in a rough area of town."

Carlita's stomach knotted. "She's in a tough spot," Carlita whispered. Tears welled in the back of her eyes as she thought about the young mother, down on her luck.

"She is." Annie lowered her gaze. "I don't know if she has family. Obviously, no one she can turn to for help."

Carlita slowly nodded. "I see."

"Would you like to meet her? She's in my office filling out papers," Annie said. "It's up to you. If you don't want to take that low of a monthly rent payment, she understands...I understand."

"No." Carlita sprang to her feet. "I would like to chat with her."

Rambo and Carlita followed Annie out of the courtyard, across the street and into the real estate office where a young woman sat with her back to the door. A small child with light brown hair sat in the chair next to her.

The child spun around and then hid behind the top of the chair, her eyes following them as they made their way inside.

The woman turned and then quickly stood, a shy smile lifting the corners of her mouth.

"Shelby, this is Carlita Garlucci. She owns the apartment you just looked at," Annie said. "I briefly explained your situation."

"Hello Mrs. Garlucci." The woman extended her hand and Carlita took it.

"Hello Shelby."

"I'm Violet," the small girl piped up.

"Hello Violet." Carlita bent down to eye level and smiled at the innocent young face. "What pretty pink hair bows in your hair."

Violet lifted a hand and patted the bows. "Mommy fixed my hair."

"She did a wonderful job," Carlita said. "You look like a princess." She turned to Shelby. "I heard you are looking for a place near downtown and you just got a job."

Shelby nodded. "Yes, ma'am. I've looked at a few places, but..." her voice trailed off as she glanced at her young daughter. "The apartments we can afford are not safe. I-I know your apartment rents for a lot more, but I hoped perhaps we could work out an arrangement."

471

Carlita nodded, listening intently.

"I was thinking if I could pay you what I can afford right now and then when I move into a full-time position, I'll be able to start paying a higher rent and then a little extra to catch up." Shelby clasped her hands and laced her fingers together. "I – It's such a nice area and safe..."

If she only knew...well, it was mostly safe.

"Annie told me you're living in a shelter right now," Carlita said.

"I have a lot of friends to play with, but sometimes they don't share toys," Violet said solemnly.

"I'm sorry to hear that dear," Carlita said. She turned back to Shelby. There was a look of determination in the young mother's eyes. It was a look that Carlita recognized in her own eyes, ever since her husband's death.

It was apparent the woman needed help...a small hand up. Carlita swallowed the lump in her throat and blinked, willing herself not to burst into tears as she forced a watery smile. "Annie will still need to run a background check. If you pass the screening, I'll rent the apartment to you on a couple conditions."

Shelby was visibly relieved. "Yes, of course."

"One." Carlita lifted a finger. "You pay what you can, the agreed $800/ per month and two." She lifted a second finger. "We agree the amount is full payment with no back rent due, but if, and when, you get back on your feet, we will adjust your rent to the current market rate."

"I...yes." Shelby's lower lip began to tremble and she burst into tears as she dropped her head into her hands.

Violet bolted out of the chair, ran over to her mother and wrapped both arms around her legs. "Mommy, don't cry."

The tears rolled down Carlita's cheeks at the sight and she stared at Annie helplessly. Annie was crying too.

Carlita wrapped her arm around the young mother's shoulders. "It's okay, Shelby. This is a good thing," she said.

"I know," Shelby sobbed and then sucked in a deep breath. "It's just that I need a break so bad," she whispered.

Annie handed a tissue to Shelby, another to Carlita and then dabbed at her own eyes. "Lordy, we're a mess," she said.

"That we are," Carlita agreed.

"Thank you, Mrs. Garlucci. You won't be sorry," Shelby whispered.

Violet tugged on the edge of her mother's blouse. "Can I pet the doggy Mommy?"

Carlita had almost forgotten about Rambo. "Rambo wouldn't hurt a flea," she assured the mother.

"Yes, you can pet the dog," Shelby told her daughter as she swiped at her eyes.

Violet tiptoed over to Rambo, who was sitting on the floor near the desk. "Mambo."

"Rambo," her mother corrected.

"Rambo." Violet said. She patted his head. "Nice doggy."

Rambo licked the side of Violet's arm and she started to giggle. "That tickles."

Violet petted his ear and then suddenly wrapped both of her small arms around the dog's neck, placing her cheek against the side of his face. She closed her eyes.

Carlita could've sworn Rambo smiled as he let out a low, happy moan. She released her grip, patted his head one more time and then skipped over to her mother. "He likes me."

Rambo followed her, anxious for more attention. "He sure does," Carlita agreed. "We better get out of here so you can finish the paperwork."

Shelby thanked Carlita a half a dozen times before Carlita exited the office, promising her she wouldn't regret giving her and her daughter a chance.

Annie followed Carlita to the sidewalk, closing the door behind her. "I didn't have time to tell you that I have another appointment scheduled in about fifteen minutes."

"Good," Carlita nodded and then glanced through the front glass door where Shelby and Violet sat close together in one of the chairs.

"Thank you for telling me about their situation," Carlita said.

"You're welcome, and I'll stop by if anything comes of the second showing," Annie promised before heading back inside her office.

Carlita returned to the apartment and found Mercedes sitting on the edge of the recliner, remote in hand. "Have you seen the taped recording of our picket yet?"

"No. Honestly, I forgot all about it." Carlita unhooked Rambo's leash. "Did you?"

"Yeah." Mercedes chuckled. "I'm glad we recorded it. We'll have to keep this one handy for the times we need a good laugh."

The first section of the clip showed a quick shot of the group chanting and marching as they held their signs. The camera panned to the reporter, who stated Carlita's case bluntly, how she was a new business owner in Walton Square who had applied for a building license to open a pawnshop and the district office was dragging its feet.

"You look good," Carlita told her daughter as the camera zoomed in for a close up of Mercedes as she waved her sign back and forth and then began talking to the reporter.

She watched Ken and Faith Colby as they marched behind Mercedes. Ruby McKinley was next.

Annie was behind Ruby, followed by Steve and Autumn. Carlita brought up the rear.

When the manager and the uniformed police officers burst onto the scene, the camera zoomed in. Carlita remembered most of the district office manager's speech and when Mr. Yates made his way down the steps, stating his reason the department hadn't issued the license yet, Carlita's ears burned.

She wondered why Mr. Yates had not been forthright in his reason for not issuing the license instead of hem hawing around, making excuses.

The toupee incident was the highlight of the clip and Carlita grinned.

After the recording ended, she turned the television off and reached for her cell phone, determined to take the bull by the horns.

Carlita left another message, asking more firmly for Rodney Yates to return her call and then jabbed the end call button. "Ugh. There's one thing I miss about having a house phone and that's being able to slam the phone down."

Mercedes popped out of the chair. "I gotta get going or I'll be late for my interview." She gave her mother a quick hug and darted out the door.

With time on her hands, Carlita wandered into Mercedes' room to use the computer. She settled into the chair, and reached for the mouse. The dark screen disappeared and the screen opened up.

She scrolled to the search bar when something caught her eye. *"Murder, Mayhem & the Mafia."* The icon was one Carlita had noticed once before.

"Should I or shouldn't I?" Carlita had never been one to snoop on her children. She trusted them, she trusted Mercedes. Curiosity won out. She clicked on the icon and a Word document popped up:

Murder, Mayhem & the Mafia. A Mob Daughter's Confessions by Author Mercedes Garlucci.

Carlita's hand flew to her throat and her eyes widened as all of the pieces began to fall into place. All of the times Mercedes hid out in her room, always closing her computer when her mother came in the room and insisting her mother get her own laptop.

Mercedes was writing a book.

Carlita hovered over the "x" at the top to close the document, before changing her mind. She began reading the first paragraph.

"Sophia Marucchi slipped into the back of the pool hall. All eyes were focused on the front as she made her way across the room undetected.

Her father, who was conducting a business meeting near the front, would be furious if he knew his only daughter had followed him, but she had to know. Had her beloved father offed her boyfriend, Jimmy? She'd heard the whispered rumors but couldn't believe her father was a ruthless killer.

478

Sophia eased behind the bar area. Her heart began to pound as she heard someone mention Jimmy's name."

Carlita clicked out of the document, closed her eyes and placed the palm of her hand on her forehead. She had always believed her daughter had been sheltered from her father and brother's chosen careers and never really been exposed to the "family" business...or had she?

All these years, Carlita tried to shield her daughter, but perhaps it had backfired, piquing Mercedes' curiosity about her family's business dealings.

Carlita tried to focus on researching recipes but her mind kept wandering to her daughter's book, torn between confessing to her she'd read a small part of it and pretending she hadn't seen it.

She didn't want her daughter to think she was a snoop or that she was under her mother's thumb. Finally, she decided if her daughter wanted to tell her about dipping her toes in the literary world, she would do so when she was ready.

She managed to find a couple intriguing recipes before clicking out of the search screen, closing the lid on the computer and heading back to the kitchen.

She was halfway there when the doorbell rang so she changed direction and headed to the front, gazing through the peephole as she reached for the doorknob. It was Annie.

Carlita flung the door open. "You're not going to make me cry again."

"Nah. I might have more good news," Annie smiled and shook her head.

"Come in. Have a seat." She led Annie into the living room and motioned Annie to the sofa. "Can I get you a bottled water? A cup of coffee?"

"Water would be great."

After bringing Annie the bottled water, she settled into the recliner. "Did you show the second apartment?"

"Yes. I showed both the front and the back unit." Annie unscrewed the cap on the bottle of water and took a big swig. "I like to think I'm a good judge of character so I'll give you my honest opinion."

"And?"

"I think the second potential tenant could be a royal pain in the rear."

Chapter 7

"Pain in the rear?"

Annie ticked off her mental list. "It's a single woman. She seems extremely picky, nosy, arrogant and rude, and those appear to be her redeeming qualities."

Carlita wrinkled her nose. "You're kidding."

"Okay. Maybe not that bad. Let's just go with she may be trouble." Annie shifted to a more comfortable position. "She's concerned about noise, whether pets are allowed and every time I tried to answer, she cut me off. I barely got a word in edgewise."

"Let's hold off on giving her an answer for a few days," Carlita said. "Maybe we can find a more promising prospective tenant in the meantime."

"I agree."

The women chatted about the neighborhood and the recent vandalism. Annie hadn't heard about the incident at Steve's tattoo shop. "We should form a neighborhood watch," Annie said. "We can all buy Segways to patrol the neighborhood. I see your daughter zipping around on one and it looks like fun."

Carlita grinned. "It's all fun and games until someone plows you over."

"Your daughter plowed you over?" Annie gasped.

"No. Autumn, Steve Winter's sister, did." Carlita told Annie the story of how she met Autumn when the young woman knocked her over with her Segway. "Mercedes just bought one and has been bugging me to give it a go, but I'm not sure yet. It would be nice to be able to get from one end of town to the other quickly."

They chatted about life in Walton Square and how much they enjoyed the neighborhood. Carlita told Annie how grateful she was for the support of the others.

"Thank you for helping me screen tenants," Carlita smiled. "I owe you lunch."

"No need," Annie said. "I think you're so sweet to allow Shelby and Violet the chance for a better life. I'll let you know as soon as I hear back on Shelby's background check."

The women discussed the tenants for a few moments before Carlita turned the conversation to Annie. "Do you have family in Savannah, Annie?"

Annie lowered her gaze and shook her head. "No. No family. I lived in Atlanta most of my life but got tired of the big city so I started to do some research about five years back. When I stumbled upon Savannah, I visited for several days and fell in love." She shrugged. "I've been here ever since."

"So your family is in Atlanta?" Carlita asked.

"I don't have a family," Annie spoke softly. "It's just me."

"I…" Carlita stared at the woman across from her, at a loss for words.

"You're sorry." Annie finished her sentence. "Don't be. I have a great life, wonderful employees and close friends. I have everything I need." She gave Carlita a half-hearted smile as she twisted the lid on her water bottle. "Better to have no family than one who doesn't love you."

Annie's words were light but her somber expression just the opposite. There was some deep pain inside the woman and the last thing Carlita wanted to do was open old wounds for her new friend.

"Friends can be just as important as family," Carlita said. She didn't know what else to say and thankfully, Annie's cell phone chirped. She pulled it from her purse and stared at the screen. "My assistant, Cindy, just texted me. Shelby passed her background check. She's clean as a whistle."

Annie looked up. "I'll have Cindy contact Shelby to have her come back in, sign the paperwork, secure the deposit and first month's rent and then give her the key you gave me."

"Yes." Carlita nodded. "As soon as you have everything in order, Shelby and Violet can move in. I would wait on the other one. Hopefully, we'll get someone who is not so...particular."

Annie's phone began ringing. "It's Cindy."

She turned her attention to the phone. "Hello? What was that?" She rolled her eyes. "You're kidding. Okay thanks for the heads up. I'm on my way back to the office."

Annie stood. "The woman I showed the apartment to earlier has called four times and now she's demanding to speak to the owner of the property. Something about discrimination because of her sex."

"She thinks she's being discriminated against?" Carlita gasped. "How can I discriminate? I've never met the woman. Plus, I am a woman!"

Annie patted her arm. "Don't worry. I'll take care of it."

Carlita walked Annie down the steps, through the store and out the front door before heading back to the apartment.

Bob Lowman, the construction supervisor, stepped out of one of the rear units as Carlita was reaching for the doorknob.

"We're almost done, Carlita. I caught a glimpse of yesterday's protest on the late night news. Hopefully, the district office will get a move on and make a decision on the license."

"I hope so, too."

"Are you planning to start working on the restaurant now?" There was one property left to renovate, the former Denny's Diner. The restaurant was in the worst condition construction-wise and Carlita was on the fence about starting renovations until she had a firm answer on the business license for the store.

"I thought I would put it off until I have a clear idea of what to do downstairs."

Bob nodded. "No problem. I have a couple other jobs I can send my guys to. I'll check back with you in a couple weeks."

Two of his men stepped out of the unit and descended the steps. "I have one final draw, a small one, which is due when we finish a final walk-thru of the last unit in the back this afternoon."

"Two-thousand and some change?" Carlita asked. She remembered looking at the contract not long ago.

"Yes ma'am."

"Perfect." Carlita nodded. "Just in time. I have at least one unit rented."

They chatted for a few moments before Mercedes came blowing through the downstairs back door, dragging her new Segway behind her. "Oh my gosh. You'll never guess what."

Chapter 8

"You got the job," Carlita guessed.

"No. Mr. Tanner said he would let me know," Mercedes said as she whipped her helmet off and then hung it on one of the Segway handles. "I stopped by Colby's Corner Store on the way here and someone dumped their dumpster over last night. There's trash everywhere."

Carlita's heart sank. "You're kidding."

"Nope. I tried to help but since I was wearing my interview clothes, I didn't want to ruin them so I'm going to change and go back to help."

"I'll go too." Carlita told Bob good-bye before Mercedes and she hurried to their apartment.

After throwing on old clothes, they made the quick ten-minute walk to Colby's. When they arrived, there were several other volunteers combing the area and collecting trash, which was scattered everywhere.

Ken, who was filling a trash bag near the back of the tipped dumpster, looked up when Carlita and Mercedes approached.

"We're here to help," Carlita said.

"We'll take all the help we can get." Ken handed each of them a trash bag and pointed to the end of the alley. "We have a bunch of our old flyers blowing around the next block."

"We're on it." Carlita lifted her hand in a small salute and then Mercedes and she hurried to the adjacent alley. There were sheets of the ad everywhere, buried in bushes, stuck in doorways.

Mercedes picked up a pile of crumpled papers. "Someone is targeting Walton Square. First us, then Steve-O and now the Colby's."

Her daughter was right. The neighborhood was a target of vandals. It didn't make sense. The odd thing was they weren't breaking in to rob the businesses, just vandalize.

"I wonder who'll be next." Carlita thought of Annie and her real estate office. "Annie and I were discussing setting up a neighborhood watch."

Mercedes picked up a crumpled scrap of news ad and shoved it in her garbage bag. "That sounds exciting." She looked around and lowered her voice. "Can we carry our guns?"

Mother and daughter had visited a shooting range before moving from New York, but Carlita wasn't 100%

certain she could hit a target, although she might come close.

"I'm not sure about a gun, Mercedes," her mother said.

"Taser?"

Carlita frowned.

"We have to carry some sort of weapon," an exasperated Mercedes said. "What if we're attacked?"

"True." Mercedes had a valid point. What if the culprit stepped up their game and grew more brazen, robbing, attacking or even murdering one of the neighborhood residents? "I wonder if anyone else has fallen victim."

She thought about Ruby and her souvenir shop. There was also an ice cream shop, A Scoop in Time, which was only open in the evenings and on weekends.

Carlita and Mercedes had visited the ice cream shop several times and Carlita had attempted to meet the owners, the Fischers, but they were never around.

Carlita suspected their children ran the ice cream shop and she'd even caught a glimpse of a forty-something man sweeping the sidewalk out front but by the time Carlita ran over to introduce herself, he was gone and the ice cream shop closed.

Mother and daughter made quick work of cleaning the alley and then headed around the side, where they discovered several more sections of the flyer scattered about. They finished their cleanup by circling the entire city block before heading back to the alley.

Several men were tipping the dumpster upright and it landed with a loud bang, causing the ground to shake.

Carlita tossed her bag of flyers in the recycle bin and then helped the others toss bags of garbage inside the trash bin.

When they finished, Ken thanked everyone for their help and the crowd dispersed.

Carlita and Mercedes waited until Ken was alone. "Is there anything else that we can help with?" She was anxious to repay the favor since Ken and his daughter had picketed alongside them.

Ken wiped his hands on the front of his jeans and shook his head. "No. I think we got it all." He gazed at the dumpster. "I guess I'll have to put a padlock on it. Can you believe it? Having to put a padlock on a dumpster?"

"Did you hear Steve-O's tattoo shop was vandalized?" Mercedes asked.

"No," Ken shook his head. "I hadn't heard."

Carlita told him how one of his back store windows had been busted out, someone had snuck in and then sprayed paint all over the floor, cash register and counter. "First me, then Steve and now you. I wonder who'll be next."

"We're tossing around the idea of starting a neighborhood watch," Mercedes said.

"It's a thought," Ken said. "Only thing is, I wouldn't want Faith to patrol alone."

"We could do it in pairs," Mercedes said.

"I guess if the vandalism continues, we won't have a choice. It's either that, or stand back and let the thugs keep targeting us." Ken thanked them again and the women headed home.

Carlita had left her cell phone in the apartment and the first thing she did when she arrived was check to see if Mr. Yates had returned her call, which he hadn't. She left another message, telling him at the very least, she deserved to see a copy of the anonymous letter so she could defend herself.

Mercedes hurried to shower first while Carlita waited out on the deck. Rambo and their new cat, Grayvie, followed her out.

She patted Rambo's head and picked up Grayvie, who began purring loudly and sniffing her stinky shirt. "You like the deck, don't you," she cooed and scratched Grayvie's ears. "Maybe one day, I'll take you out to the courtyard to let you explore."

Mercedes and her friend, Autumn, had rescued Grayvie from Norma Jean Cleaver's place not long ago, after the woman's body had been found on their property.

Carlita determined Grayvie would make a nice addition to the family but decided the right thing to do was to see if Norma Jean's family wanted to claim the cat. They had sent a letter to Norma Jean's address to the "next of kin" but no one ever responded.

She set the cat down and watched as a familiar sports car pulled in behind the town car. It was Glenda Fox, her friend, and one of the Savannah Architectural Society members.

"Hey!" Carlita hollered after Glenda exited her Alfa Romeo and shut the door.

Glenda waved and Carlita hurried out of the apartment, down the steps and unlocked the back door. She gave her friend a brief hug.

"I tried calling," Glenda said.

"That's odd. I just checked my phone and didn't see a missed call." She motioned Glenda up the steps and into the apartment.

Rambo waited by the door. "Hey buddy." Glenda patted his head.

"I'll fix coffee."

Carlita tugged on the corner of her t-shirt. "Sorry about my clothes. We were over helping Ken Colby. Someone tipped his dumpster over and Mercedes and I were helping him clean up."

"Oh no." Glenda followed Carlita into the kitchen. She crossed her arms and leaned her hip against the side of the cabinet. "It looks like you've got your hands full between your instant celebrity-dom from the protest and trying to get your pawnshop license."

"Whew." Carlita blew air through thinned lips. "It's like pulling teeth. Did you see the clip? Mr. Yates said someone sent an anonymous letter, stating I was involved in possible drug dealings."

If Carlita's husband, Vinnie, had been alive, that may have been a possibility, but Carlita had moved away from Queens and the mafia lifestyle. The last thing she needed was for someone to start snooping around in her past.

"That's why I'm here. I've been promising to invite you over to see my home so I'm planning an afternoon tea. I think I can kill two birds with one stone. Throw a fabulous afternoon tea party plus help move your cause along."

Carlita filled the coffee pot with tap water and dumped the water in the reservoir before filling the basket with fresh coffee grounds and turning the machine on. "I can use all the help I can get."

"My idea is to invite you and your daughter, along with a couple of the district office elected officials, plus members of SAS for afternoon tea. Vicki Munroe is the mayor's sister. Perhaps we can butter her up and she can pull some strings," Glenda said.

"That would be awesome," Carlita reached for clean coffee cups. "I would be forever grateful."

"I owe you one." Glenda smiled. "An SAS afternoon soiree is long overdue. Now that Betty Graybill is gone and Vicki moved up to President, I've been nominated as Vice-President."

"Congratulations," Carlita said. *"Movin' on up,"* she sang.

"Ha. Plus, we have a new member coming on board. It would be like a welcome to SAS, a meeting with one of Walton Square's business owners and perhaps help you out, too."

"Oh. A party." Mercedes strolled into the kitchen, hairbrush in hand. "We finally get to check out the Fox's swanky digs," she teased.

Glenda grinned. "I hope you're not too disappointed. I was thinking next Monday around four."

"Perfect for me," Carlita said.

"Me too," Mercedes piped up. "I'm hoping to start working part-time at the Savannah Evening News. If I do, I'll be off around noon so I can make it."

"Reginald will be thrilled," Glenda said. "I'm on my way to SAS now and will invite them, as well. I also plan to pop some invitations in the mail as a reminder. It's kind of short notice but I think it'll still work."

The coffee finished brewing and Carlita poured two cups while Mercedes excused herself and disappeared inside her room.

Glenda and Carlita chatted about the protest as well as the recent acts of vandalism against the Walton Square business owners.

"Maybe you should contact the Savannah police about stepping up patrols around here," Glenda suggested.

"Good idea. I'll do that."

The women chatted easily and finally, Glenda stood, glancing at her watch. "I should head over to the office."

Carlita walked her to the lower level and waited until Glenda was safely inside her car before closing the door behind her. When she got back upstairs, she checked her phone again and there was a text message from Rodney Yates. Her heart began to pound as she clicked on the message:

"Per your request, attached is a copy of the letter I received."

There was a photo attachment and Carlita tapped on the photo before enlarging it:

"210 Mulberry Street is the home of a New York drug cartel."

Carlita could've sworn her heart stopped beating. "Oh. My. Gosh."

She absentmindedly made her way to Mercedes' bedroom door and tapped lightly on the outside.

Mercedes flung the door open and gazed at her mother. "What? You're white as a ghost."

"This is the anonymous letter Mr. Yates received." Carlita turned the phone so her daughter could read the words.

Mercedes' mouth dropped open. "You're kidding. But how did...do they know..." Her voice trailed off. "I don't believe it. It's just a freaky coincidence."

"I hope you're right, Mercedes. I hope you're right."

***

Carlita was a nervous wreck the rest of the afternoon, certain someone was lurking in the neighborhood who knew her history, knew Mercedes' history.

Bob stopped by and he and Carlita completed the final apartment walk-thru, after which she paid him the rest of the money owed for the apartment renovations.

She was going to miss Bob and his men, and for the umpteenth time she wished she had the business license in her hot little hands so she could move forward. Right now, it was more like her hands were tied and it was frustrating.

Mercedes and Carlita's dinner consisted of the fresh gazpacho soup Carlita had made that morning. She served it with a batch of fresh shrimp she'd recently purchased at Colby's and some crusty bread for dipping.

After dinner, Carlita watched a little television while Mercedes holed up in her room, working on her novel, Carlita was certain.

She was barely able to keep her eyes open for the eleven o'clock news, and headed to bed right after the local weather forecast.

Grayvie had claimed the end of the bed and Carlita's feet as his territory and he curled up while she crawled in. Rambo settled into his doggie bed in the corner.

Before Carlita drifted off to sleep, she offered up a quick prayer that the anonymous note was a fluke, a shot in the dark by some unknown person and that they wouldn't have any more incidents in Walton Square.

***

Carlita's eyes flew open. It took her a minute to realize someone was knocking on her bedroom door. She flung back the covers, almost tripping over Grayvie who had leapt off the bed.

She opened the door to find Mercedes on the other side. "Oh my gosh. Did I wake you? I thought I heard you moving around."

"It's okay, Mercedes. It was time for me to get up," her mother replied.

"I think I figured out who's behind the mysterious note to Savannah-Burnham District Office and the reason we don't have our business permit yet."

Chapter 9

Carlita blinked rapidly, trying to clear the fog from her head. "Who?"

"Paradise Pawn. I was doing a little research online and found an article from a couple weeks ago. They applied for a permit to expand their business. My thinking is when they applied down at the district office, someone tipped them off that we applied for a permit and they either paid someone off or know someone."

Carlita yawned, covering her mouth. "I wonder how we can find out."

"I already texted Autumn to see if she could nose around down at the newspaper. She also has a few connections with Savannah-Burnham PD."

"Good idea. You need to use the bathroom?" Carlita asked.

"Nope. It's all yours."

Carlita had just finished getting ready when she heard a loud *THUNK*. It rattled the picture on the bathroom wall.

"What was that?" Carlita hurried from the bathroom and over to the front door where she peered out the peephole. She caught a glimpse of Shelby, struggling to carry a bulky box through the door of the apartment.

Mercedes bolted from her room. "Did you hear that noise?"

"Yes. It's our new tenant. She's moving in," Carlita said. "What time is it?"

Mercedes glanced at the living room clock. "Eight-fifteen."

Carlita straightened her back, lifting her hands over her head. "I need a cup of coffee," she groaned. "This is going to be a long day." She was halfway to the kitchen when she heard another loud *THUNK*.

Rambo began to howl.

Carlita did an about face, momentarily forgetting about her much needed cup of coffee. "I should take Rambo out first."

"I already did, while you were in the bathroom," Mercedes said. "What do you think of the new tenants?"

"I think you'll like them. Her name is Shelby Towns and her daughter's name is Violet." Carlita briefly explained their situation. When she got to the part where the little girl was excited to be moving out of the women's shelter, Mercedes' eyes watered.

So, we're not making as much as we originally thought," Carlita finished.

"Money isn't everything," Mercedes said. "I wonder what forced her to move into a women's shelter."

"I don't know," Carlita confessed. "All I know is she and her little girl needed a safe place to live and Shelby passed the background check.

"I should grab a bite to eat and then offer to help." Carlita sliced a thick piece of lemon coffee cake and placed it on a paper napkin while she waited for the coffee to brew. After the coffee finished brewing, she carried a fresh cup and the sweet breakfast treat to the deck. She set the cup and napkin on the small side table and made her way over to the deck railing.

The only car in the alley was hers. She wondered if Shelby owned a vehicle. Obviously, she had to get around somehow. Carlita gobbled her breakfast, gulped her coffee as soon as it cooled and then carried her empty cup to the kitchen, rinsing it in the sink and placing it inside the dishwasher.

She hurried across the hall and knocked on Shelby's apartment door but no one answered. Carlita ran back to the apartment, scribbled a note, asking Shelby if she needed help moving and then shoved it under the door before returning to her own apartment.

Mercedes wandered into the living room. "I think it's time to do a little sleuthing on Paradise Pawn."

Vinnie, Carlita's son, had scoped it out during his brief visit some time ago, but Carlita hadn't been there yet and, as far as she knew, neither had Mercedes. "Sure. Let me grab my purse."

Rambo was waiting by the door. "Sorry Rambo. We can't take you with us, but when I get back, I'll take you to the park." Rambo thumped his tail on the floor and then slunk to the living room rug and flopped down.

"Let's take the Segway," Mercedes suggested.

"You take the Segway. I'll walk," Carlita countered. She still didn't trust the contraption.

"Nah. I guess we can walk." Mercedes gazed longingly at the Segway, parked off to the side in the hall below as they made their way into the alley.

"Maybe I'll give the Segway a try someday soon," Carlita said.

Paradise Pawn was located a block away from City Market, historic Savannah's shopping and restaurant district.

The building was a two-story brick structure with large bay windows facing the street. It reminded Carlita of a boutique store.

Mercedes reached for the front door handle. "This is nicer than I thought it would be."

"You're right," Carlita said. It was not what she had expected.

The doorbell tinkled as the women stepped inside. To the left of the entrance was a large, long glass counter. There was an identical one on the right hand side. In the center were shelves, crammed full of items for sale.

Near the back of the store were another door and a sign overhead that read "Antiquities and Artifacts."

The women started on the left, perusing the display case, filled with jewelry, watches and loose gems.

The center aisles sported a variety of items including small appliances, electronics, power tools and video games.

The display case on the right hand side showcased various collector's items, baseball cards, autographed posters and old books. Behind the counter and lining the walls were flat screen television sets in all different sizes and brands.

"They have a nice set up," Mercedes whispered in her mother's ear.

"I'm getting some great ideas." Carlita glanced around. The coffee she'd consumed had gone right through her. "I need to use the restroom." She pointed to the corner. "I see it over there." She headed to the restroom while Mercedes lingered off to one side, perusing the merchandise.

When Carlita returned a short time later, Mercedes was holding a shopping bag.

Carlita pointed at the bag. "You bought something?"

"Yep." Mercedes dangled the bag from her wrist. "I found it a few minutes ago. Had to barter since I didn't have enough cash to pay full price but finally, the clerk and I were able to agree on a price. Only twenty-five bucks. I've been researching these online and even saw this exact same one so I know I got a good deal."

"What is it?"

"A surprise." Mercedes grinned. "The bartering business is kinda fun."

The women finished inspecting the second display case before wandering into the antiquities room, filled with antique furniture, lamps and gilded picture frames.

There was even a rack of vintage clothing and hats. A musty smell lingered in the air and it reminded Carlita of her basement back in New York.

Mercedes ran the tip of her finger across the rim of a feathered cap. "This looks like some cool period clothing."

"Can I help you find something?"

Carlita spun around and came face to face with a smiling young man. "We're just browsing. You have a very nice store," she complimented.

His smile widened, displaying a dimple in his chin. "Thank you. My grandfather started this business over twenty years ago. I've been helping out here since I was a kid."

He pointed to the rack of women's clothing. "We're always in the market for period clothing if you want to clean out your closets."

Mercedes snorted. "Ha. We already did that before we moved down here."

The young man placed both hands behind his back. "You're locals?"

"Yes," Carlita nodded. "We own property on the other side of town, in Walton Square."

"Walton Square. Say, you're not the woman who recently moved to Savannah and began fixing the property over on Mulberry Street?"

Carlita's heart began to beat faster. She hadn't meant to let the owners of the pawnshop know who she was. Her eyes widened.

Mercedes piped up. "Yes. We just finished renovating the second floor apartments. We're also going to start working on fixing another building and perhaps open a restaurant." She didn't mention the pawnshop, but she didn't have to.

"Ah." The young man rocked back on his heels and nodded. "We heard you applied for a pawnshop business license down at the district office."

"We're tossing around the idea, but it's not set in stone," Carlita said, which was the truth. Carlita wasn't 100% sure they were planning on opening a pawnshop...just 99.9% sure, if they were able to get the necessary license.

"I see." The young man glanced behind him, to the front of the store. "Got a customer to wait on." He didn't wait for an answer as he made his way out of the room.

Mercedes tugged on her mother's arm. "Let's get out of here before we're cornered again."

The women made a beeline for the exit and made it within a few feet of the front door when a burly man with long dark hair, pulled back in a ponytail, blocked their path.

"Can I help you find something?"

"No. Uh. We were just leaving," Carlita replied. She attempted to sidestep the man, an employee wearing a nametag, *Ralph*.

The man didn't budge. "I overheard you talking to my son. You're Mrs. Garlicky."

"Garlucci," Carlita corrected. "Carlita Garlucci."

"Ah." He nodded his head. "Heard you applied for a pawnshop business license."

"Yes. We have." Mercedes nodded. "I'm sure there are enough customers in this town to support two pawnshops."

The man smiled evilly. "Guess you haven't heard."

"Heard what?" Carlita asked.

"The district office is going to turn down your request."

Chapter 10

"What a bunch of baloney," Mercedes argued. "We're still waiting for them to contact us."

Ralph shrugged. "Suit yourself. You'll find out soon enough."

Mercedes squared her shoulders, shot the man a dark look and then stomped out of the store and onto the sidewalk out front.

"I think he's lying," Mercedes said when her mother joined her. "If not and he pulled some strings down at the district office, I'll plan a second protest, except this time we'll protest a corrupt government."

"Aren't they all?" Carlita asked. "Corrupt, I mean." She sucked in a deep breath. "Maybe we should move onto 'Plan B' for the property."

"We don't have a Plan B," Mercedes grimaced.

"Well, we need to create one." Carlita pondered their predicament. Maybe God didn't intend for them to open a pawnshop. Maybe he had something better in mind. "Let's stop by the church you mentioned the other day. I've been meaning to check it out."

The women detoured, two blocks over, to the Cathedral of St. John the Baptist. It was a magnificent structure. A sign out front read *"Open for Visitors."*

Carlita pointed to the sign. "We can go in." She opened the door and held it for her daughter before closing the door behind them.

They could hear the faint echo of voices and followed them from the vestibule, through a large set of double doors where they stopped in their tracks, gazing into the sanctuary.

The upper walls of the sanctuary were lined with intricate woodcarvings depicting the Stations of the Cross. Beneath the carvings were stained glass windows. Each window consisted of vibrant, detailed frescoes.

Carlita lifted her gaze. Adorning the ceilings were stunning murals and soaring gothic arches. "Will you look at that," she whispered.

At the front of the sanctuary and off to one side, was a large confessional constructed of wood and etched glass.

Carlita nodded to the woman, a volunteer, seated at a table near the entrance before Mercedes and she walked down the center aisle to the front.

They scooted into a nearby pew. "I would love to come for Mass," Carlita told her daughter.

"Of course," Mercedes said. "I had no idea the inside of this place was like this." Although the outside was grandiose, it gave only a small inkling as to what the inside looked like.

The women sat quietly praying and finally, Carlita reluctantly stood. "We better get going." She slowly walked to the left, past the confessional and down the side aisle, which gave her a closer view of the Stations as she made her way to the back.

A small sign near the exit suggested a two-dollar donation. Carlita pulled a five-dollar bill from her purse, slid it in the round cylinder and twisted the knob. The money disappeared.

"We'll be back," she told the woman before mother and daughter walked out of the church.

They stepped out onto the sidewalk. The weather was starting to turn and dark storm clouds began to gather. "We better get a move on."

Mercedes and Carlita picked up the pace as small drops of warm rain splashed onto Carlita's face and arms. She breathed a sigh of relief when the alley and the back of their building were in sight.

Her relief was short-lived when she noticed someone hovering in the doorway. It was a gray haired woman, her hair pulled back and a scowl on her face.

"Can I help you?" Carlita asked.

"I'm waiting for Carlita Garlucci." She pronounced it "gar-Lucy."

"I'm Carlita Garlucci."

"Huh. I'm Elvira Cobb. I filled out an application yesterday to rent your apartment. I've been calling the real estate agent who showed me the apartment but she hasn't called back yet. Is the apartment still available?"

A bolt of lightning shook the ground nearby, saving Carlita from having to answer.

Mercedes quickly unlocked the door and the trio darted inside. She slammed the outer door behind them as the skies let loose and sheets of rain pelted the ground.

"I hoped to take a second look at the apartment. Since your agent is slacking off, I decided to track you down myself," Elvira said as she brushed drops of water off her arms and turned her attention to the stairwell. "I don't care for all of these stairs."

She sniffed the air and wrinkled her nose. "It smells musty in here. You would have to do something about the odor if I moved in." She clutched her throat. "Mold is bad for my asthma."

Elvira didn't wait for an answer as she grasped the handrail and slowly climbed the stairs.

Mercedes tapped her mother's arm, pointed at the woman's back and shook her head. Carlita shrugged helplessly as they followed the woman up the steps.

Elvira stopped in front of Shelby Towns' apartment door and reached for the knob.

Mercedes lunged forward. "We have a tenant occupying this property."

"What?" Elvira screeched. "I wanted that unit. The view of the courtyard from the back unit is obstructed by a tree."

"I'm sorry, but the front unit is occupied. The only unit available is the back unit." Carlita was leaning heavily toward not renting to the woman. She hadn't stopped complaining since she'd opened her mouth.

Elvira waved her hand dismissively. "I guess it will be all right. You'll have to cut the tree down so it doesn't block my view."

"I don't think so." Carlita shook her head.

Elvira ignored Carlita's comment and strode to the rear apartment. She stared at Carlita expectantly. "You're going to show the unit to me."

Mercedes slipped past Elvira and stood in front of the apartment door. "I don't think this apartment is a good fit for you, Ms. Cobb."

Elvira crossed her arms and took a step closer. "Have you rented the unit?"

"We are not going to make a decision on the next tenant until later this week," Carlita countered.

"Do you have other applicants?"

They didn't and somehow, this woman knew it.

"It doesn't matter," Mercedes insisted. "We aren't making a decision today."

"You're discriminating against me because of my age," Elvira argued.

Carlita chuckled. "I'm older than you."

"My weight," she shot back.

"Good heavens." Carlita rolled her eyes.

"I'm not a religious person."

"That's no surprise," Mercedes whispered under her breath.

"I'm going to report you to the ACLU," Elvira threatened.

Carlita blinked rapidly. "ACLU?"

"Don't play dumb with me." Elvira pulled her cell phone from her purse. "I'll call them right now."

The last thing Carlita needed was someone else investigating her. She held up a hand. "This is ridiculous." She decided to call the woman's bluff. "Go right ahead. You can't force me to rent my apartment to you."

The woman dropped the phone. Her expression instantly transformed as tears welled up in her eyes and her lower lip began to quiver. "Please. I have nowhere to go. My landlord is refusing to renew my lease. My daughter doesn't have room for me. I'm going to have to sleep in my car after tonight."

Carlita chewed her lower lip as she studied the woman. How could she live with herself or sleep at night, knowing this woman was living on the streets and she was partially to blame?

Despite the warning bells clanging loudly in her head, Carlita sucked in a breath and nodded. "Okay. But you cannot complain about every single thing."

She lifted a finger. "One. I will not cut the tree in the courtyard. Two. There's nothing I can do about the smells so you're going to have to decide whether you can live with it. This building has been completely remodeled, from top to bottom. Three. Annie told me you don't like pets. Pets *are* allowed. In fact, I have two of my own. Rent is $1500 per month, due the first day of the month. You must pay me first, last and one month security deposit before I turn over the key and you'll have to sign a six-month lease."

"But..." Mercedes was going to remind her mother they wanted a year lease, but quickly realized her mother didn't want this woman to sign a year's lease.

"Okay," Elvira nodded and reached for her purse. "I can pay you now."

Carlita held up her hand. "Sorry. No personal checks. Since you're moving in tomorrow, I need a cashier's check, money order or cash."

Elvira opened her mouth to complain, but noted the look on Carlita's face and quickly closed it. "I'll have to go to the bank. In the storm. I don't have an umbrella and my car is parked on the street."

Carlita cut her off. "Have the money to me by five o'clock today or you can't move in."

"At least let me look at the apartment one more time," Elvira bargained.

"Fair enough," Carlita said.

"I'll get the key." Mercedes disappeared into their apartment, returning moments later with the key in hand.

Mercedes opened the door and stepped to the side while Elvira made her way in. Carlita brought up the rear.

Elvira slowly walked through the living room and dining area before making her way into the kitchen where she opened the fridge and inspected the inside.

She did the same with the oven before walking to the living room window, lifting the corner of the blinds and peering out. She mumbled something under her breath.

"I'm sorry. I didn't catch that, Elvira," Carlita said.

"Oh nothing," Elvira replied lightly. "I'll take a quick peek at the bedrooms and bath." She hurried into the hall and disappeared into one of the bedrooms.

Mercedes leaned close and whispered in her mother's ear. "Are you crazy? This woman is going to be a major pain in the rear."

"I hope not," Carlita sighed. "I'm a sucker for sad stories."

"Let me handle potential tenants next time," Mercedes said.

"I might have to."

Mercedes didn't have time to reply. Elvira had returned. "I'll take the apartment. It's a little smaller than I remember and I prefer gas stoves to electric, but I got a new job downtown and I need to live close by."

Carlita opened her mouth to speak.

"But beggars can't be choosers." Elvira glanced at her watch. "I better head down to the bank unless you can wait..."

Carlita shook her head. "Nope. Today." She glanced at her own watch. "It's almost four. You better hurry."

Elvira frowned and then exited the apartment. She turned back once, as if she were about to say something but the look on Carlita's face changed her mind and she disappeared down the stairs.

Moments later, the outer door slammed shut.

Carlita's shoulders sagged. "What have I just gotten us into?"

Chapter 11

Carlita opened the apartment door and stepped inside.

Mercedes bent down. "What's this?" She picked up a slip of paper.

"I stopped by to see you."

The paper was signed, "Shelby Towns."

"Shoot!" Carlita stomped her foot. "I was hoping to have you meet Shelby and also offer to help her move."

Carlita crumpled the note and tossed it in the trashcan. "I guess I better rustle up some dinner. How does a sandwich and leftover gazpacho sound?" She asked her daughter as she passed the empty cat food dish on her way to the fridge. "Rambo, have you been eating Grayvie's kitty food again?"

Rambo, who had followed Carlita to the kitchen, slunk away, his tail low and his ears drooping. She had caught him eating Grayvie's cat food, but knew she couldn't be too upset with him since she'd also caught Grayvie eating Rambo's dog food. "What am I going to do with you two?"

She opened the fridge and peered inside. "How 'bout a hot ham and cheese?" she hollered into the living room as she reached for the packet of deli meat and sliced cheddar cheese.

When no one answered, Carlita peeked around the corner and noticed Mercedes' bedroom door was shut.

She pulled the loaf of bread from the pantry, counted out four slices and grabbed the frying pan from the cabinet next to the stove.

Two sets of eyes stared up at her. "Okay, but only a small snack." She counted out three extra pieces of ham, giving two to Rambo and one to Grayvie.

"Now for some of your own food." Carlita filled both pets' food dishes, and then added fresh water to their water dishes before focusing on the task at hand. She assembled two sandwiches, carefully placed them inside the frying pan and then turned the front burner on.

Mercedes emerged from her bedroom. "I didn't know you were making dinner already. Why didn't you holler? I would've helped."

Carlita waved the spatula at her daughter. "I did holler and you didn't answer so we're having hot ham and cheese with what's left of the gazpacho."

Mercedes set the table while her mother finished cooking the food. They settled in at the table and Carlita reached for her spoon. "When do you hear if you got the job?"

"I was hoping to hear something this afternoon." Mercedes bit into her sandwich. "I'm having second thoughts though. I don't want to leave you high and dry with the businesses."

"Don't worry about it, Mercedes. Even if the district office issues the license, it will still take some time to order equipment and set up shop."

The women discussed the license and recent vandalism in Walton Square, certain someone was targeting their neighborhood.

Carlita popped the last bite of sandwich into her mouth and reached for her napkin when a loud banging noise shook the floor. "What on earth?" She scrambled out of her chair and ran to the front door before peeking out the peephole. "You're kidding."

"What?" Mercedes hovered off to one side.

Carlita didn't answer. Instead, she flung the front door wide open.

Elvira was in the outer hall, half-carrying, half-dragging a large, square metal box.

"Let me help." Carlita swooped down, grabbed the other end and the women lifted it. "What are you doing?"

"Moving in," Elvira gasped. "I figured why waste a trip? I could bring some of my things up with me."

"Let me get the apartment key." Mercedes darted back into their apartment, returning moments later with the key in hand. She hurried to unlock the door and then held it open while Elvira and Carlita carried the heavy box into the living room.

They carefully set it on the floor, just inside the door.

"What is that?" Mercedes asked.

"It's an ozone machine. It purifies the air. I use it all the time what with my allergies." Elvira reached inside her pocket and pulled out two cashier's checks, handing them to Carlita. "First month's rent, last month's rent and security deposit. Four thousand, five-hundred smackeroos."

Carlita glanced at the checks. "I have a copy of the rental agreement on the computer. I'll go print it off and bring it back for you to sign." She was about to tell Elvira not to move anything else into the apartment, but Elvira was already out the door, heading down the steps.

"I'll print it off," Mercedes offered. "You might want to help Elvira."

"I suppose I should." Carlita wondered what all she planned to move in, but she didn't have to wonder long. She ran into Elvira on the stairwell. She was dragging a futon cushion up the steep steps.

Carlita reached for the other end and the women struggled to drag it to the top.

"I hope these floors are clean," Elvira grumbled.

"If not, you're cleaning them now," Carlita quipped.

They dropped the cushion on the living room floor, next to the ozone machine and Elvira dusted her hands off. "That's it for the big stuff tonight. I'll bring the rest tomorrow. Wayne, my former landlord, is helping me move."

"He must..." Carlita was about to say, *want you out pretty bad to help you move* but held her tongue. Once again, she wondered what she'd gotten herself into.

Elvira crossed her arms in front of her and studied the apartment. "I put the water and power in my name already so the only thing left is to hook up satellite. You do have a satellite dish?"

Carlita shook her head. "No. We have cable. Savannah Cable One."

"That won't work."

"Why?" Carlita asked.

"They banned my account."

"Imagine that," Carlita murmured. "Sorry. We're using cable only. I don't want someone attaching a satellite dish to my brand new roof."

"But..."

Carlita frowned.

"All right." Elvira stomped out of the apartment and into the hall. Carlita followed her out, closing the door behind her. "I'll go grab my suitcase. Might as well get settled in."

"I thought you were moving in tomorrow."

"I already switched my power and water over today." Elvira's eyes widened. "Technically, I can move in after midnight. You're not going to make me wait until midnight? I'll have to sleep in my car. The drive back to my old place is too far from here."

Visions of the woman sleeping in her car in the alley filled Carlita's head. There was no way she could do that to Elvira. "Of course not."

Mercedes returned with the rental agreement and handed it to her mother. "I filled in the blanks. The rent is $1500 per month with a six-month lease."

"Thanks Mercedes." Carlita scanned the four-page document. Most of the wording was mumbo jumbo and she had trusted Annie to make sure they were covered.

She checked the move-in date, the expiration date, the monthly rental amount, the deposit amount and the signature line before handing it to Elvira. "It looks as if you'll only have to sign and date the last page."

Elvira fumbled inside her purse, pulled out her reading glasses, slipped them on and studied the agreement. She shifted her gaze to Carlita. "I'll take it over here to sign."

A red flag flew in the back of Carlita's mind. It wasn't that she didn't trust Elvira, but she didn't trust her. She followed her new tenant to the kitchen counter and flipped the light switch.

Elvira hunched over the agreement, blocking Carlita's view of the document. She watched as the woman scribbled something, flipped to the back page, signed her name, dated the agreement and handed it back with flourish. "Signed, sealed and delivered."

"Huh." Carlita eyed her suspiciously, as she flipped through the pages. She stopped when she noticed something had been crossed out and initialed on page three:

~~The tenant shall not destroy, deface, damage, impair, or remove any part of the premises or property therein belonging to the landlord nor permit any person to do so.~~

"You crossed out and initialed the section on destroying my property." Carlita remembered Elvira's comment about the beautiful Japanese maple trees in the courtyard. "Do not even think about touching those trees," Carlita warned.

Mercedes snatched the pen from Elvira's grasp and re-wrote the section the woman had lined out. "Sign and initial." She handed the pen back to Elvira.

"I wasn't going to take the tree out, maybe trim a couple branches so I would have a view."

Carlita glared at Elvira. "Sign or I rip up the contract and haul your stuff right back out of this apartment."

Elvira reluctantly signed and handed the papers to Carlita. "Sheesh. You'd think I was committing a crime. The tree isn't even that pretty."

Carlita felt the tips of her ears start to burn. She turned to Mercedes. "Let's go." She stomped out of the apartment.

Mercedes hurried after her mother. "Don't sign off on the paperwork tonight," she said. "Sleep on it. You can always change your mind since you haven't signed."

"You're right. I need some fresh air. C'mon Rambo." Rambo trotted to the door and Carlita met him there. "We're heading down to the courtyard for a few minutes. Would you like to go with us?"

"Sure. Let me get my cell phone." The rain had finally stopped and the women exited the apartment and made their way down the steps.

Carlita was grateful they did not to run into Elvira again. She'd had enough of her new tenant to last for a good long time. Somehow, she had a sneaky feeling she would deeply regret her decision.

They moseyed out of the alley and onto the sidewalk. The rain had cooled the air and it was a welcome relief from the brutal heat. Carlita would be glad when the summer season ended.

Business was booming at A Scoop in Time ice cream shop across the street and there was a line of customers. The Fischers had placed several small café tables out front, all of them occupied. "Let's have some ice cream." Carlita tugged on Rambo's leash and the trio crossed the street.

The line moved quickly and soon they were standing at the window. A man with sandy brown hair and a wide grin greeted them. "What can I get you lovely ladies?"

"I'll have the four-legged special for my dog, a small vanilla cone dipped in chocolate swirl." Carlita turned to Mercedes.

"I'll have a single scoop blueberry cheesecake," Mercedes said as she plucked several napkins from the napkin dispenser sitting on the counter.

"That'll be ten dollars and fifty cents," the man said.

"Shoot. What was I thinking? I forgot my purse," Carlita turned to her daughter. "Do you have any cash?"

"Nope." Mercedes reached into her front pockets. "I'll run back to the apartment and grab some money."

"Wait." The man behind the counter leaned forward. "Are you the new owners across the street? Carla something." He pointed toward their building.

"Carlita. You must be Mr. Fischer," Carlita said.

The man extended his hand. "Stu Fischer. Pleasure to meet you." He pumped Carlita's hand. "Don't worry about paying. My treat. Welcome to Walton Square."

"Thank you. It's nice to finally meet you. We've stopped by a couple times but you weren't here."

A young girl slid around the man and handed Rambo's treat to Carlita first. She returned moments later with Carlita and Mercedes' cones. "I see you've got some tenants moving in upstairs."

Carlita took her cone and handed the other to Mercedes. "Yes. We finished renovations and two of the units are now occupied."

Mr. Fischer nodded. "I've been meaning to stop by to chat but we were busier than the Savannah trolleys today." He leaned his elbows on the small counter. "I drove by your place early this morning and I could've sworn I saw someone walking around inside the building. When I circled the block for a second look, he was gone."

Chapter 12

The woman standing behind Carlita tapped her on the shoulder. "Can we order now?"

Carlita stepped to the side, a million questions swirling around in her head. Rambo's treat had started to melt and a sticky trail trickled down the side of her hand. They shuffled to the side and Carlita held the cone out while Rambo licked his treat.

She attempted to balance his cone while licking her own.

Mercedes shuffled closer to her mother. "We need to find out who was wandering around inside the store this morning." She shivered. "That's creepy. Do you think it was Bob Lowman or one of his men?"

"I don't know but I intend to find out." The line to order ice cream grew. There was no way to talk to Mr. Fischer again. "Let's head to the courtyard. We can swing back by after we're done. Maybe we'll be able to talk to him then."

Mother and daughter, accompanied by Rambo, crossed the street, passed by the store and stopped in front of the wrought iron gate. "Hold this." Carlita handed her cone to her daughter, reached in her pocket and pulled out the key. She unlocked the gate and cautiously pushed it open.

Rambo trotted in first, followed by Mercedes. Carlita brought up the rear, closing the gate behind them. The dog headed straight for the fountain in the back, which was no longer working and now sat empty.

"We need to get a new fountain," Mercedes said as she settled into one of the refurbished bistro chairs. Her mother sat across from her. "We will. I'm hoping we can figure out who is behind the vandalism before we do it, though."

Carlita and Mercedes enjoyed the rest of their ice cream while Rambo patrolled the courtyard perimeter.

They discussed the break-ins and anonymous letter to the district office. Mercedes was convinced it was the owners of Paradise Pawn and Carlita had to agree. Motive and opportunity. They had motive for sure, but she wasn't sure about opportunity. Were the owners spying on them, watching their every move?

A flash of light caught Carlita's eyes and she turned her gaze upward, toward the apartment windows.

"She's watching us," Carlita said.

"Who?"

"Elvira. She's staring at us out her apartment window." Carlita gazed skyward and for the umpteenth time wondered why she had rented the apartment to the troublesome woman.

"You haven't signed the contract yet." Mercedes read her mother's mind.

"I know. I decided to sleep on it." Deep down she knew she would sign. There was no way she could sleep at night, knowing the woman, although irritating as all get out, was sleeping in her car.

"Let's start the first neighborhood patrol tonight," Mercedes whispered. "We'll wait 'til dusk. I'll map out a route, based on the recent incidents. We can also keep an eye on our storefront."

Mercedes bit the side of her cone. "What if Mr. Fischer saw an apparition? It wouldn't be the first time we heard someone was haunting the place."

It was true. The first day Mercedes and Carlita arrived in Savannah, an employee at a gas station right off the highway had told them the place was haunted. Autumn had made a similar comment. "I've never noticed anything," Carlita said.

"But we've never been in the store at night," Mercedes pointed out.

"You're right," Carlita said. "I'm going to check with Bob to make sure none of his men were here early. Tomorrow morning, I'm going to track down Annie and get a copy of Shelby's background check and see if she can run one on Elvira, something I should have done in the first place."

They finished their ice cream and headed out of the courtyard. The ice cream shop was even busier than before and the line extended all the way to the curb and then snaked along the sidewalk, abruptly ending in front of Annie's real estate office.

"We should try to speak to Mr. Fischer tomorrow, too," Mercedes said.

Carlita nodded. "Maybe he'll still be around when we start our first patrol."

The upstairs hall was quiet. Carlita opened the front door and the three of them headed inside.

Carlita tossed her keys on the small table just inside the door. "I wish Vinnie was still here. I would feel a lot safer."

"Me too," Mercedes agreed. "We'll need to be cautious until we can figure out who is lurking around, targeting Walton Square and determine if someone is wandering around downstairs."

"Not to mention sending mysterious notes to the district office." Carlita shivered. "What if a trail of crime followed us here?"

***

Mercedes emerged from her room at 8:45 wearing black jogging pants, a loose-fitting black shirt with an odd bulge in the front and a pair of running shoes. "Ready to start the patrol?"

Carlita inspected her daughter's outfit and reached out to pat the front. "What is that?"

Mercedes took a step back. "Nothing. Hopefully you won't have to find out." She changed the subject and pointed at her mother's outfit. "Your white capris might stand out, but then I'm not sure. Are we trying to avoid detection or blend in with the crowd?"

"I would say after dark, you'll be hard to see, but if someone spots you, they're going to wonder what in the world you're doing wearing a black knit shirt and black jogging pants in the dead of summer."

"I never thought about that," Mercedes said. "Maybe I should change." She turned to go.

"No. As long as you don't think you'll sweat to death, I say we go as is."

"Okay," Mercedes nodded. "Let me grab my cell phone." She disappeared in her room, returning moments later.

"You're sure you don't want to tell me what's under your shirt?" Carlita asked.

"I'm sure," Mercedes mumbled.

"I don't want to know, do I?" Carlita asked.

"Probably not," Mercedes answered. "Ready?"

"Probably not," her mother said.

Mercedes grinned. "Good. Let's see if we can track down a vandal or two."

Chapter 13

The sun had already set by the time they started their patrol. From the corner of the store, they crossed the street, passing by Riverfront Real Estate on the left. When they reached the corner, they turned left, walking adjacent to the main thoroughfare with the Savannah River on the opposite side of the street.

At the next corner, they made another left, passing several buildings Carlita had never paid attention to, although they were still technically in Walton Square.

There was a donut shop, a hair salon and a travel agency. On the other side of the travel agency was a store that caught Carlita's eye, *The Book Nook.* She stopped abruptly in front of the brick building.

The store had closed at six. "I had no idea this was here," she said excitedly. "I need to come back during business hours." She noted the store hours and mother and daughter continued their patrol.

"I wouldn't mind checking it out myself," Mercedes said.

They passed Colby's Corner Store on the left. The lights were on. The store was open until nine, something

Carlita filed away for future reference. When they reached the corner, they made another left.

Shades of Ink tattoo shop was several stores down the block. The lights were on but Carlita couldn't see anyone inside.

"Keep a sharp eye out," Mercedes said. "We need to be looking for suspicious activity."

"Like what?" Carlita asked.

"The usual, anyone hovering around doorways, trying to break into buildings, crawling through windows, the sound of glass breaking," Mercedes rattled off. She patted the front of her shirt as she talked.

"I hope you didn't bring your gun," Carlita said as she watched her daughter nervously pat her shirt.

"Well...technically, no. I don't have my *gun*, in the sense that you're thinking," Mercedes said.

They passed between Steve's tattoo shop and A Scoop in Time ice cream shop, now closed.

"Wait." Carlita flung her arm out to stop her daughter. "Let's head to the alley."

They strode between the two buildings, emerging into the alley out back. It was getting dark now, the closest light coming from a mercury light on the corner, just beyond Annie's real estate office.

Mercedes caught a movement out of the corner of her eye. "I think I saw someone dart behind the building," she hissed. "Let's go."

Mercedes waved her mother forward as she crept along the side of the alley.

Carlita, following her daughter's lead, tiptoed behind her.

Mercedes abruptly stopped. "I saw them again." She pointed to a basement window well. "Let's hide down here."

"Down there?" Carlita's eyes widened as she gazed at the rectangular opening, surrounded by metal and a small section of wrought iron. "I dunno about that."

"We don't have time." Mercedes grabbed her mother's arm and pulled her into the hole.

Carlita hit the ground with a muffled *thud*. "Oh my gosh. I think something is crawling on me." She began frantically swatting at the back of her bare ankles.

"Shh." Mercedes held a finger to her lips. She craned her neck and peered over the top, focusing her gaze on two sets of legs. The figures were moving slowly along the back of the ice cream shop, as if trying to find a way inside.

"I think it's the vandals," Mercedes whispered in a low voice. She reached for the bulge under her shirt.

Carlita focused her attention on the dark figures. Her daughter was right. There was someone lurking not far away and it appeared they were trying to access the building. A chill ran up her spine as they crept closer and closer, until they were within striking distance.

Carlita dropped to her knees and squeezed her eyes shut, certain they were about to be spotted by the thugs. They were so close now that she could hear the gravel crunch beneath their shoes.

Mercedes elbowed her mother and Carlita silently gasped as she clutched her ribcage. Her eyes flew open, just in time to see her daughter lunge out of their hiding spot, gun in hand.

"No." Carlita gasped as her daughter pressed the butt of the weapon against the leg of the closest person, the larger of the two.

ZAP.

"Ahh." The figure stumbled backward, arms flailing as the person lost their balance, hitting the ground with a loud *THUD*.

When the figure hit the ground, Carlita realized two things: Her daughter had shot someone and that someone was Steve Winter.

"Steve!" Autumn screamed as she dropped to her knees and leaned over her brother's still body. "Are you okay? Can you hear me?"

She jerked her head and stared at Mercedes, still holding the weapon. "Mercedes? Y-you shot Steve!"

Mercedes, realizing what she'd done, gazed at her weapon in horror and dropped it like a hot potato. It landed near Carlita's sandal.

Carlita bent down and picked it up. It didn't look like any gun she'd ever seen. "What is this?"

"A stun gun," Mercedes said. "I only zapped him." She scrawled to Steve's side. He was moaning loudly.

"I'm so sorry. I thought you were one of the vandals." Mercedes jerked the stun gun's prongs from Steve's bare skin as she apologized. "I had no idea."

"What happened?" Steve moaned as he tried to lift his head.

"Mercedes thought we were the thugs vandalizing the neighborhood and she zapped you with her Taser," Autumn turned to Mercedes. "Why were you hiding down there?" She pointed to the window well.

"Mom and I were patrolling the neighborhood. We saw you two lurking nearby so we hid in the window well. It was so dark, I couldn't tell it was you," Mercedes said. "Why didn't you let us know you were on patrol?"

"We tried," Autumn said. "We stopped by your apartment, but no one answered when we rang the outer doorbell. I also sent you a text," she told Mercedes.

"It's apparent we need a neighborhood watch schedule," Carlita said as she helped Steve, who was beginning to recover from the stun, to an upright position. "We can't go around shooting each other." She gave her daughter a pointed stare.

"At least I didn't use a real gun," Mercedes said in her defense.

They waited several more moments for Steve to recover and then helped him to his feet. Mercedes held one of his arms while Autumn held the other as they slowly shuffled down the alley.

"I should have double checked before stunning you," Mercedes said. "I feel so bad."

"Don't worry about it." Steve limped along. "Autumn probably would've done the same thing if she'd had a stun gun."

"I would not," she gasped. "Well...maybe." Autumn turned to Mercedes. "Mind if I check out the gun?"

The four of them stopped under a street light. Carlita, who had picked up the gun when Mercedes dropped it, held it out.

Autumn turned the dark gray weapon over in her hand. "At first glance, this looks like the real deal."

"I've been eyeing this particular model online and when Mom and I were in Paradise Pawn scoping it out, I saw they had one and it was a great price," Mercedes said.

The women admired the stun gun for several moments and then Autumn handed it to her friend. "Maybe when you guys open your pawnshop, you can get a few in stock and I'll buy one."

They walked the short distance to the tattoo shop entrance. Steve reached in his front pocket for his keys as they stood under the tattoo shop's porch light.

"Are you feeling okay?" Carlita fretted. "You look a little pale."

"I'll be fine," he said.

"I'll make it up to you," Mercedes said as she touched his arm. "Mom can make your favorite pasta dish," she volunteered.

Mercedes and Carlita waited until Steve and Autumn were inside the tattoo shop before heading across the street to their apartment. "Remind me to never lurk around the apartment building after dark," Carlita joked as she opened the outer door. "That thing has some real juice in it."

Mercedes brandished her new weapon. "It has a lower setting." She eyed her mother. "Hey. What if you let me try it out on you?"

"Oh no." Carlita shook her head. "Your brother, Tony, called earlier. He's planning a visit soon. Why don't you try it out on him?"

"I will." The dimple in Mercedes' cheek deepened. Tony had been Mercedes' childhood nemesis, while Vinnie, Carlita's oldest child, had always been protective of his only sister.

Paulie, the youngest of Carlita's sons, had been more of a playmate to Mercedes since they were closest in age.

Carlita had to admit that being the only girl, and a daddy's girl at that, had caused the two siblings to be at odds, although both loved each other and, for the most part, had outgrown the rivalry.

They finished the evening watching some television and finally, Mercedes hopped off the couch. "I'm going to play on my laptop before hitting the hay." She leaned over and hugged her mother before disappearing inside her room.

When Carlita got ready for bed a short time later, she prayed for protection, for her children in New York, that the vandals would be caught and no one else would get hurt.

***

Carlita spent a restless night, lying awake for hours, listening to every creak and groan, convinced someone was either lurking right outside her door or wandering around downstairs inside the empty store.

Rambo woke her for his seven o'clock-ish morning bathroom break, and as they exited the apartment, Carlita noticed a dim light beaming out from under Shelby Towns' door. She shifted her gaze to Elvira's front door. It was dark.

They descended the steps and made their way into the alley, to Rambo's usual morning spot, near the small tenant parking lot. There was only one car parked in the lot besides Carlita's town car. It was a subcompact Ford and the inside, including the passenger seat, was crammed to the ceiling with stuff. "The car must belong to our new tenant, Elvira."

Rambo sniffed the side of the tire, deemed it non-interesting and then ambled to his favorite spot in the corner. Every morning, there was a new pile of discarded trash in the parking lot. Someone was using her alley as a shortcut and dumping their trash on her property.

Carlita picked up an empty Styrofoam drink cup. "I wish I could catch the litterers red-handed."

They hung around in the parking lot for a few more minutes and then headed back inside. Carlita noticed beams of light poking out from under both tenants' doors as she made her way back inside the apartment. She closed the door and locked it behind her.

Mercedes shuffled into the hall that separated their bedrooms, lifted her hands over her head and stretched. "There you are."

"You're up early." Carlita unhooked Rambo's leash.

"Not by choice. Someone was pounding on our door. I thought maybe you locked yourself out."

"Who was it?"

Mercedes pointed toward Elvira's unit. "It was the new tenant, Elvira what's-her-name. She said she didn't have any hot water and asked if she could use our shower."

"Our shower?" Carlita blinked rapidly and shifted her gaze to the bathroom door. She took a step closer and could hear muffled humming coming from the other side.

Mercedes shrugged helplessly. "She took me by surprise. I didn't know what to say."

"No. Just say no."

"Sorry Mom."

Carlita sucked in a breath and rolled her eyes. "I probably would've done the same thing."

The humming abruptly stopped and a short time later, the bathroom door popped open. Elvira emerged, her hair wrapped in a bright pink towel, one of their towels. She was wearing a pair of purple stretch pants and a sleeveless blue blouse. "Good morning. My hot water wasn't working and your daughter graciously offered to let me shower here."

The woman unwrapped the towel and began drying her hair with it. "I forgot to bring my toiletries so I hope you don't mind. I used a bottle of shampoo I found in the shower, the one that smells like wildflowers."

She went on. "Hopefully, I don't break out in hives. I'm allergic to certain flowers."

Elvira finished toweling her hair and began running her fingers through her shoulder length gray locks. "Your towels are a little scratchy. You should probably use a better grade fabric softener."

Carlita unconsciously clenched her fists and began silently counting to ten. *One...two...*

"I should head back to my apartment." Elvira smiled breezily. "Busy day today, moving and all."

"I'll follow you over to check your hot water," Carlita said. "Maybe the workers forgot to turn your hot water tank on." When they reached Elvira's apartment, the first thing Carlita noticed was an odd smell. "What is that weird smell, I mean non-smell?"

"It's my ozone machine. It sucks out all the bad air."

"Huh." Carlita hurried to the utility closet in the hall, opened the door and studied the front of the compact hot water tank. "Ah. Yep. It just needs to be turned on." She turned the knob and the heater began making a small ticking sound.

Elvira peered over her shoulder. "Huh. I had no idea. You can have your towel back." She handed Carlita her dirty towel.

Carlita stared at the wet towel. "Let me know if you need anything else." The words slipped out of her mouth before she could bite her tongue and she silently berated herself.

Elvira walked her to the open front door. "You'll be the first to know." She glanced out into the hall and then waved Carlita back inside. "I heard a child screaming last night." She pointed to the wall separating Shelby's apartment from hers. It wasn't a little whimper. It was more like a shrill high pitched scream."

Chapter 14

Carlita gasped. "Oh no. It must have been Violet, the new tenant's young daughter."

"I'm surprised you didn't hear it," Elvira said. "I thought about going over there but it was late. Hopefully someone didn't break into their apartment and rob them."

"They better not try to break into my apartment," Elvira continued. "I'll shoot them first and ask questions later."

Carlita mentally filed the fact Elvira was packing heat for future reference. "Thank you for sharing that." She quickly exited Elvira's apartment and hovered in the hall, torn between making sure Shelby and Violet were all right and minding her own business.

Mercedes was at the dining room table, eating a bowl of cereal. "Did you figure out her hot water problem?"

"Yes, but now we have another one," Carlita said. "Elvira told me she heard screams coming from Shelby's apartment last night."

Mercedes dropped her spoon in her bowl. "You're kidding."

"I wish I was." Carlita headed to the kitchen to get her cell phone. "I'm calling Annie right now. I think we need to take a closer look at Shelby's background check. I might as well see if we can get one on Elvira while I'm at it." She picked up her cell phone and dialed the real estate agent's number.

Annie didn't answer so Carlita left a message. "I'm going to head over to Annie's office. Surely, Cindy has Shelby's information on file."

Mercedes nodded. "I'll hold down the fort."

Carlita hurried out of the apartment, down the steps and across the street to Riverfront Real Estate. Annie's convertible was nowhere in sight but she could see Cindy sitting at her desk through the front window.

She waved to Carlita when she stepped inside. "Good morning Mrs. Garlucci. I was getting ready to call you. We've had several more interested parties who would like to see your vacant apartment."

"It's not vacant anymore," Carlita said.

"Oh? I thought Annie told me one of the units was still vacant," Cindy shook her head.

"It was, until late yesterday when Elvira Cobb showed up on my doorstep, giving me some sob story about how she was going to have to sleep in her car and was in dire need of a place to live."

"You didn't," Cindy gasped.

"I did," Carlita said. "And I've regretted it almost every second since."

She went on. "That is why I'm here. I want a copy of Shelby Towns' background check and I need you to run one on Elvira if you can, which I should have done in the first place. This whole landlord-thing is going to be a learning curve."

"Of course. It will only take a few minutes." Cindy opened the side drawer, reached inside and pulled out a manila folder. She set the folder on the desk and then began typing on her computer. "Ms. Cobb filled out some preliminary papers yesterday."

Carlita wandered over to the window and stared at her building across the street while she waited.

"All done," Cindy announced a short time later. "Shelby's application looks good. Is there a problem with her, too?"

"Elvira said she heard screams coming from Shelby's apartment last night."

Cindy's hand flew to her mouth. "Oh no." She fumbled with a file folder, pulled several sheets out and then hurried to the copy machine behind her. After she made a copy of the papers, she handed the copies to Carlita. "I'll have Annie give you a call."

Carlita glanced at the papers and then folded them in half. "I've already left her a message. Hopefully, the little girl was just having a bad dream." Still, for Elvira to have heard the screams was disconcerting, although one of the bedroom walls was directly behind Elvira's bedroom wall.

"So I guess I can tell the other parties interested in the apartments that they've already been rented."

"Yes. It's too late," Carlita made her way to the door. "Thanks for this." She waved the papers in her hand before exiting the office and closing the door behind her.

"It's time to take a closer look at who's living under my roof," Carlita mumbled under her breath as she crossed the street.

When she reached the apartment, she made a beeline for Mercedes' bedroom, knocking on the closed door.

The door flew open and Carlita took a step back. "It scares me every time you open the door that fast."

"Don't stand so close," Mercedes teased. She gazed at the papers her mother was holding. "You got the background checks?"

"Yes." Carlita handed the papers to her daughter. "Can you do a little research?"

"I would love to." Mercedes took the papers from her mother. "By the way, you just missed Glenda Fox. She said she was on her way to work and wanted to remind you of her afternoon tea."

With all the tenant issues popping up, Carlita had almost forgotten about her business license fiasco and the fact Glenda was going to try to help. "I'll give her a call."

Mercedes took the papers and headed to her computer while Carlita made her way to the kitchen to grab her phone.

Glenda answered on the first ring. "Good morning Carlita. How are you?"

"I've been better," Carlita muttered. "I'm sorry I missed you."

"Me too. I wanted to let you know the party plans are moving forward. I'm mailing the invitations today. The party is at 3:30 Monday afternoon. Dress is resort casual, nothing fancy."

"Resort casual?" Carlita had never heard the term "resort casual" and decided it must be a southern thing.

"It means a summer dress and sandals or flats. No blue jeans or shorts."

"Ah." Carlita made a mental note to check her closet. She may have to take her first clothes-shopping trip since moving south. "Thanks for the tip."

They chatted for a few moments, with Glenda promising to drop by in the next day or two for a visit and then they hung up.

Mercedes stepped out of her room, papers in hand. "Did this Elvira mention that she just moved here from Charleston, South Carolina?"

"No." Carlita shook her head.

"She has bounced around a lot, moving about every six months," Mercedes said.

The information wasn't a surprise and Carlita had a sneaky suspicion it had something to do with the fact she drove her previous landlords crazy and they kicked her out or refused to renew her lease.

Mercedes studied the papers. "She's forty-two years old. I'm assuming divorced since she has a couple previous last names. There's also a small list of people here in Savannah who may be related to her."

Mercedes lowered the sheet. "That's about it. Oh. There's one more thing. I'm not sure where this came from, but there's a small note at the bottom with one word and I can't figure it out. 'Socia,' whatever that means."

"You don't think they misspelled it and it should be 'sociopath,'" Carlita joked.

"That's the first word that came to my mind." Mercedes grinned and handed the papers to her mother. "I don't know what to think. Under possible employers, it lists none found."

"So where does Elvira get her money?" Carlita asked.

"Hopefully we don't have a deadbeat tenant on our hands," Mercedes grimaced.

"I hope not either," Carlita said.

If they only knew that was the least of their worries.

Chapter 15

"I spoke with Glenda and the afternoon tea is 'resort casual.' According to Glenda, casual would be a summer dress paired with perhaps sandals." Carlita flung her closet doors open and frowned at the contents. All of the clothes Carlita owned had come from New York.

Mercedes followed her mother to her closet, reached inside and pulled out a drab gray dress with a burgundy collar and plain black buttons. She wrinkled her nose as she held up her mother's dress. "This looks..."

"Frumpy," Carlita suggested.

"Yeah." Mercedes hung the hanger back on the rod and then perused her mother's wardrobe. "None of these seem particularly summery."

"I agree." Carlita frowned at her clothes. "I can't remember the last time I went clothes shopping. Maybe we should take a trip to the outlet mall near the highway."

With nothing else pressing and still waiting for Annie to call back, they headed to the car, parked in the back alley and climbed in.

Carlita pulled the door shut. "You still remember how to drive?"

"Yep." Mercedes started the car and reached for her seatbelt. "We should try to drive the car at least once a week so the battery doesn't die." She shifted into reverse, backing out of the small parking lot and alley as they headed out of town and toward the freeway.

The outlet mall was only a few miles up the road and Mercedes parked the car near the center of the parking lot. The afternoon flew by as the women perused the stores, trying on bright, colorful casual dresses.

Carlita found two; the first was a purple chiffon with a slight V-neck and the second a light coral sleeveless gauze maxi dress with a double ruffle surrounding the neckline. She also found a pair of summer sandals, the tops of each sandal adorned with a small gold seashell.

Mercedes picked out a couple pair of neutral dress slacks and button down blouses she could mix and match, as well as three summer dresses, all of which were appropriate for an afternoon tea.

When they finished shopping, they placed their shopping bags in the trunk and climbed back into the car. "That was fun," Carlita said. "We should get out more often."

They had not wandered from downtown Savannah since Carlita's son, Vinnie, had left.

The afternoon had been a welcome escape from the worries of the business and the recent Walton Square vandalism, not to mention her odd tenants.

Carlita briefly wondered if perhaps her tenants weren't odd after all. Maybe she was the one who was odd.

Cash flow from the rentals would be put to good use, although she was not going to make as much in monthly rent since she'd allowed Shelby Towns to move in, paying what she could afford.

Carlita still had a chunk of change from the sale of her home in New York as well as a small retirement account she and her husband had accumulated over the years.

Mother and daughter also had several precious gems hidden in their secret hiding place, the fireplace, which was the perfect spot to stash them until they decided to fire it up in the fall.

Mercedes eased the town car into the alley and Carlita gazed out the window at Elvira's compact car. The inside of the car, which had been full, was now empty. Elvira had finished moving in...lock, stock and barrel.

Annie had left a message while Mercedes and Carlita were out shopping, letting her know she was in the office for the remainder of the afternoon so after taking their bags into the apartment, Carlita took Rambo out for a walk and then they headed over to Annie's real estate office.

Cindy, the receptionist, was nowhere in sight and Annie was the only one there. She looked up when Carlita and Rambo opened the door.

"You got my message."

Carlita nodded. "Yes, and I'm sure Cindy told you that Elvira strong-armed me into letting her move in."

Annie leaned back in her chair. "I heard. Don't say I didn't warn you."

"She's a trip. She tried to cross out part of the lease agreement, complained about every stinking thing, used my shower this morning because she didn't know how to turn on her hot water tank and I think she's spying on us."

"That's it?" Annie teased. "She sounds like the model tenant."

Carlita snorted. "And she told me she heard loud screams coming from Shelby's apartment last night."

Annie's eyes widened. "You're kidding. Oh my gosh. You don't think she's abusing her young daughter..."

"I don't know what to think," Carlita admitted. "She seems like a good mother and the little girl doesn't seem to fear her mother."

"Carlita, I am so sorry," Annie apologized. "Would you like me to talk to Shelby?"

"No." Carlita waved a hand. "I say we wait to see if it happens again. Now that I'm aware of the situation, I'll be sure to keep an eye out." She reached into her pocket and pulled out her checkbook. "I owe you for helping me with the rentals and I want to settle up."

"It's two-hundred fifty per signed lease which makes the total five hundred dollars," Annie said, "although I may have to end up paying you instead."

"Nah." Carlita grabbed a pen off the desk, scribbled out the amount, signed her name and then tore off the check before sliding it across the desk. "I only signed Elvira for a six-month lease. She's on probation."

The women chatted about the recent vandalism to the neighborhood and Carlita told her of the incident the previous evening with Steve and Autumn and the Taser.

Annie's hand flew to her mouth. "Poor Steve."

"Poor Steve is right. Mercedes got him good." Carlita also told her about the conversation she'd had with one of the owners of Paradise Pawn and how she wondered if perhaps he wasn't pulling some strings to ensure Carlita wouldn't get her pawnshop license.

"You don't think the pawnshop owners are behind the vandalism, trying to give Walton Square a bad rap so that even if the district office does issue the permit, no one will want to visit our side of town because of recent crimes?" Annie asked.

Carlita hadn't considered that angle. It was true. Perhaps Paradise Pawn was behind all the recent incidents. She still couldn't understand why the pawnshop would be so against her little shop. What was wrong with a little friendly competition? Of course, Carlita had absolutely zero business experience and its cutthroat ways. She had a feeling she had a lot to learn about the business world.

She thanked Annie for all of her help, reassuring her once again, she wouldn't hold her responsible for her tenants' actions and then Rambo and she headed out, deciding to take a leisurely stroll around Morrell Park before heading home.

When they finished their walk and reached the storefront, Carlita noticed a car she didn't recognize. She wondered if perhaps it belonged to Shelby.

Carlita made her way around to the back where Mercedes and Mr. Yates were chatting.

"There she is now." Mercedes pointed to her mother.

Rodney Yates turned to face Carlita. "Mrs. Garlucci," he said. "I'm here to discuss your license application."

"Yes. Of course. Thank you for coming by. Can I get you a cup of coffee?" Mercedes led the way, Carlita followed behind and Mr. Yates brought up the rear. She couldn't resist the urge to take a quick glance at the top of his head to see if his hairpiece was in place.

She started to grin and then caught herself so she cleared her throat and pretended to cough. "I hope you have good news."

They ascended the stairs and stepped into Carlita and Mercedes' apartment.

"I do." Mr. Yates studied the interior of their home. "This place looks nice."

"Thank you," Carlita and Mercedes replied in unison.

"We love it," Carlita said. "Would you like coffee?"

Mr. Yates shook his head. "No. Thank you. After careful deliberation, I'm going to recommend that the committee approve your business license application."

"Yes!" Mercedes pumped her fist in the air triumphantly.

"Thank you." Carlita wanted to hug the man, but held back. "I appreciate it."

"I could find no trace of evidence supporting the anonymous claim of nefarious activity so we closed the investigation. I'm sorry for any inconvenience," he apologized.

Carlita sank into the dining room chair. "Thank the Good Lord."

Mr. Yates continued. "Your request will be brought to the next Savannah-Burnham District Office meeting where members will vote but I don't see a problem. There will only be one minor hurdle before the license is issued."

A cold chill ran down Carlita's spine. The other shoe was about to drop.

"We have to run a background check."

Chapter 16

Carlita clutched her chest. "On me? You have to run a background check on me?"

"Why?" Mercedes asked.

"Because of the nature of your business. The district office wants to make sure you're not fencing goods."

Mr. Yates leaned in, studying her over the top of his glasses. "This won't be a problem, will it?"

"N-no." Carlita's mind raced. She was almost one hundred percent certain she had a clean-as-a-whistle background, despite her family history, but there was still the slightest chance something unexpected might pop up.

If she told Mr. Yates she was opposed to it, it would definitely send up a red flag.

"O-of course not," Carlita stammered.

"I knew George Delmario, the previous owner of this property, quite well." Mr. Yates clasped his hands in front of him and studied Carlita thoughtfully. "Mrs. Garlucci, not every fine, upstanding citizen in every community is as they appear to be."

He paused to let his words sink in. "Everyone has a skeleton or two in his or her closet. I don't think your background check will be an issue."

Mr. Yates continued. "If you'll send me your email address, I'll have my office email a copy of the information needed to run the check." He glanced at his watch. "I have another appointment."

Carlita walked him to the door. "Thank you Mr. Yates. I appreciate your time. I'm sorry about the protest the other day."

Mercedes started to laugh and quickly covered her mouth.

"I have to say you're a tight knit group over here in Walton Square." Mr. Yates reached for the doorknob and then slowly turned. "Ralph Silva, the owner of Paradise Pawn, won't be pleased but he'll get over it."

The door opened and Mr. Yates stepped into the hall. "I'll have those papers sent over later. By the way, I don't think your outer doorbells work. You may want to look into that."

"Thank you." She followed him down the steps and out into the alley, waiting for him to disappear around the side of the building before turning her attention to the small buttons on the side of the outer door.

Carlita hadn't considered that now she had tenants, she would need to have the individual buzzers repaired so Shelby and Elvira would know when they had visitors.

After a quick call to Bob Lowman, who promised to send one of his workers before the day ended, Carlita headed upstairs.

Mercedes was in her room, the door closed. Carlita stepped into the hall and lightly knocked. This time, she took a step back, prepared for the door to fly open. She wasn't disappointed.

"Have you had a chance to study Shelby Towns' background information?"

"I did." Mercedes nodded. "There was information on previous addresses, her age, and occupation."

Carlita interrupted. "What kind of occupation?"

"It lists her as a restaurant employee."

"Huh. That would be hard with a small child at home."

Mercedes shifted, resting her hip on the doorframe. "There was one thing that caught my attention. There were several relatives listed and at the top of the list, a husband named Robert."

"I wonder what happened to the husband," Carlita said. "Speaking of that, I should run next door to check on them, say hello and make sure they're settled in."

Carlita turned to go and then turned back. "What did you think of Mr. Yates' statement about skeletons in the closet and his comment about George Delmario?"

Mercedes picked at the edge of her fingernail thoughtfully. "He knows something about Mr. Delmario's past and possible connections."

"Which means he suspects ours," Carlita shrugged. "I just thought it was an interesting choice of words."

"Me too," Mercedes agreed.

"I better head next door." Carlita didn't wait for a reply as she walked out of the apartment, stepped out into the shared hall and made a beeline for the apartment across the hall. She rapped loudly on the front door and waited.

The door opened a crack and Carlita caught a glimpse of Shelby's long dark hair. "Hi Shelby."

The door opened wider. "Hello Mrs. Garlucci."

Carlita smiled. "You can call me Carlita."

A small face peeked out from the side. It was Violet. "Hello Violet."

"Hello." Violet was eating an orange Popsicle.

"Your Popsicle looks yummy," Carlita said.

Violet held up her half-eaten treat. "You want a bite?"

"No thanks. You keep it." She smiled at the child and turned to Shelby. "I wondered how you were settling in and if you needed anything." Carlita gazed past Shelby's shoulder and into the almost-bare apartment. "Are you still moving in?"

"No ma-am," Shelby shook her head. "We're all moved in."

"We got to sleep on the floor," Violet said. "It was hard."

Carlita's heart sank. "My goodness. You don't have beds?"

"No," Shelby said, her eyes lowering. "The women's shelter is donating one for each of us. They should be here sometime today."

"I'm sorry to mention this, but your new neighbor thought she heard Violet crying last night. Is everything okay?" Carlita asked.

"Yes," Shelby nodded as she smoothed her daughter's hair. "Violet had a bad dream."

Violet nodded solemnly. "Monsters were chasing me but Mommy helped them go away."

Carlita nodded, relieved to hear it was only a bad dream. "Mommies are good at scaring away monsters." She shifted her attention to Shelby. "What other furniture do you need?"

"Mrs. Garlucci...Carlita, you've already been so kind to Violet and me," Shelby said.

"Shelby." Carlita used her best "mother" voice. "Let me, let my daughter and me help."

Tears welled in Shelby's eyes. "Whatever you can spare," she whispered, her voice cracking. "We don't have much." She opened the door wide and Carlita gazed inside.

Shelby was not exaggerating. There was no sofa, no chairs, no dining room furniture or lamps. Carlita had a feeling the bedrooms looked about the same. "What did you say the shelter was donating?"

"Two beds and one dresser. They already donated some linens and household items. When I get the money, I plan to buy furniture and maybe even a television."

"That settles it," Carlita said. "We're going to run out and buy you a few things. Let me go grab a pen and paper so I can make a list." She didn't wait for a reply as she headed back to her apartment, returning moments later, pad of paper and pen in hand.

She jotted down everything she thought the young mother might need and despite Shelby's protests, proceeded to the kitchen to take stock before heading to the bathroom and bedrooms.

She returned to the living room where Shelby and Violet were standing. There was nowhere to sit. "You stay here and wait for your bedroom furniture. Meanwhile, my daughter and I will visit the used furniture store on the edge of town. I might not be able to have the stuff delivered today."

Shelby was shaking her head. "I can't let you do that Mrs.-Carlita."

"You can't stop me," Carlita insisted. "I'll be back."

Carlita was a woman on a mission as she strode into her apartment to grab her purse. "We need to make a trip to the used furniture store," she told Mercedes, who was standing at the kitchen counter, slicing an apple. "Okay."

There were plenty of funds sitting in the mother's and daughter's joint checking account, enough to cover purchasing the necessities for Shelby and Violet. She explained to Mercedes what she'd discovered inside the apartment during the drive to the store.

It was a whirlwind shopping trip and Carlita hoped Shelby would approve of their limited choices, but was certain the young mother would be grateful for whatever she got.

Carlita was able to talk the store manager into delivering all of the items before the end of the day, with an added incentive of extra cash and when they walked out of the store, Carlita thanked God she was in a position to help the young woman.

They stopped by Shelby's apartment when they got home and Shelby told them the beds had been delivered, along with bedding, a dresser and they had even thrown in a couple area rugs.

Carlita wanted to surprise Shelby and was vague about the purchases, only telling her that by day's end, she would have something to sit on.

She paced the apartment the rest of the afternoon, anxious for the delivery truck to show up. Finally, it did and she peeked out the peephole as she watched the delivery men bring all of the items Mercedes and she had purchased into the apartment across the hall.

Mercedes hurried from her room to the peephole as they took turns watching. After the last piece was delivered, Carlita watched as Shelby signed the delivery ticket, her hand trembling and then she burst into tears in front of the two men.

Tears welled in Carlita's eyes and trailed down her cheeks. "Dear God, please help them," she whispered.

Rambo nudged Carlita's hand and she patted his head. "I need some air." They headed to the deck where Carlita eased into the lounge chair while Rambo flopped down near the railing. Grayvie made an appearance as he climbed onto Carlita's lap and began to purr.

She absentmindedly stroked Grayvie's back and stared out into the alley as she thought about her young tenant.

Carlita's thoughts drifted to Mr. Yates' statement about background checks and skeletons. Would the district office find anything? What if Carlita's deceased husband Vinnie's name popped up and they decided to check on him, as well?

She could have Annie run a check on her first, to see what showed up, but then Annie would wonder why and Carlita didn't want to have to explain.

The license was only the first hurdle for Carlita. She'd never run a business before. What if she screwed everything up? Mercedes had done a great deal of online research on starting a pawnshop. The information had been overwhelming and most of it had gone right over her head.

What if she failed? What if she opened the shop and no one came? Perhaps Steve Winter, her neighbor and owner of Shades of Ink Tattoo Shop, could help her get started.

She wondered what her Vinnie would think if he could see her now. Would he be proud? She hoped so. She knew he would be surprised. Heck, she was surprised she'd actually gotten this far on her own.

The move had been good for her, for Mercedes, who had always lived a sheltered life. She was starting to think for herself.

She hoped her son, Vinnie, would decide to move to Savannah. He was hem hawing around and Carlita was the first to admit it was a big move, a big decision.

Carlita thought about the afternoon tea Glenda Fox had planned. It wasn't necessary now, but a little too late since Glenda had told her the invitations had already been sent.

The Savannah Architectural Society was attending, as well as Mercedes and Carlita, but she wasn't sure whom else Glenda had invited. She couldn't wait to see the inside of Glenda's magnificent home. Carlita had never attended an afternoon tea. Hopefully she wouldn't embarrass herself.

Carlita shifted to the side, lifted Grayvie from her lap and then set him on the deck before heading inside to phone Glenda with the good news that she was one step closer to getting the license.

"That's wonderful news, Carlita," Glenda replied, "But I'm still looking forward to afternoon tea. So is Reginald." She lowered her voice. "Not that you'll get him to admit it. He and Mary, our cook, have been working on the menu for days now. It's going to be fabulous."

"I'm looking forward to it." After she hung up, Carlita rambled around the house restlessly.

Mercedes emerged from her room and watched as Carlita dusted the top of the fireplace. She ambled over to the couch and plopped down. "Whatcha doing?"

"Nothing much. I'm going stir crazy."

"Shelby and Violet stopped by to thank us for the furniture," Mercedes said. "You were out on the deck and she didn't want to disturb you so I told her I would let you know."

Carlita's daughter sat up. "I have an idea." She hopped off the sofa and ran to her room, returning a short time later, waving a sheet of paper. "Let's take the riverboat cruise. We've been talking about it for weeks now."

Carlita paused, dust rag midair. "Really? When?"

"Now. I can make reservations online. The Mystic Queen starts boarding at six-thirty."

"Sure. Let's go." After Mercedes completed the online reservation, mother and daughter each changed into one of their new "resort casual," outfits and headed out.

It was a quick walk to Morrell Park and to the other end of the riverfront area. They arrived at six-thirty on the dot, tickets in hand.

Carlita hadn't asked how much the cruise cost. She probably didn't want to know. After they boarded, the women headed up the stairs to the viewing deck and over to the railing. The sun was still blazing hot so they hovered under an expansive awning and gazed out at the deep murky water.

There wasn't much to see so Mercedes and Carlita wandered along the rail, stopping to peruse the small gift shop but didn't purchase anything and then headed back outside to an empty bench near the rail.

Finally, the riverboat set sail and Carlita and Mercedes wandered to the railing for a better view.

The captain narrated as they sailed, telling of the port's long history and sharing some fascinating facts. The riverboat passed under the Talmadge Bridge before circling around past the waving girl. They even managed to catch a glimpse of Fort Jackson.

The captain finished his narration by announcing that dinner was being served on the lower level and the passengers descended the deck to the dining area.

At the bottom of the steps, a uniformed employee led them to a table for two near the window. He pulled out Carlita's chair and she slid in.

Mercedes seated herself and reached for her dinner napkin, placing it on her lap. "This is so cool. I've never taken a riverboat cruise, let alone a dinner cruise."

Carlita hadn't either. It was something she would've enjoyed with her husband. She swallowed hard as she thought of her husband, Vinnie, and forced a smile. "What a great idea, Mercedes. We should plan a new activity every week."

"I agree." Mercedes lifted her glass of ice water. "A toast."

Carlita lifted her glass. "A toast to new adventures." She sipped her water before carefully placing the glass next to her silverware. "Where are the dinner menus?"

"No menus." Mercedes shook her head. "According to their website, they only serve a dinner buffet. The food gets great reviews."

The women each ordered a glass of lemonade and then headed to the end of the buffet line where Carlita grabbed a small salad plate, filling it with lettuce, tomatoes, cucumbers, onions and then drizzling the top with ranch dressing and a sprinkle of croutons.

Mercedes followed suit and they both headed back to the table. She wiggled into her seat and then picked up her fork. "I was eyeing the fried chicken. It looks delicious."

Carlita stabbed a tomato wedge. "So does the baked fish."

Carlita finished her salad first and then waited for Mercedes to finish hers. They returned for their second round where Carlita loaded her plate with small portions of several things, anxious to taste a little of everything.

Mercedes did just the opposite. She placed two large pieces of fried chicken in the center of her plate, surrounded the chicken with a large scoop of loaded mashed potatoes, a heaping spoonful of creamy macaroni and cheese, a dinner roll and two scoops of brown rice.

"I'm starving," Mercedes said as she settled into her seat a second time. She sawed a piece of chicken breast off and bit the end. The outside of the fried chicken was crispy with the perfect amount of salty goodness. The white meat was juicy and tender. She closed her eyes in pure bliss. "This is so good," she moaned before taking another bite.

Carlita nibbled on her baked fish first. The fish was flaky and tender with a hint of lemon flavor. She finished the small piece before moving onto the fried chicken. "You're right. This is good. It's all good."

After they cleaned their dinner plates, they headed to the dessert station where Carlita selected a small dish of mixed berry cobbler while Mercedes grabbed a chocolate chip cookie and a bowl of ice cream. "I'm almost too full to eat this." Mercedes patted her stomach. "But somehow, I'll manage," she vowed.

The server brought coffee to accompany their desserts and after they finished eating, mother and daughter headed back upstairs where a band was playing reggae and blues music, and several couples had already hit the dance floor.

It was a fun evening, and although Carlita didn't "cut a rug," she enjoyed watching the other passengers.

It was dark when the riverboat finally docked and the passengers exited the ship. "It's a good thing we don't have far to go," Mercedes said.

When they reached the apartment building, Carlita unlocked the back door and they stepped inside.

Mercedes flipped the deadbolt and then tugged on the door to make sure it was secure. "This has been one of the best days I've had in a long time," Carlita said.

"Me too," Mercedes grabbed the handrail and they headed up the steps. When they got to the top of the stairs, they both stopped abruptly.

Elvira Cobb was lying on the floor in front of their apartment door, fast asleep.

Chapter 17

Elvira must have heard the creaky stairs or felt their presence as mother and daughter stared at her in disbelief.

She snorted loudly and then began to stir, opening her eyes. "You're home."

"We are. What are you doing?" Carlita shuffled forward, asking the question but already knowing the answer. "Is something wrong?"

Elvira shifted to a sitting position and reached for the pillow she'd had under her head. "Something attacked me."

"Attacked you," Carlita gasped. "Someone attacked you?"

"No." Elvira shook her head. "Not someone...something. It's in my apartment." She rolled over onto her knees and then stood. "I was in the kitchen cooking dinner when I felt something whoosh by my head. At first, I thought I was imagining things until it happened again. Then I caught a glimpse of something black dive bombing me."

"Oh no." Carlita remembered the bat infestation. During renovations, Bob Lowman had discovered the upper level was inhabited by the pesky creatures. Apparently, the exterminator had missed one. "I think I might know what it is."

"I'm not going back into my apartment until you get rid of it," Elvira insisted.

Carlita shifted her gaze to her daughter. She would be on her own on this one. Mercedes hated flying critters. "I'll see what I can do." She started toward Elvira's apartment and then turned back. "I'll need something to swat at it."

"You can use my tennis racket." Mercedes darted into the apartment, returning moments later with the tennis racket in hand.

Carlita took the tennis racket from Mercedes and slowly inched toward Elvira's apartment door. She tightened her grip on the handle of the racket and reached for the doorknob. "Here goes nothing." She sucked in a breath, opened the door and then paused as she stood in the doorway.

"Don't let it out!" Elvira screeched as she shoved Carlita inside her apartment and slammed the door shut behind her.

"Chicken liver," Carlita muttered at the door and then turned her attention toward the living room. She hunched forward, her eyes gazing fearfully at the shadowy corners of the living room. A pungent odor, the smell of dirty socks, filled the room and Carlita wrinkled her nose.

"Here batty, batty, batty," she cooed. "Come out, come out, wherever you are." Carlita crept toward the dining area, keeping one eye overhead.

She shifted the tennis racket to her right hand and listened carefully but Elvira's blaring television set drowned out any other noises.

Carlita shuffled into the dining area. On the left hand side of the room, covering every square inch, was a tall wall of what appeared to be black bins...black *blinking* bins. The low hum of electricity was coming from the wall. "What in the world?"

Carlita shook her head, still unsure of what she was looking at and continued a slow walk toward the kitchen.

When she reached the kitchen area, Carlita ran her hand along the side of the wall, searching for the light switch. "That smells so bad," she muttered as she gazed inside the saucepan, sitting on top of the burner. It resembled a pan of baked beans, covered in a gooey substance. It reminded her of melted marshmallows.

Carlita shifted her gaze to the dark, overhead beams. "I should've brought a flashlight." She circled around the dining room table as she made her way back into the living room and then the small hall where she checked both bedrooms and the bathroom.

If the bat was still lurking somewhere inside the apartment, he was doing an excellent job of hiding.

She zigzagged around several boxes as she made her way to the front door and into the hall where Mercedes and Elvira were hovering off to one side.

"Well?" Elvira took a step forward.

"I couldn't find the bat. He either went up the fireplace or he's hanging out in the rafters."

"I can't sleep there tonight with a bat in my apartment."

Carlita couldn't blame her. She wouldn't want to either, but she knew exactly where this conversation was going. "I'll go with you, back into your apartment to grab some overnight things. You can sleep on our couch. First thing tomorrow morning, I'll have an exterminator come by and then call my construction guy to check to make sure your fireplace chimney is covered."

Mercedes headed to their apartment to set up the sleeper sofa while Carlita and Elvira entered the apartment.

Carlita kept a firm grip on the tennis racket in case the flying creature decided to make an appearance and she could take it out. She almost hoped it would so Elvira wouldn't have to stay with them, but she wasn't that lucky.

Elvira quickly packed a small suitcase before turning off the bedroom light and heading to the hall. She stopped abruptly and gazed into the kitchen. "I was making dinner and I'm starving."

Carlita eyed the smelly pan on the stove. More than anything, she didn't want the stinky stuff in her apartment. "I can fix you a sandwich," she offered.

"But my dinner is already done and it's my favorite food," Elvira whined. "I have digestive issues. Why just last night..."

Carlita held up a hand, cutting her off. "Okay. Bring it with you." She followed Elvira to the kitchen, keeping one eye on the ceiling and her other on her new roommate.

Whompf. A large toolbox Carlita hadn't noticed before stuck out beneath a dining room chair. Carlita collided with the toolbox, the corner stabbing her in the ankle. She hopped up and down. "Ouch!"

"Watch out for the toolbox," Elvira said.

"That is an accident waiting to happen." With the tip of her sandal, Carlita nudged the toolbox back, knocking over a can of spray paint in the process. The can hit the wood floor and began to roll.

Carlita reached down to set it upright. "I hope you're not planning on painting this place."

Elvira scooped her smelly food into a plastic bowl and then placed the lid on top before setting the empty pan in the sink and filling it with water. "No. I dabble in art, painting and other stuff."

"Huh. I never would've pegged you for an artist," Carlita murmured.

"I'm ready," Elvira announced as she extended the handle on her suitcase, juggling the suitcase in one hand and holding her dinner in the other.

The blinking black bins caught Carlita's attention. She pointed at the wall. "What...is that?"

"What's what?"

"This wall of..." Carlita was at a loss for words. "Equipment."

"It's just some old computer equipment I play around with," Elvira answered vaguely. "I use it for a little hobby of mine."

"Huh." Carlita's eyes narrowed. "I have hobbies, too, but they don't take up half my apartment." She gave up trying to figure out what all the bins meant, followed Elvira out of the apartment and waited while she locked the door.

Mercedes had left the door to their apartment open.

Elvira stepped inside, easing her suitcase next to the sleeper sofa and then followed Carlita to the kitchen. "This is a nice unit. It looks bigger than mine."

"It's the same size."

Carlita's tenant placed her food dish on the counter. "Can I borrow a fork and paper towel?"

Carlita handed her the items and watched as she removed the lid, centered the paper towel over the top of the container and then opened the microwave, setting it inside. "You're not going to cook that?"

"It's cold. I can't eat cold food," Elvira said as she closed the door.

After the food warmed, Elvira pulled it out of the microwave. The rancid smell of moldy cheese and dirty socks poured from the microwave.

Cough. Carlita began to gag and pinched the end of her nose as her stomach churned. "Oh my gosh."

"It's an acquired smell and taste," Elvira said calmly. "The dish has excellent health benefits."

Carlita took a step back as Elvira carried the dish and silverware to the table. The rancid smell engulfed the room.

Rambo, who had been sleeping on his bed in the dining room, scrambled onto all fours, ran to the slider door and began pawing in a desperate attempt to escape the smell.

"I'm right behind you." Carlita ran to the slider, shoved the door open and darted onto the deck, gasping for air.

She spun around when she heard a choking sound coming from inside the apartment, certain the smell had overpowered Elvira after all, but it was Mercedes.

She ran into the living room. "What is that disgusting smell?" she gasped in horror.

"Natto. It's a Japanese dish. Would you like to try it?" Elvira held up a heaping spoon of the stinky substance.

"No thanks." Mercedes eyes widened. She darted across the room, joining her mother on the deck, and then closing the slider door behind her.

"This is too much. The woman is like a caustic case of poison ivy."

Carlita placed the palms of her hands on the railing and shrugged her shoulders in a sign of defeat. "I don't know what to do. We can't make her go back to her apartment. What if the bat bit her?"

"And that would be a bad thing?" Mercedes asked. "I'm kidding." She tugged on the ends of her hair and gazed at Elvira through the glass. "First she showers at our place, now she's eating and sleeping here."

"I'll have an exterminator here first thing in the morning." Carlita patted her daughter's shoulder. "For tonight, you can hide out in your room. I wish I could join you."

A movement caught Carlita's eye. Elvira had finished her meal and was carrying her dirty dish to the kitchen where she began washing it. "She seems to have settled right in."

The women headed back inside. Carlita turned every single ceiling fan on high in an attempt to rid the apartment of the disgusting smell.

Afterwards, Mercedes and she made up Elvira's bed. "You're all set," Carlita said after she placed a blanket on top of the clean sheets.

Elvira eyed it suspiciously and cautiously eased onto the edge before sprawling out on top of the sleeper sofa. "The metal bar is hurting my back."

Mercedes rolled her eyes. "I'll get more blankets." She stomped into the hall, returned with an armful of blankets and tossed them on the center of the bed.

Carlita piled the bed with the added blankets and finally, their guest settled down and the women headed to bed.

For the first time in a long time, Carlita set her alarm. She wondered how much it would cost for expedited pest removal and then quickly decided it didn't matter. It would be worth every penny.

Chapter 18

Aagh.

Carlita bolted upright in bed, her eyes darting around her dark bedroom. For a minute, she thought she'd been dreaming and then she heard it again.

Aagh.

Carlita flung her covers back and scrambled out of bed. She ran to her bedroom door, wrenching it open, certain something terrible had happened to Mercedes.

Mercedes met her in the small hall. "What was that noise?"

"I..." Carlita was about to say "don't know" until she spotted their overnight guest cowering in the corner of the sleeper sofa.

"Shoo! Shoo!" Elvira was waving her hands in an attempt to get Grayvie, who was reclining on the right hand side of the sleeper sofa, off. He eyed the interloper with mild interest before yawning lazily and closing his eyes.

"What is going on?" Carlita hurried into the living room.

"That...cat. He jumped up on my bed and scared me half to death."

Mercedes walked over to the couch, picked Grayvie up and held him close. "He wouldn't hurt a fly."

"Achoo." Elvira sneezed and rubbed the end of her nose. "I'm uh, uh..." She sneezed again.

"Lergic," Carlita offered. "I'm sorry. He usually sleeps with me and must've snuck out of my room."

Rambo, excited that everyone was up and around, began circling the sofa.

Elvira started to shoo him. "Shoo."

Rambo barked.

At that precise moment, the alarm in Carlita's bedroom began beeping. She took one look at Rambo - "Stay there," and ran back to her bedroom to shut off the alarm. "Unbelievable," she muttered under her breath.

By the time she returned to the living room, Mercedes had herded the pets into the dining room and Elvira was no longer cowering on the couch. "This place reminds me of a farm."

"More like a zoo," Carlita quipped. She glanced at the living room clock. "I plan to call an exterminator at eight on the dot." *And not a moment too soon.* She didn't wait for an answer as she headed to her bedroom to grab some clothes and then onto the bathroom.

When she emerged, Mercedes and the animals were nowhere in sight and Elvira was standing on the deck, in her pajamas, gazing into the alley. "The bathroom is all yours," Carlita said.

Elvira turned. "I think you should add a deck to my apartment, too."

"It would block the view of the courtyard," Carlita pointed out.

"What view? The trees are in the way."

Carlita held up a hand. "We're not having this conversation again. The bathroom is free," she repeated before heading back inside and began mentally counting to ten. The woman was wearing on her last nerve.

She tapped on Mercedes' bedroom door. "I'm taking Rambo for a walk." The door opened and Rambo trotted out, heading right for the front door.

They made their way down the steps, along the alley to one of Rambo's favorite spots and then walked around front. They stopped abruptly when Carlita spotted a sign propped up against the front of her building. *Property for Sale. Riverfront Real Estate.*

"What in the world?" Carlita shifted Rambo's leash to her other hand and picked up the sign before glancing across the street at Annie's real estate office.

She carried the sign around back, propping it against the wall in the back alley before heading inside and up the steps. Carlita made a beeline for her bedroom. It was just after eight so she scrolled through her phone list and dialed Annie's number.

The phone rang several times and Carlita was about to give up when a breathless Annie picked up. "Hi Carlita."

"Hi Annie. I'm sorry to bother you so early."

"No bother," Annie groaned. "You're the least of my worries. What's up?"

"Well, I thought I would let you know, I found one of your For Sale signs propped up in front of my store."

"Oh no," Annie groaned. "Not you, too. You're the third person already this morning who told me they found my signs in front of their businesses."

Carlita began to pace back and forth. "You're kidding." She headed to the slider. "Let me guess. Colby's grocery, Shades of Ink tattoo shop or Walton Square Souvenirs also had signs."

"Close. Colby's and Shades of Ink. Could be Ruby's place, too and she just hasn't called me yet." Carlita hadn't noticed if there were signs in front of the ice cream shop and gift shop, but then she hadn't been looking, either.

Annie continued. "I can only guess someone pulled my signs from legitimate properties that are for sale and then placed them in front of your place as well as the others."

"This is ridiculous," Carlita said. "We need to get to the bottom of this."

"I agree," Annie said, "But how?"

Elvira had emerged from the bathroom. She was wearing Carlita's favorite spa bathrobe and waving her hands frantically.

"I gotta go, Annie. Your sign is in my back alley, right next to the door."

Carlita disconnected the line but held onto the phone. "I'm getting ready to call an exterminator. What's the problem?"

"You're out of toilet paper," Elvira said. "I searched the bathroom cabinets but couldn't find any."

Carlita frowned. "Out of toilet paper? There were two rolls in there yesterday."

"Well," Elvira tightened the belt on Carlita's bathrobe. "Remember when I said I have a finicky digestive system? I...uh."

"Never mind." Carlita held up a hand as she headed to the linen closet in the hall, opened the door and pulled out an unopened four-pack of toilet paper. She handed it to Elvira. "This should last you a while."

"Thanks." Elvira disappeared inside the bathroom, closing the door behind her.

Thankfully, Carlita was able to speak to a real live person the second call that she placed to a local exterminator and begged the receptionist to send someone out as soon as possible, claiming it was a matter of life and death...Elvira's death.

The woman on the other end was able to contact one of their crew via radio and he promised to be there within the hour. Carlita disconnected the line and then uttered a prayer of gratitude.

Mercedes emerged from her room. "Well? Did you find someone to come out right away?"

"Thank heavens, yes. Someone put a for sale sign in front of our building last night," Carlita told her daughter. "I talked to Annie and someone also put one in front of Steve's tattoo parlor and Colby's grocery store."

"This is crazy," Mercedes said. "Paradise Pawn is going to a lot of trouble to harass us."

"But how can we prove it's Paradise Pawn?" Carlita's eyes slid to the closed bathroom door and the sound of Elvira banging around inside.

"We should check with the neighbors to see if anyone happened to notice suspicious activity," Mercedes said. "

"I'll go with you but I'll have to wait until the exterminator leaves."

"No hurry. I'm still waiting to use the bathroom." Mercedes tipped her head toward the bathroom door. Elvira was inside, humming.

"Hopefully, there's still toilet paper left by the time it's your turn," Carlita joked.

"Huh?"

"Never mind. Let's have a bowl of cereal while we wait." Carlita carried the carton of milk and box of corn puffs to the table while Mercedes grabbed a couple bowls and spoons from the kitchen cupboard. They settled in at the table, but not before Mercedes poured a small amount of milk into a bowl and set it on the floor for Grayvie.

"You're spoiling that cat."

"I can't help it," Mercedes said. "He's just so darned cute. Look at that adorable face."

Grayvie's small pink tongue lapped the milk while he gazed at Carlita with his big, green eyes.

The women ate their breakfast and discussed the rash of vandalism, how excited they were that they were one day closer to getting the pawnshop business license and how relieved they would be when Elvira's apartment was free of varmints and she was out of their hair.

The bell rang a short time later. "I'll clear the table," Mercedes offered as her mother hurried down the steps to answer the outer door. She peeked through the peephole overlooking the alley and then opened the door to let a young man, dressed in a gray uniform, inside. "Thank you for getting here so quickly. One of the tenants has a bat in her apartment." *Not to mention her belfry.*

Carlita led him up the steps and to the apartment in the corner. "Hang on. I'll go get the key." She darted into her apartment. Elvira was in the living room, watching television. "The exterminator is here. I'm going to let him into your apartment."

Elvira jumped out of the recliner. "I'll do it. I want to make sure he doesn't mess with anything. You know how careless some service people can be."

"Be my guest."

Elvira hurried out of the apartment, dragging her suitcase behind her. Carlita closed the door, leaning her head against it. "Good riddance. I hope they find the critter. If not, I'll move into her apartment and she can have this one."

The exterminator knocked on the door mid-morning and Carlita had almost forgotten about him. She ushered him inside, glanced into the hall and then shut the door behind him. "Did you track down the bat?"

"Yes ma'am. Actually there were two of them." The man juggled his clipboard and began writing on the sheet, attached to the front. "I ain't gonna charge you for an emergency service call. I call this charity work." He shook his head. "That woman, she would drive me right up the wall."

He tore off the top sheet and handed it to Carlita. "That'll be one hundred twenty-five dollars."

Carlita glanced at the sheet. "It's worth every penny. Let me go get my checkbook." She hurried to her room, returning moments later, check in hand. "Thank you so much. Can you tell me how they got in?"

"Yep. My guess is a small gap in the top where the chimney meets the roof. Your tenant wanted me to climb up there and check but I can't do that."

"You did your job and I thank you for getting here so quickly," Carlita said. "I'll have it taken care of today."

She walked the young man out and then headed back upstairs where she promptly called Bob Lowman, who promised to send one of his guys to check it out before the day's end.

"Ready to go?" Mercedes emerged from her bedroom.

"Go?"

"To talk to Walton Square business owners, try to get to the bottom of who is harassing us," Mercedes patiently explained.

"I forgot." Carlita grabbed the keys off the hook and headed to the door.

Carlita caught a glimpse of Stu Fischer, who was in front of his ice cream parlor, sweeping the walk. "Perfect. We'll start with Mr. Fischer." She grabbed the real estate sign, deciding she would help Annie out by setting it next to the real estate office's back door before hurrying across the street.

Stu Fischer stopped sweeping as they approached. "You must have read my mind. I was going to finish sweeping the walk and then stop by. I have something I'd like to discuss with you."

Chapter 19

"I noticed you had a sign out front and wondered if you decided to sell your property, after all," Stu Fischer said.

"I'm not selling." Carlita shifted the real estate sign she was holding, balancing it against her right leg. "Some practical jokester stole one of Annie Dowton's signs and stuck it in front of my property. From what she told me, several other business owners in Walton Square discovered Riverfront Real Estate signs in front of their businesses this morning, as well."

Stu Fischer propped the broom against the side of his ice cream shop. "I didn't have a sign and I didn't notice any others on my way in this morning, other than yours."

He went on. "So you're not selling?" Stu looked disappointed.

"Nope. Not now that the district office is close to issuing my pawnshop license. Mr. Yates told me he processed my application and is sending it to the council for approval."

Stu lifted a brow. "Pawnshop? I thought you were opening a corner grocery."

"That was the original plan," Mercedes said. "We figured a pawnshop would be easier to manage than a grocery store."

"Huh." Stu rocked back on his heels and nodded his head toward Walton Square Souvenirs. "What does Ruby McKinley think of that? Seems like you'd have two stores competing against each other."

"If she minds, she's hiding it pretty darn good. She picketed with us in front of Savannah-Burnham District Office the other day," Carlita said. "If anyone is unhappy, it would be Paradise Pawn on the other end of town near City Market."

"True." Stu nodded. "From what I've heard, they're kind of a rough bunch. Rumor has it the owner has had a few run-ins with the law." Stu picked up his broom. "Let me know if you ever decide to sell. Like I said, I might know someone who is interested."

"Who is that?" Carlita asked.

"Me. This place is small and business has taken off the last year or so. I'm tossing around the idea of expanding, adding a sit down ice cream parlor and sandwich shop."

Carlita promised she would keep him in mind if she ever decided to sell and then mother and daughter continued walking toward Riverfront Real Estate. They circled around back to drop off the for sale sign since the office wasn't open.

"What if it's Mr. Fischer?" Mercedes whispered. "Think about it. He isn't around for weeks. Now all of the sudden he's here all the time. Not only that, he's the only one who ever sees anything."

"True." Mercedes had a point. Stu Fischer was the one to tell them he spotted someone walking around inside the store early in the morning, not to mention he noticed the sign...or perhaps he was the one who had put it there.

He claimed ignorance about their pawnshop application. What if he had been the one who sent the anonymous note to the district office, trying to stop them from getting their license?

"We need to keep an eye on him," Carlita said. "I wonder if he knows I plan to eventually open a restaurant next door."

"Anyone could have told him," Mercedes pointed out. "Steve-O, Annie, Ken Colby. I think we even mentioned it to Ruby."

After dropping off the sign, they stopped by Walton Square Souvenir Shop. The store wasn't open and the small plastic clock on the door said they were opening at eleven. "We'll stop back later."

Mercedes and Carlita passed by the ice cream shop a second time on their way to Shades of Ink, Steve Winter's tattoo shop. Steve was the only one inside and when he caught a glimpse of the women, he waved them in. "Let me guess. You had one of Annie's for sale signs in front of your place, too."

"How did you know?"

"Because I saw the one in front of Colby's and guessed the Walton Square vandals had struck again."

"Yep," Carlita nodded. "How are you feeling?"

Steve grinned and glanced at a red-faced Mercedes. "No worse for the wear after the incident the other evening."

Steve waved them to the barstools in front of the counter as he settled into the chair behind it. "Have you heard any news on our picket the other day?"

Carlita brightened. "Yes. As a matter of fact, Mr. Yates said he processed the pawnshop license. Now all we're waiting on is for the district council to approve it during their meeting early next week." She didn't mention her background check.

Mercedes plucked a pen from the holder on the counter and began clicking the end. "What do you think of Stu Fischer?"

Steve shrugged. "He's an okay guy. His ice cream shop has been around for a few years. Told me one time he started the business to keep his teens out of trouble. Why?"

Carlita told him how Stu Fischer said he had noticed the sign out front and offered to buy the building if she ever wanted to sell, telling them he was considering expanding his ice cream shop and adding a sandwich shop.

"Does he know you plan to open a restaurant in the other building? I don't think you want a competitor right next door," Steve said.

"Me either. I told him about the pawnshop and he didn't seem thrilled."

Steve drummed his fingers on the counter thoughtfully. "I'm sure he didn't. I remember when I was trying to open this place and someone was fighting it. I always figured it was a business owner here in Walton Square. Think about it, ice cream, pawnshops and tattoos."

Carlita hopped off the barstool. "We're on our way to Colby's Corner Store to talk to Ken. Annie said he had called to tell her there was a for sale sign in front of his store this morning too."

They headed to the door and Steve walked them out. "Good luck on that permit." He turned to Mercedes. "I heard you didn't get the job at the newspaper."

Mercedes had told Carlita earlier that morning, during breakfast, that she'd received a voice message from the manager down at Savannah Evening News, letting her know they had decided to hire someone else.

"Yeah." Mercedes shrugged. "I guess it wasn't meant to be."

The women exited the building and turned right, heading to the other end of Walton Square and Colby's Corner Store. Mercedes stopped abruptly. "What if whoever this is isn't targeting all of Walton Square, just those of us who picketed in front of the district office the other day?"

Carlita slowly turned, studying her daughter. "You're right. Now that you mention it, it has been only us. The ice cream shop hasn't been hit."

The women picked up the pace, turned the corner when they reached the end of the block and then stepped inside Colby's.

Carlita caught a glimpse of Faith, Ken Colby's daughter, in the back.

She waved when she spotted them. There was no one in the front of the store so mother and daughter headed to the small café in the back. "We heard you're selling the grocery store," Mercedes teased.

Faith rolled her eyes. "Oh my gosh. When Dad saw the sign this morning, he almost flipped his lid. How did you know?"

"Because we had a sign in front of our place, too, and so did Shades of Ink, Steve Winter's tattoo shop."

Faith lifted a brow. "You're kidding. You should tell my dad. He's in the back."

The young blonde hurried through a door in the back, emerging moments later with Ken Colby. "Faith said you were targeted again last night, too."

Carlita repeated the story of how she had found the for sale sign in front of the building and called Annie. She mentioned how the tattoo shop had been targeted and then told them how they had talked to Stu Fischer on their way here and what he had said. "What do you think of Stu Fischer?"

Ken shrugged. "Don't know him all that well since he's on the other end of Walton Square. Faith and I have been down there a few times for ice cream. Seems like his business is growing."

Carlita interrupted. "He told me he was interested in buying my store, to expand his ice cream shop and add a sandwich shop."

"What did he say when you told him about the pawnshop?"

"He didn't seem too keen on the idea," Carlita admitted. "I can't sell him my building to expand his place. I'll be the first to admit I have zero business experience, but I can't imagine opening my Italian restaurant and having an ice cream shop / sandwich shop right next door."

Ken rubbed his chin thoughtfully. "Have the vandals targeted him?"

"That's another thing," Mercedes piped up. "As far as we know, his business hasn't been targeted, just those of us who picketed the other day."

"That stinks," Faith said.

"We're going to get to the bottom of this," Carlita vowed. "But for now, while I'm here I have a few things to pick up."

Faith and Mercedes chatted in the back while Carlita grabbed a hand basket and made her way up and down the aisles.

She carried her purchases to the front of the store where Ken was waiting behind the checkout counter. He reached inside the basket and pulled out a bag of bagels. "Any news on the license?"

"Yes." Carlita told him what Mr. Yates had told her. "It looks like we'll be moving full steam ahead in the next few weeks."

Ken smiled, the dimple in his cheek deepening. "I'm happy for you Carlita. It's nice to see a good guy...girl catch a break."

Carlita smiled back and her cheeks warmed. "Thanks. I appreciate your support and vow that a pawnshop will not bring riff raff to our neighborhood."

After Ken bagged her groceries, she handed one of the bags to Mercedes who had wandered to the front, and then reached for the other one. "If you want, we can drop Annie's sign off on our way home," Carlita offered.

"That would be great. Faith and I will be stuck here all day and I'm not sure if Annie needs it. I'll go grab it and meet you out front."

Ken strode to the back of the store while Carlita made her way out the front door. She waved at Faith before stepping onto the sidewalk.

Mercedes followed her mother out and then pulled the door shut behind them. "He's such a nice man," her daughter whispered. "I almost asked Faith about her mother but didn't dare."

Carlita had wondered the same thing, but she didn't want to pry. It was none of her business, but still, she was curious.

Ken rounded the corner, carrying the sign. Carlita handed her bag of groceries to Mercedes and reached for the sign.

"Thanks for taking this to Annie. Tell her I said 'hi' and she doesn't have to worry. She'll be the first person I call when I'm ready to sell."

He winked at Carlita and then followed a customer inside the store.

"He winked at you," Mercedes teased after the grocery store door shut.

"At us," Carlita corrected. "It was an innocent gesture."

On the way back to their side of the square, the women discussed Stu Fischer. In Carlita's mind, he was making his way to the top of the list of suspects, closely followed by the owners of Paradise Pawn.

The lights were on inside the real estate office and the front door unlocked.

Carlita carried the sign inside and Mercedes followed.

Cindy looked up from her computer before hopping out of her chair and running over to grab the sign. "Annie told me what happened. What kind of jerk would steal the signs and then place them in front of buildings that aren't even for sale?"

"The same jerk that dumps dumpsters, and breaks into courtyards and tattoo shops," Carlita said. "Did Annie ever figure out where they came from?"

"Yep." Cindy nodded as she propped the sign against the wall behind the desk. "Someone had taken them from several businesses over in Freedom Square."

"Freedom Square." Carlita frowned.

"It's on the other side of town, near the City Market."

"Near..." Carlita's head was spinning.

"Near Paradise Pawn." Mercedes snapped her fingers. "I knew it. It's them behind all of this."

"Don't jump to conclusions," Carlita warned. "We have no solid proof that it's them. Maybe it's a coincidence."

They chatted a few more moments and then headed back out. When they reached their back alley, Carlita glanced at the tenant parking lot. Elvira's car was gone. "Whew. It looks like we've been blessed with a few minutes of peace and quiet."

"Carlita! Mercedes!"

Carlita spun around. Steve-O was hustling across the street. He stopped abruptly and paused to catch his breath. "I think we just got a break in the case."

Chapter 20

"We could use a break," Carlita said.

"One of my regular customers, Cody, just left. I was telling him about the recent vandalism, how someone had broken in and sprayed paint on my floor and splattered my cash register, then someone tipped over Colby's dumpster and, last but not least, your courtyard break-in."

"He said it was funny I should mention that. Cody had overhead his younger brother bragging about making some quick cash by vandalizing properties. When they mentioned my tattoo shop, it caught Cody's attention."

"Someone hired teens to vandalize our properties?" Carlita blinked rapidly.

"Yep. He tried to find out who it was. You know, without raising too much suspicion, but the only other thing he found out was that the boys had been hired a few times by the same person...same MO."

Mercedes stomped her foot. "Turds. So it is the same person."

"Right." Steve-O nodded. "Well, I got to thinking...what if we ask Cody to help us set up some sort of sting where we pretend to hire them? Maybe we can meet with them and find out who is behind it."

"Great idea," Carlita said, excited for their first big break.

Steve promised to work on it. He glanced at his watch. "I've got another appointment coming in, but I'll keep you posted."

The rest of the day was uneventful, for which Carlita was grateful. In fact, the rest of the week and weekend was quiet and uneventful. Carlita's new motto was, "no news is good news."

Mercedes' disappointment over not being hired by the Savannah Evening News was short-lived. By Monday morning, she'd managed to land another job interview for a part-time position, this time at the Savannah-Burnham Police Department, only a few short blocks from the apartment.

Mercedes changed three times before sticking with a black skirt, pale blue button down shirt and sensible flats. She had first come out wearing heels but when Carlita reminded her she would have trouble balancing on the Segway, she agreed and ran back to her room to switch shoes.

Carlita managed to convince her daughter to eat half a breakfast bar and then watched as she disappeared down the steps.

Rambo and she stepped out onto the deck to watch Mercedes leave and it reminded Carlita of Mercedes' first day of kindergarten, where she had walked her to the small elementary school, watched her join the throngs of other young children and then disappear inside the school.

She swallowed the lump in her throat as her daughter slipped the helmet on, tucking stray strands of dark hair underneath before hopping on her Segway. With a small wave of her hand, Mercedes was gone.

Carlita patted Rambo's head. "I guess it's just you, me and Grayvie today." She took Rambo for a long walk, through Waverly Square, Rollins Square, all the way to Oldsmar Square where they turned around and retraced their steps.

Today was Glenda Fox's afternoon tea and Carlita was looking forward to it. Mercedes would be home in plenty of time to get ready and the two women planned to walk to Glenda's place.

Glenda had told her the members of Savannah Architectural Society had been invited under the premise they were celebrating Vicki Munroe's recent promotion to president.

She had told Carlita the members were not aware the Garlucci women had been invited, too.

Mercedes arrived home shortly after noon and ate the other half of the breakfast bar she'd left behind, along with a small sandwich. She chattered excitedly about the interview and told her mother that the woman who had interviewed her had given her a tour of the station.

Carlita had already decided if Mercedes wanted a part-time job, apart from working at the pawnshop when it opened, then she would hire outside help.

"I'm so excited about high tea at Glenda Fox's home."

"Afternoon tea," Carlita corrected. "While you were gone, I did a little research and the British take this tea thing very seriously. I picked up a few pointers."

"Like what?" The last thing Mercedes wanted to do was embarrass herself, or her mother.

"Make sure you place your napkin on your lap, don't clink your spoon against the china and don't eat too much," Carlita rattled off.

"We're not supposed to eat?"

"You can eat. Just don't finish all your food," Carlita said. "You're not supposed to appear hungry. This is more of a social event. If all else fails, copy whatever Glenda does."

"I thought I would like high, I mean afternoon tea, but it sounds kind of pretentious."

"Let's look at it as an adventure and if we screw up, we won't have to worry about a second invitation," Carlita joked.

"I guess I better start primping," Mercedes said. "Don't want to appear shabby."

Carlita was beginning to grow nervous as well. Her old neighborhood was so completely different from Savannah high society. Perhaps she and her daughter were in over their heads, but it was too late now.

They were going to afternoon tea, like it or lump it.

***

Carlita sucked in a breath and grasped the round brass knocker on the impressive front door of the Fox residence. "Here goes nothing."

Mercedes tugged on the sides of her summer dress and frowned, wishing now she'd chosen the pastel floral pattern instead, which would hide stains if she happened to dribble tea or drop food down the front of her.

The door abruptly opened and Reginald Higgins, Glenda's butler, peered down at them. "May I help you?"

Carlita fumbled inside her purse and pulled out the invitation. "Yes. We're here for afternoon tea."

Reginald stared at the invitation, nodded faintly and then took the invitation from Carlita before taking a step back as he opened the door. "Do come in."

Mercedes, followed by Carlita, stepped into the massive hall and gazed around in awe. Gleaming black and white tiled floors flowed from the entrance, down the hall and to the back where Carlita caught a glimpse of a butler's pantry.

"Follow me." Reginald turned, the sharp rap of his heels echoing on the tile floors. The tinkle of laughter floated in the grand entrance as they walked toward the sound.

He led them through an arched doorway, down a spacious hall where exquisite paintings adorned both sides of the crimson-colored walls.

They entered a large room with a wall of windows overlooking a sparkling blue swimming pool, surrounded by a meticulously manicured courtyard.

"There you are." Glenda spied her friends.

Reginald cleared his throat and lifted their invitation. "Announcing the arrival of Mrs. Carlita Garlucci and daughter, Mercedes Garlucci."

"Thank you Reginald." Glenda touched the man's arm before taking the invitation from him and lightly hugging Carlita. "You're right on time."

She continued. "We're only waiting for one more member of the society, our newest member, to arrive before we head to the parlor."

Carlita heard Carol Weatherbee before she saw her, her back turned toward Carlita and her signature bright red beehive hairdo towering high atop her head. "We should have taken a vote and conducted a more thorough check before allowing a new member to join," Carol sniffed.

"Some things never change," Carlita said.

Carol spun around, her eyes wide. "You! What in heaven's name are *you* doing here?" she screeched.

Glenda folded her arms in front of her. "I invited Carlita and Mercedes. No introductions necessary, I see."

Carol scowled while Vicki Munroe stepped forward, her hand extended, a warm smile on her face. "Mrs. Garlucci. How nice to see you again." She shook Carlita's hand and then turned to Mercedes. "And your beautiful daughter."

"Glenda has such a lovely home. Wasn't that kind of her to invite us to tea? I can hardly wait to tour the place."

Carlita relaxed her shoulders. "Yes. I agree."

The doorbell rang and Reginald disappeared from the room. There were other women in the room and Glenda introduced them as Kim Phelps, Savannah-Burnham District Clerk and Renee Visser, District Mentor. They were both genuinely friendly and seemed intrigued that a new business entrepreneur in Walton Square was a woman and daughter duo.

"We need more women business owners in Savannah," Kim Phelps told Carlita. "I heard Rodney Yates is presenting your business license request to the district's council tomorrow."

"Yes," Carlita clasped her hands. "We're anxious to continue moving forward with our business."

"A pawnshop," Glenda added.

"Announcing Ms. Elvira Cobb."

Carlita spun around. Her jaw dropped as she locked eyes with her new tenant.

Chapter 21

Elvira slowly crossed the room. "I...you..." Her voice trailed off. The woman was clearly just as surprised by Carlita's presence as Carlita was by hers.

The pieces began to fall into place. "Elvira. You must be the new member of Savannah Architectural Society."

"I am." Elvira blinked.

"You two know each other?" Glenda asked.

"Elvira is one of my new tenants," Carlita explained.

Glenda stared at Carlita and then Elvira. "No wonder you were throwing such a fit the other day about contacting the district council to raise a ruckus about Carlita's business license application."

"You." Carlita's eyes narrowed.

Elvira lifted her head defiantly. "As not only a concerned SAS member and tenant of said property, it is my opinion that opening a pawnshop under the same roof as my home is not in the best interest of either of Savannah-Burnham District Office or me."

For the umpteenth time, Carlita wished she had never allowed Elvira Cobb to talk her into renting an apartment. "I have half a mind to..."

Mercedes grabbed her mother's arm and pulled her off to the side. "Not now. We can discuss this later." All eyes were on them, including the butler's eyes.

"You're right."

Glenda hurriedly spoke. "Well, now that we're all here we can adjourn to the parlor."

Reginald led the way and the others fell in line with Glenda jumping in between Elvira and Carlita. "I had no idea," Glenda whispered to Carlita. "I guess when I mailed Elvira's invitation I should've realized that was your address."

They passed through a library and approached a set of large wooden double doors.

Reginald flung the doors open and stepped aside.

Clusters of overstuffed Victorian chairs dotted the room. There was a massive brick fireplace in the center of the far wall and large wingback chairs faced the fireplace. Despite the spaciousness of the large room, the rich mahogany wood-paneled ceiling gave the room a cozy feel.

To the right of the double doors was a trio of tables covered in crisp linen tablecloths. On top of the tables were tiered trays of delectable treats.

On the smaller tables were four hand-painted teapots, surrounded by antique teacups and matching saucers.

Directly in front of the pots of tea was a tent card. Carlita leaned in:

Cream Colored Pot – Twinings
Pink Pot – Yorkshire
Sapphire Pot – PG Tips
Yellow Pot – Tetley

The only tea Carlita recognized was Tetley.

Mercedes reached into her small hand purse, pulled out her phone, turned it to camera mode and then snapped a picture. "This is so cool."

"Ahem." Reginald, who stood off to the side, cleared his throat.

"Sorry," Mercedes smiled. "I couldn't help myself. This is so awesome."

A shadow of a smile flitted across Reginald's face before being replaced by a solemn expression.

Mother and daughter stepped over to the large table with tiered treats. There was another tent card, this one even larger:

A Selection of Freshly Made Farmhouse Sandwiches:

Italian Baked Ham with Country Tomato Chutney
Smoked Salmon
Cucumber & Cream Cheese
Savory Ham
Chicken Finger
Farmhouse Mature Cheddar Cheese Savoury

Freshly Baked Scones with Cornish Clotted Cream & Strawberry Jam

A Selection of Homemade Mini Desserts including:

Italian Lemon Verbena Cake
Walnut & Sultana Farmhouse Cake
Luxurious Macarons
Zesty Lemon Meringue Tart

Mercedes snapped a picture of the menu, the large food tray, as well as the smaller food trays and then slipped the phone into her purse as she gazed at the carefully arranged petite treats. "They're almost too pretty to touch."

Carlita, not wanting to be the first to dig in, hovered off to the side.

Carol Weatherbee glared at Carlita and headed to the table where she picked up a small dessert plate, and loaded it with one of everything.

She stomped off, her tower of treats teetering precariously. Carol placed the plate, along with a linen napkin, on a small side table before approaching the teapots.

Glenda eased around Carol. "These are all British teas. If you like strong tea, I suggest Twinings. The others are milder."

"Thanks." Carol reached for the Tetley, which was the one Carlita was going to sample. Carlita was more of a coffee drinker, although she loved a cool glass of iced tea.

Mother and daughter watched as the other SAS members, followed by Kim Phelps and Renee Visser, approached the tables. The other guests took their tea and delicacies to the nearby tables. Only Glenda, Mercedes and Carlita were left.

"Thank you so much for inviting us," Mercedes said. "I hope you don't mind, but I took pictures."

Glenda grinned and then winked at Reginald who was standing near the back of the tables in the event a guest needed assistance. "Absolutely not. I'm sure Reginald was tickled, although he won't admit it."

"Miss Mary made the sandwiches," Reginald said.

"And you made the tea," Glenda added.

The women each picked up a small plate and Carlita perused the offerings. She decided to stick with something that sounded remotely familiar, the Italian baked ham, cucumber and chicken finger sandwiches. She slid a small piece of the Italian lemon verbena cake next to her chicken sandwich before picking up a napkin and slowly walking over to the last empty table in the far corner of the room.

"I'll get the tea." Mercedes followed her mother. She placed her plate on the table and returned moments later with two cups of tea.

Carlita smoothed the napkin on her lap, picked up her tea and daintily sipped. It wasn't too strong and a little on the sweet side. "I didn't know the tea was sweet."

"It isn't." Mercedes eased into the seat across from her mother and leaned forward. "Everyone else was adding sugar and milk so I added some to ours."

Carlita took another sip and wrinkled her nose. "I like cold sweet tea but I'm not sure about this."

Mercedes sipped hers and quickly set it back down as she curled her lip. "You're right. Sorry."

"Don't worry about it." Carlita picked up the cucumber sandwich and nibbled the corner. "Not bad." She ate almost all of her small sandwich before remembering not to appear hungry.

Carlita set it on the plate and reached for the chicken finger sandwich. The Italian baked ham sandwich ended up being her favorite and she threw caution to the wind and finished the entire sandwich. She quickly downed the sweet, now lukewarm, tea.

"Well?" Glenda wandered over, plate in hand. "What do you think?"

"I like my sweet tea cold," Carlita admitted and Glenda laughed. "Me too," she whispered conspiratorially, "but don't tell Reginald."

"The sandwiches are delicious," Mercedes said as she took a bite of the smoked salmon sandwich. "Too bad we can't eat it all."

"Why can't you eat it all?" Glenda asked.

"Mom did a little research and read that it's not proper British manners to finish your food," Mercedes explained.

Glenda chuckled. "Well, we're not in Great Britain so feel free to lick the plate," she teased. Their host finished making her rounds while Carlita and Mercedes finished their food.

Mother and daughter refilled their teacups, minus the milk and sugar, and then chatted with the others. Carlita immediately took a liking to Renee Visser, the Director of Tourism, and Vicki Munroe, the President of the Savannah Architectural Society.

Glenda formally introduced Elvira as the newest member of the society to a polite round of applause.

Elvira, deemed it the perfect opportunity to blather on about her opinions, how she vowed to police the Savannah-Burnham district and crack down on violators of Savannah's strict architectural codes. She droned on about her goals and her certainty the society would not regret their decision to hire her.

Carlita had begun to tune her out, when something caught her attention "...and I plan to start by ensuring tattoo shops and pawnshops are no longer allowed to tarnish the beloved City of Savannah's impeccable image."

Chapter 22

Mercedes shoved her chair back and started to stand but her mother reached out and stopped her. "Remember, Mercedes. We can handle this later," she said in a low voice.

Finally, Elvira stopped flapping her gums and sat, and an uncomfortable silence followed.

Carol Weatherbee was the first to leave. She glanced at her watch. "I should get back to the office. Thank you for a lovely afternoon tea and *mostly* lovely company." She shot Carlita a glare before Reginald escorted her to the front door.

Vicki Munroe was the next to leave, followed by Elvira.

Kim Phelps and Renee Visser hovered near Carlita. "Don't worry about that bag of hot air," Renee said. "Rumor has it her bark is worse than her bite."

"Yeah," Kim agreed. "Rodney Yates said your license is only a matter of formality now." She patted Carlita's arm.

Reginald walked both women to the door leaving only Glenda, Mercedes and Carlita in the parlor. "Thank you again for the tea. It was lovely," Carlita said.

"I'm sorry about Elvira. I had no idea you knew her let alone that she was your new tenant."

Carlita waved a hand. "It's not your fault."

They strolled out of the room. "I completely forgot about the tour," Glenda said. "If you have time, we can do it now."

"Yes." Mercedes clasped her hands. "I would love to see your magnificent home."

"Perfect. Let's start upstairs." Glenda led them up a large, curved, carpeted staircase and they toured several bedrooms, bathrooms, as well as a small movie theater. "I would show you the master bedroom, but it's a mess. I didn't get around to straightening it since I was busy this morning preparing for the tea."

"No worries," Carlita said. "I'm sure it's as lovely as the rest of your home."

They made their way back down the grand staircase with a tour of the kitchen where mother and daughter met Mary, the cook. They gushed over the goodies they had eaten and Mary beamed.

After departing the kitchen, the trio toured the library, the formal dining room, the formal living room and a sunroom on the back of the house. Off the sunroom were French doors leading to the courtyard.

Glenda opened one of the doors. "This is my favorite part of the house."

Stepping into the courtyard and pool area was like stepping into another world. There was a small grotto tucked into one corner of the pool and on the other side of the grotto, a large hot tub with glass block walls.

To the left of the pool was a gourmet outdoor kitchen, complete with built-in gas grill, small refrigerator and a prep area. It even sported a large wine cooler.

The meticulously manicured gardens were filled with a rainbow of roses, sculpted shrubs and blossoming trees. "This is beautiful," Mercedes gushed. "It's my favorite part of your house, too."

Back inside, they chatted for several moments. "We should get going," Carlita said and then turned to Glenda. "Thank you for the invitation to tea and for showing us your lovely home."

A small smile played on Glenda's lips. "Thank you for your friendship. It's hard to make friends with the SAS members. It seems like each of them have their own personal agenda." She sighed.

"It's refreshing to have friends without all the baggage," Glenda added.

Mercedes began to cough and pounded her chest. If only Glenda knew how much baggage that her mother and she had. She thought back to their home in Queens, to their previous life, to her brothers' lives...

Carlita patted her daughter's back.

"I swallowed wrong," Mercedes gasped.

"I'll walk you out." Glenda led the way to the front door. "Perhaps we can get together for coffee or tea next week."

"Mom and I were thinking about taking in more historic Savannah sights, maybe touring one of the haunted houses or trying another local restaurant."

"Ah," Glenda nodded. "If you're going to do a haunted tour, I highly recommend Sorrel-Weed house. It's been featured on several national television shows."

"Sounds cool," Mercedes said.

"Sounds creepy," Carlita shook her head.

"I'd love to do lunch," Glenda said, "but will skip the haunted tour. We could try the Pirate House. I haven't been there in eons."

They said their good-byes after Glenda opened the front door, and Carlita and Mercedes began the walk home.

"What do you think Glenda would say if she knew about our past?" Mercedes asked.

"I don't know, Mercedes. It's hard to tell." Carlita grinned. "What do you think Elvira would say if she knew?"

"Ha," Mercedes snorted. "I don't even want to think about it."

"Neither do I," Carlita said. "Neither do I."

Chapter 23

Mercedes and Carlita beat Elvira back to the apartment and the only reason Carlita knew was that she heard heavy footsteps tromp up the stairs, moments before a hall door slammed. At least she guessed it was Elvira since she'd barely heard a peep out of Shelby and Violet across the hall.

Carlita had settled into a dining room chair when the doorbell rang. She headed out the slider and peered over the side. It was Annie.

"I'll be right there." Carlita hurried to the outer door, letting a frazzled Annie inside.

"Nothing like spending most of my day putting out for sale signs that some jerk decided to redistribute for me."

"I'm sorry Annie. I think we may be onto the culprit or culprits who are vandalizing Walton Square."

Carlita led Annie up the stairs and into the apartment. "Would you like a glass of tea? Unsweet this time." Sweet tea was starting to grow on Carlita, but she decided she needed to drink a little more of the unsweetened variety and skip the unnecessary calories.

"Sure." Annie settled into a dining room chair. "You think we may be able to figure out who is vandalizing us?"

Carlita poured two glasses of tea, set one in front of Annie and then eased into the seat across from her. "Yeah. One of Steve Winter's customers told him that he overhead his teenage brother talking to a friend about vandalizing Walton Square properties. He was going to get back to me when he had more information. From what he said, someone was hiring these teenagers to destroy our property."

"Who would do such a thing?" Annie asked.

"I wish I knew. What I find odd is not everyone in Walton Square has been hit." Carlita thought of Stu Fischer, who so far hadn't had anything happen.

Carlita lifted a finger. "Us, you, the Colby's, Steve. I don't think this is random."

"You don't think..." Annie's voice trailed off.

"Think what?" Carlita prompted.

"The protest," Annie said. "Remember when we protested in front of the district office? What if the person or persons saw our protest on television and that's how we became the targets?"

"Mercedes and I thought the same thing," Carlita said.

Annie twirled the straw inside her glass. "It started with you. An anonymous person contacted Mr. Yates to try to stop you from getting your pawnshop license. Those of us who are supporting you have been targeted."

Perhaps it was Paradise Pawn, or maybe it was Carlita's new tenant, Elvira Cobb, or even Stu Fischer.

"Steve's broken window, his painted floors, cash register and counter, Colby's dumpster disaster, your courtyard figurine, my signs." Annie ticked off the list of incidents.

Carlita slapped the palm of her hand on the table causing Annie to jump. "Wait a minute. When I was in Elvira's apartment the other day, she had a bunch of cans of paint on the floor. I think we just figured out who has been up to no good."

The more she thought about it, the angrier Carlita became. Here she had been feeling sorry for the woman and all the while, she was wreaking havoc in Carlita's life.

"It was right around the time Elvira filled out the rental application that someone destroyed the statue. Not long after, everything else happened, one incident at a time. How convenient."

She remembered how Elvira had wanted to cut down her courtyard trees and had tried to scratch out a section of her rental agreement.

"We need hard evidence," Annie said. "We should wait until Steve sets the trap to lure the suspect into the open using the teenagers as bait."

A knock on the front door interrupted their conversation, which meant it could only be one of two people, Shelby or Elvira. "That's probably her now." Carlita marched to the door and swung it open. Elvira was on the other side.

"Yes," Elvira said coolly, "I would like to use the courtyard. I need a key." She held out her hand.

Carlita stared at her hand, the sudden urge to slap it washed over her. Instead, she clenched her fists. "Wait here," she gritted out.

She headed over to the key rack, removed the skeleton key and carried it back to the doorway where she dropped it in Elvira's open hand. "Make sure you lock it when you're done. We've had a rash of vandals destroying business property, including my fountain and we don't want you to be blamed." Carlita leaned in, studying Elvira's expression, which was blank.

She was good…real good. Cool as a cucumber. "I'll be sure to do that." Elvira turned on her heel and returned to her apartment.

Carlita waited until the door closed before closing her own.

Annie glanced at her watch. "I should go. Cindy is at the office holding down the fort and I told her I wouldn't be long."

"I'll walk with you. I want to stop by Steve's place to see if he has heard anything yet."

"I'm going over to Steve's," Carlita hollered toward Mercedes' room. She heard a muffled response and taking that for a yes, Carlita and Annie exited the apartment.

Carlita twisted the knob to make sure the door had locked before heading down the steps and out the building.

"I'll run over to Steve's with you before heading back to the office." The women crossed the street and headed left. As they walked by the front window, Carlita could see Steve bent over his worktable; a customer was lying on the table.

He glanced up when they stepped inside. "You must have read my mind. I was going to give you a call."

He turned his attention back to his customer, the buzz of the tattoo gun echoing in the small shop. The sound reminded Carlita of a dentist drilling teeth and she cringed at the noise.

Annie, on the other hand, seemed fascinated by the procedure and stood off to one side to watch. "I always wanted a tattoo but I'm a big chicken. I have a low pain threshold."

They waited for Steve to finish the procedure. The customer sat up, adjusting the sleeve on his shirt so it wouldn't touch his new tattoo and then eased out of the chair. "Thanks a lot man. I owe you one."

Steve clasped the man's hand in a tight grip and gave it a firm shake. "I appreciate you, Cody. You get us hooked up and we'll call it even."

The young man nodded and then exited the building, closing the door behind him.

"That's the guy whose brother has been hired to target us," Carlita said.

"Yep. I offered him a free tattoo in exchange for talking his brother and his buddy into coming over here so we can have a little chat with the fellas."

Carlita hoped no one would get hurt. She thought of her own sons, Tony and Vinnie. If it had been them, she was certain it would involve a few broken bones and some bloodshed to teach the culprits a lesson. "No one is going to get hurt..." her voice trailed off.

"Nah." Steve waved a hand and then rubbed his thumb back and forth across his other fingers. "It may cost a few bucks and I may have to toss in another tattoo or two, but it'll be pain-free."

"Good," Carlita nodded. "So now what?"

"We wait. He promised to bring them by around seven tonight."

***

"How are we all going to fit in here?" Carlita asked as she studied the cramped bathroom inside the tattoo shop.

"I'm claustrophobic," Annie said.

"Stand on the toilet and open the window," Mercedes suggested.

"I'll take the side of the sink," Autumn offered.

Annie squeezed in first, followed by Autumn. Mercedes shuffled to the front of the toilet and Carlita pulled the door almost all the way shut.

"I have to go to the bathroom," Mercedes whispered.

"You're kidding," Autumn hissed.

"Yeah. I'm kidding."

Carlita groaned. "No one gets to use the bathroom, cough, sneeze or hiccup. Those boys mustn't know we're here." She turned her attention to the front of the tattoo shop. "They should be here any minute."

Cody, Steve's contact, had texted to say they were on the way and should arrive within minutes. The plan was for Steve to bribe the teenagers to rat out whoever was paying them to vandalize the neighborhood.

If that didn't work, he would resort to threatening to contact police, telling them he had evidence, linking them to the crimes.

"It's getting hot in here." Annie began fanning her face with a folded newspaper she found on the back of the toilet seat.

"You do know that is Steve-O's bathroom reading material," Autumn pointed out.

"Ew." Annie dropped the paper and wiped her hands on her slacks. "Disgusting."

"Shh. Someone just walked in." Carlita placed her index finger to her lips. Through the crack in the door, she barely made out the young man she'd seen earlier.

He stood next to two younger boys, their shoulders hunched. They looked uncomfortable. She wasn't able to hear what was being said, but hoped Steve was persuading them to reveal their client.

When he reached into his back pocket, pulled out his wallet and opened it up, Carlita knew he had been successful. She couldn't see how much he paid the teenagers but handed both of them some bills before closing his wallet and sliding it back inside his pocket.

The three exited the shop and Carlita burst out of the bathroom.

Steve grinned as the women hustled out of the cramped quarters. "I have some good news and some bad news."

"Bad news first," Carlita said.

"Good news first," Annie said.

"The bad news is the boys don't have a name. Their 'client' always pays in cash, wears sunglasses over the top of regular glasses and they're pretty sure a wig. According to their vague description, it's a woman. She's short, a little on the chunky side and I'm not sure if it matters, but both boys said she swung her arms when she walked."

"Swung her arms?" Carlita asked.

"Like this." Steve strode across the room, his arms swinging wide as he walked. When he reached the far wall, he walked back, still swinging his arms like an Army soldier.

Carlita couldn't remember ever watching Elvira walk any sort of distance. She was usually pounding on her apartment door.

"So what's the good news? Autumn asked.

"Well, they said it was a woman and they never saw a car when she approached them in the skate park."

"So the perp either parked close by or walked," Mercedes said.

"Or lives close by," Steve agreed. "Last, but not least, she was always adamant about the timeframe of when the vandalism took place."

"So she knew everyone's schedule," Mercedes mused.

"Yep. Think about it. It's in this one square block," Steve said. "It's a woman who knows everyone's schedule."

"That knocks out Stu Fischer," Carlita said.

"Unless it's Stu's wife," Annie said.

"Or Elvira Cobb." Mercedes said.

"I have one more piece of good news I saved til last." Steve smiled.

"What?" The women echoed in unison.

"The 'client' told them yesterday at the skate park she has another job for them coming up."

"Cool. All we gotta do is hang out at the skate park when the boys are there. When the 'client' shows up. Busted." Autumn snapped her fingers.

"We can take shifts," Annie suggested.

"But work in pairs for safety," Steve said.

Steve and Autumn offered to take the evening shift. "I don't have any more appointments scheduled for tonight so we can take the first shift," Steve said. "We'll have to get going, though. The boys were on their way to the park to see if she shows up, which is usually around 7:30 - 7:45 p.m."

Carlita and Mercedes quickly decided they would take the following night's shift.

"If we need another night, I'll go with Annie," Carlita said.

With a plan in place, the group parted ways. Annie made her way back to her office. Carlita and Mercedes headed home while Steve and Autumn headed to the skate park.

"I can't wait to see the look on Elvira Cobb's face when we bust her," Mercedes said.

"I can't wait to evict her," Carlita added.

Chapter 24

Carlita was on pins and needles the rest of the evening and she kept checking her cell phone to see if either Steve or Autumn had called or texted. Finally, she gave up and headed to bed.

She tossed and turned all night. Visions of Elvira creeping around, trying to break into their apartment filled her head and every little noise made her wonder if it was the woman.

Sometime after midnight, she fell into a fitful sleep.

Rambo woke her early the next morning. They wandered to their usual areas and she watched as her pup sniffed at the weeds and the front tire of Elvira's car.

She was almost convinced Elvira was behind the vandalism. Still, until they could catch the person in the act, she couldn't say with one hundred percent conviction. Innocent until proven or found guilty. What if she was wrong?

She thought about Stu Fischer. He wasn't keen on Carlita opening a pawnshop either. Not to mention Paradise Pawn, whose owner definitely didn't want Carlita to set up shop.

The fact the woman was always adamant on the time the teenagers vandalized Walton Square businesses was a clue. It was also a clue that only Carlita's friends, the local business owners, had been targeted...the Colby's, Steve, Annie and Carlita.

It was too much of a coincidence that Elvira was desperate to move into the apartment at the same time the incidents started to occur. The fact that she was on the Savannah Architectural Society committee and dead set against the pawnshop was also a clue, not to mention the paint cans Carlita had spotted inside Elvira's apartment.

Everything pointed to Elvira.

With all that had gone on, Carlita had forgotten all about contacting Rodney Yates to see if her license had finally been approved.

When she reached the apartment, she started a fresh pot of coffee. She had purchased a bag of bagels from Colby's the last time she'd shopped there and was looking forward to trying the everything bagel. She sliced the bagel and popped it into the toaster.

Carlita could hear Mercedes moving around in her room. She wondered how her daughter's novel was progressing and several times, she'd almost asked her, but held back. She didn't want Mercedes to think she was spying.

She also needed to call her middle son, Tony, who said he was planning a visit. It would be nice to see him, to see all of her children. As soon as she had the license in hand, she would press Vinnie for an answer on whether or not he was moving to Savannah.

If he wasn't going to move to Savannah, she would go ahead and rent the last apartment, but make sure the next tenant was thoroughly screened before having them sign on the dotted line.

The bagel popped up and Carlita pulled both pieces out before placing them on a small plate and then reaching inside the fridge for a tub of whipped cream cheese. She slathered a thick layer on each side and then pulled a coffee cup from the cupboard.

Rambo and Grayvie sat near the edge of the kitchen, eyeing her every move.

"You get a treat, too," she told them as she pulled the boxes of dog treats and cat treats from the cupboard. "You want to eat on the deck?" she asked them before carrying her bagel and pet treats in one hand and cup of hot coffee in the other.

Carlita set the bagel and coffee on the small stand before placing the treats on the deck. She settled into the chaise lounge and reached for her coffee.

The day stretched long ahead of her and a pang of loneliness filled her. She missed Vinnie, the sound of his voice, his smell. There were times at night she would reach over and touch the other side of the bed, only to realize he wasn't there.

A tear trickled down her cheek and she quickly swiped it away. She didn't want Mercedes to see her cry.

Carlita pushed the melancholy thoughts out of her mind and focused on her sons. She was excited Tony was planning a trip.

She finished her everything bagel, deeming it one of her new favorites before draining her coffee cup and heading back indoors.

Mercedes was standing over the sink, eating a bowl of cereal.

"Why don't you sit at the table?" her mother asked.

"I'm lazy," Mercedes mumbled between mouthfuls. She scooped the last spoonful of cereal into her mouth and dumped the milk down the drain before rinsing her dishes and placing them in the dishwasher.

"Where are you going?" Carlita asked as she eyed her daughter's Bermuda shorts and t-shirt.

"It's a surprise." Mercedes grabbed her keys that were dangling from the hook by the door before hurrying out.

"I'll lock up after you," Carlita yelled through the open door.

"Thanks." Mercedes said. The alley door opened and then slammed shut.

Carlita turned to Rambo. "Let's go down to the courtyard. I need to water the flowers before I forget."

The two of them trailed behind Mercedes, out through the back door before rounding the side of the building.

The lights inside A Scoop in Time ice cream shop were burning brightly as were Walton Square Souvenirs and Riverfront Real Estate but Shades of Ink tattoo shop was dark.

They rounded the corner of the building and headed to the gate where Carlita pulled the key Elvira had slipped under her door the night before from her front pocket and stuck it in the keyhole. "We should put one of those combo locks on here. I'll have Tony do it when he gets here."

Rambo's ears perked up at the mention of Tony's name. Rambo had originally belonged to Tony, and Carlita had inherited him several months back when someone was breaking into her home in Queens.

Carlita waited for Rambo to trot into the courtyard before closing the door behind them and turning the lock. Her gaze automatically focused on the second story apartment windows.

"Maybe I should put decks on these units and move into one of them." It would give her a little more privacy when she was out in the courtyard, leaving only one other apartment that overlooked her serene oasis.

Her scalp tingled, a sure sign she was being watched, and a shiver ran down her spine.

Someone...Elvira...had moved the bistro table and it now sat off in one corner. Carlita dragged it back under the tree.

Rambo patrolled the perimeter of the courtyard while Carlita pulled a few stray weeds. She'd brought the previous day's Savannah Evening Newspaper with her and settled into one of the chairs to catch up on local news while enjoying the still relatively cool morning.

They stayed in the courtyard for a long time until finally, her mental to-do list no longer allowed Carlita her morning peace and quiet and she decided it was time to head back up.

"Ready to head home?" Rambo was sniffing the broken statue. "We'll replace it soon," she promised her pooch.

Carlita folded her paper and patted her leg. "Let's go." She pushed in the chair and something caught her attention. There was an outline of black spray paint on one of the courtyard walls.

"What in the world?" She stepped closer and studied the pattern. It looked as if someone had placed something against the cement wall and then painted it.

Only one word...one name...came to mind. "Elvira," Carlita gritted between clenched teeth. She glanced up at the window before stomping out of the courtyard. She marched down the sidewalk and back inside the apartment building.

When she reached the top of the stairs, Carlita made a beeline for the apartment across the hall and in the back where she rapped sharply on the outer door.

The door opened and Elvira gazed out. "Yes?" she said coolly.

Carlita didn't bother beating around the bush. "You spray painted the side of my building."

"I don't have any idea what you're talking about," Elvira replied haughtily.

"The courtyard. When you used it yesterday, you must have painted something and now there's black spray paint on my wall."

Elvira eased the door shut, obscuring the view of the inside of her apartment. "Prove it."

"Let me see inside your apartment if you have nothing to hide," Carlita said.

"It's a mess right now."

"I like messes."

She stared her tenant down. "All right." Elvira opened the door wide and Carlita and Rambo stepped inside where Carlita spotted a freshly painted canvas propped against the fireplace. "Aha! You *were* painting in the courtyard."

"It's not against the law," Elvira argued.

"But defacing my property violates the terms of your rental agreement giving me grounds to evict you," Carlita said.

The defiant expression on Elvira's face vanished, replaced by a look of pure fear. She clasped her hands. "Please, I have nowhere to go."

"Maybe you can move in with Carol Weatherbee." Carlita grinned evilly at the thought.

"I'll paint the wall," Elvira bargained. "Any color you want. It'll look like brand new."

"Let me think about it," Carlita said. She turned to go and then turned back. "In the meantime, do not, I repeat, do not paint anything else."

Chapter 25

Carlita puttered around the apartment, still seething over Elvira's complete disregard for rules and property. She tossed around the idea of punishing her by forcing her to paint the entire courtyard.

Mercedes bounded through the front door at quarter past noon, carrying a large box.

Carlita had just finished chopping a bunch of vegetables. She was in the process of mixing a tossed salad for lunch. "Right on time. Would you care for a salad?"

"Sure." Mercedes nodded. "Let me wash up." She carried the box to her room before she disappeared inside the bathroom, returning moments later to set the table. "I talked to Autumn earlier. She told me no one showed up at the skate park last night."

Carlita carried the large bowl of tossed salad and a bottle of ranch dressing to the table. "I figured as much, so I guess our turn is tonight."

"Seven o'clock on the dot."

Mother and daughter sat across from each other at the table. "I talked to Tony earlier. He'll be here next week for a visit."

Mercedes smoothed her napkin in her lap and reached for her fork. "Yay. We'll have to take him around, show him the sights. Speaking of that, are we still going to take that haunted house tour?"

"Do I have to?" Carlita reached for the tongs and then loaded a heaping pile of mixed salad onto her plate.

"No, I guess not." Mercedes' shoulders slumped. "I've never been inside a haunted house."

"What if you live in one?" Carlita handed her daughter the salad bowl. "Okay. I'll go with you, but if I start having nightmares, it's your fault."

"Well, we can't go tonight because we have a stakeout. How 'bout tomorrow night if I don't have another stakeout?"

It would give Carlita a day to psych herself into it. "It's a deal." While they ate, she told her daughter about the spray paint on the side of the building inside the courtyard and how she'd confronted Elvira, only to find out she had painted a picture.

"She's an artist?" Mercedes wrinkled her nose. "Huh. Never would've pegged her for one." She shrugged. "We may not have to worry about her if it turns out she's hiring those teenagers to vandalize Walton Square businesses. Plus, it'll be one more nail in her eviction coffin."

After lunch, Mercedes and Carlita straightened the kitchen. "I'd like to see what Elvira painted and then I have a surprise for you," Mercedes told her mother.

They headed to the courtyard with Rambo in tow. Mercedes shook her head as she stared at the paint-splattered wall. "I think we should make her paint all the walls."

"That's what I was thinking," Carlita said. "Or, we throw her out on her ear and add another project to our to-do list."

"Let's have her paint first and *then* kick her out," Mercedes joked. They wandered out of the courtyard and Carlita double-checked to make sure she had locked the gate.

When they reached the front of the building, Carlita noticed Annie's convertible parked in front of her real estate office. "I'm going to chat with Annie. I'll meet you inside."

Mercedes and Rambo continued walking toward the alley while Carlita crossed the street.

Both Cindy and Annie were inside the office. "Any news?" Annie asked when Carlita stepped through the front door.

"Nope. Looks like Mercedes and I are on deck for tonight," Carlita replied.

"On deck for what?" Cindy asked.

"Nothing much. It's a small project we're working on," Annie answered vaguely.

"Oh no." Cindy eyed her boss suspiciously. "Not another project."

She glanced at Carlita. "Has Annie ever shown you one of her projects?"

Annie began shaking her head.

"C'mon. Let me show her." Cindy hopped out of her chair and waved Carlita to the hall. "Check this out." She flipped through the key ring she was holding, inserted a key in the closet door and then flung the double doors open.

Carlita peered around the side of the door. Shelves lined half of the closet. Tucked inside the other half was a tall metal box with wheels. On top of the box was what appeared to be some sort of vent cover. Poking out of the four corners of the vent were small propellers.

"Check this out." Cindy reached inside the closet and pulled out a small square box. She flipped a switch on the front and the box began flashing. Round blue discs lit up. They looked like eyes. "Stand back."

Carlita stepped back and the box moved forward. "What in the world?"

Cindy shifted the stick and the box turned before rolling down the hall toward the front of the office. When they reached the front, Cindy handed the box to Annie. "Show her the rest."

"Okay." Annie took the remote. "Promise you won't laugh." She pressed a button and the robot turned, the base of it spinning as it rolled to the desk. Annie pressed another button and one of the metal arms shifted up, and then awkwardly flopped down on a sheet of paper. The robot backed up, carrying the sheet with it.

"How did you..." Carlita started to ask.

"Pick it up?" Annie asked. "I'm still in the testing phases. I had to put sticky stuff on the ends of the arms and Tinker is only able to pick up lightweight objects like papers or paper clips."

"Tinker," Carlita said. "You named your robot Tinker?"

"Cool, huh." Cindy said. "Annie is working on voice commands but so far, Tinker only spins in circles when she tries to get it to do something."

"You're a mad scientist," Carlita joked.

Annie turned a tinge of pink. "I love tinkering with stuff. I have other smaller projects but this is my biggest one," she admitted.

"You should see the custom drone Annie has been working on," Cindy said.

"I would love to see it," Carlita said.

"Maybe next time," Annie said as she guided Tinker back to the closet. "Cindy and you are the only two people who know about Tinker."

"My lips are sealed." Carlita made a zipping motion across her lips. "That is so clever."

Annie walked Carlita to the door. "I'll let you know if tonight's mission is successful," Carlita promised before exiting the building and stepping onto the sidewalk. "I wish I had a special talent."

"You do," Annie said. "You just haven't figured it out yet." The door closed and Carlita started down the sidewalk. She passed by Walton Square Souvenirs. The lights were on but the door was locked and when Carlita peeked in the window, she couldn't see anyone.

She passed by the ice cream shop. Business was booming and, once again, Carlita wondered if Stu Fischer...and his wife were behind the vandalism. Carlita looked both ways before crossing the street and heading back to the apartment.

When she got inside the apartment, she called Rodney Yates' office. He didn't answer so she left him a message, inquiring on the status of her license.

She also called Paulie, her youngest son, but held off on calling Vinnie. Hopefully, Mr. Yates would return her call and she could call Vinnie with the good news.

Mercedes hurried from her room, holding the box she'd brought home with her earlier. "Are you ready to see your surprise?" She didn't wait for a reply as she placed the box in the center of the dining room and lifted the lid.

Carlita peered over her shoulder. "What is it?"

"A laptop," Mercedes grinned. "I got a great deal on it. This is a closeout model. Now all I have to do is get it set up for you." She removed the plastic cover, placed the laptop on the table and lifted the lid.

Carlita ran her hand over the top. "Wow. It looks new."

"It is. Like I said, it's a closeout model," Mercedes said. "It might take me a little time to get you up and running, but I think you're gonna love it."

Mercedes spent the rest of the afternoon in front of the computer while Carlita grew restless about the stakeout. What if the woman never showed up again or the teenagers were just pulling their legs, wasting their time?

Something was gnawing in the back of Carlita's mind. It was the fact that perhaps it wasn't Elvira after all. She was annoying as all get out, but it didn't make her a criminal. Still, she knew for a fact her troublesome tenant did not want her opening a pawnshop, but then, neither did Paradise Pawn or Stu Fischer.

Finally, early evening rolled around and Carlita was anxious to get the show on the road.

Mercedes had put aside working on the computer and emerged from her room wearing khaki shorts and a lavender sleeveless blouse. She eased the strap of her small handbag over her head and then patted the front. "I'm packing heat."

Carlita lifted a brow. "You're carrying a gun?"

"It's the small one."

"I don't want anyone to be shot," Carlita said. "In fact, I don't think we should confront the suspect. We're there to observe and follow."

"That sounds boring," Mercedes said. "I was hoping to surprise them with a gotcha."

"What if they freak out?"

"That's why I'm bringing a weapon," Mercedes said.

"You can bring the weapon, but we're not going to approach them."

"Party pooper," Mercedes said. "Maybe I'll bring the Taser instead."

Rambo waited for them by the door. Carlita patted his head. "Sorry buddy. Maybe next time."

The dog slunk across the room and flopped down on the floor to pout.

"I hate it when he does that," Carlita turned her attention to her daughter. "Let's roll."

Chapter 26

The skate park was two squares over, which consisted of six city blocks, not a bad stroll on a late summer evening.

The skate park was busy, busier than Carlita thought it would be considering she assumed most kids spent their time hanging out indoors, playing video games and watching television.

She spotted Cody's brother, Keith, and his friend sitting on top of one of the cement pads, holding their skateboards. They were talking to a couple other teenagers, paying no mind to mother and daughter who settled in at a picnic table nearby.

Carlita nervously glanced at her watch. "We have ten minutes," she reported and then rubbed her sweaty palms on top of her shorts. "Hopefully this isn't another wasted evening."

"Maybe we're too close," Mercedes suggested. "If the perp spots us or recognizes us, they may turn right around and leave."

"True." Carlita hadn't thought about that. She was almost one hundred percent certain whoever was behind the acts of vandalism was someone they knew. They hopped off the picnic table and headed to a tree several yards away.

Carlita kept a visual on the teenagers, still sitting in the same spot. She glanced at her watch again. "Maybe it's going to be another no-show."

"Wait." Mercedes grabbed her mother's arm. "I see someone walking fast toward Keith and his friend."

The friends the teenagers had been talking to were gone and now it was just Keith and his friend. They looked up as the lone person approached.

Carlita had come prepared and pulled a small pair of binoculars from her purse, placed the lenses to her eyes and adjusted the dial on the front. "Short, roundish. Swinging their arms. Definitely wearing a wig but not sunglasses with regular glasses. Just regular glasses," she reported.

Mercedes whipped her cell phone from her back pocket, clicked it to video and began recording the exchange. "I wish I had a zoom lens."

Elvira didn't wear glasses, at least not that she knew of. Carlita handed the binoculars to Mercedes who adjusted them to her eyes and studied the person. "The person is handing something to Keith. It looks like an envelope, but I can't be certain."

Carlita tilted her head to the side and studied the exchange. It could be Elvira...

Her eyes grew wide as it dawned on her there was someone else who looked a lot like this person, someone with a business in Walton Square, someone she would have least suspected...someone who wore glasses. "I think I know who that is. Let's go."

Carlita flipped over and began crawling on all fours until she was hidden behind the tree. Mercedes was right behind her. "Where are we going?" Mercedes hissed.

"To Walton Square. We're gonna head her off at the pass."

When mother and daughter reached the cover of a row of hedges, Carlita sprang to her feet and began sprinting down the sidewalk.

"Wait for me." Mercedes groaned. She quickly caught up with her mother, and the two of them raced down the sidewalk.

Carlita and Mercedes didn't stop running until they reached the apartment building.

"Over there." Carlita gasped as she pointed to Ruby McKinley's Walton Square Souvenir shop. "I'll bet a million bucks the person we saw wasn't Elvira and that she's home."

"I'll check." Mercedes bolted up the apartment steps and pounded on Elvira's door.

The door flew open. "What?" Elvira growled.

Mercedes took a step back, her eyes wide as she gazed at the thick layer of creamy green goop that covered Elvira's face and neck. "Nothing. I thought you were looking for us."

She didn't wait for an answer as she hurried down the steps taking them two at a time.

Carlita was on the sidewalk, pacing. "It wasn't Elvira."

"You don't think she beat us here?"

"No way." Mercedes shook her head. "Not the way she looked."

Carlita studied the exterior of the souvenir shop. "I want to surprise Ruby. You hide out by her back door and I'll hide in Annie's doorway."

"We need walkie-talkies," Mercedes said. "What if it's not her?"

"Oh, it is. Now that I think about it, I'm almost positive it's Ruby McKinley."

Mercedes and Carlita hurried across the street and parted ways with Mercedes heading to the back of the building while Carlita hovered in Annie's dark doorway.

She dialed Mercedes' cell phone. "Hello?" Mercedes whispered.

"Are you in place?" Carlita whispered back.

"Yes. You?"

"Yep. Let's stay on the phone so we both know what's going on."

"Good idea," Mercedes said.

Carlita ducked down, peering over the top of the window ledge so that she had a bird's eye view of the souvenir shop's front door.

Sure enough, ten minutes later, Ruby sauntered down the sidewalk. Carlita could hear her whistling as she stopped in front of her store door and began to unlock it. "She's at her front door," Carlita said.

"I'll be right there." The line disconnected.

Carlita sprang into action and quickly strode to the front of the souvenir shop where Ruby was fumbling with the lock.

"Hello Ruby," Carlita said.

Ruby jumped, clutching her chest. "Oh my goodness. You frightened me. How are you Carlita?"

"Just dandy." She gazed down the sidewalk nonchalantly. "Nice night for a stroll."

"Yes. Yes, it is."

"Even to say, visit some other squares," Carlita said.

Ruby twisted the doorknob and pushed the door open. "I agree."

"The skate park a couple blocks over was busy."

Ruby froze. The color drained from her face.

Carlita moved in for the kill. "Keith and his friend, they told an interesting story, Ruby, of how someone was paying them to vandalize Walton Square businesses."

She went on. "My place, Ken Colby's, Steve Winter's and Annie Dowton's real estate office." Carlita crossed her arms. "You know, I almost thought perhaps my new tenant was behind the vandalism, but I got to thinking, there were only a couple people right here, right near my place, whose businesses weren't vandalized...yours and Stu Fischer's ice cream shop."

"H-how do you know my shop wasn't vandalized?" Ruby challenged. "Maybe I just didn't say anything."

Carlita ignored the question. "Yeah, it had to be someone who was able to keep a close eye on us. What a perfect spot, right across the street." Carlita shifted her gaze. "Why, I would think from your front window, you have a crystal clear view of the front and back of my building."

"I joined your protest," Ruby argued. "I was right there in the trenches, fighting the district office."

"Were you?" Carlita asked. "Or were you pretending to help, all the while doing whatever you could to stop me from getting my license? You don't want me to open a pawnshop because you think I will compete against you for business." She caught a movement out of the corner of her eye.

Mercedes, accompanied by Steve Winter, were rapidly approaching. Mercedes' purse was open and her hand was inside. Carlita knew her daughter was gripping the handle of her gun.

"You can't prove it," Ruby argued. "It's your word against mine."

"The glasses. The boys said you typically wore sunglasses over the top of regular glasses, but tonight you were wearing only regular glasses." Carlita pointed at Ruby's eyeglasses. "Mercedes recorded your meeting with Keith and his friend. Would you like her to show you the recording?"

"This is ridiculous. Now if you'll excuse me."

Steve reached out to stop her. "The gig is up, Ruby. We won't file a police report if you promise to stop vandalizing our properties."

The door to the store slammed in their faces. Carlita could hear the lock turn. "Well, that went well."

Steve turned to Mercedes. "Let me see the recording."

Mercedes turned her phone on, switched to the recording screen and handed it to Steve. He watched in silence. "You sure it isn't your tenant, Elvira? It kind of looks like her."

"Nope." Mercedes shook her head. "Elvira is in her apartment with a thick layer of goop on her face. No way would she have had time to make it back to her apartment, change and cover her face with a toning mask."

"Now what?" Carlita gazed at the store door.

"I have a feeling we've seen the last of the Walton Square incidents," Steve said. "Once Ruby finds out you got the license, I have a feeling Annie will have a new customer and Ruby will decide to sell."

Steve shook his head. "You never know about someone, do you? What secret lives they lead."

Carlita and Mercedes exchanged a quick glance. "You can say that again."

Chapter 27

Carlita headed to the district office the next morning to pick up her freshly minted pawnshop business license from the clerk. Rodney Yates had left her a message, letting her know she'd passed her background check with flying colors and the license had been issued.

Things were going to get busy now that Carlita had her license. Tony would be heading down in a couple days and he promised to help his mother get everything set up.

Steve was partially right about Ruby McKinley and Walton Square Souvenir shop. There was a for sale sign in the window the morning after the confrontation, but it wasn't Annie's Riverfront Real Estate sign. It was another local real estate agent's sign.

Carlita passed the sign as she headed to Annie's office and stepped inside.

Annie was behind the desk and Cindy at another desk. They looked up as Carlita walked into the office, closing the door behind her.

"I see Ruby is selling her business, after all."

Carlita had called Annie the evening before to tell her all that had transpired while Steve promised to call Ken Colby.

"It's a shame she didn't ask you to list the property," Carlita said.

"Right? I guess I'm not surprised. After all, she targeted me, too. She probably didn't want to have to apologize."

"True." Carlita eased into the seat across from Annie. "I'm sure the property won't sit on the market for too long. This is such a great neighborhood."

"A book store or coffee shop would be fun," Cindy chimed in.

"That's a great idea," Annie said. "Carlita can buy it and open a book store."

"Oh no," Carlita groaned. "I've already got my hands full." Her phone beeped and she glanced at the screen. There was a text message from Mercedes. "Bob Lowman my construction manager just showed up. I better head home."

She told her friends good-bye and stepped out onto the sidewalk, pausing long enough to gaze proudly at her soon-to-be pawnshop.

A small smile lifted the corners of her mouth. Things were looking up for Carlita Garlucci. She couldn't wait to see what wonderful adventures life in Savannah had in store for her and her family.

The end.

If you enjoyed reading this book, please take a moment to leave a review. It would be greatly appreciated. Thank you.

The Series Continues-Get "Swag in Savannah," Book 4
hopecallaghan.com/books/swag-in-savannah/

Books in This Series

Made in Savannah Cozy Mystery Series

Gazpacho Recipe

<u>Ingredients:</u>

4 cups tomato juice
1 yellow onion, minced
1 green bell pepper, minced
1 cucumber, peeled and chopped
2 cups chopped tomato
2 green onions, chopped
1 clove garlic
¼ cup chopped fresh basil (optional)

3 tablespoons fresh lemon juice (I used lime)
2 tablespoons red wine vinegar or apple cider vinegar
¼ teaspoon garlic powder
1-1/2 teaspoons Italian seasoning
1 teaspoon white sugar
Salt and pepper to taste

<u>Directions:</u>

In blender, mix onion, bell pepper, cucumber, tomatoes, onions, garlic and basil. Add 1 cup of tomato juice for better blending. Blend to desired consistency and pour into bowl.

Add the rest of the tomato juice, lemon or lime juice, vinegar, garlic powder, Italian seasoning, sugar, and salt and pepper.

Chill.

Enjoy!

Get Free eBooks and More

Sign up for my Free Cozy Mysteries Newsletter to get free and discounted ebooks, giveaways & soon-to-be-released books!

hopecallaghan.com/newsletter

Meet the Author

Hope loves to connect with her readers! Connect with her today!

Never miss another book deal! Text the word Books to 33222

Or visit hopecallaghan.com/newsletter for special offers, free ebooks, and soon-to-be-released books!

Email: hope@hopecallaghan.com

Facebook: www.facebook.com/authorhopecallaghan/

Hope Callaghan is an author who loves to write Christian books, especially Christian Mystery and Cozy Mystery books. She has written more than 50 mystery books (and counting) in five series.

In March 2017, Hope won a Mom's Choice Award for her book, "Key to Savannah," Book 1 in the Made in Savannah Cozy Mystery Series.

Born and raised in a small town in West Michigan, she now lives in Florida with her husband.

She is the proud mother of one daughter and a stepdaughter and stepson. When she's not doing the thing she loves best - writing books - she enjoys cooking, traveling and reading books.

Made in the USA
Coppell, TX
06 December 2022

88010794R00402